P9-CMY-753

Third and Indiana

A NOVEL BY STEVE LOPEZ

Third and Indiana

VIKING

VIKING
Published by the Penguin Group
Penguin Books USA Inc., 375 Hudson Street, New York, New York 10014, U.S.A.
Penguin Books Ltd, 27 Wrights Lane, London W8 5TZ, England
Penguin Books Australia Ltd, Ringwood, Victoria Australia
Penguin Books Canada Ltd, 10 Alcorn Avenue, Toronto, Ontario, Canada M4V 3B2
Penguin Books (N.Z.) Ltd, 182–190 Wairu Road, Auckland 10, New Zealand

Penguin Books Ltd, Registered Offices: Harmondsworth, Middlesex, England

First published in 1994 by Viking Penguin, a division of Penguin Books USA Inc.

10 9 8 7 6 5 4 3 2 1

PUBLISHER'S NOTE: This is a work of fiction. Names, characters, places, and incidents either are the product of the author's imagination or are used fictitiously, and any resemblance to actual persons, living or dead, events, or locales is entirely coincidental.

Grateful acknowledgment is made for permission to reprint excerpts from the following copyrighted works:

"Thinkin' " by Steve Forbert. Copyright 1977 Steve Forbert. Rolling Tide Music (ASCAP).

"As One Listens to the Rain" from *A Tree Within* by Octavio Paz. Copyright © 1987, 1988 by Octavio Paz and Eliot Weinberger. Reprinted by permission of New Directions Publishing Corp.

"It's Only a Paper Moon" by Billy Rose, E. Y. Harburg, and Harold Arlen. © 1933 Warner Bros. Inc. (renewed). Rights for the extended renewal term in the United States controlled by Glocca Morra Music, Chappell & Co. & SA Music. Rights for the world, excluding the United States, controlled by Warner Bros. Inc. & Chappell & Co. All rights reserved. Used by permission.

LIBRARY OF CONGRESS CATALOGING IN PUBLICATION DATA
Lopez, Steve.
Third and Indiana : a novel / by Steve Lopez.
p. cm.
ISBN 0-670-85676-2
1. Runaway teenagers—Pennsylvania—Philadelphia—Fiction. 2. Mothers and sons—Pennsylvania—Philadelphia—Fiction. 3. Drug traffic—Pennsylvania—Philadelphia—Fiction. 4. Teenage boys—Pennsylvania—Philadelphia—Fiction. 5. Philadelphia (Pa.)—Fiction. I. Title.
PS3569.0673T48 1994
813′.54—dc20 93-49815

Printed in the United States of America
Set in Garamond No. 3
Designed by Katy Riegel

To my parents and my sons

From across the fields
they will have seen
this one lighted room
and travelled towards it.
A summer night's inquiry.

—Michael Ondaatje,
In the Skin of a Lion

My thanks to Maxwell King, editor of the *Philadelphia Inquirer.* And to Nan Graham, my editor at Viking.

Also to Mike Maska, Fran Dauth, Robin Clark, Marsha and Ingo Schamber, and Lev Fruchter.

A special thanks to my agent, David Black.

—Steve Lopez

Third
and
Indiana

One

The weather came up from the south, a warm passing rain that left the October sky clear and the pavement steaming, and from a distance it looked as though the woman on the bicycle, her black skirt rippling in the liquid breeze, was riding through the clouds.

Gabriel stood in shadows thrown by the overhead tracks of the Market-Frankford El and watched her come through the mist, pedaling east on Lehigh Avenue. Even at half past midnight, before he could see a clear shape or a face, there was something that gave her away.

Maybe it was the way she made the street lonelier than it was before she got there. Maybe it was the way the air cleared a path for her thoughts, which moved in a cushion around her, a swirl of confusion. Whatever it was, Gabriel could tell from two blocks away that the woman coming at him in darkening shades of gray, as if growing out of a dream, was his mother.

Her grace fell away as she drew closer, close enough that he could see her struggle. Either she was too big or the bicycle was too small, because she bulged over it like a circus bear. The handlebars wiggled in her hands and the bicycle staggered along in nervous spasms, waiting for her to remember how to ride.

Gabriel stepped deeper into the shadows as she approached. He tugged at his Sixers cap and smiled, half out of pride, half out of fear.

Maybe he should have gotten her a bigger bicycle. It had been a birthday present six months ago. Get some exercise, he had told her. She had put on so much weight since his father walked out on them without a word or a warning. Get some exercise, some fresh air, whatever. Just get out of the house. A person could suffocate in there, it was filled with so much unspoken disappointment. But Gabriel never really expected her to ride the bike. She'd be too self-conscious, for one thing. And she'd wonder where he got the money.

He didn't know her as well as he thought he did. Not only was she riding the bicycle, but she was riding it in the middle of the night. Looking for him.

Damn, Gabriel thought. She shouldn't be out here at this hour. Not in this neighborhood.

Gabriel was fourteen, a dark sliver of a boy with slow, sad eyes that could stay sad through a smile. He was going to be a lady killer, his mother had been telling him since before he knew what it meant, and she had said it again a week ago. The night before he ran away.

His first thought was to run to her now. His second was just to run. His right foot made the decision, a slow backward step on the toe of his sneaker, and then he wheeled and was gone, lost in the darkness beyond the El as a train rattled over Philadelphia rooftops, past the steamed windows of sleeping babies and past corners owned and ruled by drug gangs.

Ofelia Santoro of Diamond Street fought the bicycle to a stop at the intersection of Lehigh and Kensington, her chest rising with each breath. She looked left and then right and then left again, tracking invisible footsteps.

He was close. She felt it. Somewhere close.

She stood with one foot on a pedal, one on the ground, frozen in indecision. A postcard of her life.

She didn't need this. She was lost enough in her house, and shouldn't have to be out here where the city, with all its ghosts, all its secrets, could play with the ones you already had inside of you.

3

The cops and prosecutors had a name for this part of town, which took in areas of Kensington and North Philadelphia and was good for several shootings a night and a drug trade that rivaled the gross national product of a dozen small nations. They called it the Badlands.

If her husband were still around, he'd be the one out here searching the Badlands. If her husband were still around, Gabriel wouldn't have run away. That was the way she looked at it.

The world wasn't worth living in, Ofelia thought, if it was a place where Gabriel could be dead and her husband could be alive. If that were the case, she'd have to find a way to get word to him. He had a right to know.

And then, when he showed up, she'd kill him.

Ofelia ran a hand through straight, matted black hair. A yellow, drizzly light fell on her from the streetlamp and her shadow spilled around her like a great black cape. Her face, lit now by the silver light of the moon, was anything but simple. It could go from pleasant to pretty to stunning and back again without looking the same twice, without knowing it had changed. Everything that had ever gone right in her life was on it, and everything wrong, too.

There was a time in her life when she broke hearts, and it was still there, glimpses of it, a deep beauty that showed more of itself with each look, coming through the things she'd wrapped herself in. On a crowded train platform, on a busy city street, she was the one who made everyone else disappear. She was the one who drew stares from strangers who couldn't explain why. Women wanted to have that look and men wanted to sleep with it, and Ofelia Santoro of Diamond Street was oblivious to both.

The look she wore now was none of that. Only worry and regret. She'd told Gabriel a million times what was out here, and what it could do to the two of them. And when she'd felt him moving toward it, she stopped telling him to stay out of trouble and began asking instead. Maybe that was when she lost him.

When Ofelia had caught her breath, she wondered if she looked as ridiculous and awkward as she felt, trying to ride a shiny red bicycle through these streets in the middle of the night. Looking north, in the direction Gabriel had just run, she told herself that was the way to go. And then she turned south, convinced her decision had to be wrong.

The new bicycle jerked along Kensington Avenue like a jewel in a junkyard, under the grimy tracks of the El and past littered storefronts. The rain had raised the street, a smell that was the city.

Ofelia's knuckles were white from squeezing the grips of the bicycle she had refused to ride before this night. As she rode, stiff and uncertain, her eyes scanned unlit alleys and slumping sidestreets for her runaway son.

"Happy birthday," he had said when he gave her the bicycle.

Happy birthday my ass. That's what she thought six months ago as she dragged the bicycle down to the basement of their little brick row house. She wanted it out of sight. Happy birthday? She was fat, her husband was gone, and her son had just given her a present he couldn't possibly afford by any legal means.

And there the bicycle stayed, leaning against the water heater in the basement, until this night. Until the eleven o'clock news.

The big story on Channel Six was seven people being shot in three apparent drug-related incidents in the Badlands. The anchorman said something about the summer of blood running into the fall, and Ofelia went clammy.

In the next story, city officials were trying to figure out who was spray-painting the outlines of bodies in the middle of North Broad Street, a major north-south artery that ran along the western boundary of the Badlands and all the way down to the doorstep of City Hall. Ofelia had seen the bodies one day on her way to work at the diner, and felt sick to her stomach.

A police flack was saying that every time a minor was killed in a drug-related shooting, a new body appeared on the street. The bodies were about six to ten feet long depending on the age of the kid who was killed, and the age was painted somewhere in the body. Fifteen. Nine. Seventeen. Twelve. There were four or five bodies per block, painted like the chalk outlines at murder scenes, except that these seemed to float, limbs extended, as if they were falling through space. It was powerful and disturbing, a Temple University art professor said, the way the bodies seemed ghostly and lifelike at the same time, extending in a chain down Broad Street toward the heart of Center City's spectacular new skyline. Eventually, the professor noted, the bodies would be piled at the doorstep of City Hall.

Ofelia felt a shiver as the announcer said the Broad Street colony now included twenty-seven bodies. A Liberty Bell was painted after the tenth, and Independence Hall was painted after the twentieth. And still, the identity of the artist was a mystery to all.

Ofelia walked to the door that led from the kitchen to the basement. It had been seven days since Gabriel disappeared without a warning or a clue, just like his father. Seven days, the house growing quieter each time the sun fell out of the sky. And after watching the news, Ofelia promised herself that if it stopped raining, and maybe even if it didn't, she'd get on the bicycle her son had given her, no matter how he got it, and pedal through every corner of Philadelphia searching for him.

And there she was, hauling it up from the basement, wincing at the feel of it in her hands. A cold skeleton.

The pedals scraped the walls on the way up. In the kitchen, the new rubber tires squeaked on the linoleum floor, laughing at her.

She pushed the bicycle across the room toward the door, but felt as if it were pulling her. She'd always had weird sensations, back to when she was a child, as if she were somehow the second one to learn about her own thoughts. And she'd always had premonitions, too. But nothing like what she'd been having since Gabriel ran away.

Ofelia stopped before she got to the door and held the bike still, so the laughing would stop. She squeezed the frame, as if choking it, stalling for time to decide she didn't really want to go out there. She was afraid of what she might find. But she was afraid, too, of what might happen if she didn't get to Gabriel soon.

The kitchen held a simmering smell of pork and beans, even though she wasn't cooking. It had buried itself in the furniture, the walls, and the woodwork, that stuffy and stale kind of smell you don't notice until you go outside and come back in.

Ofelia took a deep breath and moved through her kitchen again. But it was the same as before, as if the bike were pulling her. As if everything that happened was beyond her control.

Near the door, she grabbed the stick of blue chalk on the bureau and held it in fingers that had decided not to get fat with the rest of her, fingers dipped in blood-red polish. Ofelia steadied the bike with one hand and with the other she raised the chalk to the wall and made a vertical slash, one foot long, on wallpaper the color of unearthed bones. She was counting the days Gabriel had been gone, and this was the seventh.

Above the marks were the words Ofelia had written the first day the feeling came over her, rising up from a place she didn't know about. The words still held the tremble of her hand.

EL NADA EN LO OBSCURO.

The thing that troubled Ofelia, aside from the involuntary urge to scribble a message on her kitchen wall, was that she didn't write or read Spanish. She never had. And so she had stared at the words, written by her own hand, wondering what they meant.

Ofelia's father was Dominican and her mother Canadian, but Ofelia grew up neither. Her father had come to the states as a young man and left a part of himself on the island. Looking Hispanic was bad enough, but the white factory bosses would slam the door in your face for sure if you sounded like you'd just gotten off the boat. He made sure that Ofelia, his only child, would have English as her first language.

Ofelia had picked up some Spanish from the neighborhood over the years, but not enough to read her kitchen wall. She bought an English-Spanish dictionary and flipped through it, but still couldn't decipher the message. On the fifth day, she had made a diagonal slash through the first four marks, leaving a neat cluster of five. That was the day she called in a neighborhood boy named Wilfredo to read her wall.

He was about ten, and when Ofelia led him into the kitchen and told him what she wanted, he looked at her as if he knew he'd have nightmares the next ten years.

Vandals did it, she told him. They broke in, threw things around, and wrote on the wall.

The boy looked up at Ofelia, a long look, and nodded. Then he looked at the wall.

"He swims in darkness," the boy said, and then he left, not another word, leaving the door open behind him as he jumped down the front steps and ran into the street, never looking back.

He Swims in Darkness.

What Ofelia had seen, the day she wrote those words, was a flash of blue. And in a way she couldn't explain, even to herself, she knew it to be a vision of death. In the blue haze, she felt Gabriel close, and then far away. She called to him, but he didn't hear.

The slow chill that crept through her in that moment had stayed, hiding in places she couldn't get to. It was hard to know what was real. For a week, it had been hard to know. The Spanish words. The blue haze. The bicycle pulling her across the room.

Was the Spanish a warning from the ghost of her father? Was it all a dream? She had to get out.

Ofelia locked the door behind her and walked the red bicycle to the middle of the street, where she stood over it a while, troubled by the geometry of throwing her leg over the frame. It didn't help that she wore this loose black skirt and sandals. She had taken to wearing black every day since the blue flash, though she couldn't recall her choice of colors as a conscious decision.

On the sidewalk, she looked back at the two-story red brick row house and something about it struck her as absurd. Here's this spinning planet, a tiny speck in the galaxy, and you need a place to keep your stuff. An address in the universe. This one seemed as strange a place as any. A little house on Diamond Street to hold you and your thoughts.

It was a classic Philadelphia block. Ofelia's house was a copy of every other one on the street, thirty-two identical stalls connected to each other in two unbroken rows, sixteen on each side of Diamond. They warmed each other in winter and suffocated each other in summer and had spent sixty years holding each other up, though some were sagging now, weary from the fight.

Six houses were boarded up and the city had come out and sealed two others with concrete because they were crack dens. Neighborhood kids, who used to be younger at this age, it seemed, bounced balls off of what used to be doors and windows.

Three other houses were open caves, and the walking dead would crawl into them for drugs, cheap wine, malt liquor, sex, a night's sleep. It wouldn't be long before a cement truck would pull up and close these houses off to he world, because that was what the city did. Ofelia, on her darker days, toyed with the idea of sneaking into one of the houses just ahead of the cement truck.

Ofelia had walked halfway down the block, lost in thoughts too scattered to identify, when she stopped and looked at the bike as if she had just realized it was there.

With a sudden burst—she just told herself to do it, as if speaking to another person—she threw her leg over the back wheel and slid confidently, though uncomfortably, onto the seat. It struck Ofelia that it was uncommonly wide. Maybe the designers had made a mistake thinking there was so much space in that particular area of the human body. Maybe it was just that nothing else had been there for so long.

Ofelia pinched her waist, recalling a story about how much fat you're supposed to be able to grab. It was in a magazine she'd bought because of a headline about twenty-five exciting new dessert ideas with strawberries. She was glad she'd waited until this late hour to ride, because none of the neighbors would be out, those nosy assholes, to see her struggle like this.

What was Ofelia up to? What was she doing on a bicycle at this hour? And was it true, this rumor about scribbling on her kitchen wall? That was probably why Gabriel had run away. His mother was a witch.

Fuck them, Ofelia thought. Fuck all of them.

Ofelia's hair rode the breeze behind her, catching the glow of flickering streetlights and neon signs. She had no idea where Gabriel might be, and so she pedaled without a plan, cursing the bicycle, wrestling it, and turning when something inside her said to turn.

And now here she was at Lehigh and Kensington, ten minutes into the ride, and feeling something at this intersection. Feeling Gabriel's presence.

Something of him was here.

And then gone.

And she, thinking left, goes right.

Ofelia couldn't remember the last time she'd ridden a bike, but it felt like a hundred years and the bike seemed to want to squirm out from under her. She shifted her weight to one side and then the other, looking for balance, and the bike suffered along, sharing her uncertainty.

A parked car was coming up on the right, and although Ofelia saw it clearly, her bicycle was in a zig when it should have been in a zag and she sideswiped it, taking some of its paint with her. She managed to stay up, but overcompensated and veered too far into the roadway just as a taxi roared up on her from behind, its horn blasting as the driver swerved around her, tires screeching.

"Learn how to drive," Ofelia screamed at the driver. And then, through clenched teeth, "Asshole."

Most of the lost souls on the street were oblivious to Ofelia, if not to themselves. But a few of them turned to look, and Ofelia felt their eyes on her. It was not a common sight, a forty-year-old overweight woman dressed all in black and riding a bicycle, after midnight, in the Badlands. At this hour you were a dealer or a buyer or a whore, somebody begging to make the news.

Kensington Avenue, the commercial center of the neighborhood, was skid-row ratty and rundown, especially at night, though it wasn't as scary as a lot of the row-house streets. It sat in eternal darkness and gloom under the El, and the tracks were supported by an archway of rusted iron crablegs, a symbol of the city's industrial death.

Ofelia passed a tavern, a hoagie stand, a twenty-four-hour shop that replaced glass and installed burglar bars. Coming up on her right was the store where Gabriel said he had bought the bicycle—Deals on Wheels.

She seemed to be finding a better balance now—it was coming to her gradually—and she was able to look down for a moment at all the levers on the handlebars. She didn't remember any of this stuff on the bikes she rode as a girl.

Gabriel had bought her an all-terrain model with eighteen gears, seventeen of which Ofelia didn't know how to use. As far as she knew, she'd be using only one kind of terrain. The city was mostly flat, so it seemed kind of a waste, unless there was a special gear to shift into for pothole terrain. Philadelphia had a lot of that.

Looking left, into the darkness of a stairwell to the El platform, Ofelia saw a dance of movement. It was like one of those shows where the performers wear black and a dark background hides them from the audience. Ofelia saw a man's light colored shirt, and just under it, a pair of earrings throwing light.

A hooker at a man's crotch.

At the next corner, a boy stood alone, his eyes holding Ofelia as she rode by. He couldn't have been much older than Gabriel. He nodded as she approached, not a hello but an offer, and when she didn't react, he made a stronger sales pitch, pursing his lips around an imaginary crack pipe and sucking in air as if the air itself was a drug.

In a way, it was a relief to Ofelia. She couldn't see Gabriel standing on a corner like that, selling crack to pipers. She couldn't see him anywhere in this midnight carnival of freaks.

An hour into it, the riding was smoother. Ofelia began to trust the bike under her and feel the wind in her face.

A smile appeared without her permission.

When she began to tire, it was a sweet feeling, warm in her veins. She closed her eyes for an instant, letting the bicycle pull her through a dream, and wondered if it was possible to fall asleep while riding. And then she closed her eyes again, a few seconds longer this time, enjoying the danger in it. Feeling connected to him now.

"Gabriel," she called out, her voice fading into the overhead rattle of an approaching train, the sound of a million pots and pans tumbling out of a cupboard.

When the train was gone, she called Gabriel's name again, her voice bouncing off of buildings and going thin, the way sound does at night. In the distance, she heard a gunshot, and the howl of frightened dogs.

Colder air had moved in behind the rain, and the wind picked up, blowing out the fog. A tin can blew across an alley and the sound of it, hollow and empty on the pavement, seemed eternal.

"Damn you, Gabriel," Ofelia whispered, her tears running cold.

She rode in mournful grace, black skirt flapping, dark hair flying, a mother in search of her child.

"Ga-bri-el," she called loud, her cry carrying over rooftops and rising in silent, unanswered prayer.

"Ga-bri-el."

Two

The ringing of the phone filled the house, startling Eddie Passarelli. He was onstage somewhere in his mind, a nice place, not some hole, playing guitar to people who were actually listening.

By the second ring the fantasy was over and his career was shit again. He picked up the phone.

"Joe Pass, it's Mike. I got a truck."

They called him Joe Pass in the South Philadelphia neighborhood where he grew up, after the jazz guitarist.

Eddie could hear his own breathing on the phone. Nervous breathing.

He looked toward the kitchen wall at a photo of his boys, Anthony and Dominic. The older one eleven, the little one nine. Anthony, dark brown hair in a spike cut, had his father's look of unwarranted confidence. Dominic, with his mother's fair skin and hair, seemed lost in thought over the alignment of the planets, a dizzy thing Eddie attributed to the genes on his wife's side.

The boys were at school now, his wife was at work. And Eddie, trapped in a marriage that had gone stale ten years ago, was trying to find the nerve to make a break while his family was gone, and move in with his girlfriend.

"I thought you said you couldn't get a truck," he said to Mike Inverso, unable to keep the disappointment out of his voice. Eddie had a clear, crisp voice, but it went too nasal when he tried to sing, which was one of the things that had led him to jazz. It also went nasal when he was scared or uncertain.

"I got it, Eddie. I borrowed it off of Thin Jimmy."

Eddie sat down hard, and when he opened his mouth, it sounded like he had a sinus infection. "Thin Jimmy?"

"Thin Jimmy," Inverso said. "You got a problem?"

"Thin Jimmy the wiseguy," Eddie said, not asking, but saying it like it was a dumb idea.

"You want the fucking truck or you want I should tell Thin Jimmy Eddie Passarelli says no thanks he don't want no wiseguy's truck?"

It was with you forever, that's what Eddie was thinking. You get out of South Philadelphia, move to Roxborough, it doesn't matter. You can't leave downtown.

Eddie had grown up with Mike Inverso, but they were never buddies. Eddie's parents always told him it was best to stay away from kids whose fathers everybody whispered about.

They got a little closer, though, when they ended up in the same ethics class at Community College of Philadelphia. Inverso's father had been a ward leader and then, after prison, became a big deal political consultant, and his driver took Inverso to school every day in a black Lincoln Town Car. Eddie would hitch a ride and sit for a few seconds after Inverso got out, because Inverso always stepped out of the car like he owned the fucking school and Eddie didn't want anybody to know they were together. He didn't mind the association when it came time for grading, though. Neither one of them was nailing the ethics class, but Inverso's father had a guy in administration and they both got A's.

Inverso ended up going to work for the city and managed to get Eddie a few gigs through his contacts. But for the most part Eddie tried to avoid him. Not so much because Inverso was going to sleep in the big trunk in the sky one day, but because of the constant bullshit. Inverso was one of those South Philly guys—the ones standing on corners scratching themselves—who could always get you a deal on something through a cousin. Shoes, toasters, golfballs. It didn't fucking matter. It was a twenty-four-hour hustle. Everybody downtown had something going on, a piece of this or that, and it was a culture Eddie got sick of. That's why he had taken his family to Roxborough, where fewer guys scratched themselves in public and there wasn't as much whispering.

But if Eddie was going to move into this new place, he needed a truck to pick up some furniture. And he knew Inverso would have a connection.

"Fuckin' mob truck," Eddie said to himself, still thinking it over. Thin Jimmy was the number-two or -three guy in one of the two gangs that were shooting it out for control of sports betting, numbers, prostitution, and loan sharking. A guy he knew to say hello to, but that was all. "All right," Eddie said to Inverso. "Give me twenty minutes."

Eddie got off the phone and looked around the house at twelve years of marriage. He was looking for a reason to stay and not finding it.

The marriage had become the half-moon indentation where the doorknob had plugged the wall for nine years. The faded yellow spot on the dining room rug where one of the dogs pissed five years ago. The wooden plaque with ducks and geese and a smiling, talking sun that said WELCOME TO OUR HAPPY HOME.

The air in the house had gotten tighter over the years, to where Eddie couldn't wear a turtleneck or do the top button of a shirt because that was where the air was tightest. At his neck.

Twelve years of marriage.

The dogs were watching Eddie. He'd gotten them at the pound six years ago, two black labs, and named them Monk and Mingus after the jazz giants. They were looking at him as if they knew what was going on, and Eddie had to turn away, because he knew he was the kind of guy who'd second-guess his life based on the way two dogs looked at him.

The thing Eddie hadn't worked out yet was whether he was leaving to be with his girlfriend or because he couldn't be with his wife anymore. Something told him he should probably know the answer to that, but Eddie was the type of person who wasted most of his thinking on the problem instead of the solution, and never figured things out until it was too late to do him any good.

He'd been having the affair for a year. Her name was Sarah and the way he met her, she came to a club near Independence Mall one night while he was playing. It was one of a dozen places where Eddie had pissed off the management and was on his last chance. He was supposed to play background music, but Eddie always pumped it up to be heard over the rattle of dishes and the smalltalk of people who weren't paying attention. He spotted Sarah sitting alone at the bar and crying while he played "Autumn Leaves," and he read her response as a testament to his creative achievement. He took a break after the song and sat down next to her, asking if it was a favorite number of hers.

"Who are you?" she asked, wiping her eyes.

"I'm the guitar player."

"I didn't know there was live music," she said.

She apologized for not crying over his music, but said she might have cried if she had noticed it. She said she came into the club every once in a while for a good cry, because it was the last place she and her fiancé had gone to before he dumped her for a gentile.

For Eddie, being with Sarah was like waking up from a long nap. She read poetry in her underwear and knew about music and hated curtains, plaques, or anything else with ducks and geese on them. She liked to have a good argument, veins bulging, and then, before the veins went back into her skin, make love on top, riding Eddie hard and lapping at his face with an open mouth and a wet, hanging tongue.

With his wife, they never even argued. Marie, she was a downtown girl. The high hair, the gum, the whole nine yards.

Sarah was five-eleven, red-haired and green-eyed, and never did her nails, which set her apart from all the girls Eddie had known in his life. He liked that she was Jewish because it took him farther from where he came from. He wondered if all Jewish women were like her, but he would have bet they were different across the river in Cherry Hill, where the Jews seemed more like Italians with two-car garages.

Sarah was forty-three, five years older than Eddie. She studied music at Temple, worked as a substitute teacher, and shared an Old City apartment with a friend from school. Eddie had stayed there a couple nights a week, telling his wife he had out-of-town gigs. The plan now was for Eddie and Sarah to move into a house in Kensington, a house his slumlord mother owned and had trouble renting because the neighborhood was so bad. Eddie told his mother he wanted the house for a friend who needed a break on the rent for a couple of months. He didn't say the friend was a lover, or that he was moving in with her. Eddie and his mother didn't get along so well. She didn't understand the music thing, and she'd always come at him with a job she heard about, some bullshit thing like unloading trucks at the Food Distribution Center or being a mailman, something like that.

Eddie's moving out, or at least the idea of it, had been in the works a month or so. Sarah had been busting Eddie's balls with it lately, telling him he was too scared to pull it off and letting him know she wasn't waiting around forever.

Eddie had decided this was the day, for no particular reason. "Let's go," he said to Monk and Mingus, leading them to the back door and putting them out in the yard. If he was going to do it, he had to do it.

He grabbed his guitar, a hollow-body Gibson he'd bought used five years ago for two thousand dollars. It was worth three times that now. He patted his pocket for his keys, grabbed the overnight bag he'd left at the foot of the stairs, and walked out.

He didn't get far. Something froze him on the front step, he wasn't sure what. He went back in and looked around again. From the fireplace mantel, Eddie grabbed two framed pictures of Anthony and Dominic in their Little League uniforms, hats too big for their heads, gloves big as baskets on their hands. He threw them into his bag and then he walked out the door and into a new life, still not sure what the hell he was doing.

Inverso lived a couple of blocks from the Mario Lanza Museum in South Philadelphia. When Eddie pulled up in his disintegrating 1978 Cutlass, he didn't remember having driven there. He didn't even remember if there had been any traffic. He had spent the whole time trying not to think about anything.

Inverso saw Eddie parking his car and came outside, a cat after a mouse. His hairline started three-quarters of an inch over his eyebrows, which charged across the bridge of his nose without a break. Southern Italian. Eddie was north.

Inverso was five-foot-four and had a long stride he thought made him look taller. He also had that South Philly swagger, the cock as a fulcrum, with every other joint swinging from it. And the two things together made it look like he was coming out of his Italian loafers.

When he wasn't talking he was usually whistling "The Lady Is a Tramp," or anything Sinatra. Inverso wore three gold necklaces and they threw off cheap slices of sunlight. He was smiling his asshole goombah smile as he bent toward the window, waiting for Eddie to roll it down.

"You rat bastard," he said slowly, a cadence perfected through years of shit-giving. "What're you, stupid?"

Eddie didn't say anything. There was no way to respond to a guy like Inverso calling you stupid or a rat bastard.

"You got a family," Inverso continued, lecturing now. "You got kids, you stick it out, douchebag. What're you, nuts? Come on, talk to me you stuttering prick. Talk to the man."

Now he was into *stuttering prick.* You knew Inverso was warmed up good when he started with the *stuttering prick.*

"You don't fuckin' shatter your kids, wreck your home, for a little piece of ass. Where's your morals?"

Mike Inverso on morality. Eddie had to look away.

"Let me explain something," Inverso continued. "What you do, you keep the girlfriend on the side, throw her the bone a couple times a week, everybody gets what they want. The wife, the girlfriend, the kids. Where'd you come out of, a tree?"

Eddie gave him a laugh. Not that he was amused, but Inverso was the kind of guy who was going to bust your chops for five or ten minutes no matter what the situation. If you let him know it was getting to you, he'd just keep teeing off.

Besides, Eddie needed the truck, and he also needed the jobs Inverso had been getting him since he became a supervisor in the Recreation Department. Inverso was running a scam in which he set up musical entertainment for things like senior citizen socials. He'd tell the groups the city had a flat rate of two hundred dollars payable in cash only, then he'd give half to Eddie and pocket the rest.

"So tell me, Romeo," Inverso was asking now, "why you wanna fuck up your life like this?"

Eddie had to say something or Inverso might keep at it until the sun went down. But he spoke without thinking, just spilling what was in his head.

"I think I'm in love with her."

Jesus fucking Christ. How did he always let this happen? That was the worst thing he could have said. It was as though being in Inverso's presence cost Eddie twenty IQ points. He said the dumbest things, and stepped into every trap Inverso laid.

Inverso stood back from the car, giving himself room to jump on the softball Eddie had just tossed him.

"You think you're in love with her," he said.

The words were low and flat, setting up the motion. His head was bobbing now, hands flying, shoulders swiveling. The cock had everything going. He was grabbing himself for punctuation.

Then he got serious all of a sudden, like he always did when he felt obligated to share a solemn truth. He walked back up to the car and bent down at the window.

"Didn't you learn anything downtown, junior?"

Eddie was shaking his head. Not as an answer. Just shaking his head at the situation.

"You think you're in love," Inverso said. "Well I didn't invent it, but guess what, douchebag. I got a little piece of advice for you. Don't fuck with your brain, and don't think with your dick. You see what I'm saying?"

Inverso stepped back and threw his arms out, as if he'd just passed on a new theory of relativity.

Eddie got out of the car

"Where you moving at?" Inverso asked, realizing it was time to change the subject or he might get smacked. Eddie was half a foot taller. "You comin' back downtown? It's about time you got out of Roxborough, all those fuckin' 'mericans."

"Kensington. I'm going to Kensington."

"Get the fuck outa here."

"No, really. I'm going to Kensington."

Inverso stared him down.

"You gotta be shittin' me. You're movin' to Kensington?"

"I'm going to Kensington," Eddie said.

"What the fuck is the matter with you, junior? You lose your mind?"

"It's one of my mother's places," Eddie said. "It's just for a while, till I get a place."

"You oughta have your fuckin' head looked at. You know who lives in Kensington? It's fucking Moolengians and Portarickens up there, alls they do is sell crack, fuck their cousins, and shoot each other in the head. What are you, stupid? Tsutsoons and Portarickens. Even the white people are niggers. They got these Appalachian white trash niggers. You take everybody in Kensington, you can't make one set of fuckin' teeth."

Eddie didn't respond. He was actually giving some thought to what Inverso had said. You got kids, you stick it out. Damn, was he that fucked up that he needed advice from Inverso?

"Where's the truck?" he said.

"Around the corner," Inverso said.

Eddie started in that direction and Inverso followed him like a lap dog, nipping at his heels and still busting his balls.

"They all got baseball bats up Kensington," he was saying. "Everybody thinks they're Joe fuckin' DiMaggio. You walk down the street, *ba-da-boom, ba-da-bing,* some ignorant Polack's crackin' your melon with a club, the prick doesn't have a tooth in his fuckin' head."

"Where's the goddamn truck?" Eddie said.

"Right here," Inverso said, pointing to a brand-new baby blue Ford pickup that almost blinded both of them with sunglare. "That's the cocksucker."

"Shit," Eddie said, walking a circle around the truck. "You didn't tell me it was brand new. It's still got the paper license. What'd you tell Thin Jimmy?"

"What'd I tell him? I told him, Yo Thin Jimmy, that stuttering prick Eddie Joe Pass wants to borrow your truck because he's banging some kike that reads poetry in her fucking drawers. She's got him so fucked up he puts on a yarmulke to pull his pud. You wanna know what I told Thin Jimmy? That's what I told him. Just don't get a fucking scratch on his truck. That son of a bitch is crazy enough, he'll kill both of us. Shit, I knew it was Kensington, I wouldn't of even asked him. Jesus, Eddie. You grow up downtown, some refinement, a little class. What the hell went wrong with your life?"

Eddie picked up the furniture at a discount house in northeast Philadelphia and was headed south on I-95. Ahead of him, the skyline sprouted over row-house rooftops and church steeples. One Liberty Place rose above the Center City bouquet, steel and glass playing catch with the sun.

Eddie's eye followed the Benjamin Franklin Bridge, all Tinker Toy blue, across the river to Camden. Sailboats puffed over the Delaware, slowing time the way sailboats do, their candy-colored sails dressing up worn-out Camden. Eddie wished he could be out there on the river, feel the sun, float all the way down through Delaware Bay and out to the Atlantic, maybe get lost at sea. But he'd never been a lucky type of person.

He'd call later and explain things to Anthony and Dominic and his wife. Soon as he figured out what the hell to say. Shit, he'd rather not think about it. It was hard enough trying to figure out whether, by moving out, he had balls or he was a coward. And it didn't seem fair that the one could be confused with the other.

Thin Jimmy's gleaming new Ford was a prize among the cars that rolled down the highway, but it ran like it ought to be recalled. It coughed and hesitated, like maybe they left out a few sparkplugs at the factory. All Eddie wanted to do was dump the furniture and get it back to Thin Jimmy as soon as he could.

Eddie turned on the radio and Thin Jimmy had it tuned to WPEN, which played a lot of Sinatra and Tony Bennett. Eddie switched it to WXPN and the news came on.

Two days after his heart attack, Mayor DeMarco, the former police commissioner, was listed in serious but stable condition in Holy Redeemer Hospital. If ever there was a guy who used power as a license to steal, Eddie was thinking, it was that fat fuck of a mayor. The news said the head of the local mob had stopped by the hospital to pay his respects to the mayor and his wife Angela.

"Meanwhile," the newscaster said, "in a continuing story that still gathers attention and baffles authorities, three more bodies have been painted on North Broad Street, bringing the total number to thirty. A police spokeswoman confirmed that three more juveniles had been killed in apparent drug-related incidents in the Badlands over the last week, and that the additions on Broad Street seem to correspond to the actual deaths, as has been the case since the paintings were first observed around the beginning of June. The spokeswoman said it remains unknown which person or persons are responsible for the paintings, and that no effort is being made to solve the mystery."

The Badlands, Eddie thought. That's where he was moving. He was moving to a place where bodies were piling up in the street.

After the news, a Steve Forbert song came on. Before jazz, Eddie had gone through every phase of rock, and back when he was playing coffeehouses he covered a lot of the stuff on Forbert's *Alive on Arrival* album. The lyrics were always sharp and Forbert's guitar was precise and heartfelt at the same time. This song was called "Thinkin'."

> Well don't you go thinkin' and thinkin' and thinkin' and
> Thinkin' so much till you're stranded behind.
>
> Don't you go thinkin' and thinkin' and thinkin' and
> Thinkin' so much til you're losing your mind

Eddie's hollow-body Gibson sat next to him on the passenger seat, locked up in its hard black leather case. Eddie always strapped the seatbelt and shoulder harness over it, like it was a person. Himself, he never used a seatbelt.

> All the tension inside has gone through to your face
> You're flashing your madness all over the place

You stand in the hallway and try to explain
I look in your eyes and see shackles and chains

Eddie checked the mirror to make sure the furniture was okay and caught a glimpse of himself. Damn, he was a mess. The unwarranted confidence was gone, replaced by the look that was in the song—flashing madness. Eddie realized he'd been yanking at his wavy brown hair, the way it stuck up here and there in nervous clumps. He smoothed it back with his hand and checked the mirror again. Sarah had told him he looked like President Clinton, which he didn't necessarily take as a compliment, considering how gray and fat-faced the president was.

But it was true that at thirty-eight, Eddie could pass for mid-forties. His scraggly beard was going gray in patches and looked like those lawns that got too much fertilizer in one spot and not enough in another. His hairline was climbing his forehead, too, but Eddie thought it gave his face a balance it had never had.

When he was fourteen, his mother encouraged him to wear hats, maybe even a fedora. It would give him some character, she said. Since that day, he was convinced there was something too plain and dull about him. He'd gone with a ponytail in his late teens. Not a full-blown horse thing, just a little tail for some character. A musician thing. It was an un–South Philly way to go, and he liked that. His whole life, Eddie had been trying to break out.

The whole thing in South Philly was to get over on somebody or strike it rich. But it had nothing to do with creative achievement or honest enterprise. The way to make it big was to hit a lottery, pick a longshot horse, or come into a once-in-a-lifetime scam.

Years ago in South Philly, a kid named Joey Coyle had gotten rich when an armored car hit a bump and a bag of money fell out the back. He was a hero, even after he got caught with wads of bills stuffed in his boots, and an understanding Philadelphia jury bought Joey Coyle's plea that all that money made him too crazy to know right from wrong.

It seemed to Eddie that as long as you stayed in South Philly, you were waiting with everyone else for the next bag of money to fall in the street.

Behind his face in the mirror now, Eddie saw the price tags flapping around on the furniture he'd just purchased. And then there was the sticker that was glued to the sofa and said: CAN'T BEAT THIS.

The sofa was a color the manufacturer had specified as Deep Sea Blue. It was made of foam rubber and opened into a bed, or actually a mattress that sat flush on the floor. The whole thing weighed only twenty-five pounds, which was a nice feature, unless you happened to be going down a highway.

In the mirror, Eddie watched the centerpiece of his new ensemble levitate off the bed of the truck. It was just a few inches, but it looked for a moment like he'd lose the whole load.

"Son of a bitch," he said, easing up on the gas of Thin Jimmy's new Ford.

They wanted to sell him a rope at the store, but Eddie was pissed off they didn't throw it in, so he said no.

Now that he'd eased off the gas, the sofa sat down and behaved. He'd just take it easy, that's all, and everything should be okay.

Eddie also bought two of what the store called oatmeal flipchairs. They could be chairs or beds, depending on whether they were flipped out flat or folded up square. Eddie figured he as at a point in his life where he needed that kind of versatility in his furniture.

He had wedged the flipchairs between the sofa and the sides of the truck bed, binding the whole mess against itself to hold it all in. Riding along behind him, the whole deal coming in under two hundred fifty dollars, was a living room or a bedroom, whatever the situation called for. Anthony and Dominic could sleep on the flipchairs when they stayed over, and he'd sleep on the sofabed.

Sarah would be moving in tomorrow. She hadn't met the kids, but she didn't seem concerned about it. Eddie, on the other hand, was worried about how it would go over. He imagined the four of them sitting on the sofabed and flipchairs waiting for somebody to know what to say, and then Anthony and Dominic starting a fight over something stupid, like whether one of them spit on the other, as Sarah looked on in horror.

Something moved in the rearview mirror now, catching Eddie's attention. When he looked, he almost ran off the road.

The oatmeal flipchairs had worked themselves free, and the entire bedroom/living room ensemble was levitating off the back of Thin Jimmy's baby blue pickup. A highway magic show.

Eddie clutched at the dashboard instinctively, as if there were a lever to crank the furniture back down. He took his foot off the gas, but it was too late. The moment the furniture nosed above the cab, the wind caught it.

And everything was slow motion.

Eddie caught glimpses of the CAN'T BEAT THIS special dancing across his rearview mirror as he pulled Thin Jimmy's truck onto the shoulder. The sofa tumbled end over end in the slow lane, with the oatmeal flipchairs tagging along after it.

Seeing it in the mirror made Eddie think that somehow it wasn't happening. When he turned to look, it was hard to separate the furniture from himself. That was him, Eddie Passarelli, bouncing down the highway. His marriage, his career, his life.

The only salvation was that the sofa and chairs, not having the properties of conventional furniture, such as wood and other natural products, did not explode on impact. They reacted more like cartoon furniture.

Eddie saw one flipchair open, close, open, and close again as it cartwheeled along Interstate 95, as if it were demonstrating for passing motorists why it was called a flipchair. The other one caught a gust and sailed up high before spiraling out of the sky like a padded meteor and landing on the shoulder of the road.

It bounced once, hurdled the roadside railing, and fell out of sight below.

Finally, after what seemed like roughly six weeks, everything stopped. Eddie felt a headache growing, with roots in the eyeballs.

Just get out of here, he thought. It was a sign from God. It had to be. Get on the highway, take the truck back to Thin Jimmy, and go home. Nobody'll be back yet and you can pretend you never left.

In his gut, Eddie knew this was one of those critical moments in life when the decision you make, without benefit of wisdom, without knowledge of the consequences, can fuck you up for years. And it was fitting, he thought, that in his moment of truth, his hand would be forced not by some spiritual awakening, not by some cosmic revelation, but by cheap furniture falling off a gangster's truck.

Steve Forbert wailed.

> You're chasing some notion you've misunderstood
> You're trying so hard can't you tell it's no good
>
> You analyze everything into a no
> You're falling apart, you got nothing to show

It was the sound of screaming tires, the tires of a late-model BMW swerving around Eddie's twenty-nine-dollar oatmeal flipchair, that pulled him out of the truck.

He stood there a moment, wondering if there were a way to make it look like he was helping some other dumb bastard whose living room just got scattered over the highway.

Now he was wondering how long it took the traffic reporters to find out about this stuff. Maybe *Traffic Update* was already on the air: "Please be careful on southbound I-95, about a mile north of the Girard Avenue exit, where we have a report that Eddie Passarelli, an unemployed, pudgy, balding musician, who just walked out on his wife and kids, is retrieving discount furniture from the slow lane. Looks like a sofabed and some oatmeal flipchairs."

Eddie walked back toward the furniture and then broke into a gallop, seeing that it was a good couple of hundred yards back. Almost there, he stopped. Shit. He should have driven Thin Jimmy's truck back along the shoulder in reverse, because what the hell was he going to do with the sofa and chair once he got to them, carry them back to the truck on his head?

Eddie thought about just throwing himself onto the sofa and waiting to take a hit. Maybe a big rig would come along. But then he thought about how it would be written up in an obituary, and he imagined his kids telling their own children, years later, how he'd been snuffed out in a collision between a truck and a sofabed.

A guy in a passing car rolled down the window and laughed like a horse. Eddie flipped him off. He picked an old sneaker up off the shoulder and threw it at the car, too late to hit it.

Eddie dragged the sofa and flipchair off the highway and onto the shoulder. The beauty of it was you couldn't see the slightest sign of damage. Maybe a scuff mark or two was all.

Eddie saw this as symbolic, the furniture going through a traumatic experience but emerging intact. He took it as a sign that he was doing the right thing.

He remembered the other flipchair now, the one that bounced off the highway, and walked over to the railing to look down.

Down into his new neighborhood.

As far as he could see in any direction, it was boarded up row houses, graffiti, mounds of trash. The streets were paved with broken glass. Maybe he should have checked out the neighborhood first. He hadn't been to the house in a couple of years.

Eddie saw three kids down there, early teens, sitting on the stoop of a house with its roof burned off. A fourth kid was on the sidewalk in front of them. He had the oatmeal flipchair flipped out and was on his back, hands behind his head, like it was a day at the beach.

"Hey, that's my chair," Eddie yelled.

The kids looked up. The sun was behind Eddie and they couldn't see his face, just his silhouette. A cloud of black smoke drifted over the highway behind him.

"It fell off my truck," Eddie said. "I'm coming down to get it."

Eddie put the other flipchair on top of the sofa and tried hoisting the two of them onto his shoulder. The weight of the furniture wasn't a problem, but the package was too bulky. He'd have to go get the truck and back it up.

Eddie smelled something burning but didn't pay attention. He was thinking about whether he should ask the kid with the chair to meet him at the off ramp. He probably should, if he expected ever to see the flipchair again.

He walked back over to the railing and looked down.

Shit. All four kids were gone.

Eddie slumped down on the sofa. Looking south on I-95, in the direction he'd been traveling, he saw the smoke for the first time, and seeing it made the smell of it sharper. A black cloud mushroomed into the sky and dark shadows moved over the highway.

It was coming together in Eddie's head. The truck hesitating, missing. Maybe something in the electrical system.

Eddie jumped up, took two steps, and then broke into a sprint. When he got to within fifty yards, the heat was a wall.

Traffic had stopped and Eddie ran alongside the backed-up cars, circling the smoke and the heat to the upwind side of the fire. He heard crackling sounds and smelled the burning and the melting.

Thin Jimmy the gangster's new Ford wasn't baby blue anymore. It was charcoal gray, and half barbecued.

Eddie watched as the hood burped itself open and flames shot out from under it. Windows shattered and tires blew.

Then he remembered his guitar.

He raced to the passenger door, holding his hands in front of his face against the heat. Through the smoke, he saw the top of the guitar case and without thinking, he grabbed for the door handle.

It was white hot.

Eddie ran up the shoulder, looking for a rag or something, anything, so he could open the door. Another window shattered and Eddie looked back as the fire sucked air through the new hole, feasting on the rush.

Devouring his guitar.

Eddie sat on the ground and held his head in his hands, as if it might come apart otherwise. His eyes were closed when he heard the voice.

"I got your chair."

Eddie looked at the kid. A handsome boy, big brown eyes. A scar on his right cheekbone in the shape of Italy's boot. He was the kid from over the railing.

The boy set up the flipchair next to Eddie, in case he wanted to consider his life from a more comfortable position. Eddie didn't move; didn't say anything. He was coming up with a plan.

Thin Jimmy wouldn't want to hear an explanation. He'd want his fucking truck back, or another one just like it.

Maybe Eddie could get Inverso to tell Thin Jimmy a bomb went off.

Somebody must have planted it on the car, intending to blow up Thin Jimmy. Eddie Passarelli, by borrowing the truck, had actually saved his life.

Shit, Thin Jimmy wouldn't go for it.

Eddie looked up at the kid. The boy seemed to sense that something besides the truck was burning.

"You look like Anthony," Eddie said to him.

Something popped just then in Thin Jimmy's truck. A small explosion of gas or oil. Eddie and the boy turned toward it and then toward each other, just looking, respecting that there was nothing either one could say.

After they'd turned from each other, the boy spoke.

"No," he said. "My name's Gabriel."

Three

It was ten in the morning. Eddie kissed Sarah on the cheek when she left.

"I've got a few errands to run," she said.

"I won't be here when you get back," Eddie said. "Inverso got me that job at eleven thirty. A senior citizen Halloween dance or some goofy thing, almost two weeks early."

"I know," she said. "I'll see you later."

One week, they'd been together in Kensington. It hadn't gone quite as well as Eddie had hoped. Now that they were living together, he realized Sarah had stretches where she needed to be alone. He kept asking if everything was okay and she kept saying sure, she was fine.

Eddie figured it would just take time. This was a big transition for both of them, and she still hadn't met Anthony and Dominic. But Eddie felt okay about things. After a year of sneaking around on his wife, this was honest, at least.

From the beginning, he'd been flattered, if not puzzled, by Sarah's interest in him. She was pretty, smart and wise. She challenged him, and he felt better about himself when he was around her.

One night not long after they met, he thought he had embarrassed himself. They were talking about music and he tried to explain that he thought he had things inside of him that he wasn't sure how to get out. He couldn't put words to his thoughts, though, and apologized for not being more articulate about it. But Sarah said she knew exactly what he was talking about. You're an artist, she told him. An artist.

It was the first time in his life anybody called him that.

She said she had the same kind of frustration when she wrote short stories and poetry. A feeling of unfulfilled potential, and a fear, too. A fear that she'd never get it out. Or worse, that she'd find there was nothing there.

Eddie knew exactly what she meant.

Back when Eddie used to stay at the Old City loft Sarah shared with a roommate, she had often read poetry to him. She'd just grab a book off the shelf—she had more books than anyone Eddie had ever known—and flip to something she liked.

Eddie loved it. For a kid who grew up where nobody read anything but the racing form or the sports page, this was all new. They talked politics and religion, music and literature. Sarah brought Ivy League smarts to all those subjects, and Eddie brought a blue-collar street sense, and each one was intrigued by the other's perspective.

But the truth was, with the poetry thing, Eddie didn't always get it. One night Sarah had read Emily Dickinson, and Eddie thought it was the worst stuff he'd ever heard.

Forbidden fruit a flavor has
That awful orchard mocks;
How luscious lies the pea within
The pod that duty locks!

"That's nice," Eddie said, shifting in his seat and downing half a bottle of Yuengling in one gulp. Maybe if he drank a lot of beer, it would open his mind to this stuff.

Sarah had this habit of kicking off articles of clothing while she read, sometimes getting all the way down to panties and a camisole. It didn't seem like flirting at first, it seemed like she was just getting more comfortable around him. But whatever it was, Eddie wasn't going to risk losing it by criticizing her choice of poetry. He told her he thought Emily Dickinson was great.

Sometimes while Sarah read, they played *Kind of Blue,* by Miles Davis, or *Blue Trane,* by John Coltrane. On warmer evenings, when they knew her roommate wasn't going to be around, Sarah would sit curled like a question mark in the window well of the loft, which looked out on the Ben Franklin Bridge. The bridge was beautiful at night, with soft blue lights outlining the towers, the cables, and the gently arched span.

Eddie would study the way Sarah's hair fell over her shoulders and the way she ran her tongue over her lips every few minutes while reading. Every time he saw her she looked different, no matter where she sat, no matter what she was doing. She looked different the way the sky is always different and the ocean is always different. Familiar but slightly different.

The first few months they knew each other, Sarah and Eddie worked their way through Walt Whitman, e. e. cummings, Lawrence Ferlinghetti, Anne Sexton, Charles Simic, and Sylvia Path. And then one night Sarah introduced Eddie to Octavio Paz.

First she went to her bedroom, kicked off her sneakers, and unzipped her blue jeans. Eddie watched from the next room as fingers of light found her through the half-open door.

Off came the jeans, and then Sarah's fingers worked the buttons of her blue oxford shirt. The white T-shirt was next, Sarah peeling it over her head. Her hair fell out of the shirt and cascaded over her fair shoulders. She put on her favorite hat, a San Francisco Giants cap, and wearing only panties she walked slowly across the living room—a walk Eddie would never forget—and climbed into the window well.

The blue of the moon found her there, and she began to read.

> Listen to me as one listens to the rain
> not attentive, not distracted,
> light footsteps, thin drizzle,
> water that is air, air that is time
> the day is still leaving
> the night has yet to arrive,

figurations of mist,
at the turn of the corner,
figurations of time
at the bend in the pause . . .

Eddie walked over to her. He ran a hand through Sarah's hair and stroked her neck. With the back of his other hand, he brushed her breasts, her nipples hardening in the creases of his fingers.

She kept reading.

night unfolds and looks at me,
you are you and your body of steam,
you and your face of night
you and your hair, unhurried lightning . . .

Over the next two hours, the last spoken words, "unhurried lightning," hung in the room.

Sarah wore moonlight, and Eddie realized he had fallen in love with her sometime around Emily Dickinson.

Eddie couldn't believe that his mother expected to rent this place to anyone. The front door had warped shut the day after they moved in, and Eddie and Sarah had been crawling in and out of the side window. The rug, which might have been the color of chianti at one point, was now the color of the Delaware River. And as if the house weren't already dark and gloomy enough, half the light fixtures were broken.

Eddie put Monk and Mingus out the back door. He'd brought them to Kensington when his wife said they were going to keel over from hunger because they were his dogs and she wasn't going to lift a hand to feed them. Eddie was in the kitchen when the phone rang, and he had to think about where it was. In the living room somewhere. There. On the floor next to the sofa.

"Hello?"

"Yeah, pal, hold on a minute." Eddie didn't recognize the gruff voice. "Here we go. Lerner. You got a Sarah Lerner there?"

"She's not here right now," Eddie said. "She just left to run a few errands."

"Well listen, pal, could you tell her we're running ahead of schedule?"

"You're what?"

"Another job got done a little early is what happened."

Eddie had no idea what this guy was talking about.

"Who are you?" he asked.

"The movers."

"Movers?"

"Esposito Moving. Look, we're supposed to be there at twelve, but we'll be there in a half hour, like ten thirty, if you could let her know."

Son of a bitch.

"Yeah," Eddie said. "I could let her know."

Eddie dropped the phone on the floor. The blood drained from his face and he felt like he did when he watched Thin Jimmy's truck go up in flames.

"That bitch," he said, thinking about Sarah's last words to him before she left: "I'll see you later."

Much later, apparently. And he had to find out from the movers.

Eddie wanted to strangle her. Why hadn't she said something? They talked about everything. That was what made it so good. Hell, he could remember her grabbing him by the collar if he tried to go to sleep on her without settling an argument. "You're not going to treat me like your fucking wife," she'd say. "Talk to me, you son of a bitch."

And now she'd pulled this.

Eddie looked around the room for something to throw. His guitar was the closest thing, a beatup no-name steel-string with a crooked neck. He'd picked it up at the pawn shop, unable to afford anything remotely resembling the Gibson hollow-body that had gone up like kindling.

Hell, if he was going to throw something, it ought to be something of hers. He looked around the room again.

The menorah would be good. Her fucking menorah. Eddie went over and picked it up off the shelf.

The one thing she had said, in the way of a clue, was that she couldn't tell her parents about him. Not having to meet them was okay with Eddie, but he had a problem with the reason.

Judaism wasn't just a religion, Sarah had told him. It was a culture, an ethnicity, a history. A history that fades a little bit every time somebody marries outside. Her parents wanted her to marry a Jew and raise Jewish kids. Anything less and their hearts would be broken.

Jesus, Eddie had thought at the time. The Jews sounded like bigger bigots than the Italians.

"Then what the hell are you doing with me?" he had asked Sarah. "What am I, your goy toy?"

"I love you," she told him. "That's why I'm with you."

Damn, she was fucked up. Maybe he was better off without her.

Eddie put the menorah back. It was a religious thing, and he was afraid something terrible might happen if he threw it.

Sarah had some books on the shelf under the menorah, and Eddie spotted the perfect projectile. He grabbed the book, cocked his arm, and let it fly.

Emily Dickinson sailed out of the living room—mocking orchard, pea within a pod, forbidden fruit and all. The book carried over the dining room and crash-landed in the kitchen, where Monk and Mingus chased it as if this were a game of fetch.

Eddie trembled. He looked around, realizing this was it. He and this house, alone together.

The light was pale, the walls dingy. With his nostrils flared, he picked up a strong whiff of the damp, mildewy smell that filled every room, upstairs and down. All right, so it wasn't a penthouse, and the neighborhood was like Beirut. But Eddie thought it was kind of romantic, starting off in a place like this. And it wasn't as if Sarah was putting out a nickel for rent, so she had no complaints there.

With a quick inventory, Eddie realized three-fourths of the furniture was Sarah's, and it'd be gone in a couple of hours. In a couple of hours, he was going to have an empty shack, a shitty guitar, and a debt to the mob. And he'd probably be playing "Achey Breaky Heart" at a Halloween dance for senior citizens.

He never should have left his family. And he'd really fucked things up, the way he walked out.

Last week, when Eddie went back to Roxborough to get the dogs, Anthony and Dominic still didn't know he'd moved out. He'd been gone only two days at that point, and they figured he had been out of town on a job.

"You tell them," Eddie's wife told him. "You're the one walking out."

The kids were playing outside when Eddie got there. They didn't have a clue. That's what really hurt. They didn't see it coming, and it smacked them.

"Guys," Eddie said after calling them into the living room, "your mom and I . . ."

His wife ran in from the kitchen when she heard that. She'd been cooking and had a cleaver in her hand. It looked like she wanted to fillet Eddie right then and there.

"No," she said to the kids, pointing the knife at Eddie with fire in her eyes. "Not your mom and dad. Your dad. Just your dad. Your dad is moving out on us."

The boys looked at their mother, their mouths open, worried about what she might do. And they looked at Eddie with those looks he'd never forget.

It isn't true. Tell us it isn't true.

When they realized it was, every muscle in their little bodies went limp. They slumped down on the floor and rolled over on their sides and cried and cried. There was no anger in them, only hurt and fear.

Eddie hugged them and told them he loved them. He said he'd still see them all the time, don't worry. And then he left, with that Steve Forbert song playing in his head.

When Eddie drove back to Kensington and crawled in the window, Sarah handed him the phone.

"It's your wife," she said, fire in her eyes, too.

"If you expect to ever see my sons again," his wife screamed into the phone, loud enough for Sarah to hear, "you better hit the lottery. Because you're going to need a team of fucking attorneys to get within six blocks of this house."

Eddie looked at the clock. He had about an hour before the Halloween dance. He decided to call his wife.

Monk and Mingus had a look in their eyes, as if they were thinking, "What a loser."

"Fuck you guys," Eddie told them, and then he dialed.

"How you doin'?"

His wife said she was fine.

Maybe they could get together, Eddie said, talk it over. Work this thing out.

"You think so?" she said.

"Yeah, I think so," Eddie said. "I really think so."

He'd made a mistake. He wanted another chance, now that he realized what was really important.

"So the slut dumped your ass?"

Eddie was startled.

"What?"

"You heard what I said."

Jesus, was he that obvious?

"No," Eddie said. "I've just been thinking it over."

"Well guess what," she said. "I was thinking it over myself, and you know something?"

"What?"

"You can go fuck yourself."

Shit.

"Look," Eddie said, "what if I come over now and we talk about this?"

"I don't think so."

"I think we should at least talk about it."

"I think you're a lousy piece of shit."

"I can come right over."

"No you can't."

"Why not?"

"Because that's not how it works."

"Look, I made a mistake, that's what I'm saying."

"And it's as simple as that? All you gotta do is say you made a mistake, and everything's all right again?"

"I thought we could just talk."

"Eddie."

"Yeah?"

"I got company."

"You got company?"

"Yeah, I got company."

She had to be kidding.

"You're busting my balls, right?"

She didn't answer.

"Get the fuck out of here," Eddie said. "You're kidding me, right?"

Still no answer. Eddie was starting to burn.

"One week, and you got fucking company?" he said.

"Geez, I'm sorry, Eddie. I meant to check with you first, get permission, you know? I don't know what came over me. Hell, I meant to ask you about it, and I was going to ask your girlfriend there, too, see if it was all right with the two of youse. Geez, can you forgive me, Eddie?"

"Who is it?" Eddie asked. He could feel his heartbeat in his ears.

"You're a piece of work," she said. "You know that, Eddie? A real piece of work."

"Who is it?" he insisted, contempt in his voice.

She went nuts with that.

"It's none of your fucking business who it is," she screamed. "But just so I don't have to hear your pathetic ass calling up here every day, asking who it is, it's Paulie Rego."

Eddie's shoulders slumped and his chest caved in. He put his hand to his head, feeling an aneurism coming on.

"Paulie Rego?"

"You got a problem with that?"

Paulie Rego was another guitarist. He and Eddie put a band together in high school. The first band either of them was in. Later, they both went into jazz. Things were okay between them until about ten years ago, when Rego's career started to take off. In the last five years, he'd put out a couple of CDs, toured Europe, and earned a good living.

Eddie said it was a sellout. Rego did cocktail stuff and would even throw in pop bullshit, whatever the audience wanted to hear. If Eddie had made any peace with his own failures, it was only by blaming the Paulie Regos of the world for corrupting the art.

And now Paulie Rego wasn't just stealing Eddie's jobs. He was fucking his wife.

"This is to get back at me," Eddie said to his wife. "You're with Paulie Rego because he's hotter in the clubs."

"No, honey," she said. "That ain't it at all. I'm with Paulie Rego because he's hotter in the sack."

Eddie threw the phone against the wall.

He'd never in his life been left by a woman. Now he'd been left twice in five minutes.

He paced the room, end to end, with Monk and Mingus following behind him. He almost tripped over them as he turned to start another lap.

Maybe he could work on Sarah. It sounded like his wife was gone for sure, but Sarah could be persuaded. Hell, it wasn't some damn fling they were having. They were natural together and could talk about anything. Anything at all. She'd even told him about the guy who dumped her, and he'd told her about his fucked-up marriage.

Maybe that was what poisoned it, bringing the past into it. But Eddie liked what she had to say. She didn't decide things for him, she just got him to where his questions about himself sounded more and more like answers.

"You've got two choices," she said one day. "Fix your marriage, or get out of it. But you can't leave it like this. This is no good for any of you."

Eddie picked up the pawnshop guitar and started to fiddle with it. He had his music, anyway. He'd lost two women, and his good guitar, but he still had his music, and that was all he needed. Music gave back what you put into it. It didn't walk out on you.

The doorbell rang.

The movers? Sarah? What would he say to her? Part of him wanted to tell her off, part of him wanted to beg her to stay.

It couldn't be Sarah. She would have come in through the window.

Eddie asked who it was through the door.

"Hey man," Gabriel said.

Shit, this kid again.

"What do you want?"

"Nothing," Gabriel said.

Nothing. Here he is, knocking on the door at a time like this, and what does he want? He wants nothing.

Gabriel had helped Eddie carry the furniture to his house the day the truck burned, and he had come back the next day to show Eddie where the best pawnshops were.

"Look," Eddie said. "I'm really busy right now. I've got a job in about a half hour, I don't even know where the fucking place is."

"What's the name of it?" Gabriel asked.

Eddie pulled out his wallet and looked at a note he had scribbled. "The Girard Rec Center."

"I know where that is," Gabriel said through the door. "I could show you."

What the hell, Eddie thought. Nobody else would have him, but for whatever reason, the kid kept coming back.

Four

Ofelia had been awake half an hour, staring through her thoughts, before she rolled out of bed. Her feet landed in the footprints they'd matted into the rug over the years, her toes feeling the morning coolness of the shag carpet. She took a deep breath and blew it out.

Three weeks she'd been riding, every night, and not a trace of Gabriel. She'd try to get to sleep about ten each night, toss and turn under blankets made of lead, and then go out on the bike at midnight or after. Sometimes she rode until it was time for her morning shift at the diner. Today she had the lunch and dinner shift. A chance to sleep in. But there was no way.

She wore a gray Temple University T-shirt and white panties. A stiffness climbed the backs of her legs as she stood up and moved through the room. There was a mattress on the floor, no box spring, no frame. Against the back wall, a nicked pine dresser. Next to that, Johanna Farms milk crates, four gray ones, stacked like shelves. They held clothes that didn't fit in the dresser.

Ofelia walked through the aches in her legs, stretching the muscles with each step, moving now past the only painting in the house. It was a Monet and it hung on the wall near the door, a window to another world. She paused to look at it.

The Monet was slightly crooked; a nail nubbed out of the bottom left corner of the pine frame. One day, about a year ago, she'd gone to Center City to see *Casablanca* at the Roxy Theater, and a crazy man jumped in front of her as she turned a corner. He began screaming at Ofelia, his eyes wild. He foamed at the mouth and said he wanted to give her a shampoo. Ofelia ran into the Salvation Army thrift shop at Twenty-first and Market to get away from him, and there it was. Ten dollars, frame and all. Ofelia recognized the painting from an art history book she kept at home and often leafed through with Gabriel.

Ofelia hoped one day to find out more about her own talent. She'd always had an interest and a knack, but never pursued it because her parents didn't encourage it and her husband didn't appreciate it. This history made her all the more supportive of Gabriel. From the time he was able to hold a crayon, he was going to be an artist. He knew it, she knew it.

This was one of the cool, brooding pieces Monet did in London, a period in which, Ofelia was certain, he had been dumped by a lover. The Parliament building was emerging through a foggy, purple dawn. Or maybe it was falling dark at sunset. That's what she was trying to figure out now. Was it the end of one day or the start of another? Either way, Ofelia liked the way the filtered light transformed the mood of the building, revealing a different part of its beauty. And though she knew better, she held on to the corner of a dream—that it was an original, and she had a million-dollar painting on the wall of her house in Kensington.

She remembered the day now when she raced in the door with it, anxious to show Gabriel what she'd found.

"Gabriel," she called from the kitchen. No matter where she was, her voice filled the house. It was a voice that went with her body. Husky and full when she raised it, sexy and warm when she lowered it. "Gabriel, come here."

She'd become even more convinced of his talent when he was five or six. He had moved beyond stick figures before the other kids, had begun shading his subjects and giving them perspective. Drawing eyes that could look off the page.

Gabriel was convinced Ofelia's Monet was the real thing. He ran to the living room for the art history book and flipped to the painting.

"Look," he said. "This is it."

Take it to the art museum, he pleaded. Take it and let them look at it. If it was real, he'd split the money with her, since it was her painting and his idea.

He always had a deal, a cut, a plan. It worried Ofelia, the way his mind divided up all the things in the world.

Ofelia was a little embarrassed to admit to the same dream. She told Gabriel she wasn't going to bounce into the art museum like some nutcase and ask them what they thought of her ten-dollar thrift-shop painting.

"We'll never know if you don't ask," Gabriel said, giving her those eyes. "Don't you think there's a chance?"

She wanted to hug him, but he was getting too old for that. He'd be embarrassed.

"Yes, I think there's a chance," she said, answering a question bigger than the one he'd asked. "Sometimes I do."

Ofelia went to the bathroom and drew a bath. In married life, she had always taken showers. But back then the only purpose was to get clean. Now it was therapy. She'd slip down to where her head floated just above the suds, six inches away from disappearing, and run her fingers over the surface of the water. She could practically hypnotize herself with the sound.

Ofelia brought a soapy hand out of the bubbles and picked at a few nubs of crust in the open pizza box on the hamper. She wondered if it was okay to eat a dried glob of cheese that had been sitting there since yesterday, when she finished an entire pie while bathing. But she drew her hand back, thinking better of it. The cheese might have gone bad. And besides, she needed discipline in her life, if she was going to get herself together. She might as well start now.

She returned to her room wrapped in a towel, wet hair glistening, face flush from the hot water. In the places where they had hurt, her legs were warm and felt better than the rest of her. She was getting into decent shape with all this riding. Gabriel would be proud.

Ofelia closed the blinds on the window that looked into the yard of a house that was a backward image of her own. Two boys had lived there, and Gabriel had been friendly with them until Ofelia ordered him to stay away. She could always see it in kids, like there was a sign over their heads that only she could read. Ofelia could just walk down the street and separate the living from the dying.

The oldest one was dead at seventeen, shot two years ago in the street in front of his house while his mother smoked crack at the kitchen table. The younger brother, fourteen at the time, kneeled over his brother as he died, slapping his face and screaming that he didn't want to be left alone. He had not been seen since that night.

A frameless mirror sat on top of the pine dresser and Ofelia looked at her reflection, hair down to the tops of her breasts. As she lifted her arms to brush it, the towel fell from her body.

Ruben had liked to pretend he was still asleep when she came out of the shower. And when she peered into the mirror, he would be suddenly behind her, sniffling at that fresh smell of clean soft skin, his breath tickling the small hairs on her neck.

With a magician's touch, he'd pull at the tuck in the towel and it would slip from her body, and before it landed in a sigh, his hands were on her breasts.

In the mirror, she saw him behind her, his dark head buried in the curve of her neck and shoulder, his nakedness cool on her bath-warmed body. She could feel him there now.

One of his hands—they were big hands, strong and graceful—dropped from her breast and floated smooth against her skin. His fingers were water, teasing down over her stomach and drawing a wave through her, and she felt it in the place it was going to before it got there.

Angry with herself, Ofelia shook the thought from her mind. How many times had she shaken it? Two years, he'd been gone. Two years.

She had met Ruben at a wedding reception in the old Dunfy Hotel on City Avenue. She knew the bride, he knew the groom, and she knew the instant she saw him what is possible in the world. Ofelia had been living with another man for two years. It was all comfort and security, but no passion, and although Ofelia was young she knew she would always be the type of woman to trade the two for the one.

He was tall and handsome and strong, a halfbreed like herself, Cuban and Italian, with smoldering eyes that made love to half the women in the room. And his legs, an athlete's legs. Ofelia wanted to bite him.

She was something to look at herself, Rubenesque in all her dark and youthful beauty, the kind of beauty that doesn't know it's there. And people talked about the way they looked together, Ofelia and Ruben, a couple to put on top of a wedding cake.

He held her hand on the dance floor and Ofelia twirled on her heels, natural as the spinning of the planet, long hair flying wild, the room racing in a hot circle and Ofelia drunk with the limitless possibilities of lust and fear. Fear, because in his handsome darkness, and in all the unkept promises she saw in his eyes, there was a danger Ofelia had already given herself to.

"Arthur, you have to move out," she told her limp and lukewarm lover when she got home from the party that night.

Arthur did so without question, and with no apparent trace of regret. He was gone inside of three days, affirming Ofelia's conviction that safe men had no self-respect. And to think she'd wasted two years of her life on Arthur when Ruben the Cuban was eligible and unclaimed.

In the three days it took Arthur to clear out, time moved backward for Ofelia. She ached with desire, dizzy with the thought of her bedroom spinning like the dance floor.

Ruben said he would be there at eight o'clock on a Wednesday night, and Ofelia spent the entire day undoing things she'd just done. First she hid her *Cosmo* magazines in embarrassment, and then hauled them back up and put them where he'd be sure to see them, thinking it would suggest she was well-versed on what men really want.

First she put pots and pans in the drainer, to make him think she could cook, and then she put them away so he wouldn't think she was a slob.

She dug into her wardrobe, pulling out seven different outfits over the course of two hours, trying on each one, and then tossing the clothes into a mounting heap on the floor of the closet.

She took two showers, not happy with the way her hair looked after the first. At seven forty-five, she ran a stick of antiperspirant under her arms for the sixth time, not certain she had done it yet. Her armpits were beginning to sting.

He didn't come at eight.

He didn't come at nine.

He didn't come at ten.

At eleven, Ofelia began trashing the apartment she had worked half the day to clean. She tore up the *Cosmos*, littering the floor with ribbons of fashion trends and sex surveys. She even found herself missing Arthur at one point, but pinched herself for the thought.

Finally she tore off the seventh outfit and put on a torn T-shirt and baggy sweatpants and scrubbed off the makeup and just then the doorbell rang, and five minutes later, though she was sure Ruben carried the scent of another woman's lust, they were swimming inside each other.

A child was conceived that night. A child they called Gabriel.

In six months of courtship and all the years of marriage, Ruben's sense of timing never changed—he was late, he forgot things—and neither did Ofelia's memories of that first night, a restless night in which her underarms burned and she dreamed in two-dimensional black and white of intimacy and betrayal.

But all it had taken for her to gamble on Ruben was the realization, when she rose with the morning sun that first day and opened her eyes, that the lean and muscular bare ass next to hers was not Arthur's.

She wondered now, alone in her bedroom and trapped inside her mind, why she so often forgot the pain Ruben had brought her when they were together. The distant eyes, the stone silence, the touch gone cold. She had been tormented by the fear that he hadn't married her for love, but because she was pregnant. And how foolish it had been of her to think, despite all the evidence, that he'd change.

But she didn't really expect any of it to seem rational or make sense. If Ofelia had learned anything, it was this: Love is mental illness going in and mental illness coming out. In between, you do a lot of laundry.

Fuck him.

Ofelia sprinkled powder on her chest and smoothed it over her skin. Now she took hold of the small bottle of toilet water on the dresser, something she seldom used, and shook a few drops onto her hand. She stroked her neck, anointed her shoulders, dabbed between her breasts. The moisture left frosted fingerprints in the powder.

She brushed her hair once more and it took body this time, soft waves. She studied the look in the mirror, turning her head from side to side. Not bad, she thought. For forty, she didn't look bad. At some point, she could see herself with another man. If her mother were alive, she'd be pushing, and Ofelia knew exactly what she'd say.

Ruben leaving wasn't the worst thing that happened in your life. It was the best.

Ofelia put on a pair of blue panties from her top drawer, and a black T-shirt from one of the milk crates. The black skirt was thrown over a folding chair at the foot of the bed and she put that on too, and then her shoes. Black hightop sneakers of soft leather. And then Ofelia went down to the kitchen in the black-on-black outfit that had become her uniform. She was not entirely comfortable with the flowery smell of perfume that followed her. It turned into something else in the kitchen, where it mingled with lingering drifts of pork and beans to create what smelled to her like men's cologne.

Ofelia put on a pot of coffee and turned the radio to KYW for the night's weather forecast. A story came on about the condition of Mayor DeMarco, who'd been in the hospital since his heart attack two weeks ago. The announcer said something about a blockage and some surgery they were going to have to do. The forecast was clear and cold, with possible frost in the northern and western suburbs.

The fresh coffee overpowered the other smells, and Ofelia moved the pot out of the way and caught the flow with a cup. With her first sip, she looked at the phone book on the table. She had thumbed through the yellow pages after getting in from last night's bike ride, looking up churches. It was just an idea, not a decision. She needed help.

Her eyes traveled from the phone book to the slash marks on the wall. They startled her every time, as if she'd never seen them before. Ofelia put a finger to her mouth, nibbling at a nail. Sometimes she felt as if she were a spectator in her own life.

There were twenty-seven now. Five clusters of five, one of two.

The red bike was against the door, its shine gone. Ofelia took the chalk in her hand and made the twenty-eighth mark.

She hadn't seen the blue haze since the first time, but she often felt as if she were being watched, and connected that feeling to her premonition of Gabriel's death. In those moments, alone to the world, she was convinced that it wasn't a premonition at all. It had happened. And maybe Gabriel was watching her now, from another place.

Her theory was that time isn't linear, the way most people like to think of it. It sort of piles up on itself, sometimes making the past, the present, and the future indistinguishable. Gabriel was alive, and that was real. But she'd seen him die, and that was real, too.

In better moments, Ofelia liked to think she had read the signs all wrong, and that it wasn't Gabriel, but she, who swam in darkness. To encourage the notion, she had scribbled an offering on the wall, above EL NADA EN LO OBSCURO. She couldn't say exactly when, because the whole wall-marking thing seemed like the work of someone she didn't know.

TAKE ME. That was what she wrote. TAKE ME.

If one of them had to die, did it have to be Gabriel?

Ofelia thought about calling the neighborhood boy back to rewrite her offering in Spanish, because whatever was out there, threatening her, seemed to have a preference for Spanish. But she wasn't sure how she'd explain the situation this time, or whether the boy would even be willing to set foot back in the house after his first visit.

The taste and the smell of the coffee made Ofelia think about her job at the diner. It was easier to keep her mind occupied there, partly because Stella, her best friend, always seemed to know exactly when to tease her or trash one of the customers or tell her some dumb joke.

Stella had told one yesterday. Why did the Siamese twins move from New York to London?

I don't know, why?

Because the other one wanted to drive.

Stella, that's your worst.

You know you'll be tellin' it, Stella said.

Ofelia had been at the diner five years, and the entire time, she'd told herself she was going to take night classes at Temple University, maybe get into the nursing program. There just wasn't time, though. Especially after Ruben left. Ofelia had to almost double her hours at the diner, and still, she and Gabriel barely made it month to month.

Ofelia looked around the kitchen. Three empty pizza boxes were on the counter. A saucepan sat in the sink, a reddish film floating in it. Except for the smell of coffee, the kitchen air was thick and stale, same as in the other rooms. The house had no side windows, being in the middle of a row-house block, so it got no cross-ventilation. Ofelia was convinced the furniture had soaked up the scent of everything she had ever cooked. Especially the worn, shapeless, green plaid sofa in the living room. Every time someone sat in it, it sent up a drift of dinner from last month or who knows when.

Ofelia's eyes went back to the phone book. She had drawn a circle around the name of one church.

Holy Ghost Roman Catholic Church.

The words took her into the church. Even though she'd never been in there, she could see it.

It was empty, with a silence that fell through itself. Ofelia listened to her footsteps on the red tile, the sound traveling up, like prayer, and gathering under a high ceiling.

She shook her head. The thought of church was haunting. Weddings and funerals and holy ghosts.

Ofelia brought herself out of the church and back into the kitchen. It was scary here, too, she thought. But writing on the wall and seeing things in blue didn't seem any stranger than a church calling itself Holy Ghost.

She wondered what she'd say if she called.

Hello, my name is Ofelia Santoro and my son has been kidnaped.

No.

Hello, my name is Ofelia Santoro and I'd like to talk to someone about becoming a regular parishioner.

No way.

Hello, my name is Ofelia Santoro, my husband left me, my son ran away, the devil is in my kitchen, I haven't had it since the Reagan administration, and I'd like to know more about the concept of the Holy Ghost.

She liked that one. She liked it a lot.

Ofelia poured herself another cup of coffee—black and strong—and took a sip. Then she picked up the phone and dialed.

"Can I help you?"

Ofelia wanted to hang up, but didn't let herself. A secretary transferred her to a priest.

Ofelia held the cup with both hands, squeezing the warmth out of it as she waited.

The priest's voice was kind.

"Yes, ma'am, how can I help you?"

She was surprised by how easy it was to tell him she had tried to do right, had told her son to stay off the streets. She was surprised, too, by how easy it was to say she was afraid, and that she didn't know who else to call.

It felt good to say she was afraid.

Yes, she'd called the police, they were no help at all. No, she had no family. No, she didn't know where her son's father was.

The priest listened patiently. When she was done, he said, "I see."

It didn't sound to Ofelia like a judgmental and condescending "I see," which was what she expected.

He waited for her to continue.

"Well, I'm not even sure why I called, or what you can do."

He asked if she'd like to come in and talk about it.

"I'm not in the parish," she said. "I've never even been to the church."

Shit. Now he'll probably tell her to forget it.

"Can you make it at noon?" he asked.

Ofelia looked at the clock. It was eight thirty, and she wondered what she'd do for three and a half hours.

Five

Gabriel was on his back when he opened his eyes, and the first thing he saw was Michael Jordan upside down and blurry, flying across his bedroom. The poster was over his bed and Gabriel was staring up at it, goop in his eyes from sleep, wrinkles matted into his clothes. He always wore the next day's clothes to bed to save time in the morning.

His father had gotten him the poster at the Gallery, and for the longest time, Jordan had had the wall to himself. But Gabriel couldn't ignore Charles Barkley, who played for the Seventy-Sixers and later was traded to the Phoenix Suns. Barkley didn't have Jordan's grace or moves, he was more like a bull on rollerskates. But he was good, and he told people what he liked or didn't like about them, whether they asked or not. Gabriel, who was more inclined to paint his thoughts than tell them to someone, didn't necessarily admire that, but he was intrigued by it.

One month after his father left, Gabriel had gone to the Gallery and bought a poster of Barkley. He wasn't sure what to do with it at first. He felt like he was dishonoring a trust between himself, his father, and Michael Jordan by letting someone else hang on the same wall. Five weeks went by before he decided to put Barkley four or five feet away, off to one side of his bed, and about six inches lower than Jordan.

Gabriel lay still, listening for the sound of his mother moving through the house. She should be up by now, getting ready for work at the diner. Then she'd make sure he was up, try to get him to eat breakfast, and tell him to have a nice day at school.

She had to be onto him by now. She must know he skipped school half the time, even though his grades were mostly Bs. The problem he had with school was, what's the point? You didn't see many grown-ups in Kensington with jobs, and it wasn't like a high school diploma was going to change that.

And school was boring. The last time he'd gone, they had a quiz in industrial arts.

"What is technology?" was the first question.

Gabriel had looked around the classroom. Thirty-two kids. Most of them lived within a block or two of a drug corner. They'd all thrown themselves to the ground, or to the floors of their houses, when they heard gunshots. Most of them had a relative in prison. Most of them had no car unless someone in the family was selling drugs. A lot of them had no electricity, and Gabriel knew of two classmates who had no running water.

The second question was, "What is a system of technology?"

Gabriel could always bullshit his way through those kinds of tests. And if they were going to ask stupid questions like that, questions the teacher got from those reviews at the back of each textbook chapter, that's what they deserved. A bullshit answer. Besides which, he was going to be an artist. What did he need with technology?

When Gabriel was in second and third grades, his father would walk him to school because it was near the El station where he caught a train to work in a hat factory in North Philadelphia. His father was tall and strong—it seemed like nothing in the world could scare him. Gabriel would hold his dad's hand, and when he saw friends on the way to school, he'd call out to them, proud to be seen with his father.

His dad said very little on those walks, but that seemed normal to Gabriel. His dad was the same way with his mom, holding most of himself back. Every day, though, when they got to the steps of the school, his father would look down and say something to him.

"Pay attention. You don't wanna end up like your old man."

Same words, day after day. Gabriel never questioned it, but he didn't understand.

He wanted to be just like his dad. Exactly like him.

The hat factory shut down when Gabriel went into fourth grade, and he had walked to school alone after that. He could still remember the disappointment, those first few weeks of going to school without his father at his side. It seemed like it changed everything. His father stayed home, circling jobs in the morning newspaper and making phone calls. He found jobs here and there, but never anything safe and secure. Never anything so steady that he could walk Gabriel to school again.

"Gabriel?"

His mother was calling from down the hall. She had a voice that sounded just as clear whether she was in the same room or across the street.

"You up?"

He didn't feel like answering. Most people said a lot more than they needed to, as far as he was concerned. He got out of bed, opened the door, and then threw it shut. The noise would be his answer.

She had cried again in the night, but he hadn't gone in this time. This time, something changed in him. He had lain awake in the dark, hearing an occasional gunshot, and then a siren, and feeling closer to his father than he'd felt since the disappearance. Not angry now. Seeing, for the first time, the edge of the reasons for his leaving.

His mother had cried him back to sleep from the other room, and in Gabriel's dream, Michael Jordan raced up court and then took off, not just jumping but flying, staying up in the air longer than anyone is supposed to.

Gabriel stood at the mirror over his dresser, running his hands over himself to smooth wrinkles out of his blue oxford shirt, which he buttoned all the way up to his neck. He wore faded, baggy blue jeans low on his butt. That was the look. He was lanky to begin with, but with pants low, and shirt tucked in, he looked like one of those freaks in a funhouse mirror. All torso.

His Sixers cap was a good one, all wool, and it was fitted, not one of those cheap jobs with the adjustable plastic belt in the back. Gabriel hated those. This one was black, with a red bill, and he wore it pulled down low, to where he'd have to tilt his head back to see the ceiling. His face was all eyes and mouth under there. Small and dark.

Gabriel opened the top drawer of his dresser and his father looked up at him. Gabriel had done the sketch about a week ago. Whenever he did a new one he threw the old one away. There were no photos of his father, none that he knew of, anyway. So he was always working from memory, and from the last sketch he'd done.

He looked at his father's eyes, and then in the mirror at his own. The same. Sad. Burning low. Somewhere else.

He wondered if his father looked anything like this sketch. It had been two years. He might be gray now. His face might be fuller. He might be dead.

Two years and not a call.

His mother didn't acknowledge him when he went into the kitchen, and Gabriel wondered if she was mad at him for not going into her room when she cried. She was near the door, digging into her purse for keys.

"I'll bring something from the diner tonight," she said. She hated to cook, which was okay with Gabriel. He'd eaten enough of her cooking to know her heart wasn't in it. "What do you want?"

She still hadn't looked at him, but Gabriel was looking at her. She was getting fatter. He wished she'd start riding the bike, but she always did this with the presents he bought her. She pretended she had never got them.

"Have you seen my sketchpad?" he asked.

"How about meat loaf, or chicken?"

"Fine," Gabriel said. "Have you seen my sketchbook?"

"How come I never see you with any homework besides art?"

"Meat loaf," he said.

"What?"

"Meat loaf. For sandwiches."

"Okay. But answer my question. How come you never have math or science or English? You can't ignore those things just because you can draw. What do you want for breakfast?"

"I'm not hungry."

"There's cereal. You could make toast."

He didn't answer.

"You're not hungry and then you go and eat junk," she said. "Pretzels, pizza. You better start eating right. You don't want to end up like your mother."

Some days, Gabriel wondered who he was supposed to end up like.

When she was ready to leave, she turned to him, and he could tell. She wasn't going to bring up last night, but it was there.

With his eyes, he apologized for not going into her room. With her eyes, she apologized for expecting him to.

Gabriel was glad he hadn't gone in. She had to do this on her own. Sometimes it seemed like the hardest thing wasn't that his father was gone, but that they had to share the house with the part of him he'd left behind. Gabriel had drawn them that way, many times, in sketches—him and his mother on either side of his father, who wasn't filled in. He was hollow. An outline.

"I love you," his mother said to him, kissing him on the cheek.

She never said that. It was understood, but unspoken. Gabriel didn't know what to say back. He looked away, and she was out the door and gone before he had to decide.

Nefario's Market had a newspaper rack at the door, and Gabriel grabbed an *Inquirer* and a *Daily News.* There were four lollipop stools at the counter, and two formica tables with three chairs each. Gabriel sat at one of the tables with his papers, and when the waitress looked his way, he nodded.

She brought coffee as he spread the *Inquirer* business page over the table. She set the coffee down gently, but slapped the cream and sugar onto the table, first the two creams, then the two sugars.

"You know what?" she said, bringing her eyes down to his. "You're getting more stupid every day."

Gabriel didn't look up from the business page. Marisol had a year and a half on him and this was his edge, reading the news. He'd gotten hooked on the papers in a sixth-grade history class, when they had had to bring in current events. The teacher had a reporter from the *Inquirer* come in and the reporter said something about how thirty-five cents bought you a pair of eyes and ears in every city in the world, and it had struck Gabriel as a good deal.

He didn't give a shit about the business news, but he figured it was the section that would make the biggest impression. In this neighborhood, Marisol couldn't know too many guys who drank coffee and shook their heads over a twelve-point drop in the Dow Jones average.

He didn't respond to her insult. Didn't even look up. Not until she walked away.

This was the pose he'd drawn her in. A hundred times. A thousand. Moving away from him at that same angle, black hair splashing over a perfect shoulder. Her lips full, skin like cream, face in a pout. For him.

She came back his way now. Tight blue jeans. A loose white Temple Wrestling T-shirt. Hightop sneakers.

Red lipstick.

"I'm telling you, Gabriel," she said. "You better get your narrow brown ass to school."

He liked that she was concerned about him. And he liked pretending he didn't notice.

And he wondered if she knew that he loved her.

She took him to sleep every night and she was there when he woke up. When he wasn't a virgin anymore, she was going to be why.

"You don't fucking love her," his buddy Ralph had said. "You get a hard-on, that ain't love, dickhead."

Gabriel didn't see a distinction. For two years now, he'd been in love with Marisol. He was sure it was love.

"I don't see your ass in school," Gabriel said as Marisol dropped his food on the table. Bacon and egg on a roll, salt and pepper.

"How many times I told your ass," she said. "I got to help out my mom and dad. Plus, I go to the night program. Don't see your ass in no night school neither."

For the first time in his life, Gabriel found himself wanting to take showers. He had even thought about hanging his clothes up instead of sleeping in them.

When he was done and up to leave, Marisol shook her head at him, disgusted. And then her face broke into a sweet smile. She couldn't help it.

Gabriel let it mean what he wanted it to mean.

Gabriel walked home from Nefario's knowing that was it. There was no one moment he could look back on and say that was when he decided to leave. It sort of built up without him knowing it was building up. One thing was, with his new job, it would be impossible to account for all his time away. His mother would know what was up, and there was no way he could live under the same roof with her while he was selling drugs.

The question was: Should he write her a note?

Gabriel went up to his room and sat down on the end of his bed with a pen and his sketchbook.

"Dear Mom:"

He sat there a long time, looking at the morning light that fell through his window. A half dozen ideas went through his head, none of them any good.

He got up and scanned the room to see what he would take with him. Maybe he should throw some things into a bag. Extra socks or underwear? Nah. Another shirt? Nah. His toothbrush? Hell, what he had on his back was about all he'd need.

Blue jeans. Black hightop sneakers. An oversize Army jacket that hung halfway between his waist and his knees. The Sixers cap.

He went back to the bed and picked up the sketchbook and looked at "Dear Mom:"

Still, nothing came to him. This wasn't going to be a forever kind of thing, though. He wasn't leaving the country or anything. Hell, he wasn't even leaving the neighborhood. He was just going to be gone a while. Maybe that's what he'd write. He'd be back soon, don't worry.

Don't worry?

Gabriel tore the piece of paper out of the book and crumpled it in his hand. Without thinking, he began sketching his mother. He drew her beautiful, which was how he saw her. But there was a sadness in her eyes. She was trapped inside herself, and tormented by the company.

Gabriel tore the drawing out of the book and tossed it in the wastecan. He pulled a sock out of his drawer. Inside was a wad of money. One hundred fifty dollars. His last payday for working lookout.

On his way down Diamond Street, Gabriel tried not to admit to himself that he wasn't sure about this. And he wondered if his father had been.

Gabriel had started out two years ago, right after his father left. He was twelve.

Kids at school had new sneakers. They had starter jackets. They bought pizza slices and pineapple soda after school. With his father gone, he and his mother didn't have that kind of money. But it wasn't money that got him into it. So many kids did it, a lot of the wrong was taken out of it. It was instead of baseball or a movie. Instead of homework.

And beyond that, it was all so obvious. It wasn't something that happened behind closed doors or in secret hideaways. Drugs were peddled around the clock on public streets. The cops knew it, City Hall knew it, the goddamn White House knew it, and still it went on, a Chinese army of young dealers waiting in the ranks to feed a national thirst, selling drugs the way kids once sold lemonade. And something about the openness suggested a degree of social acceptance that made it easier for Gabriel to become a part of it.

Some parents knew their kids were involved, but they liked the money the kids brought home and pretended they didn't know where it came from. Gabriel never had it that easy. His mother warned him. Pleaded. Especially after the kid who lived behind them got killed.

In that first job two years ago, Gabriel was a decoy. He was posted inside a house that customers used as a smoking lounge. He had to peek out the window the whole time, looking for a signal, which was kind of boring. If police came, his job was to run. The idea was that the police would go after him, giving the handlers time to hide the drugs back in the house, and giving customers time to clear out. Even if the police caught him, which they only did once or twice, there was nothing they could do to him. It wasn't against the law to run down the street.

For this, he made twenty dollars a day.

He was nervous and scared at times, only a sixth-grader and working for a drug gang called Black Caps, the color of the plastic tops on the inch-long crack vials. But there was something about it that gave him a sense of power and control.

The two people he cared about more than anything in the world had split up. Over that, he had no control. On the streets, Gabriel loved his father and he hated him. The danger, and the fact that he wasn't supposed to be out here, made the love greater and the hate greater, too.

In his next job, Gabriel worked as a lookout for fifty dollars a day. His responsibility was to yell "Five-oh" if he saw a cop, or *"Agua,"* which meant to throw water on a hot corner.

Gabriel, who'd always had a good memory, was an especially good lookout because he never forgot a face or a vehicle. If plainclothes cops jumped out of a car at the next intersection and threw a drug crew against a wall, kicking at their insteps to spread their legs, Gabriel would wander in close enough to study the faces of the officers. He'd remember a mole, a scar, a tattoo. Sometimes he drew sketches for the crew supervisor. He drew sketches of the unmarked cars, too, detailing a small dent, a missing hubcap. And he'd be the one to suggest that a car with a real estate name on the side of it was a fake. Same with an exterminator's truck. They were cops.

That's why he was being promoted. Gabriel was looked upon in his drug gang as something of a rising star, and beginning today, he was a dealer. His new job would be to stand on a corner and sell drugs to people who drove up in an endless stream, half of them in nice cars from Jersey or the Pennsylvania suburbs. Fucked-up white people.

His pay would be one hundred fifty dollars a day.

They hadn't told him what corner he'd have, so Gabriel was headed north, on his way to the stash house where the drug boss had been staying lately. As he made his way across Kensington, Gabriel started adding up the money in his head. They generally had you work six days, sometimes seven, and six times a hundred fifty was nine hundred dollars. Hell, if he saved up for a few months, they'd have enough for a down payment on a house in a better neighborhood. All he'd have to do is come up with an explanation. Maybe tell his mother he won it in the lottery or something.

Gabriel's new sneakers were stiff, and raised a blister on the rise of his heel. For eighty-five bucks, he was thinking, you'd think they could make them so they didn't rip your skin off.

It was a sunny day, but brisk, a trace of fall in the air. In this part of row-house Philadelphia, there weren't enough trees to tell you it was autumn, but the season still had its colors. On trash-covered lots, men with nothing to do lit barrel fires and stared into the orange and yellow flames. They fed scraps to the blaze and held their hands to the warmth, their eyes red and watery from the smoke.

Gabriel stopped at Eleventh and Germantown to watch a wrecking crew take the block apart. He'd read about this in the morning papers. Almost every house on the block was either a stash house or a crack den. The houses had been abandoned and police had stormed in a dozen times to make arrests, and either the same people were back the next day, or new people came in to replace them. The city had decided this was the only sure way to get on top of the situation.

A giant metal claw grabbed the edge of an upstairs window, clamping down on red brick. It jerked its catch toward the street in a deep, wrenching groan, peeling back the entire upstairs wall in one piece and exposing a bedroom with a mattress on the floor.

On the mattress, exposed now to the world, a sleeping crack couple lay naked, tangled up in each other. The wall being ripped off hadn't roused them.

Several street people began pointing up there, whistling and hooting, and for some reason, the couple heard that. They rose unashamed in bed, looking out on the street, and flipped off their audience. Then they disappeared into the back of the house.

A junkie watching from across the street threw an empty whiskey bottle at the tractor operator. The bottle exploded harmlessly on the back of the yellow rig.

Gabriel looked toward the end of the block, where ten people held signs and walked in a circle.

10,000 HOMELESS IN PHILADELPHIA.

END ILLNESS—BULLDOZE HOSPITALS.

WELCOME TO AMERICA.

Gabriel thought it was cool. The protesters didn't look like neighborhood people, but here they were, making a statement.

A lot of things about the neighborhood bothered Gabriel, but he wasn't sure what to do with those feelings. He wasn't the type to walk in a circle with a sign. Too shy. But he respected it. In a way, reading the papers and learning about the world made living in Kensington harder for Gabriel. It made him aware that things weren't supposed to be this way.

Gabriel walked down Fourth Street and turned east on Cambria. He knew the drug boss was somewhere on that street, but he didn't know which house. They kept moving every week or two, to stay one step ahead of the police.

Gabriel saw a new white Trans Am in front of one house and figured that must be it. The guy who owned the car, Diablo, bought a new car every month or so. He was the the street supervisor for the Black Caps, which meant he was in charge of about twenty four-man crews.

Gabriel knocked at the door. No answer.

He knocked again. Nothing. When he sat down on the top step, the door opened.

A pink-faced white guy stood there, about twenty years old. He had a face like a picnic ham. Gabriel hadn't seen him before.

"Diablo here?" he asked.

The ham face was annoyed.

"The fuck are you?" he asked.

"Gabriel. Gabriel Santoro."

The ham face retreated into the house, leaving the door open. Gabriel assumed he was supposed to follow. Just inside, he stepped carefully around a growling pit bull that guarded the door.

The house smelled of stale smoke, passed gas, spilled beer, and the dog. Diablo was asleep on a sofa, and the guy with the picnic ham on his shoulders was tapping the boss lightly, trying to wake him.

Scattered on the floor in front of the sofa were syringes, crack vials, glass pipes, beer bottles, used condoms, and chicken bones. If everything Gabriel heard was true, and he had no reason to doubt it, the house was used every night by whores who turned five-dollar tricks and then smoked their brains out. If there was anything left of the whores when Diablo got in after working the streets, he would take it, whether they were awake or not, conscious or not, fucking them like a savage and then dragging them across the floor and dumping them out the front door.

A fish tank sat on a wooden crate near the sofa. Inside the tank were four bundles of crack vials, a nine-millimeter semiautomatic, and two snakes. The snakes slithered over the bags of crack vials and the gun. One of the snakes was sticking its head into the muzzle of the gun.

Diablo woke up groaning and rubbing his eyes. When he stood up, his prick popped through the fly in his boxers. He let it hang there, proud of it, and walked over to Gabriel, scratching his ass as he made his way across the room.

Even at night, when darkness hid part of him, Diablo was the ugliest person Gabriel had ever seen. Now, in the light of day, he was hideous. His hair looked like sea grass after an oil spill, and the left side of his face was a landslide of melted skin, marbled flesh dripping onto his neck.

As Gabriel had heard the story, there'd been a fight between Red and Black over the ownership of Ninth and Pike, and the day after the shootout, somebody torched Black's stash house while Diablo was asleep inside. Diablo ran out of the house with his head on fire and rolled in the street, rubbing his face on the pavement. Those who saw it swore he was grinning the whole time.

Diablo had stalked the torch for three days, and when he found him he shot him four times, three in the head and one in the balls. That was his calling card, shooting a guy in the balls, and it was always the first shot. Then he drove down to Penn Treaty Park, where William Penn and the Leni Lenape Indians had worked out an early turf agreement three hundred years ago, and dropped the torch off the fishing pier, with cast iron motor parts tied around his neck. The torch's body sank like a rock to the mucky bottom of the Delaware, where it joined a growing colony of hoods, all of them twenty-two or younger, some as young as twelve, who had crossed Diablo and now slept with fish.

Diablo's face was two inches away from Gabriel's. When he opened his mouth, he belched.

Gabriel didn't react.

Diablo turned and walked back toward the sofa, stopping at the fish tank. He took the pizza box off the top and reached in.

Gabriel didn't know what kind of snakes were in there, but they were slender and greenish, about a foot long. When Diablo's hand popped in, they coiled, ready to strike. Gabriel assumed they were poisonous. The gangs were always looking for new ways to protect guns and drugs. In a lot of stash houses, drugs were booby-trapped with explosives. Gabriel's buddy Ralph told him the Red Caps gang kept their drugs in washing machines, guarded by pythons.

One of the snakes flicked at Diablo's hand, but he didn't flinch. Gabriel couldn't tell whether he'd been bitten or not.

Diablo pulled his gun out of the fish tank, put the pizza box back on top of it, and walked back with both his gun and his dick pointed at Gabriel. He moved in close, like before, and Gabriel could smell the sleep on him and see something growing in Diablo's stare, speeding up from the back of his head.

Gabriel saw the hand rise, but didn't move. Diablo backhanded him hard across the face, the hand with the gun in it. Gabriel felt the impact in his skull. His face was on fire, his ears ringing. His eyes began to water, but he blinked tears away.

Diablo laughed a psycho tough-guy laugh, but there was some respect for Gabriel in it. If this kid was weak, Diablo seemed to be saying, he wasn't showing it.

"What're you, fucking ignorant?" Diablo asked.

Gabriel said nothing.

"When it's dark, asshole. You got the night shift. The fucking night shift."

Gabriel still said nothing. Diablo was bringing the gun up now, his finger on the trigger, a homicidal grin on his face.

He made a quarter turn toward the door, leveled the gun, and shot the dog.

The sound of the gun stayed in the room a long time, and it stayed in Gabriel, too, ringing off the walls of his head.

"I don't know where we're getting these little assholes," Diablo said, telling it to the ham face, who looked relieved it was the dog that got shot instead of him.

"I don't know, either," the ham face said, part of his voice missing.

Gabriel had the ham face fixed for a complete idiot. A spineless yes-man.

"This is supposed to be our new ace, he don't even fucking know when to show up," Diablo was saying as he walked over to watch the last bit of life go out of the dog.

The dog, sprawled on its side, let out a little yelp, a final, involuntary act. A grayish-pink ooze dripped out of its ear.

Diablo turned to the ham face with a smile and said: "Go get me another dog."

The yes-man scooped up the dog in his arms, as if it were something he'd done before, and was out the door in an instant. And now it was just Gabriel and Diablo.

Only a few nights ago, Diablo had come by the corner to tell Gabriel about his promotion, but he didn't say when or where he'd be working. Gabriel was just trying to do the right thing, dropping by to get his assignment, and here was Diablo, going nuts on him.

Gabriel wasn't sure what he was supposed to do. Diablo hadn't dismissed him, but maybe he was just supposed to get out.

"Okay then," Gabriel said. "Tonight. I'll be back tonight." He was afraid to ask the question he was about to ask. But he had to. "Do I just come here, or go to a certain corner?"

Diablo came face to face with him again and grabbed his arm, digging his fingers in. He still held the gun in the other hand, and jabbed the muzzle into Gabriel's chest.

"The first thing," he said, talking through broken yellow teeth, "you don't fuckin' breathe without I say so. This is your family now and I'm your fucking old man. Fuck your brother fuck your sister fuck your mother. I'm your daddy. The second thing, you cut me on the street, you cut me one fucking cap, you cut me ten cents, you and that dog are gonna be best friends."

Gabriel nodded and Diablo told him to be at Third and Indiana at six o'clock.

Third and Indiana. Shit, that was their hottest corner.

Gabriel took a deep breath when he got outside. He looked left, in the direction of his house, and then went right. Halfway down the block, he put his hand to his face and felt the welts from Diablo smacking him.

He'd heard a lot of stories about Diablo. He was a maniac. He was a lunatic. His father, in prison for a triple murder, used Diablo as a mule when he was five and had him dealing when he was eight. The general thinking among Black Caps gang members was that Diablo would shoot his mother just to scare the shit out of whoever was watching.

But Gabriel had never seen that part of him. The only times he had seen him, Diablo would come up and say he'd heard nothing but good things about the job Gabriel did on lookout. When Gabriel thought about it at all, he just assumed it would always be easy for him. Like it was when he was a decoy. Like it was when he was a lookout.

As he walked down the street now, his face hot and his ears ringing, he realized he had crossed a line he hadn't seen. The control was gone now. He thought about all the times his mother warned him. And he thought about Marisol. Damn, he wanted to make love to her.

Six

Gabriel pulled his Sixers cap down tight, put his hands in his jacket pockets, and walked on, not sure where he was going. It was all a blur, the streets, the graffiti, the people, Gabriel moving through Kensington in a daze brought on by the events of the day.

He couldn't get that line out of his head: "This is your family now and I'm your fucking old man."

His thoughts moved in circles. Diablo, his mother, Marisol.

If he tried to just blow off the whole thing, never show up at Third and Indiana, Diablo would send someone after him. Maybe Diablo himself would show up at his house on Diamond Street. In his mind, Gabriel saw his mother answering the door, looking at Diablo, and then turning to Gabriel. Her face unforgettable.

Gabriel still didn't know what to do, where to go. Someone had left a barrel fire going, full blast, in a vacant lot. Gabriel held his hands to the heat, his thoughts lost in the flames. When he backed away, he had no idea how long he'd been standing there. He had to look around to see where he was, and hearing the rattle of the El, he walked toward the sound. There was something comforting about it.

Gabriel paid the station attendant and waited on the platform for a train to Center City. He liked to ride the El, even if he had no particular destination. Sometimes he'd just ride it to the end of the line in West Philadelphia and come right back. He liked the rocking motion, the hum, and he liked to imagine himself without the train around him, his reclined body whisking over the city, the air-suspension boy.

A train came along in five minutes and the city was flying by him now, all rooftops and steeples and empty factories. A water tower caught his attention because it had a ladder from the top of the roof all the way up to the tank, maybe fifty feet of ladder. Gabriel wondered what would happen if you were standing on the very top of the tower when it fell over, but you jumped off a split second before it hit the ground. He wondered if that would save you.

He had a whole car to himself. He liked that best, when he could pretend it was his own private train. He took out his sketchpad and began to draw. A boy on his side, a boy on his back, a boy on his stomach, their eyes open, bubbles coming out of their mouths. One on top of another at the bottom of the river, piles of arms and legs. An eel slithering by. He gave the eel Diablo's face.

At the Spring Garden stop, two older kids got on, both about sixteen. Out of eighty seats to choose from, one sat right behind Gabriel and the other sat across the aisle from him. He pretended not to notice, but he knew something was up.

The train started to move again and the one across the aisle tapped Gabriel on the arm. "Nice kicks," he said, nodding toward Gabriel's new sneakers.

Gabriel didn't answer.

"Looks like my size," said the one behind him.

Gabriel needed just a few more seconds. The Second Street stop was coming up and if he could hold on until then, he could make a break for the door. It was coming up now, fifty yards away, forty, twenty, ten.

Now.

He didn't feel himself fall, it happened so fast. But on the floor of the car, face down, he knew the one to his side had tripped him.

The door opened and Gabriel started to lift himself off the floor. He was going to make a run for it. But the guy on his side pushed him back down with a foot to his back.

If somebody gets on, Gabriel thought, it'll be okay. These assholes would let him go.

But nobody did. The door slid shut with a whoosh, sealing him inside.

"Sneaks like that, the homeboy should be able to run faster," said the one who had tripped him. The other one pulled at one of Gabriel's shoestrings.

It was a simple deal. All he had to do was give them up. He had a hundred fifty dollars in his pocket they didn't even seem interested in finding out about. He could replace the sneakers.

What he couldn't replace, it came to him as he went from being scared to being angry, was the other thing they would take. The thing Diablo had already taken a piece of that morning.

Gabriel turned onto his back. His mouth bled from hitting the floor. He ran his tongue across a chipped tooth, feeling over the rough edge.

"Go ahead," he said, offering his left foot.

"This one's not as stupid a fuck as he looks," said the guy who had tripped him, relaxing and smiling to his buddy as he pulled off Gabriel's left sneaker.

Gabriel shifted when the left sneaker was off, as if he was going to offer his right one. And when the target was in place, he brought his knee up hard, a quick pop.

It caught the mugger solid, right under the chin, and blood sprayed in a neat arc. He spit out part of a tooth along with skin and blood.

"You motherfucker," he groaned, grabbing Gabriel by the hair and pulling his head off the floor.

When the door opened at the Fifth Street stop, a woman looked inside, screamed, and backed away.

Gabriel threw a punch at the bloodied face of the one who held him by the hair and squirmed free as the train started up. Now he was bulling the other guy. He wrestled him down and was trying to jam his head through the floor of the train when the bloody one pulled him off and threw him across a seat. Gabriel slid into the wall and his head snapped back, cracking the window.

Each of them grabbed a foot and Gabriel lost his other sneaker. He kicked and squirmed as they dragged him off the seat, and he fell hard to the floor, lifting his head so his back took the blow.

One of the muggers hooked his arms under Gabriel from behind, lifting him to a standing position, and the other drew back a fist.

Gabriel turned as it zoomed at his nose. It caught him flush on his cheek and ear, rocking his head.

He kicked, still trying to break free, but now the guy who punched him was pulling out a knife and stepping back in a slow tease. Gabriel felt the train slowing and knew that it was the Market East station, where a lot of people would be waiting to board. The closer the knife came, the slower the train moved, and now Gabriel could see dozens of people waiting on the platform. When the doors opened, both guys ran.

In his stocking feet, Gabriel walked through the Gallery. He washed himself in the bathroom next to McDonald's, checking the damage to his teeth and face. It didn't look too bad. And then he went up to Foot Locker and bought the same sneakers.

On the train ride home, Gabriel sketched the moment when his knee exploded into the mugger's chin. The mugger was all pain and surprise, and his partner was stunned. The sketch was filled with movement.

It was just after noon when he got back to Kensington. Four hours ago he had been home, getting a kiss from his mother. Since then he'd been smacked by his boss and mugged by two hoods. Life as a runaway wasn't going so well.

Gabriel went to a pay phone on Kensington Avenue and called Marisol to see if he could drop by. He told her he had a little accident and needed some help.

"You need somebody to look at this, in case you got a concussion," Marisol was telling him twenty minutes later. She was feeling the bump on the back of his head, where he cracked the window, as she led him up the stairs. She and her family lived above the market.

"No," he said. "No doctor."

She ran warm water over a towel in the kitchen and touched it to his lower lip, which was split. With her free hand, Marisol cradled the back of his neck as she worked his face with the towel.

Gabriel closed his eyes. It was heaven.

When he opened them he saw her head moving toward his, in soft focus, and he prepared to kiss her. But apparently she was only getting a closer look at his lip.

"You seen the *Daily News?*" she said. "The late edition?"

He hadn't.

She opened it to page three. The headline read: STUDENT KILLED FOR GOLD CHAIN.

The story said a thirteen-year-old seventh-grader at Fitz-Simons Middle School was knifed to death at a subway station by two teenage robbers after they grabbed at her necklace and she resisted. She was stabbed in her heart in the Erie station on her way to school and died right there in a puddle of blood.

Gabriel knew the station. It smelled of piss and damp filth. He imagined the girl on the cold stinking pavement.

The story said police thought the same two robbers might be involved in a rash of train robberies involving jewelry, jackets, and sneakers. At the bottom of the story, a school counselor said that over the last twelve years, thirty-four Fitz-Simons students or former students had been killed, counting the one that morning.

Gabriel's left eye was swollen shut. Through his right eye, Marisol was in soft focus again. He closed that eye and imagined the space between them closing. He imagined the feel of her breasts against his chest, the smell of her hair, the touch of her skin. There seemed to be a connection between his pain and her beauty, a connection that made no sense but didn't seem like something he needed to understand.

She asked him again to go to the doctor and to the dentist, too. Gabriel said he didn't have time. He thanked her and she led him back downstairs.

The early afternoon sun fell on Marisol's face and lit her hair when Gabriel opened the door to leave. He walked away with that picture burning warm inside, the picture of an angel in light.

Third and Indiana wasn't just the hottest Black Caps corner, it was one of the hottest corners in the whole city. And one of the most dangerous, too, because Blue and Red were on the next two corners, and when customers were backed up in traffic, there were disputes about which corner they were headed to.

Six or eight times the first week, Gabriel heard gunshots. Every now and then they came close enough that he had to take cover, diving behind a car and holding his hands over his head as the bullets zinged by.

One night, toward the end of the week, the weather was great for October and it seemed like everybody in six states was celebrating by getting high. Gabriel had a traffic jam almost his entire shift, no less than a half dozen cars lined up for crack at any time. When the shift was over, the crew captain, the one in charge of the corner, came up to him.

"It was a motherfucker out here tonight," he said.

Gabriel didn't respond. He was suspicious of everybody, even his own gang, and generally said nothing unless he had to.

"Man, where'd you go," the crew captain asked, "fucking sales school?"

Gabriel assumed that was supposed to be some kind of compliment, but it wasn't as if he had anything to do with the number of customers who showed up each night.

The crew captain was about twenty-two, eight years older than Gabriel. But he seemed uneasy, as if he felt his job security was uncertain because Diablo had stuck this hotshot kid with him.

"You heard about Kiko, man?" the captain was saying now.

Gabriel had heard, but pretended he hadn't.

"Kiko?"

"The kid working Fourth and Cambria."

"What about him?"

"Cocksucker fucked up, man. Say he want out."

That's what this was. A threat. Maybe the captain had picked up on something in Gabriel, because he was letting him know that if he tried to back out now, there'd be a price to pay.

"Myself, I think he was too young for the job," the captain said. Kiko was fifteen, and the captain knew Gabriel was fourteen. "That's what happens, you get boys out here 'stead of men. You see what I'm saying?"

Gabriel nodded.

"Pussy learned his lesson. Diablo sent out somebody with a baseball bat, fucked up his legs so bad the boy couldn't even walk home to his mama."

Gabriel nodded again. The image of that made him queasy, but he didn't let it show.

A car drove up in a rush, the driver rolling down the window as he pulled to a quick stop.

"I got twenty dollars," he said. He was wearing a coat and tie.

Gabriel reached inside the pocket of his army jacket and handed him four vials. The driver pulled over a half block away and lit up, smoke curling out the window.

Third and Indiana was nothing like the corner where Gabriel had worked lookout, about a half mile away. At that corner, where he had worked afternoons instead of nights, there was still some recognition of social contracts. Even among dealers, there was a respect for the neighborhood and the people in it. A dealer might even go and track down a parent if he saw a young kid trying to buy drugs.

At Third and Indiana, no laws applied, and there were no social contracts. People would stroll down the street with a gun out. Like it could have been a newspaper or a loaf of bread. Houses and streets were crumbling and graffiti ran from one end of the block to the other, broken only where houses had burned down or fallen in on themselves. Half the houses were sealed to keep out squatters and pipers, and the air always smelled of something dead. Gabriel hoped it was a big rat or a dog or something, instead of a human being. Unless it was Diablo.

On every one of those blocks, no matter how bad it was, several families, decent people, held on. Not by choice, but because they were trapped. Some had paid as much as twenty thousand dollars for their houses, but couldn't give them away now. And even if they could, they couldn't afford to move anywhere else. They were prisoners here. They kept their kids inside, pretended they didn't see what was happening on the street, and dropped to the floor when they heard shots.

Gabriel thought about those people when he worked a shift. It bothered him that they hated him. It bothered him that they were afraid of him. He wanted to go around telling them he wasn't what they thought. He wanted to tell them he lived in a good house with his mother, and he did pretty well in school and he was going to be an artist. More than anything, he wanted to walk away. But he realized, as that first week wore on, that he was a prisoner here, too.

Gabriel's only escape was to lose himself in the daily routine. Just after sundown each day, a drop-off man would deliver a trash bag filled with drugs. Gabriel would hire a couple of extra lookouts during delivery, because you couldn't risk getting caught with all the drugs on you. The crack came in bundles, twenty vials each. Gabriel and the crew captain would stash the bundles in a hiding place, usually an abandoned house, sometimes a car. And intermittently throughout the evening, the crew captain would visit the stash and deliver a fresh bundle to Gabriel.

Gabriel also had to know where the crew captain hid the gun each night. Behind some trash, inside a car, under the lip of a bumper. They moved it every day or two. The thing you never wanted to do was have drugs and the gun on you at the same time, because it was automatic prison. The cops did high fives on the street when they caught somebody dumb enough to carry a gun and drugs.

If shooting broke out, Gabriel would be expected to go for the gun and defend the corner first, the drugs second, and the supervisor third. When the crew captain explained this and asked Gabriel if he'd shot a gun before, he said of course he had. A million times. How would they know, one way or the other?

Aside from all these concerns, the job was simple. The cops would come by every night and know exactly what was going on, but unless they saw a transaction, there was nothing they could do. The lookouts spotted just about every cop that came through, uniformed and plainclothes, and Gabriel gave big tips at the end of each shift. He felt guilty about getting kids involved that way, the same way he had gotten involved, but he had a selfish consideration. He didn't want to get caught.

Even if you were inept enough to get picked up, though, chances were you'd spend no more than two hours in custody. Even if you had a whole bundle on you, the street value was only about one hundred dollars. And with the jails overcrowded, and court orders to keep the population down, you could get arrested and be back on the street before your shift was over.

As for the customers, it was like feeding babies. Gabriel hated them. He hated the ones with the nice cars and blank suburban faces and he hated the neighborhood dopers who sold their food stamps for a two-minute high and he hated the crack whores who sucked cock in abandoned houses so they could buy rocks. He knew some of them, the crack whores, and knew that their kids had to steal food when they were hungry.

Sometimes while working a shift Gabriel would try to come up with a way to get out, but he couldn't think of one. If you went to the police, the gang would know in ten minutes and you'd be at the bottom of the river in twenty. If you walked away, they'd come after you.

The only way Gabriel could see was to leave the city. But he wasn't going to abandon his mother, and he couldn't see himself going home now and telling her they had to clear out. He hadn't talked to her in the week he'd been gone.

The last night of Gabriel's first week, at the end of his shift, a white Trans Am turned onto the block. Diablo didn't look at him as he drove by and parked up the street.

He came back now, walking toward Gabriel but stopping halfway, at the stash house. He motioned to Gabriel to join him.

It was a sewer inside, like the house where Diablo had slapped him. Rats scattered as they walked in. There was dogshit on the floor.

Diablo walked to the kitchen holding a beer, with Gabriel following. The plumbing had been ripped out by a scavenger. Roaches climbed in and out of the sink drain.

Diablo looked like he'd been snorting. He lifted the beer to his scarred face and guzzled, backwash dripping down his chin. And then he cracked the bottle on the edge of the counter. Beer and glass splashed everywhere.

Without warning, he grabbed Gabriel's shirt at the chest and shoved him against the wall, lifting the jagged bottle to his neck.

Gabriel didn't move, didn't speak. He wondered what he had done now, and what it would cost him.

"I want all the money all the time," Diablo said, his nose almost in Gabriel's mouth. "All of it," he shouted with his shit breath.

"I gave it all to the captain," Gabriel said, his voice squeezed by Diablo's grip.

Diablo brought the edge of the bottle up and held it just over Gabriel's nose, and Gabriel saw something flying up again from the back of Diablo's eyes.

Diablo sniffed and laughed, and then he laid the jagged edge of the bottle under Gabriel's left eye, letting him feel its coolness. It sat there a moment—Diablo laughed again—and then came the quick flicking motion.

The blood streamed warm down Gabriel's face before he felt any pain.

"You're Black," Diablo said. "Respect it, because it's all you got now. You see Red or Blue squeeze our corner, don't fuck with it. Tell the captain. You see friends in other gangs, you don't know them no more. They're enemies. You do this job right, follow the rules, you got a future in this. You fuck up, you're dead."

Diablo backed off, reaching into his pocket, and began throwing fifty- and twenty-dollar bills on the counter. He counted out nine hundred dollars, a week's pay. And then he threw a one-hundred-dollar bill on top of it.

"That's a tip," he said. "Buy yourself some fucking Band-Aids."

His mother worked a month to clear that much money, but for the first time, Gabriel understood, really understood, why drug money was no good to her. He didn't want it himself.

Gabriel worked only one more night before they pulled him off the street. The president of City Council, who would take over if the mayor died, wanted to show that he was up to the job. Kids were still dropping like flies in the Badlands. It was chaos on the streets, which was bad for the city's image and kept tourism down. The City Council president sent a memo to the police commissioner telling him he wanted cops to bag every pusher they could get their hands on, and bust heads if they had to. In the Twenty-fifth District, where Gabriel worked, cops walked every known drug corner every night.

"It's a fucking joke," Diablo said at an emergency Black Caps gathering.

The meeting was held in front of a row of storage sheds where the gang sometimes stashed drugs and weapons. They had a good barrel fire going, and the light of it put an ugly shine on Diablo's face. About forty-five dealers, supervisors, and money handlers huddled around the fire, listening to their leader.

Diablo, speaking with more intelligence and composure than Gabriel knew he had in him, said the government was playing into their hands. There'd be a temporary inconvenience with this crackdown, he said, but as long as the ignorant fucks who ran the war on drugs kept focusing on the supply instead of the demand, the dealers would win.

They shut down one corner, Diablo said, we move to another corner. They bulldoze one block, we move to another block. The only way they could win, Diablo said, was to destroy the city they were trying to save.

Gabriel hadn't realized, before now, that the drug business was so calculated. He'd never thought about the concept of supply and demand, but he had to admit that Diablo made more sense than the politicians.

"There's more corners in Philadelphia than there is police," Diablo said. "We're going to cut back a little bit while they put on this show, waiting for this fat fuck of a mayor to die. But this is a minor and temporary inconvenience, gentlemen. That's all it is."

As expected, Third and Indiana was one of the first corners the cops shut down. They parked a van at the intersection, much to the delight of neighbors. Gabriel didn't know when he'd sell drugs again, but the gang kept him busy with other assignments, like walking Diablo's new pit bulls—he shot about three a week—or going out for pizza or hoagies. But he had a lot of time on his hands, and spent most of it hanging around with kids his age, all of them either lookouts or wannabes. To them, Gabriel—having become a dealer at his young age, and having such access to Diablo—was something of a celebrity.

"He's cranked up on coke, and so then he sticks the fucking bottle under my eye, and it's all jagged where it broke. He just looks at me, like all ugly and everything, and then he grinds the bottle into my face."

Gabriel was holding court with three lookouts who listened as if to a prophet. There was Ralph, his closest friend since first grade, and Pinto and Lalo. Gabriel knew them from school, too. Lalo was two years older than the rest of them, but he had some kind of learning disability and had been held back twice.

They were Puerto Ricans, his three friends, and they sometimes spoke in Spanish, not to hide anything from him, but because it wasn't part of their consideration that Gabriel wasn't exactly like them. Gabriel had some Latin blood in him, and for the most part he could understand what they were saying. Not by the words, but by the way they said things, and the expressions they wore when they said them. Sex was the easiest translation, followed by fear of Diablo.

The four youngest members of the Black Caps sat on the steps of a burned-out corner house under I-95 eating Italian hoagies Gabriel had paid for, talking between bites in voices awkwardly deep and squeaky with change. It was a quiet spot, except for the rumble of traffic up on the highway.

"It must be a membership thing," Gabriel was saying in a voice that still had more of the boy than of the man in it. He didn't consider himself much of a talker, let alone a storyteller. But they were asking a million questions. "It's like the Mafia, I guess, only the Mafia cuts you with a knife and makes you hold a burning match or some shit. Diablo just fucks up your face with a bottle."

The gouge under his eye had scabbed over, toughening Gabriel's otherwise smooth, innocent face. He looked a little more like a drug dealer now.

"I gotta go to court tomorrow," Gabriel said.

"You got arrested?" asked Ralph. Ralph was tall and gawky, with a neck that seemed a foot long. He was eight inches taller than Gabriel, but had a younger, more boyish look about him. He wiped mustard off his mouth with his sleeve.

"No," Gabriel said. "It's to look at the undercover cops."

Ralph nodded as if he understood what that meant. He was glad Pinto asked Gabriel why he had to go look at undercover cops.

"You sit in Municipal Court all day, Front and Westmoreland. I did it twice last week while we were still working. When the plainclothes cops testify, you just look at their face. It's so you'll know them on the street."

They shook their heads at the cleverness of it. And at how easy it was to beat the system.

"Diablo has me make sketches of the cops," Gabriel said, "and then he shows them to all the crews."

"Shit," Ralph said, "you just sit there in court, drawing pictures like that, and nobody fucks with you?"

"I sit in the back," Gabriel said. "One time there was a cop watching me, so I didn't draw nothing. I just remembered a couple of faces and drew them when I went outside."

"You drew them from memory?" Ralph asked.

Gabriel nodded.

"Somebody's drawing bodies on Broad Street, man, you see that?" Lalo said. "They kill my ass, I want Gabriel to do mine. Fuck that other artist. I wanna look sharp."

Gabriel was going to say something, but Ralph spoke first.

"How you do that shit from memory?" he asked.

"I got a good memory," Gabriel said. "My mother has a good memory. She's so good, she remembers stuff before it happens."

She'd been on his mind more in the week since he was taken off of Third and Indiana. Two weeks now, he'd been a runaway. Every day, he wanted to go home more badly. And every day, it seemed harder to do.

"Yo Gabriel," Ralph said. "I was going to tell you, man. I saw her."

"You saw who?"

"Your mother."

Gabriel tried to pretend he wasn't that interested.

"It was a couple nights ago, around midnight. I seen this person coming at me on a bike, you know, like a couple blocks away. And then when she got closer, I saw it was her. She was wearin' a dress or something, man, riding the bike in a dress."

Gabriel wished now that he'd had the sense to run to her when he saw her a week ago, instead of backing away, hiding, and watching her ride by.

"I recognized her from that time she came to the assembly at school when we made honor roll," Ralph said. "But I don't think she knew who I was."

"You didn't talk to her, did you?"

"She asked did I know her son, I said I don't know."

Gabriel looked up at the highway, squinting at the bright afternoon sky as a big truck thundered by. He shifted on the stairs and looked at Ralph.

"You told her you didn't know if you knew me?"

"I told her I knew a kid named Gilbert, but not Gabriel."

"Gilbert?"

"Yeah. I didn't know what to say."

"What'd she say?"

"She didn't say nothing. She kept riding."

Gabriel let it sit. The others were waiting for him to say something. They could tell the mention of his mother had gotten to him.

"Hey man," Gabriel said to Ralph. "You didn't make no honor roll."

"I would have. That was the time I was going to and then I got caught stealing Mrs. Orsolino's tires off her car."

"I hate Mrs. Orsolino," said Pinto.

Lalo said: "She made us read *Animal Farm.* Fuckin' animals be talking, havin' meetings. Get the fuck out of here."

"They got only one set of books," Ralph said, "so you can't take it home. Then she pops a quiz on you. I said what's this shit, you think I got fuckin' *Animal Farm* at my house?"

"Yeah," Lalo said. "She told me go the fuckin' library, check it out. I say, bitch, you been to the fuckin' library? The one on Dauphin closed, the one on Lehigh, they shut that motherfucker because of asbestos and lead fallin' on your head. They say that shit shave some IQ points, you don't even know it. Man, you could go in the library a genius and come out stupid. That's probably what happened to me."

Gabriel put his head back to laugh at the sky, and as he did, he saw something up there. The others did, too, and jumped back.

"The fuck is this?" Gabriel said as it spiraled toward them in awkward spasms, its shape changing as it fell.

They braced themselves just before it fell in the street in front of them. But it landed like a cloud, with a little *poof.*

"It's a chair," Pinto said.

"That thing's a chair?" Ralph asked. "It don't have no legs."

"Must've fell off a truck up there," Gabriel said, examining the price tag before flipping the chair open on the sidewalk and plopping down on it.

He crossed his legs and clasped his hands behind his head. He looked like a sunbather at the beach.

"You got to wonder what kind of loser buys a piece of shit like this, and then it falls off the fucking highway," Lalo said.

As he did, the four of them saw a man leaning over the highway guardrail.

"Hey," he was saying. "Hey, that's my chair."

Seven

"Stella? Ofelia."

"Where you at, hon?"

"Home. Can you tell them I can't make it in today?"

"Yeah, sure hon. It's slow in here anyways. Anything new on Gabriel?"

"No. Nothing."

"What the hell're the cops doin' with this thing, the fat bastards? We got 'em in here eatin' scrapple like they got all day to do nothin'."

"Nothing new from the police. I don't think they're going to be much help."

Stella barked at a customer, telling him the damn ketchup was next to the napkin dispenser, if he'd open his eyes.

"Yeah, there you go, Slick, the red stuff in the bottle. We disguised it today. Excuse me, hon. We got us another winner sittin' here at the counter, dumber than meat. Where's this, where's that? Like every one of my husbands."

"Stella, you think it's a good idea for me to be seeing a priest?"

"Only if he's good in the sack, hon. But I thought most of them was homos."

"Not 'seeing' a priest. Visiting a priest. To talk about Gabriel."

"Well that's another story. Do I think you should visit a priest? Yeah, I think so. I mean, don't go all religious on me or anything. But yeah, I think you should."

"Why?"

"Oh stuff it, Niko. I'll get off the phone when I'm done. 'Scuse me, hon. The boss here's growin' a horn."

"Is he going to be pissed at me?"

"Screw him. He's runnin' a sweatshop here. Do I think you should see a priest? Yeah. You should talk to people, Ofelia. A priest is as good as anybody, especially since I don't know what else they got to do all day. But yeah, you should talk about it more. You're shuttin' yourself inside that house all the time and it's makin' you crazy."

"Stella?"

"Yeah?"

"You really think I'm crazy?"'

"I'm sure of it, hon, but so are the rest of us."

"No, really. You think I'm crazy?"

"You still seein' blue creatures and scribbling on the walls, hon?"

Ofelia didn't say anything, which Stella took as an answer.

"Yeah, you're crazy. I don't think too many people see blue whaddyacallit. Aberrations."

"Apparitions."

"Right. And I don't have too many customers here writin' in languages they don't know. Half of these flounder can't write the language they do know. Yeah, you're crazy. But I love you anyhow. And listen, hon, we all got a little bit of what you got. Sometimes I get a feeling, you know, like a hunch in my bones, and then my stomach seizes up on me, and ten minutes later, sure enough, one of my exes is standing at my door asking can he borrow a few dollars till payday. He ain't blue or nothin', but he's a freakin' ghost from the past, sure as hell."

"Stella?"

"Yeah, hon?"

"Thanks."

"Don't mention it. And Gabriel's gonna be okay. Like you say, he might have just run off to find his father or something. That boy's smart as a whip and he can take care of himself. But go see the priest,

Ofelia. I'll cover for you in here. Go see the priest. And if you're not gonna do him, let me know if you think he's my type."

Ofelia Santoro rode swiftly, a small disturbance under a hazy sky. She had lost no weight to speak of, but the riding was easier now that Gabriel had been gone a month and she'd been riding every day for three weeks. She had her balance. She knew how to work the gears. Roads that had been uphill were flat now.

She banked on curves, her hair flying, skirt flapping.

Something told her he was still alive. Not a vision, but a feeling. One that she trusted.

The other feeling she trusted was that he didn't have much longer.

Kensington lay just north of Center City. Ofelia looked south, over the tops of hundred-year-old brick row houses, their wood trim shabby and their rooflines sagging, and saw the gleaming new silver high-rises of Center City in the distance. Jewelry for the sky.

Kensington looked better at night, Ofelia thought. When you couldn't see it so well. The light of day revealed one broken-down street after another, and it looked as though, if you pulled a single brick from any house, it might set off a wave, like dominoes, and reduce all of Kensington to a pile of rubble and a puff of red dust. But through all the layers of decay, Ofelia the romantic, Ofelia the naïve, saw what had been, and refused to accept that it was forever buried.

"They don't build neighborhoods like this anymore," she once told Stella.

"Thank the lord," Stella replied.

"Stella, it's classic. Don't you see it?"

In the parallel lines of row-house architecture, the hard angles of iron railing, and the swirling cornices that trimmed houses, Ofelia saw sheet music. She shared this observation with Stella, along with her notion that the past could reinvent itself.

Stella, with a pained expression, waited a perfectly timed two seconds. Then she replied. "Hon, you're out of your fucking mind. The only song in this neighborhood is 'The Party's Over.' "

Maybe so, but it almost came back to life when the few remaining old-timers talked about the way it used to be. Ofelia loved to listen, because they were talking about her childhood. Her childhood on Diamond Street, where the city was a fair on summer nights. Where adults sat on stoops or pulled lawnchairs onto the sidewalk and had crisscross conversations. What's-her-name hit the lottery again, how does she do it? And somebody traded a can of Ortlieb's for a Marlboro pulled out of a soft pack wrapped into the sleeve of a T-shirt, and the sweet smell of cheese steaks and grilled onions and peppers drifted over the block from the corner steak shop.

And every night the block would whisper at the sight of the new housewife, the one who always appeared on her porch five minutes after her husband schlepped off to the tavern for the evening. She'd stand there with ruby-red lips and crimped blond hair, wearing white shorts that barely covered her up. And when she knew everyone was looking, she'd throw a leg—she had a dancer's legs—onto the downslope of the cast-iron railing, golden flesh on a straight black edge.

The men always looked, the women always slapped them, and the blond housewife always pretended not to notice.

Every night, a glorious routine. Kids played halfball or kick-the-can, great teams of them laughing and arguing and occasionally smacking each other, and every so often a boy and girl would suddenly see something in each other they hadn't seen before and the sky would lift itself up just for them.

That was a time, people would say. And as it slipped farther into the past, they made secret promises never to forget a detail of it, especially not the little things. If anything, the few remaining old-timers recalled more and more as time passed, and were never more unanimous in their recollection of events as when someone remembered something that had never happened.

Maybe that's what drives people crazy, Ofelia was thinking. Remembering and comparing. Remembering not just what your life was, but what it was supposed to become.

She rode past a drug crew now and almost stopped to ask if anyone knew Gabriel, but she didn't want to be late for her appointment with the priest. Just up ahead, an old man with a white mustache and a newsboy hat cooked ribs and chicken on the sidewalk in a barbecue fashioned from a black metal drum. He was stabbing at the meat with a long fork as Ofelia pedaled through the sweet smoke that curled off the grill.

Ofelia pulled around a junk man pushing a shopping cart heaped over with bottles and cans and other scraps. He was on his way to join two young men, worn out before their time, who sat on a sofa in the middle of a lot, legs crossed, passing a brown bag. In the mountains of debris around them, Ofelia spotted a tub from a washing machine, a lamp shade with purple tassles, a refrigerator door, and a steering column with the driving wheel still attached and the keys in the ignition.

This had never been Ofelia's world as a child, or even as a young adult. But it was the only one Gabriel knew. She envied his not knowing what it used to be like, and she cried over it, too. He was growing up in a time when nobody here thought of the future. Only of the past.

Holy Ghost Catholic Church was coming up on the left, and the sight of it made Ofelia squeeze the brake handles, not so much to stop the bike as to slow her free fall into the flames of fear and guilt she associated with organized religion. Ofelia grew up in a parish that was closed now, and spent six years in Catholic school. But her family fell away from the church when Ofelia's father got behind in the tuition and the school threatened to expel her. She went to public school after that, and neither she nor her parents set foot in a church again except for weddings and funerals.

Holy Ghost was a brownstone with twin spires knifing above the plane of row houses in salute to the heavens. A round stained-glass window was set above the entrance—Jesus wearing a crown of thorns, blood dripping over his face.

Looking at the church reminded Ofelia of her parents' funerals. When she was seventeen, her father was hit by the Twenty-three trolley a week after her mother saw it in a premonition. A year later, her mother walked down to Penn Treaty Park and jumped into the river. Her body washed up two days later, across the Delaware in Camden.

The office was around the side. Ofelia went in with the bicycle and the smell of the room was immediately familiar. The smell of religion.

A woman sat behind a desk. She was on the telephone, peering at

Ofelia over the tops of reading glasses. She was one of those people whose voice went with her face, and Ofelia knew she was the one who had answered when she called.

The woman hung up and asked if she could help.

"Ofelia Santoro. I'm here to see Father Laetner."

"Yes, certainly. If I could get some information for our files."

She was about fifty, silver hair in a tight perm. The way she looked over the tops of her glasses, Ofelia felt like she was being judged.

"Well, I'm just here to talk to Father Laetner."

"Yes, I'm aware of that, but Father Laetner will be a bit late. He's running some errands for Pastor Killian. Pastor Killian has been called to Mayor DeMarco's bedside."

"What kind of information do you need?"

"Just a couple of things, but first of all, if you would kindly put the bicycle outdoors."

Ofelia looked at the door and then back at the lady.

"I don't think so," she said. "I'd rather keep it in here."

"Well this is an office and—"

"So it doesn't get stolen," Ofelia said, interrupting.

The woman was eyeballing her again over the tops of her glasses. She held a pen and ran her hand over a sheet of paper, like wiping a slate clean.

"Now, how long have you been in the parish?"

"I'm not in the parish."

Another look.

"But you were married here?"

"No. I got married in Atlantic City."

She might as well have said she got married in a brothel, the way the woman looked at her.

"And your son is in what grade here?"

"He doesn't go to school here."

She put down the pen.

"Mrs. Santoro . . ."

"Miss."

"Miss Santoro, we're quite backed up, and I'm not sure—"

"Look," Ofelia interrupted, "my son ran away from home and I thought I'd like to talk to someone about it. That's why I called, and Father Laetner made an appointment for me."

"How long has your son been gone?"

"A month."

"A month? Mrs. Santoro, if you'll pardon me, I think you should be talking to the police."

"Thanks for the suggestion, but I've talked to the police. A dozen times."

"Well, if the police can't find your son, how do you expect somebody here to find him?"

Ofelia took a deep breath. She didn't have much patience left. "Maybe I'm not here for my son's sake," she said.

Ofelia heard a door open and close somewhere in the building, and then footsteps, a man's footsteps, coming down the hall toward them.

He filled the doorway with an easy lankiness, and his presence seemed to push the bad air out of the room.

"Hi, I'm Father Laetner, and you must be . . ."

"Ofelia. Ofelia Santoro."

"Sorry I'm late."

He didn't look like any priests Ofelia remembered. He was about six feet tall, nice-looking, and younger than she expected. Maybe thirty-five. His left ear stuck out a little and his hair was sort of long for a priest. Stella would go nuts.

"Nice bicycle," he said.

He was dressed in Ofelia's colors, and didn't have that little white collar thing. Ofelia was relieved at that. She found those things intimidating.

"Do you mind?" he asked, taking hold of the handlebars.

Ofelia watched him throw his leg over and slide onto the seat. She smiled as he began riding through the lobby. The secretary shook her head as if he were an annoying child.

"My office is this way," he said over his shoulder.

He put a guiding hand on the doorjamb to keep from running into it as he made his way into the hallway. Before she followed him, Ofelia threw the secretary an up-yours smile.

"Great bike," Father Laetner was saying as he pedaled down the hall, coming within inches of brushing the wall on either side.

They made their way back to the kitchen of the rectory, a big room with formica counters. In the middle was a rectangular oak table with matching chairs. The room smelled vaguely of wooden wine casks, and that was a familiar odor, too. Like so many rooms in church buildings, this one, for Ofelia, was uncomfortably solemn.

Father Laetner set the bike against the wall and walked over to a coffeepot. He put his head down to it and sniffed, shaking his head.

"Same old swill," he said, pulling two cups out of the cupboard.

Ofelia could tell by the way he moved that, as a kid, he had been awkward, one of those boys who's all elbows and knees. The coffeepot clinked hard on the lip of the cup when he poured.

"Very nice bike," he said.

"From my son."

"From your son?"

"He bought it for my birthday."

"Very nice. Expensive."

Ofelia wasn't sure whether he meant to draw something out of her by saying it was expensive. But she didn't think so.

"You don't talk like you're from here," she said.

He put one cup in front of her and sat down across the table with his own.

"I grew up in California."

"I thought you had an accent," Ofelia said.

Father Laetner smiled, started to say something, and then stopped.

"I've never been to California," Ofelia said.

"Well, you probably wouldn't want to visit the town I grew up in. Pittsburg."

"Pittsburgh?"

"Pittsburg, California. Never heard of it, right?"

"Pittsburgh, Pennsylvania, I heard of."

"This one doesn't have an *h* on the end. I'm not sure why. It's near San Francisco."

Ofelia nodded.

"Anyhow, that's where I grew up. And you?"

"Right here," she said with a half-embarrassed shrug.

"Tell me about your family," he said.

She laughed because he made a face when he took a sip of the coffee. It was like mud.

"My father started out in factories, then he worked for the government in Customs. My mother was a seamstress. She worked in one of those sweatshops where you just sit and sew all day. They pay you by the piece."

"Hard work."

"She must have put a needle through her finger a dozen times," Ofelia said. An affectionate chuckle came with the memory.

Father Laetner shook his head.

"What was it like?" he asked. "Growing up around here, I mean."

"Oh, it was wonderful," Ofelia said. "I was just thinking about it on the way over here. You went out on the street at night and you knew everybody. People worked hard in the factories and mills. It wasn't a great job, but you knew it was there."

Father Laetner seemed like he was gazing off into the time she was describing.

"So how long you been here?" Ofelia asked.

"Six months. I was transferred from a little town in Illinois."

"Six months. You like it?"

He looked up at her from the coffee cup and smiled. He fingered the cup, feeling for the right words.

"I didn't expect to see some of the things I've seen," he said. "I guess it's been kind of hard to get used to."

"Like what kinds of things?"

Father Laetner leaned back and the chair creaked as the front legs rode up off the floor.

"Sometimes I can't believe it," he said. "There's no jobs, the houses are wrecked, the schools are bad, everybody has guns, there's drugs everywhere. This neighborhood needs help in every department, and you know what?"

She shrugged.

"They're closing this goddamn church."

"They're what?"

"It's one of the parishes they're shutting down."

He said it with disgust. Ofelia had never met a priest who said goddamn, or was critical of the church. She was liking him more all the time.

"Why's it closing?" she asked.

"The diocese is run by accountants," Father Laetner said. "What it comes down to is, our people don't have much for the Sunday basket."

"When is it closing?"

"Next month, the month after. Nobody knows. The cardinal doesn't even have the guts to come and tell the people directly, or to look into ways they might save the parish. They say there aren't enough parishioners anymore, but they don't do anything to change the things that drove people away, and they don't do a damn thing to find out what kind of services might bring people back."

Ofelia wasn't sure how to respond. But she didn't have to. He wasn't done.

"I just came from Saint Christopher's Hospital for Children," he said. "A six-year-old girl was on her way to the corner store to buy a popsicle when a gunfight broke out. Two gangs fighting over a corner. The bullet hit her spine and she's paralyzed. A six-year-old girl. What do you say to these people? Half the streets around here have wheelchair ramps. In six months, I've done funerals for five kids."

Ofelia didn't particularly care to hear about funerals for kids, considering the circumstances of her visit. But she didn't want to seem impolite.

"I can't get over the families," he said. "Like this family. They're sad, they're upset. But it's almost like they expected it to happen sooner or later."

"No," Ofelia said. "You don't expect it. But you fear it so much, it's almost real before it happens."

Father Laetner took another sip and apologized for the coffee. He went over to the sink and threw his out.

"Have you seen the bodies of the kids?" he said as he returned to his seat. "The bodies somebody's painting on Broad Street?"

"I heard about that," Ofelia said.

"It's incredible. It must be a mile long now and there's something about them, I don't know. I mean, it's just simple white outlines, but in the middle of Broad Street like that, where everybody drives over them every day, they're so compelling."

"They say they don't know who's doing it," Ofelia said.

"It's powerful, just for raising consciousness, because I don't think people know what's going on here. Either they don't know or they don't want to know. We've got a presidential campaign going on and the candidates don't even mention any of this. More than half the people in this neighborhood don't have jobs. Three-quarters of the kids don't finish high school. This is the birthplace of democracy? The fourth or fifth largest city in America? I wish I could figure out myself what to do about it, but I don't even know where to begin."

Ofelia didn't remember a priest ever preaching like this. She would have expected him to fit everything into some religious context, but he didn't.

"It wasn't like this where you worked before?"

He fingered the handle of the mug again.

"No," he said. "I've never seen anything like this."

He looked at her now as if a thought just came to him. "You know what?" he said. "I'm sorry. You came here to talk about your son and I'm rambling on about a neighborhood you already know about." He tugged at the ear that stuck out. It seemed like a nervous habit.

"I like listening to you," she said. "It's all right."

"Well how about if I keep my big mouth shut now and you do a little talking? Tell me about your son. It's . . ."

"Gabriel."

"Gabriel, okay. Tell me from the start."

Ofelia asked if she could have another cup of coffee first, even though she had trouble swallowing the first. He filled the cup and put it in front of her.

"Okay," she said, putting her hand around the cup for its warmth, and then she began.

She talked for forty-five minutes. The way he listened made it easier. He said nothing the whole time, not a word, but he seemed to be caught up in every detail.

She told him she called Deals on Wheels and found out the bicycle Gabriel bought her cost three hundred dollars. She told him Gabriel shined shoes at the Gallery and sometimes sold twenty-five-cent pretzels in the street, and Father Laetner nodded to let her know she didn't have to say the numbers didn't add up.

When she told him about riding her bike through the streets at night, he leaned back in his chair and pictured it.

She also told him about the blue haze, but she didn't call it that. She called it a dream. And when she was done with her story she took a deep breath, shrugged, and felt better than she had in weeks.

Father Laetner reached across the table and put his hand on hers. It was a small thing, a simple gesture. But it felt good. He didn't seem to know what to say, but she didn't really need him to say anything.

When she had composed herself, Father Laetner asked about the racial problems in the neighborhood. He said he'd never seen so many angry people, and asked her if it had always been that way.

Instead of answering in a direct way, Ofelia told him about the gruff gray men she saw in the white neighborhoods on her midnight spins, men who sat on porches with their hands wrapped around cans of cheap beer, their eyes locked in a grudge against all the factories that closed and all the white people who left and all the black and brown people who took their places. She described these men wobbling out of taverns, the walking dead on their way back to women who lay asleep in easy chairs under clouds of cigarette smoke that held the light of flickering televisions.

But the hating isn't owned by the white people, she said. Hispanics hate blacks, and blacks hate Hispanics, and together they hate whites.

"The jobs went to Mexico and Taiwan and who knows where else," Ofelia said. "I don't know if it's any politician's fault. The world just changed. But the pie gets smaller around here every day, and everybody wants the same size piece they had ten years ago."

Another thought came to her and she smiled.

"What?" he said.

"Nothing."

"Come on, what?"

"Nobody ever knew what side to put us on, so we always got along okay with everybody. My father was Dominican, my mother Canadian. My husband was part Cuban, part Italian."

"Gabriel, how did he fit in?"

She smiled again.

"He didn't have any rules. Sometimes he'd hang out with the Puerto Rican boys, sometimes the Polish boys, sometimes the black boys. There's some kids that mix, and some streets have a little of everything. But Gabriel could be with anybody. I used to tell him he should be in the movies. He could play anything, you know? A Jew, Hispanic, Italian, whatever. He has a look, something from his father. Like he's working on something, in his mind, but you don't know what. A handsome boy, too."

"Fourteen?" he asked.

She nodded. A tear filled her eye but didn't fall.

"This dream you had," he said. "Can you tell me about it?"

Ofelia was halfway through the second cup of coffee, but she couldn't take another sip of it. She pushed it away and looked at him.

"It wasn't a dream."

He waited for her to explain.

"I don't even know what I'm doing here," Ofelia said, embarrassed. She started to stand, but he reached for her hand again and it seemed to settle her.

"It wasn't a dream," she said. "It was a vision. I guess you could call it a premonition, except it was really happening."

He pulled his hand away and leaned back, creaking the chair.

"You think I'm crazy, don't you?" she said.

"No," he said. "I think you love your son."

"There's a history of it in my family," she said. "My grandmother on my father's side could tell you tomorrow's weather. You could talk to her on the phone and she could tell you what you were wearing. She completed your sentences."

"A lot of people can do that," Father Laetner said.

"My mother saw my father die," she said.

He shrugged.

"It was before he died," she said.

He didn't seem to have an answer for that.

"It was only once," he asked, "that you had this premonition about Gabriel?"

She nodded yes and the tears were streaming now. Father Laetner went to the counter by the window and came back with a box of tissues. He held one to her cheek and Ofelia reached up and held his hand.

"I miss him so much," she said. "I love him."

"I know that you do," he said.

"It's my fault. I must have made it so hard for him after his father left, when I should have been making it easier. I think I just made it harder."

She wasn't looking at him as she spoke. She was embarrassed about falling apart like this, and she let his hand go. With nervous fingers, she twisted at a gathering in her dress. Then she looked at him, his face blurry through her tears.

"But why'd he have to do this? He can't even call and let me know he's okay? A month, it's been. I try to be strong, but I'm all alone. A month."

Father Laetner moved behind her and put his hands on her shoulders.

"It's okay," he said, his voice soft and kind. "It's okay. Don't be so hard on yourself. This is a difficult place to raise kids, even if it's both parents. You're trying to do it all alone in a neighborhood where everything is working against you. You're a good mother. I know that you are."

Ofelia shook her head no.

"I'm a terrible mother. His father left and I never let Gabriel be a kid after that. He was the one who did the taking care of. He took care of me."

"It was a difficult time," Father Laetner said.

"It was a difficult time for Gabriel, and he'd hear me crying every night. I tried not to. I cried into the pillow. But he'd hear me and come in and put his hand on my shoulder, like you're doing, or sometimes he kissed my forehead. He was so sweet."

Ofelia stood up and took several deep breaths. She couldn't stop sobbing. Father Laetner put his arms around her.

"I don't even know what I'm doing here," she said into his shoulder. "I don't even go to church."

"That's all right," he said in a whisper.

"Organized religion," she said, shaking her head. "Something about it I can't stand. That it's organized, I guess."

"Sometimes," he said, pausing, "sometimes I think there's more religion in a rainfall, or a walk in the woods, than in all the Sunday sermons."

Ofelia stepped away and took another tissue. She wasn't sure she should say what she was about to say.

"I don't know if I even believe in God."

"That's all right," Father Laetner said. "It's all right. Sometimes I don't know either."

Eight

Eddie woke up at eight thirty, stiff from sleeping on his back. It was like a rubber mat thrown over concrete, this sofabed.

He had been up in the night, rolling over and reaching for Sarah, who'd been gone two weeks. She had called a few days after clearing out and said she was sorry Eddie had to find out from Esposito Moving that he was single. She told him it wasn't just religion. She couldn't see it working out with his kids. They'd resent her and she'd feel guilty, and she didn't want any part of that. They had enough to deal with right now without having another woman in the picture.

Eddie knew she was probably right, but that didn't make it any easier. Sarah had sort of left the door open to the possibility of them getting together at some point, but Eddie knew it was over. He wished he could just get pissed off at her and move on, but something was standing in the way of it. Missing her was standing in the way.

He wasn't going to let it paralyze him, though. Living in this house, with all this time on his hands, he was going to pour everything into the music now. He was going to write, he was going to practice, and he was going to start working his way into better clubs. He was going to turn the pain into music. But first he wanted breakfast.

Eddie sat up in bed, his focus coming in slow, and looked into the dining room. Gabriel was asleep on a flipchair.

That was another thing he had to do. He had to find out what this kid's story was. Gabriel had been staying with Eddie since the day Sarah left. Eddie wasn't sure why he had said yes, that first day Gabriel asked if he could spend the night. Gabriel's line was that his parents were trying to work out some problems and needed some time together. Eddie half believed him, but still didn't know why he'd given in.

Eddie hadn't trimmed his beard in two weeks, and it was on the wild side. Wild and turning whiter by the day. He wore a black Ortlieb's Jazzhaus T-shirt that stretched a bit at his paunch. From a sitting position, he pulled on a pair of blue jeans and then scratched his head. The cold in the room hit him when he stood up, and he walked barefoot and shivering to Gabriel's room, where he turned up the thermostat.

Maybe the noise of the heater would wake Gabriel. There was something wrong with it, Eddie didn't know what, but the sound from the basement was like some beast clearing its throat, and pipes rattled all through the house.

Gabriel seemed so small, curled up on that flipchair. He was sleeping on his side, a red USAir blanket over him. His Sixers cap sat on the floor beside him, next to his sketchbook. He'd drawn a picture of Eddie standing by the burning truck, and Eddie hadn't known whether to be embarrassed or flattered. It was good, though. The kid had talent.

"Gabriel."

No answer.

Louder this time. "Gabriel."

Gabriel turned all the way over onto his other side, the rhythm of his breathing undisturbed. His face was lined with the pattern of the oatmeal flipchair. The lines stopped at the scar on his cheek, the boot-shaped scar. Everyone in Kensington seemed to have a stamp, something from the street. A scar, a crooked nose, broken teeth, bruises, burns. Eddie wondered how Gabriel got his scar.

He was a nice-looking kid with a quiet charm, though with his eyes closed he couldn't get to you as easily. It must have been those eyes, those big brown eyes with no bottom to them, that made Eddie say yes, he could spend the night.

The blanket had fallen off of Gabriel when he turned over, and Eddie saw a rectangular bulge in his back pocket. It looked like it could be a wad of folded money, but a kid his age wouldn't have that kind of cash. It was probably baseball cards.

Eddie went to nudge the flipchair with his foot, but stopped. Something about children asleep. The way it brought a stillness to everything around them.

It had been a ritual with Eddie, tiptoeing into Anthony and Dominic's room when they were younger to check on them before he went to bed. Eddie would stand there ten or fifteen minutes sometimes, maybe longer, just staring down at his sleeping children. They were so small, so fragile. And yet in another way, so big, too big to have been the babies he remembered. Eddie would listen to their breathing, struck by the miracle of it. The only sound in the room. The only sound in the world.

In summer, their room had always held the sweet dried fragrance of sweat, and Eddie would watch them replace the innocence they had used up during the day, sorry he'd been pissed at them for some dumb little thing. A sadness came to him in those moments. A sadness he couldn't trace all the way back to where it came from. His wife would be asleep by then, and Eddie would go down to the basement and take his guitar out of its case and hold it, admire it, in love with the music that slept in it, waiting to be invented. The dogs would curl up at his feet.

Perfect stillness.

Eddie would surrender to the sadness and it would move through him, a lightness in his veins. And when he could feel it in his fingers, he would play softly to an audience of Monk and Mingus.

In the three weeks he'd been gone, Eddie hadn't seen his kids. He had called at first, but it got harder each time. His wife would ask why he wasn't sending any money, and he'd have to say he still couldn't afford a guitar other than this damn pawnshop junker. He'd lost some jobs, thanks to the cremation of his hollow-body Gibson. You couldn't play jazz on a steel-string guitar.

She'd start yelling at him and then she'd hand the phone to the kids, then go on yapping in the background as he tried to talk to them. And when he hung up, Eddie would wonder what she was telling them about their father and why he had left. Hoping it wasn't the truth.

The heater quieted down once it had knocked the chill off the room. Gabriel was snoring.

Eddie hadn't asked him where he went every night, or why he got back so late, or why he didn't go to school. He sensed that he had a choice between Gabriel's answers and his company.

Gabriel had gone to the pawnshops with Eddie. He didn't talk much, but he seemed to be interested in music. He asked Eddie how he had learned to play, and then he wanted to know why he played. That stuck with Eddie, that he wanted to know why. The boy seemed to ask questions that might help him find answers about himself.

Every day, Gabriel asked Eddie if he could stay one more night. His story was that he'd gone home and things still weren't right, and his parents said it was okay if he stayed with a friend another night.

Eddie would nod, or point to the flipchair, but he wasn't comfortable with it. You can't just take in a kid like you'd take in a stray animal. At some point, he was going to have to get the boy's story.

"Gabriel," he said, leaning over his sleeping body.

He was dead to the world.

Eddie wanted to get some breakfast before the ten-o'clock job Inverso had lined up for him. This one had nothing to do with the Recreation Department. It was the grand opening of a paint store on Roosevelt Boulevard. Twenty years Eddie had been studying music, and he was playing a pawnshop guitar at a paint store while Paulie Rego was playing the jazz clubs and fucking his wife.

Eddie wasn't comfortable leaving Gabriel in the house while he was gone, though he didn't know why. It's not as if there was anything worth stealing.

He was reaching down to roust Gabriel in the house when the phone rang. Eddie went into the living room, plopped down on the sofa, and picked it up.

It was his wife.

"You mind telling me what the fuck you're up to?" she asked.

"What do you mean?"

"What I mean is I got Thin Jimmy Vigilante calling here."

"Thin Jimmy?"

"Yeah, Thin Jimmy from the neighborhood. Thin Jimmy the gangster."

"He's calling you?"

"No, he's calling you. I keep telling him you don't live here no more, he says 'Yeah, I'm sure he don't,' and then he calls back the next day. What the hell are you doing that I got a gangster calling here for you? What are you, shtupping his girlfriend?"

She'd gotten more of an edge since he left. Eddie could see her lip curl. He could see her hand on her hip. Eddie's walking out seemed to have loosened something inside her, revealing someone he hadn't known. Someone he found attractive.

"You still with Paulie Rego?" Eddie asked.

"Am I still with Paulie Rego."

Not a question, but a flat, mocking refrain.

"You got nerve, Eddie, you know that? It's none of your goddamn business who I'm with. I'm asking you why in hell I got this fucking gangster calling me here, right here, in the house where I live with my sons, who, by the way, I'm suing your ass so you never see them again."

"I thought maybe we could get together and talk about it," Eddie said. "Maybe work it out."

"Yeah. We're gonna get together, Eddie. You wanna know where it's gonna be? Fuckin' court is where. And let me tell you what we're gonna work out. We're gonna work out how much you fork over. Guess what, Eddie. For the first time in your life, you gotta get a job. You fat piece of shit."

She had never called him fat. A piece of shit. But never fat.

"Yeah, I know," Eddie said, not in the mood to argue, though he had no idea how he was going to come up with any money. She'd always made more as a hairdresser than he did as a musician. "I gotta find a job."

"In the meantime," she said, "you mind telling me why I got a gangster calling me?"

"I borrowed his truck to get some furniture for this place."

"You borrowed a truck off a mafioso."

That tone again. Not a question, but an IQ assessment.

"I borrowed it off of Inverso."

"That's even worse."

"Yeah, well I borrowed it off of Inverso, who borrowed it off of Thin Jimmy."

"So what's the problem?"

"The problem is it burned."

"What do you mean burned?"

"Burned. Like in a fire."

"How did it burn?"

"I'm driving down I-95 with my furniture, the furniture falls off the truck, so I pull over and . . ."

"What do you mean your furniture fell off the truck?"

"Yeah. It just flew off."

"Jesus fucking Christ, Eddie."

"So I go back to get it, and then the truck, it wasn't running right, well, it catches fire and burns. Must have been a problem with the electrical system. It just burns right there on I-95, and there's black smoke everywhere, like from a volcano, dark clouds rolling over the highway. Burned my guitar, too. Like it was kindling."

"It's a beautiful story, you dumb shit. So what're you gonna do?"

"You got ten thousand dollars you can loan me?"

"Yeah, Eddie, sure. I'll write you a check. Maybe I'll make it fifteen grand, so you can get yourself a new guitar and maybe spend a week in Bermuda with your whore. Yeah, is fifteen enough?"

"It's not funny," Eddie said. "I'm in trouble. Maybe I can borrow some money from your parents."

It was supposed to be a joke. Her parents hated Eddie because he never had a real job, and he hated them because they were the biggest tightwads in the city. They spent half the day clipping coupons and the other half hiding money in the mattress. Eddie figured they must have a couple hundred grand under the Posturepedic, and still they'd walk five miles to save five cents on a sack of flour.

Eddie's wife didn't seem to think the joke was funny. She didn't even answer.

"I'm serious about this," Eddie said. "I'm gonna end up in a trunk with a bullet in my head."

"I'll keep my fingers crossed," she said.

And then she hung up.

Gabriel's eyes were open when Eddie got off the phone. Eddie wondered how much he'd heard.

"Get up," he said, no patience left. "I gotta go."

Gabriel folded his bed back into a chair and slid it against the wall. He put his Sixers cap on and faced Eddie, as if to say he was ready.

"What's this thing you got, sleeping in your clothes?" Eddie asked, a scolding in his tone.

Gabriel shrugged.

"You hungry?"

"Starved," Gabriel said.

The front door had jammed even tighter after the last rain. Eddie had tried to work it free with a crowbar and hammer, but it wouldn't budge, and he wasn't about to call his mother and tell her to send her fixit man. If he called, he'd have to tell her the whole story. As far as she knew, he was still living in Roxborough.

"Go on," he said to Gabriel, waiting for him to crawl through the dining room window.

Eddie wasn't so flexible at the waist. Especially in the morning. Maybe his wife was right about him getting fat. He got one leg out the window and was sitting on the sill, but the other leg wouldn't come through. He was stuck there a second, his face turning red.

"Gotta get that door fixed," Eddie said, out of breath after managing to roll through.

"Maybe you could call the owner," Gabriel said, trying to make conversation. "Who owns this dump?"

Eddie didn't answer, and Gabriel didn't press it. Eddie liked that in the kid, that he didn't talk too much. Growing up in South Philadelphia, he had learned that the people who talk the least have the most to say, and vice versa.

Puttin' on the Ritz was only three blocks from Eddie's place. Basically, the neighborhood was the shits, but that was one thing Eddie liked about the situation, having a twenty-four-hour diner so close.

Once his career picked up again, it'd be a convenient spot to get a bite after a late gig.

As they made their way up Huntingdon, Eddie saw a lone hooker up ahead, working the corner at Kensington. Eddie felt a little uneasy about walking past her with a kid. She was a light-skinned Puerto Rican or Dominican, one of those islands down there, and she had hair big enough for small animals to nest in. Her black skirt was so short it looked like a hat for her crotch, and she teased passing motorists by tugging at the zipper of her sweatshirt.

Her age changed twice as they approached. From a distance, she was a woman. Closer in, she was younger. Late teens. But when they were right up on her, Eddie could see she was worn beyond her years. She was probably eighteen and looked thirty.

She turned their way, flashing a Miss America smile, candy-apple lipstick wet and thick on her lips.

"Discount," she said, "for the two a youse together."

Eddie was embarrassed. Here he is walking with this kid, and she's offering a doubleheader.

They weren't ten feet beyond her when she called out.

"Ten dollars for you, Gabriel. Any way you want it."

Eddie turned to look at her, and then back at Gabriel.

"Friend of yours?" he asked.

"Her brother went to my school," Gabriel said.

Sometimes it felt to Eddie like he'd moved to another city. The drug scene was beyond anything he had imagined, black and Hispanic kids as young as eight or nine hanging on corners and working lookout for older kids who lived by their guns and their dicks and pimped around with that fuck-everybody look that said they had nothing to lose.

But even the white people here were different. They came from the part of Europe that got no sun, and they rolled their vowels high in their mouths and squeezed them out, instead of keeping them in the back of their throats like the downtown dagos. And it was as if, when the factories died, so did evolution. Time had stopped and maybe even backed up. You'd see people who looked like they had just had a nickel lunch at the drugstore fountain. You'd see a wiry, street-tough kid wearing a motorman's cap and looking like he ought to be hawking newspapers on a corner and sneaking smokes in an alley.

They made for an odd couple, Gabriel loping along with his pants hanging low and his hat tight, Eddie, six inches taller, with the look and stride of an outsider, maybe the boy's biology teacher. They passed a blue shack of a newsstand a block from the diner. A blue and white delivery truck pulled up as they went by, and the driver dropped a stack of *Daily News*es, tied with string, in front of the shack. Eddie noticed that the cover of the *Daily News* had a big black and white photo of one of the painted bodies on Broad Street, with a question mark superimposed over the body.

Puttin' on the Ritz sat stubborn and gritty under the El, its dimpled stainless steel dulled by time. Inside, it was all Formica and vinyl. Eight booths, plus counter service with a row of twelve stools. The lunch specials were on a blackboard behind the counter, next to a ceramic bust of Elvis.

A mirror ran the length of the wall behind the counter, and some Old World black and white photos were squeezed under the edge of the frame. Most of the people in the photos looked like they must be relatives of George, the bald, round-faced man who ran the place. One shot showed a family on a dock, maybe at Ellis Island, a ship behind them.

That was the main difference between a South Philadelphia diner and a Kensington diner. In South Philadelphia, no relatives made the wall unless they happened to be famous. Restaurant owners tacked up glossy studio shots of every two-bit celebrity who'd been within a block of the place, and there were black felt tip scrawls on every one. *All the best, Frankie Avalon. Love, Fabian. Thanks for everything, Dom DeLuise.* Anybody who'd been a TV weatherman for more than two weeks was on the walls downtown. Even the hoagie shops had them.

"Let's do this," Eddie said, sliding over a counter stool. He wanted a booth, but the only one open was fogged in with cigarette smoke that floated from the booths on either side of it. Two women in one of those booths were crying. Eddie wondered what that was about.

The man on Eddie's left, two stools over, was in that same stool every time Eddie came in, and he was known for how much coffee he drank in a day. His record was forty-eight cups, a waitress had told Eddie. And six packs of cigarettes. He was razor thin and his eyes were deep hollows in his head. Nobody ever saw him eat, nobody ever saw him use the restroom, and nobody knew his name.

"How many cups so far today?" Eddie asked.

"Sixteen," he said before Eddie was done asking. He stared straight ahead, as if his own image in the mirror looked like somebody familiar whose name he couldn't remember.

"What'll youse have?" the waitress asked. She was about fifty, one of those people who are out of breath all the time from life itself rather than from exercise. Her name was written over her right breast the way an airplane writes in the sky.

Jackie.

Jackie stood in front of them with her made-up eyes closed, a pair of blue half-moon hubcaps. She usually walked that way, too. Eyes closed. She knew her away around the place well enough that she didn't need to open them.

Eddie ordered scrambled eggs and home fries, rye toast.

"You want meat with that?" Jackie asked.

"No thanks." Eddie would have liked scrapple or bacon, but hadn't forgotten his wife calling him a fat piece of shit.

Gabriel ordered scrapple, pancakes, a side of fries, and a large Coke.

Jackie turned over Eddie's coffee cup and filled it. She took away the cup in front of Gabriel.

"I'll have coffee," he said.

Jackie opened her eyes to look at him and breathed heavier. She poured Gabriel a cup as if it were against her better judgment, closed her eyes, and wheeled toward the kitchen.

"How old are you?" Eddie asked.

"Fourteen."

"You like coffee, huh?"

Gabriel didn't answer. He was drinking it, wasn't he?

"My kids drink hot chocolate."

"Those are them in the living room?"

Eddie had put the photos of Anthony and Dominic on a milk crate next to the sofabed.

"Yeah," he said. "You remind me of Anthony, the older one. That's his name. It's Anthony and Dominic. He doesn't say much, like you. But he's always thinking something."

Gabriel stared into the notion of that, wondering if it were true.

Eddie watched him. There had to be a lot going on under that Sixers cap. It seemed to Eddie that Gabriel couldn't make up his mind whether to tell him everything or tell him nothing.

"Baseball's their favorite sport?" Gabriel asked.

"No. Basketball. They think they're Michael Jordan."

Gabriel perked up at that.

"My dad bought me a Michael Jordan poster," he said. "I got it over my bed."

"Not that they don't like baseball, my kids. They collect baseball cards, like all kids. You collect baseball cards?"

Jackie came by with coffee and Gabriel pushed his empty cup toward her. Eddie was only halfway through his.

"No," Gabriel said.

"Your friends? Your friends must have baseball cards."

"No," Gabriel said. "That's not big around here."

Eddie was wondering what was in Gabriel's pocket if it wasn't baseball cards.

"You go to Phillies games?"

"I never went," Gabriel said, and he seemed embarrassed by that. "Sixers, though. I seen some Sixers games with my dad."

The mention of his father made Eddie nervous. He'd spent two weeks with a kid who had a father and a mother somewhere, but they hadn't talked about it. They hadn't really been together that much, and when they did talk, Eddie would just tell stories about his kids or about music, simple stories, and Gabriel would listen as if he could listen all day.

Jackie stood before them with a plate in each hand. Eyes closed, she slid both to the edge of the counter.

"Your father, what's he do?"

"He worked in a hat factory," Gabriel said, going at the scrapple first.

"He works in a hat factory?" Eddie said, putting it in another tense.

"That was one of his jobs. Making hats."

The answer drew attention to itself. It wasn't an answer.

Eddie put down his fork and turned to Gabriel.

"Hey," he said, "let's not bullshit each other."

Gabriel responded as if surprised. But he wasn't. And when he spoke, there was relief in his voice. "My dad left two years ago."

Eddie took a bite of potatoes and then pushed the whites of the scrambled eggs off into their own little corner.

"And you haven't seen him since?"

Gabriel shook his head no. He took a sip of coffee.

"He played the guitar," Gabriel said, putting the cup down. "When your truck was burning, that's what I was thinking of, because I saw your guitar. That wasn't his job or nothing, but he sounded pretty good. He showed me how to hold some chords. D, I think. D, C, and G. He said you could make a lot of songs with just those chords."

Gabriel unscrewed the salt shaker and poured a little pile on his plate. Next to it, he poured a pool of ketchup. He took the french fries now, one at a time, dipping them first in the ketchup and then in the salt.

Eddie felt his blood pressure go up just from watching. Gabriel smiled at him and Eddie shook his head.

"I get to ask questions?" Gabriel asked.

"Yeah, I guess so."

Gabriel finished another snowcapped fry first.

"Why'd you leave your wife?"

Eddie picked at his eggs some more. "Sometimes things just don't work out," he said. He wanted to be careful here, because he knew what Gabriel was doing. He was trying to figure out why his own father had left his mother. "Sometimes you don't want to leave, but it's the only thing you can do," Eddie said.

Gabriel allowed time for that to make sense. When it didn't, he asked another question.

"You think you're ever going back?"

Gabriel looked at Eddie when he asked the questions, but he preferred to look away when he got his answers. He was done with his fries and took a pencil out of his shirt pocket, one of those adjustable ones, and started scribbling on a napkin. It seemed to Eddie that he did it subconsciously, the way somebody might twist his hair or jingle the change in his pockets.

"I don't know," Eddie said. He didn't think he could ever go back, especially now that his wife was sleeping with Paulie Rego, but he didn't want Gabriel to hear that. "It's not an easy thing," he said.

Gabriel nodded.

"So look," Eddie said. "You told me your parents weren't getting along, that's why you needed to stay over. If you don't level with me, we can't do this anymore. It's not right."

Gabriel set down his pencil and looked straight ahead at the two of them in the mirror. He seemed to be studying their faces for the kind of things that showed up in his sketches. Not just physical features, but emotional ones.

"Why'd you run away?" Eddie asked.

Before Gabriel could answer, they were both distracted by the sound of the women who'd been crying in the booth. A lady friend of theirs had walked in and now all three of them were crying.

Eddie turned to his left, startled to find the coffee man in conversation. He was talking to Jackie, and sounding almost normal.

"I still can't believe it," he was saying.

"He wasn't that old," Jackie said. "What, sixty-something? Let's look at TV, see if they got it."

Eddie heard more sobbing from the booth. He leaned over to the coffee man and asked what was going on.

"Where you been, pal?" the coffee man asked. "The mayor is dead."

Eddie looked at Gabriel.

"He died last night," Gabriel said, as if it was old news.

"Well why didn't you tell me?"

Gabriel shrugged.

"I just heard about it last night," he said.

Jackie came out of the kitchen dragging a stool behind her. She set it near the cash register and climbed on top of it to turn on the TV that sat on a ledge in the corner of the restaurant. She turned it to Channel Six, and a newsman was in the middle of a commentary.

"The mayor and former police commissioner was not without detractors, particularly blacks and other minorities who believe he fanned the flames of racial ignorance and fear to his own political gain. It was during his reign as the city's top cop that dozens of officers were indicted for turning their heads to drug trafficking in return for cash payments. And there were those who believed that under his reign as mayor, certain neighborhoods flourished through the channeling of manpower and tax dollars, while others were virtually ignored, their residents denied access to the city's halls of power. But to some, he was a giant, a hero. A legend. Friendly yet firm, softhearted yet courageous. A large man. Larger than life itself. A man who rewarded friends and punished enemies, and once boasted that he owned more jobs than the president of the United States. Literally tens of thousands are expected to mourn the passing of Michael Angelo DeMarco, who moved on last evening, leaving behind a wife, a son—the currently incarcerated former councilman—and six grandchildren. He was sixty-eight."

Eddie looked away from the TV and into the smoky glare of misty-eyed diners. Everyone in the Ritz was turned to the television in quiet reverence, mesmerized by the images of the mayor. One of the three women made the sign of the cross. They'd already started the funeral, right here in the Ritz.

Gabriel leaned closer to Eddie and spoke in a whisper.

"My dad used to say he was a crook."

Eddie nudged Gabriel with his elbow and laughed.

"Your dad was right," he said.

Jackie brought the bill and Eddie looked at his watch.

"Shit, I gotta run."

He reached for his wallet, but Gabriel had already pulled a ten out of his back pocket.

"Where'd you get that?" Eddie asked.

"I work," Gabriel said as they walked outside.

"He works," Eddie said, "but does he go to school?"

Gabriel put his hands in his pockets and looked at his feet.

"Your mother," Eddie said, "she know where you are?"

No answer.

"Because if she doesn't, you're not staying with me another night. If you need some time from her, that's one thing. But if you've got her worried sick over you, I don't want any part of it."

Gabriel started north. Eddie was going the other way.

"She knows," Gabriel said, calling back to Eddie. "She knows."

Eddie had turned for home to get his guitar when he heard Gabriel running after him.

"Here," he said, handing him the napkin. "This is my father."

It was the sketch Gabriel had been doing in the Ritz. Gabriel's father had a foot up on a chair, a guitar over his knee. It looked like Gabriel in twenty years.

When Eddie crawled through his window the phone was ringing.

"We gotta talk," Inverso said.

"I got this job at ten, but then I can come downtown."

"I were you, I wouldn't get within a mile of fuckin' downtown," Inverso said. "Thin Jimmy's worked up. He says it's been three weeks, and if he don't have his money in a few days, he's gonna take care of business."

"What do you mean take care of business?"

"He said he hopes you know how to play the guitar with your teeth, is how he put it. Me, they'll probably just break both my legs. And he asked me to tell you Paulie Rego says your wife is like a wild woman that broke out of chains. Like she ain't had it in years. Jimmy says maybe when Rego's done, he'll get some of it himself."

"You're all a bunch of fucking pigs," Eddie said.

It had crossed his mind earlier, but Eddie thought seriously now about getting out. Just getting in the Cutlass, that rotting piece of shit, and going. Start over somewhere else. The only thing that kept him from doing it was Anthony and Dominic.

"Look, there's no way I can raise this kind of money," Eddie said. "Doesn't Jimmy have any insurance?"

"Insurance? What're you, fuckin' stupid? This is La Cosa Nostra, junior. You think the Mafia buys fucking automobile insurance?"

Shit, how would he know?

"Look," Inverso said, "you gotta come up with this money or we're gonna wish we was with the mayor, you and me. You see what I'm saying? We gotta get together and talk about some ways to raise this."

They agreed to meet at Eddie's place. If not tonight, Eddie told him, sometime tomorrow.

Nine

Marisol didn't say a word when Gabriel walked in. She just gave him that scowl she saved for him alone. Her black hair fell over a snow-white T-shirt and she pushed it back, letting the coffee-and-cream skin of her perfect neck reveal itself.

Gabriel was taken again, as if for the first time, by the drama in her simple movements through this room. A bend, a turn, a swipe at a table with a cloth. She was all grace and light, a different part of her body tight against her clothes with each move. And she struck a fear in him unlike any he felt on the street.

Gabriel turned to the business page of the *Inquirer*. Nothing on the page registered. All he saw on it was Marisol. Many nights on the street, he would think of her, watch her walk across this room. And yet every time he saw her, just as now, she stepped outside that memory prettier, sexier, more impossible.

She was coming toward him with a coffeepot and a cup. He kept his eyes on the table.

"Your mother came here," she said in a tone that was intended as a slap.

Gabriel looked up. "When?"

There was more concern in his voice than he intended. He didn't want to blow his cool, because that was his whole approach with Marisol. He was an intelligent, self-assured guy.

"Yesterday, the day before," Marisol said, shrugging. "I don't remember."

Nefario's Market was only two blocks from his house, but Gabriel never knew his mother to eat here or shop here.

"What did she want?" he asked, too nonchalant this time. For a guy who was supposed to come off as Joe Cool, it occurred to Gabriel, he seemed to think too much.

"She's looking for your sorry ass," Marisol said. "I don't know why. If I was her, I'd disown you."

In an odd way, this was part of the attraction for Gabriel, that Marisol had his number and jerked him around the way she did. She wouldn't be this way if she didn't really care about him.

"You're a selfish piece of garbage," she said.

On the other hand, he could be entirely wrong.

He pretended to ignore her. But while staring blankly at the business page, he stepped away from himself and looked back as if through a clearing.

Was he selfish?

He hadn't thought of himself that way. He'd thought of himself as trapped, with no idea how to get away from Diablo and the whole drug scene. But maybe Marisol was right. Since he'd been gone, he had tried not to think about what it was doing to his mother.

Maybe he was selfish.

Gabriel looked at the full coffee cup in front of him. He'd just had two cups at the Ritz with Eddie, and didn't want anymore. But if he kept draining the cup, Marisol would have to keep coming back to refill it. He poured in lots of milk, cooling the coffee so he could drink it in gulps.

"I don't know why you even ran away in the first place," Marisol said when she gave him his first refill. "Like you're some bigshot or something."

He still hadn't given much thought to why he ran away. He couldn't even remember thinking it over or deciding it. But he knew, he had always known, that reasons can't be hurried. Sometimes they didn't even come until long after the decisions. At the edge of it, he knew it had something to do with the quiet in the house, and with the way the quiet was broken. All those nights she cried. And he, on the edge of the bed, falling with her like a stone in the ocean, sinking into the depths of her sadness.

"She came with a priest," Marisol said.

"A priest?"

"That's what I said. A priest."

There was no flirting in her tone now, if there ever had been. She was angry.

"What's she doing with a priest?" Gabriel asked.

"She's so worried about you, she went to a priest," Marisol said.

She'd pushed one of his buttons now and she knew it.

"The priest said he's helping her look for you. They both go out at night, asking around. The drug corners and everywhere. She rides her bike, he walks."

Gabriel looked at the door. He imagined his mother coming through it with a priest. As far as he knew, she never even went to church.

"They'll probably both get shot or something," Marisol said. "In crossfire, probably, all the shooting they been having lately. I told them it's not worth it, getting shot for you."

Gabriel thought out loud, unintentionally.

"Why'd she go to a priest?"

Marisol looked behind the deli case to see where her parents were. There was nobody in the room but her and Gabriel.

"Why're you so fucking stupid?" she said. Gabriel looked down at the newspaper, but Marisol took him by surprise, grabbing him by the face and jerking him toward her. "You're scarin' the shit out of her, asshole. If you're gonna keep your ass out there selling drugs, you could at least call her or something. Let her know you're alive. What did she do to you that you wanna torture your mother?"

She let him go.

"What'd you tell her?" he asked.

"I told her you was selling drugs."

Gabriel stood up, his chair falling over behind him.

"You told her that?"

"What's wrong, you ashamed of what you are? I told her you got your ass beat on the subway, too. And you been cutting school for two years."

Gabriel moved for the door. He stopped and turned when she said his name.

"Go ahead and run," she said. "This is just what your father did. You're a dog, just like your father."

Gabriel stared at Marisol and something rose in him. Anger, fear, confusion—it was all of those things, a feeling like nothing he'd had before.

He wanted to call her a bitch, but left without a word, slamming the door behind him. Madly in love with her.

Gabriel had been back on the job three nights, but it wasn't the same as before. Ever since the police crackdown ended, the gangs were testing the old turf agreements, and every corner was fair game. It was relatively quiet at Third and Indiana itself, but Gabriel heard shooting from all over the neighborhood. He'd try to distinguish between gunshots and echoes to guess the location, and figure out how close they were. Sometimes he'd hear a shot and imagine the feel of a bullet boring hot into his body.

The shooting attracted a lot of squad cars, and Gabriel's eyes were everywhere, looking out for police and rival dealers. But the people he really watched out for, more than anyone, were his mother and the priest. He fronted the lookouts fifty dollars each night and told them he wanted a warning for a woman on a bike.

It was early November, and Gabriel hadn't been home in five weeks. Philadelphia was getting hit with cold Canadian air and it was in the thirties every night. Most of the streetlights were broken, and with no ceiling of light, the dark sky seemed to drop right down into the streets. Gabriel shivered, the kind of shivering that is only partly from the cold. He had a bad feeling about things, as if something was happening just beyond the edge of his awareness.

He'd seen Ralph earlier in the evening, and Ralph told him to be careful. With all the squabbling among gangs, Diablo was even crazier than usual. He was talking about offing a couple of rivals, and he was also going around smacking his own people for the slightest little thing. Ralph was in the same situation as Gabriel now. He'd been promoted as another of the rising stars, and immediately realized it only meant he was all the more trapped.

Gabriel had three customers waiting now, white boys from the burbs, driving what looked like their parents' cars. They handed him money and he handed them crack, and when he turned to his left, he saw his supervisor coming toward him.

And now he was certain that something was wrong.

The last two nights, turning the money in at the end of his shift, Gabriel had picked up something in the supervisor's manner. He couldn't identify it at the time, but he could see it now. He could see it in his eyes. Gabriel had learned, in studying the shadows that moved through his father, how to read untold thoughts.

"There's a meeting at midnight," the supervisor said.

Gabriel heard the words before they were said.

"A meeting?"

"Germantown and Indiana. Diablo wants everybody there."

Lalo worked that corner. At sixteen, Lalo had been the oldest lookout. Gabriel and Ralph figured his learning disability had held him back. But the dealer at Germantown and Indiana had gotten shot a week ago, and Lalo had been filling in for him.

"What's it about?" Gabriel asked his supervisor. He hadn't seen Lalo since the day Eddie's flipchair fell off I-95.

"Some people been fucking up," the supervisor said. "Diablo wants to say something about it. It'll be quick, then we're back here till two."

What Gabriel knew, for sure, was that Lalo was about to have the shit beat out of him in front of an audience. What he feared was that Lalo wouldn't be the only one.

Gabriel hadn't stolen a nickel. He wouldn't think of it. But that didn't matter. You could get cut a dozen ways in this business, most of them involving the people on your own side. Someone below your might want your job, someone above you might think you were after theirs. You turn in five hundred dollars at the end of the night, and all the supervisor has to do is skim a hundred and tell the boss you're a thief. The first time, it might be overlooked as an honest mistake. The second time, somebody pays.

Two nights ago, the supervisor had told Gabriel he was short.

Gabriel had been resented from the day he was promoted because he was younger and smarter than most, and because something in his manner suggested that he thought of himself as different, as somehow outside this whole thing. This was part of what he hadn't anticipated when he first got involved—that cops and rival gangs could be less of a threat than your own people. The Black Caps gang, in particular, was kept in line through intimidation. It had the enforcer all the other gangs talked about. And Diablo was legendary not just for making examples, but for the pleasure he took in it.

Gabriel and the rest of his crew put all the drugs and money in the stash house at ten to midnight and then the four of them began walking to Germantown and Indiana. The supervisor, the treasurer, the lookout. Gabriel.

Nobody spoke.

Gabriel glanced down each street as they crossed intersections, studying the way the streets ended in points in the distance. He thought about his mother and his father and Marisol. He thought about Eddie. Each of them floating before him and then retreating, as if moving down those streets, their scale narrowing.

As they made their way, Gabriel dreamed of hiding. The city could lose you in a million places if you knew it, if you let it transform you. You could become one of its ghosts, a shadow sliding across the face of a building and around a corner. You could become part of its noise, a part of its movement. You could go invisible. But the city could give you up, too, because in those secret places there were other things to run from. The whispers of others in hiding. The sound of your mind at work against itself.

Gabriel wanted nothing more than to go home. Just walk in, kiss his mother good night, crawl into bed, and go to sleep as if he'd never been gone. He wanted to go in and hold her when she cried, and tell her that his father didn't deserve her. He didn't deserve either of them, and they didn't need him anymore.

Lalo saw everyone coming his way. He stood tall, but his body was already going hollow, his mind searching, as Gabriel's had, for a place to hide.

Diablo made one slow pass in his Trans Am, not looking at the gang he'd called together. He just stared straight ahead, and then he came back around the corner. He parked and stepped out, like something oozing up from the sewer, all balls and swagger and dripping melted skin. Aware of the audience, feeding off of it. But not acknowledging it.

People watched from their windows, eyeballs through slits. A small crowd of derelicts, prostitutes, and pimps gathered. Everyone looking at Lalo.

Lalo had made the decision to take it, right here, rather than let it chase him.

Diablo moved toward Lalo but then stopped at the stash house. He disappeared for a moment and then reappeared on the porch, his ugliness spilling over the street. He held a nine-millimeter in one hand, a baseball bat in the other, as if weighing the crime, considering the punishment.

He tossed the gun into the house, its thud and its slide audible on the street, and walked slowly toward Lalo with the bat. The handle in his left hand, the barrel in his right.

Lalo didn't raise a hand, didn't take a step. He made no sound. His eyes registered a certain peace, as if he had somehow anesthetized himself against Diablo, against pain, against this whole neighborhood.

All anybody heard was the bat on his legs. A sound they could feel.

One blow after another. His legs, then his arms, his ribs, his back. The sound of bones breaking, and then the sounds of Lalo's feeble breathing. The whisper of his ghost.

Diablo turned to his audience, as if awaiting applause.

Gabriel glanced at Ralph, who stood ten feet away. It looked like Ralph's eyes were filling, but it might just be the way the streetlights were hitting him. Gabriel wished he was standing next to him.

Lalo was trying to get up.

Get back down, Gabriel said to himself. Get the fuck back down.

Lalo was on his hands and knees, not a boy anymore, not a human being. Diablo stepped back, adjusted his grip, and measured his target. And then he stepped up and swung, his wrists turning, the barrel of the bat flying at Lalo's hanging head.

The sound was solid and dull, and it fell heavy over the street, penetrating everything. A young lookout dropped to the gutter and vomited.

Diablo stepped away, wiping sweat off his face with his sleeve. Now he was calling everybody to gather around. He still held the bat with two hands as Lalo lay behind him. The blow to the head had turned Lalo face up and his eyes were rolled back in his head. He was twitching like one of Diablo's shot pit bulls.

"I'd like to thank all of you for coming," Diablo said. He was grinning, floating. This was his drug.

"This is what happens," he said, using the bat as a pointer, like a science teacher. "Lalo Camacho stole money off us, and this is what happens when you steal from your family. But unfortunately, gentlemen, as it turns out, Lalo isn't the only thief in our midst."

Gabriel went limp. He was next.

Diablo smacked the bat against his hand.

"Somebody else, somebody here right now, stole money like Lalo stole money. At two o'clock, the motherfucker gets the same. All of you will be notified as to the exact location of the next performance."

He was grinning wider now, and twirling the bat like a baton.

"If you didn't steal money, you got nothin' to worry about. Just go back to work and everything's fine. Except for one of you."

They started to turn.

"And if you run," Diablo said, as everybody turned back to hear him out, "I'll track your ass down and kill you. I'll kill you and anybody who gets in my way."

As Diablo drove away, Gabriel and Ralph started toward Lalo. They weren't going to just leave him there, twitching on the street. But before they got to him, Lieutenant Bagno was there, and they backed off.

Everybody knew him. He was with East Division Detectives. Short gray hair, a U.S. Navy ballcap, an Eagles sweatshirt. The Badlands was like another tour of Vietnam for him.

There were two ways for cops to show up. There were those who arrived, and those who appeared. Lieutenant Bagno appeared. He was always there, as fresh as the crime, without anyone having seen him approach.

Among the two dozen dealers, lookouts, and bystanders, nobody talked to him. He knew they wouldn't. But he talked anyway now, like he always did, carrying on both ends of the conversation.

"Good evening, Lieutenant Bagno."

"Oh, good evening, gentlemen. How fortunate that you're here. Perhaps you can tell me how Lalo's head got squashed like a cantaloupe."

"We didn't see anything, Lieutenant Bagno."

"Now isn't that a coincidence? I just have to tell you, it seems like every time somebody gets whacked in front of a freaking audience, everybody's blinking when it happens. What are the odds on this?"

He was yelling, starting toward them, slow at first, then picking up the pace and charging like a bull, with that one vein in his forehead ready to blow. It was another Bagno trademark. He'd run up to everybody on the street, especially the dealers. Run right up to them like he was going to run through them, and then stop two inches short, screaming into their faces and spitting. It looked like he was going to chew their noses off.

"We didn't see anything, Lieutenant Bagno. We don't know anything, Lieutenant Bagno. We're complete fucking idiots, Lieutenant Bagno. Yes, Lalo is our friend and we just watched him get the shit beat out of him by an animal and we didn't lift a hand to help him because we're drug-dealing motherfucking pieces of shit, Lieutenant Bagno, and tomorrow we're going shopping for new sneakers and gold chains."

He wiped the spit off his face and went back to Lalo, crouching over him.

"Now listen to me, you cripple. I warned your ass. Your mother comes to me begging, oh, Lieutenant Bagno, you have to help me, you have to help me get my son Lalo off the street. Well I arrested him three times, Miss Camacho, I did all I could do, Miss Camacho. I'm not the boy's father now am I, Miss Camacho? But I told him he was going to die if he didn't stop. And here he is, Miss Camacho. Here's your boy. He might not be quite the same now that his brain is caved in. But we know he won't be any stupider, Miss Camacho, if it's any consolation."

Lieutenant Bagno grabbed Lalo by the collar, pulling his head off the ground, and shook him.

"Listen to me," he said. "If you're dead, you deserve it. If you're not, come see me when you feel better. I'd like to beat the shit out of you."

"On the way back to Third and Indiana, Gabriel saw the ambulance on its way to pick Lalo off the pavement. He saw Ralph only a half block ahead of him.

"Ralph," he called.

Ralph acted like he didn't hear him.

"Ralph," Gabriel called again. When he didn't turn, Gabriel ran and caught up with him.

"What's wrong?" Gabriel asked.

Ralph kept walking, staring straight ahead.

"You think he'll live?" Gabriel asked.

"What's the difference?" Ralph asked.

They walked a half block before another word was spoken.

"What's the fucking difference?" Ralph asked again. "He's luckier dead."

"How much was Lalo short?" Gabriel asked.

"Two thousand, they say. They always say two thousand dollars. They gave him two days to come up with it is what I heard. Two days, and even if you get it, that don't mean Diablo won't fuck you up."

No, it didn't. But getting the money was your only chance.

"You think he did it?" Gabriel asked.

"Did what?" Ralph asked.

"Took the money. You know, skimmed."

"Fuck if I know. If he did or didn't, it don't matter now."

Gabriel had never seen Ralph this way. He wondered if he was just upset about Lalo, or if he knew something Gabriel didn't know.

"Ralph, who's the other one?"

Ralph didn't answer. He was like Gabriel that way, not much of a talker, always holding something back. It's why they'd become close. The other kids would just roll with it all. Friends getting shot. Parents out of work. Mom on crack. Ralph never rolled with it. Like Gabriel, he thought about stuff. He thought about what he was. A drug dealer.

"You know who else gets it tonight?" Gabriel asked again.

Ralph stopped, his too-small head hanging off his too-long neck like an eight-ball on a cue stick.

"What are you going to be?" Ralph said. "Are you still going to be an artist?"

The question came out of nowhere.

"What are you talking about?" Gabriel asked.

"Is that what you want to be? An artist?"

"Yeah, why?"

"Draw fast," Ralph said.

Gabriel looked down the streets again, at the way they became points in the distance.

"I knew I was next," Gabriel said.

"We're all next," Ralph said. "It might be you, it might be me, I don't fucking know. But you're luckier than most of us."

"What do you mean?"

"You've got to hide this from your mom."

"That makes me lucky?"

"My parents, they know. I don't have to tell them, and they don't ask, but they know what I do. And they don't say a thing, because they like the money."

Gabriel had nothing to say to that.

"Look, man, I gotta go," Ralph said, and then he broke off, crossing the street to head back to his corner.

Gabriel had walked three blocks before he realized he wasn't headed back to Third and Indiana. He was headed toward home.

Something inside of him had taken over, deciding things for him, and he didn't question it.

When he walked past his school, he realized he hadn't been in it for two months. This was where he had met Marisol, and he smiled at the memory of her scolding him for skipping class. She had to love him. There could be no other reason she rode him the way she did. Dozens of kids skipped school, and as far as he knew, she didn't give them shit like she gave him shit.

He wondered whether, if he married Marisol, his father would show up. Gabriel's father had told him that he had met his mother at a wedding. Maybe his father would come to the wedding and fall in love all over again with Gabriel's mother.

Gabriel looked up at the second floor of the school and saw pictures in the window of his art class. He wondered if Mrs. Meketon, the art teacher, had sent his mother the note she showed him.

Dear Ms. Santoro:

Your son is a gifted young man. His work is beyond anything I've ever seen in a student his age, and I'd like to discuss with you sending him to the High School for Creative and Performing Arts. He has a lot of absences this year, as I'm sure you know, but I'd be happy to write a recommendation to CAPA because it would be a waste if his talent is not developed. We've been studying architecture, and I asked the kids to do a rendering of downtown Philadelphia. Gabriel sketched a skyline made of crack caps, and people on the street were in the shape of those outlines police do at crime scenes. It may sound strange, but it was brilliant. I took the class to a street near school and asked them to sketch a row-house block, and Gabriel's had human faces drawn into the moldings and cornices, like gargoyles. When I asked him who they were, he said they were kids he knew who've been killed. He is an intelligent boy, quiet and thoughtful, who sees things beyond his years. Please call me soon to set up an appointment. Applications to the special high schools have to go in by next month.

Thank you,
Mrs. Meketon

Gabriel was a block from home now. He was passing the house where his friend Jorge used to live. He hadn't seen him in two years. Jorge's backyard connected with Gabriel's, and he was the one who got Gabriel involved in the beginning, working as a decoy for twenty dollars a day.

"It's through my brother," Jorge said. He had an older brother named Tony.

Gabriel was twelve at the time, and twenty dollars didn't sound that much different than a million. So he went with his buddy Jorge, even though he suspected it involved drugs somehow, and that was the start of it.

A month later, on the very spot where Gabriel now stood, Tony was gunned down. Jorge knelt at his brother's side, slapping him in the face and telling him not to die.

That was the last time anybody saw Jorge. There were those who said he was dumped in the river because he saw who killed his brother. There were those who said he killed himself. And there were those who said he'd gone crazy and was locked up in a nuthouse somewhere. Nobody knew for sure.

Gabriel walked on, turning the corner toward Diamond Street. When he got to the end of his block, and saw that nobody was around, he moved slowly toward the house.

The light was on in the living room and Gabriel saw the dark shape of his mother move through the yellow glow. Maybe she'd just gotten back from her nightly bike ride, maybe she was just getting set to go. Gabriel watched, hoping to see her move again.

The light went off and Gabriel grew nervous. She would be able to see him if she looked out, but he couldn't see her. He stepped out of view, not sure what to do. He walked back to the end of the block, hands in his pockets. Shivering.

When Lalo was getting beaten, Gabriel had a feeling he didn't want to acknowledge, and so he had pushed it away. It was back now.

He wished he were Lalo.

Lalo had that look in his eyes, that moment of peace, right before he was clubbed. Gabriel wondered if he was still alive, and hoped, for Lalo's sake, that he wasn't. He remembered the day they had talked about the bodies on Broad Street, and Lalo had said that if he died, he wanted Gabriel to do his. He wanted to look sharp.

If Lalo died, he was going to get his wish.

Gabriel crept toward his house. He saw faded light come to the upstairs window. His bedroom. It was from his mother turning on the light in her bedroom.

Gabriel walked up the stairs to his front door. It felt right.

He was home.

He reached for the doorknob, held it, and paused.

It was two o'clock and Diablo would be after him now. He might already be watching, and Gabriel remembered him saying he'd kill anyone who got in the way.

Gabriel jumped to the sidewalk. He walked about ten paces, looking over his shoulder, and then he broke into a run, his shadow growing long at the end of the block and sliding across the face of the houses, then disappearing around the corner.

Ten

A knock at the door.

"Who is it?'

"Inverso."

"Mike, you have to come around the side, through the window."

"I gotta what?"

"The door's jammed. It doesn't open."

"You fuckin' kidding me?"

"No."

"What about the back door?"

"There's no gate to the backyard. Just come around the side."

Eddie opened the dining room window. Inverso stood out there nodding, not saying a thing, his eyes hidden behind designer shades.

When he crawled through the window, Inverso caught his shoe on the sill and was hung up. "Motherfuck," he said, hopping on one loafer while trying to free the other. Eddie tried to help, but Inverso shook him off.

"I never seen anybody can't get in their own door," Inverso was saying, a knot of irritation as he dusted off wool slacks that had creases like razors. He took off his knee-length black leather jacket and tossed it over Gabriel's flipchair, and then he examined his loafer to make sure he hadn't scratched it. When had himself back in order, he took off the shades, hung them on the neck of a sweater that was Christmas green with a pattern of red and gray diamonds, and sized up Eddie's new place.

This oughta be something, Eddie was thinking, wondering what the little asshole would say.

The house faced west, and the small amount of morning light that penetrated it was absorbed by the mud-colored wall-to-wall carpet, which was capable of absorbing the beam of a searchlight. The dining room was naked but for the flipchair Gabriel slept on, the red USAir blanket thrown over it. The other flipchair was in the living room, along with a sofabed, a lamp, and the guitar, each item made lonelier by the next. In the kitchen, a metal folding chair sat next to two milk crates stacked one on top of the other, with a cardboard pizza box for a tabletop.

Inverso drank it all in, a slow swallow, his hairline dropping down to his Neanderthal brow. When it settled into the part of him that knew everything, it loosened the cords that held him up straight. The knees broke first, and then the hands came unhinged, followed by the shoulders and the hips. And now everything was going, with the cock as the fulcrum, the head bobbing as he turned to Eddie.

"Nice fucking place."

Eddie walked away. Confronting him would only make it worse.

It was going to take time, he told Inverso, no patience in his voice. It was going to take time to replace the furniture Sarah took with her.

"No, serious," Inverso said, dripping sarcasm. "It's really a nice fuckin' place."

His hand swept over the contents of Eddie's life. Eddie's eye followed Inverso's hand, the two of them doing a quick inventory. The last item they took in was the pizza-box kitchen table.

"Let's see," Inverso said. "Three weeks ago you had a wife, kids, girlfriend, a nice house. You throw the wife away, the girlfriend drops you the first week, your guitar gets torched, and a gangster wants to cut your heart out. But you've got this."

Son of a bitch, Eddie was thinking. As if he needed this little shit to come over and bust his balls. He had a notion to take a poke at him.

Inverso seemed to sense this, but it didn't slow him down. Inverso worked from the advantage of knowing people didn't find him worth hitting.

Eddie decided to change the subject.

"The directions all right?"

"No fuckin' problem," Inverso said. "Make a left when you hit Zulu land, turn right in Beirut, pass ten fuckin' drug corners, and stop when you come to a toothless crack whore pushing a stroller. You can't miss it. Where the hell am I, fucking Portaricken Appalachia?"

Eddie was thinking it over. Maybe just one quick shot, right in the mouth.

He wanted to tell Inverso there were people here who didn't have much, but they still had more class than some of the bigmouth downtown dagos. Bigmouths like Inverso. But he knew better than to lob something like that up there.

Inverso strolled to the living room, gave it a once-over, and shook his head. He pinched his slacks at the thighs and sat down on the flipchair. When he leaned back, it took longer to get to the backrest than he expected and his feet went airborne. They did a little flutter as he paddled for balance, breaking his cool. Now he was pulling himself to an upright position and running a hand over his haircut, feeling for little hairs that might have flown out of place.

When he was settled in, Inverso saw a scrap of paper on the floor and picked it up.

"What the fuck is this?" he asked, handing it to Eddie. "You sittin' here drawing pictures of yourself?"

"A kid from the neighborhood," Eddie said.

It was a sketch he hadn't seen. Gabriel must have done it last night. It was Eddie playing guitar under a funnel of light from an overhead bulb, his eyes closed and his head back in a sort of painful ecstasy. Eddie was reminded of the nights he used to go down to the basement of his house and play.

"You mind if I ask you something?" Inverso said.

Eddie set the sketch on the sofa. "What?"

"Sarah, she's gone, am I right?"

Eddie nodded.

"And she's not coming back, am I right?"

"Why do you ask?"

"Am I right or am I right?"

Eddie shifted his weight. "What are you trying to say?"

"What I'm saying, why don't you fuckin' go back home?"

"Jesus." Eddie groaned. "What're you, my fuckin' marriage counselor?"

"I'm just trying to help," Inverso said. "I see you sittin' here alone, pulling your pud, I'm trying to help a friend."

Eddie got up to get a beer. It might take off the edge.

"You want something?" he asked, going to get a Yuengling.

Inverso said no.

"If it wasn't for the kids," Eddie said as he sat on the sofa, "I wouldn't have been there. For a long time, that's what kept me there. You tell yourself it's bad for the kids if you leave. But you know what? Sometimes it's bad for the kids if you stay." He took another sip and wiped his mouth with the back of his hand. Inverso was quiet. Maybe he was thinking about his own miserable marriage.

"We were too young," Eddie said. "We got married too young. Back then, that's what I wanted. I wanted a family, stay downtown, live there forever. Just like my parents. The life they had, I respected it, and the first girl I really liked, I married."

Inverso acted like he was personally insulted.

"And now you don't respect it? The way we live downtown's not good enough for Eddie Joe Pass?"

"I just started respecting other things," Eddie said.

Eddie reached for his guitar and pulled it out of its case. The guitar disappeared in his arms and became part of him, the neck cradled in his left hand like the head of a sleeping baby. He began playing without being aware of it.

"That don't sound bad," Inverso said. "What the hell is that?"

Eddie had to think about it.

" 'So What,' " he said. "Miles Davis."

"I'll tell you so what," Inverso said. "Myself, I don't know much about music, but we had some guy from the Settlement Music School come to one of the rec centers, put on a little program for the kids. This guy plays the guitar himself and afterwards, I'm telling him I know a couple of players myself. I mention you for one, Paulie Rego for another. And guess what. This son of a bitch tells me there's no fuckin' comparison."

"Was this Johnny Timpane?" Eddie asked.

"Yeah, it's Johnny something, I don't know from Johnny Timpane, but Johnny something. You know him?"

Johnny Timpane had taught some of the greats. Wes Montgomery, Kenny Burrell, Jim Hall, Joe Pass. Eddie had studied with him a couple of months, and learned more from him than from anyone.

"Well anyways, he says he knows the two of youse, and you got it all over Rego. He seen you play. So I says to him, hey, explain something to me. If that's the case, how come Eddie Joe Pass is playing dives and pulling his pud while Paulie Rego is playing the big clubs and fucking Eddie's wife?"

"You told him that?"

"What. Like people don't know?"

"I don't think the whole fucking world knows."

"Everybody downtown knows," Inverso said. For him, there was no difference. "But anyway, gettin' back to the story, this Johnny guy gives me this."

Inverso tapped his skull with his index finger.

"Headcase," Inverso said. "He says you're fuckin' scared. A studio player, he says. This guy cranks it up in the studio, he's great. The best in Philadelphia. He gets on a stage with some real players, he shits his pants. On top of which, somebody in a club tells him to play something they might recognize, something besides this jazz impersonation, he throws a fit."

"Improvisation."

"Right."

"He said that? Johnny Timpane said that about me?"

Some musicians might be insulted. Not Eddie.

"He seen you play a couple of times," Inverso said. "He said he could see it right away."

"That I was good?"

"No. That you was the type to find some way to waste your talent."

Eddie was still so flattered by the good part, the insult didn't sink in.

"By the way," Inverso said. "Paulie Rego? I seen him."

"What, you saw him play?"

"No, I seen him on Passyunk, goin' into Marra's."

"At least he knows a good pizza," Eddie said.

"Yeah, well so does your wife. She was on his arm."

"They're goin' out in public, the two of them?"

"The four of them," Inverso said. "Your kids were there."

Eddie set the guitar down and stood up. He ran his hand over his beard as if he were trying to wipe it off his face.

"Fuck."

His chest tightened. It was another thing he hadn't thought about, because his way wasn't to think ahead. But the idea of Anthony and Dominic being with Paulie Rego made him sick.

Eddie drained the Yuengling and went for another. When he came back, he paced the living room. Inverso let him calm down a little bit before he started in.

"Listen to me," he finally said. "This son of a bitch has taken over your family, and what have you got? Hell, if you were getting laid, it's a different deal. But you're not even getting that."

Eddie was ignoring him. He was still burning over the image of his kids going places with Paulie Rego.

"Let me tell you something," Inverso said.

"Would you shut up?" Eddie said. "Just shut the fuck up."

Inverso stood up. "No, junior. You shut the fuck up. Shut the fuck up and listen to me. You might learn something."

Eddie sat back down.

"Guess what, Einstein. Your father, my father, their fathers, you don't think they wet their whistles outside the home now and then? That's how you do it, junior. You don't pack up and leave. You think anybody loves their wife after two weeks? Get the fuck out of here. Friday, Saturday, one of those days, you keep for yourself. What're you, stupid? That's how you keep a marriage together, douchebag. That's how you keep your kids happy. Your problem is you don't have no fucking family values."

Eddie heard about half of that. He stood up in the middle of it and started pacing again. He was halfway through his second beer.

"This fucking Sarah," Inverso was saying now, surveying the living room. "She took all the new furniture?"

"What new furniture?" Eddie asked.

"The new furniture you picked up with Jimmy's truck."

Eddie looked around the room.

"This is it," he said.

"What do you mean, this is it?"

"This is the furniture I picked up. This sofa, this chair, the chair in the dining room."

Inverso looked at the three pieces and turned to Eddie with palms open, his head pulled into his shoulders.

"This is it? This is what you picked up? We're gonna have our legs broken by Thin Jimmy's gang for a flea-market sofa and two fuckin' beanbags?"

"The sofa opens up to a bed," Eddie said. "The flipchairs too. Oatmeal flipchairs, they call them."

"I got your fuckin' oatmeal right here, pal," Inverso said, grabbing himself. "I'll just call Thin Jimmy, tell him hey, pal, your truck's a piece of fuckin' toast but don't worry about it 'cuz we're gonna give you a sofabed and a couple of foam rubber fuckin' flipchairs to make it right. Yeah, you're gonna love 'em, Jimmy. Did I mention they was oatmeal flipchairs? They open up, believe it or not, just like the sofa. These are the chairs fuckin' flew off your truck right before it got smoked."

Eddie had heard enough.

"Look," he said, "I thought you came here to talk about some ideas for handling the situation."

"I did. And you're telling me about your fucking chairs that open up. Let me tell you something, pal, our heads are gonna open up, is what. I seen Thin Jimmy this morning."

"You seen him?"

"This is what I'm saying. I go to the Melrose, who should be sittin' there but the fat fuck himself. Jesus, the son of a bitch must go three hundred pounds now. He's having his eggs there at the counter, he gives me this nod, like get the fuck over here, ya know? You got three days, he tells me. Ten thousand dollars, three days. Otherwise, he says, we gotta work out some other arrangement, you see what I'm saying? I says yeah, Jimmy, look, it's not a problem. We can raise that."

The color drained from Eddie's face. He flopped back on the sofa and looked at the ceiling.

"Why'd you tell him it's no problem?" Eddie groaned.

"Whadda you want me to tell him, sign us up for the fuckin' Christmas Club? You know these kids, they ain't like their old men," Inverso said. "Those guys, they knew how to run a organization. They understood patience a little better. That's good business. It's class. It's common fucking sense. You shoot somebody in the head, how's he supposed to pay you? That's all they know, these punks, *ba-da-bing, ba-da-boom,* kill everybody looks at them the wrong way. They don't have a head for this is what I'm saying. They're out of their element, these fuckin' turks."

It was one sign from God after another, Eddie was thinking. The furniture. The guitar. Sarah. The mob. This was a hell of a penance for your marriage going bad.

"The problem I got with it," Inverso said, "you remember when we was fifteen, Eddie? Fifteen, even twenty, and these guys were ridin' fuckin' tricycles down the street? You remember that? And now they wanna tell us how to live? They're bustin' our chops, these fuckin' kids. What happened with the truck, that was a accident. These guys know we don't got that kind of money. It ain't right."

Eddie sat down again and reached for his guitar like a kid reaching for his blanket. He went back to the Miles Davis song again, "So What." And then he stopped suddenly, as if it all hit him at that moment, and looked at Inverso.

"Mike. What are we going to do?"

Inverso didn't have an answer, and that scared Eddie more than anything.

"Why don't you put on a fucking record or something," Inverso said. "It's too quiet in here."

"I don't have a stereo," Eddie said.

Inverso was coming back into his skin now. "You're a musician, you got no fucking stereo?"

"Mine's home. Sarah had one, she took it."

"She leave you your fucking shorts?" Inverso looked across the room again. "No TV either?" he asked.

"Sarah. It was hers."

"Jesus, Eddie, what the hell did you bring to the party? No wonder this girl dumped you. You don't have a fuckin' pot to piss in."

A smile scrunched Inverso's missing link of a face, and his hairline met his eyebrows. It was a downtown don't-worry-about-it smile.

"This is your lucky day," Inverso said, standing up.

"What, you got a plan?"

"No, I just remembered I got some TVs."

"What do you mean you got some TVs?" Eddie asked.

"Yeah, in the car."

"That's it? You got some TVs? I thought you had a fucking plan, you're gonna sell me a hot television?"

"We'll think of something," Inverso said. "Let me get you one of these TVs first. I know a guy, he's got a warehouse full of them. Bought 'em right off a truck. I'm gonna give you a deal on it. My cost."

Off a truck, Eddie was thinking. Off a fucking truck. Half of everything in South Philadelphia came off a truck everybody heard of and nobody ever saw. Here they were, the mob climbing up their ass, and Inverso was selling him a fucking TV.

"Look," Eddie said. "I can't afford a TV right now. Shit, I don't even want to think about a TV. We're about to get our heads cracked and what, I'm going to watch *Wheel of Fortune?*"

"Just take the fuckin' thing, you stuttering prick. I can't stand looking at this place. You got two beanbags and a half dozen fuckin' milk crates. A TV, at least it puts a little light in the room, gives you something to do besides pull your pud."

Eddie didn't say no. TV might actually get his mind off his troubles, if that was possible.

"Look," Inverso said, "you could owe it to me. I'll add it to the ten grand."

Inverso went to his car and was back in seconds, popping the TV up on the window sill.

"You wanna grab this cocksucker?" he said.

It had no box or instructions, nothing. It was just the naked television. Eddie lifted it inside.

"How many of these things you have?"

"I'm into him for thirty of these pricks," Inverso said. "Six at a time I carry in the trunk."

"Orbitron?" Eddie asked, reading the front of the TV.

"What, you got a problem? Mr. Milk Crate wants to get picky here? Orbitron, yeah. Orbitron. Same as Sony. They make all these things in the same factory, the fuckin' Japs."

Eddie brought it into the living room and set in on the floor across from the sofa. He plugged in the Orbitron and started fiddling with the built-in telescope antenna.

The picture wasn't bad. Eddie turned it to Channel Six and sat on the sofa.

"Listen, one idea I had," Inverso said, "we make a deal with Thin Jimmy. You know how these guys are all the time throwing parties. Somebody gets engaged, it's a big deal. Somebody has a baby, they do a little thing."

"So what's the point?" Eddie asked.

"The point is every time they have a party they have a band."

He had to be kidding.

"You want me to be the house band for a bunch of gangsters?"

"What, like you got a prior commitment? Look, these guys got connections. They make one call in Atlantic City, you could get a regular thing going. I mean, Christ, you're playing a freaking senior citizen social one day, a paint store the next. It's not like you couldn't use a little help with the bookings."

"You're the asshole who got me those jobs," Eddie said.

"Eddie, listen to me. You know how to play the guitar with your teeth?"

Eddie sat erect on the couch, looking at the TV.

"Listen," Eddie said. "I'm not some fuckin' Atlantic City lounge act. I'm a jazz musician."

"All right then, forget it, Mr. Joe Fucking Pass. Look, I'm thinking our best bet is we round up a few hundred dollars, that much we can borrow, no problem. And then we go to the track. My cousin, you know Mambo Joe, he's the best fucking handicapper there is. I mean this son of a bitch, he could tell you the fastest ant at a picnic. We hook up with Mambo, we play the ponies. It's our best shot."

Eddie shook his head. He was in a jam with a guy who thought their best bet was to go to a horserace.

The twelve-o'clock news was coming on the Orbitron. Inverso almost jumped off the sofa when he saw the anchor.

"Jesus, look at this," Inverso said, checking her out. She was a perky blond with a cute smile. "Mama mia, she needs some Italian sausage, this one. It's sweet, baby. Come to Mikie. Come and get it. I'd like to take a shot at this one, huh Eddie?"

Eddie felt bad for the anchor, that a mutation like Inverso would have these thoughts.

A story came on about the funeral for Mayor DeMarco. Inverso turned up the sound and tinkered with the antenna.

"The open-casket viewing begins tonight at seven at the basilica, with a mass and burial beginning tomorrow morning at ten," the anchor said.

Inverso crossed himself.

"This guy," he said, "now this was a fucking giant."

"A giant?" Eddie said.

"When he was police commissioner, the fucking Tsutsoons got their heads cracked every day," Inverso said. "You don't see that no more, and the city's a shithole. What do you think, I'm crazy?"

Channel Six was showing the front of DeMarco's house, a two-hundred-year-old three-story colonial with amaretto trim and shutters, and an oil lamp over the porch.

"Look at this," Inverso said. "Society Hill. The fuckin' guy's a cop most of his life, never made more than twenty-five grand a year till he moved up the ladder in the end. And he's got a half-million-dollar fucking house in Society Hill? You figure it out."

"The cars, too," Eddie said. "The jewelry. The women."

Eddie was one of maybe ten people who grew up in South Philadelphia and didn't think DeMarco should be beatified and sainted. The way Eddie saw it, DeMarco was just like the wiseguys, except that his parking space at City Hall had his name on it. He muscled crooks for a piece of their action, and he steered jobs and contracts to all his pals, who paid him back in spades. Nobody who ever lived did more with patronage than the mayor of Philadelphia. What set Eddie apart from average South Philadelphians was that they loved DeMarco for this.

"One time the mayor's over the house to see my dad about getting to a judge, it just so happens I was having a little problem with my wife at the time," Inverso said. "They got radar built into their fucking heads, you know what I mean? I was bangin' this waitress but good, and my wife's on to me. Anyways, we're out back at my old man's place and I'm telling DeMarco about it, and the son of a bitch puts his arm around me. 'Mikie,' he says. 'Listen to me. I may not know much, but I know women. You don't have an affair. You plow right in and you pull right out. Quick. Like a burglar.' Eddie, this is what I'm trying to tell you."

"Like a burglar," Eddie repeated, watching TV clips of DeMarco raising his right hand at his swearing in as mayor.

"This was a man," Inverso said. "A leader of men. His son, that stupid fuck, if he knew half what his old man knew he wouldn't be in the can right now. Three hundred years, and nobody who set foot in City Hall took more out of the place without getting caught than DeMarco. You gotta respect that."

Channel Six was showing the mayor's body in his casket at the Anthony Faggioli Funeral Home.

"They went to the best," Inverso said. "Look at this. Antny's got the body. Way to go, Antny."

"Where's Anthony doing business now?" Eddie asked.

"Where'd you come out of, a tree? Near Tasker, you fuck. Broad near Tasker. Same building as Congressman Fontanella, talk about stiffs. I swear to God, I'm in there one time to get some help with a parking ticket, the son of a bitch nods off while I'm talking to him. He leans back in his chair, *boom,* he's out. That cocksucker's gonna walk in the wrong door one day and they're gonna bury him."

The TV cameras were in the Faggioli Funeral Home now, where the mayor was laid out for the television audience. The announcer said this was done at the family's request, for the benefit of those who couldn't attend the viewing.

"Will you fuckin' look at this?" Inverso said, watching from the edge of his seat. "Antny's got the mayor laid out beautyful. This guy, I'm tellin' you, he's no fuckin' fluid pusher. Embalming is an art. Half the hacks on Broad Street, that's all they are, fluid pushers."

"Nice suit," Eddie said, admiring the mayor's clothes.

"Nice suit? What're you, fuckin' stupid? He didn't buy nothin' but Italian. I seen him all the time there in Boyd's. Six-hundred-dollar suits, silk ties, Italian loafers. The whole fuckin' nine yards."

Death looked good on the mayor, Eddie had to admit. It seemed like such a peaceful nap—his hands crossed over his stomach, his expression the same as the one he had carried through his political career. The look of a fat man with a half-price coupon at an all-you-can-eat buffet.

Now the TV reporter was talking about DeMarco's indictment for shaking down drug dealers. The charges had come when he was mayor, but dated back to when he headed the narcotics force. DeMarco had beaten the rap in a trial before a judge whose campaign he had bankrolled, but seven of his officers went to prison.

As the TV reporter said the word *prison,* a white light filled the TV set. Eddie thought the Orbitron was going out. But then the flash narrowed. It narrowed to where it looked like a laser.

"What the hell is that?" Eddie asked.

It was coming from the dead mayor's hands.

Inverso stood up as if in a trance. As if the flash of light was a call to him. A fat diamond on one of the mayor's rings had caught the camera light and reflected a brilliant glow all the way to Kensington, through the Orbitron, and into Mike Inverso's brain.

"Eddie," he said when the scene shifted.

"Yeah."

"Did you see what I saw?"

"What did you see?"

"I saw the end of our problems. That fuckin' rock's gonna save our lives."

"Mike . . ."

"It's our only shot," Inverso said, standing up.

"Don't even fucking say it."

"Say what?"

"Mike, we're not stealing a ring off the mayor."

"He's dead," Inverso said.

"I know he's dead."

"Then what's the problem?"

Eddie grabbed Inverso by his Christmas sweater and pulled him into the dining room. He pointed to the window. "Get the fuck out of here," he said. "Just get out."

"Listen to me, asshole," Inverso said. "What good's the ring gonna do him in the ground?"

"They're not going to bury it with him, all right? Just get it out of your head. Thc family's going to get it."

Inverso had moved toward the window, but turned back. "Listen to me, you sack of shit," he said. "This guy, his whole life, he's a fuckin' crook."

Eddie threw his hands up.

"Ten minutes ago you're telling me he's a giant."

"Yeah, well let me tell you something. That fucking ring is ours. It's yours and it's mine."

Eddie was curious now. He was curious as to how Inverso was putting the argument together in his head.

"Do we pay taxes?" Inverso asked.

"What's that got to do with it?"

"What're you, stupid? You're paying your taxes to get these fuckin' drug dealers off the street," Inverso said, pointing outside, "and guess what. This guy got paid to leave them alone."

"Your hero, you mean?"

"This guy didn't work an honest day in his life and he lived in a fucking mansion. A mansion, asshole. And guess what. You bought him the house. You and every other sucker who pays taxes. I'm telling you, Eddie, that ring is ours. We take the ring, it's practically a public service."

Eddie pointed to the window. Inverso banged his head again crawling through. "Motherfuck," he said.

He was outside now, squinting out sunlight. "Listen, Mr. Scruples," he said, putting on his shades. "While you're sittin' in that fuckin' cave pullin' your pud, think about it. Three days you got. Three days and you're a freak show, playing guitar with your teeth. You're gonna be in Atlantic City with that woman plays the piano with her tongue."

Eddie went into the living room and fell on the sofa. The Orbitron made a popping sound, and when Eddie looked up, the picture had gone out.

Eddie had never stolen anything in his life. The only solution he could come up with was to run.

Three days he had. Three days to figure out where to go.

Eleven

The sky dripped slow and steady, washing over the gray van as it made a U-turn on Lehigh Avenue and stopped in front of the Roman Catholic Church of the Holy Ghost. The driver and the man in the passenger seat got out, both in uniform and moving mechanically, but the man in the seat behind them didn't move. He waited until they slid his door open and one of them unlocked his leg chains.

He stepped out of the van, unbothered by the rain. He wore a gray suit with the pants bunched at the ankles, and his hands were cuffed in front of him. He was about five feet six and thin and his face was without expression, much like the faces of the men who guarded him. The three of them moved together, as a piece, and entered the church.

Ofelia followed them in and watched as a guard unlocked the handcuffs, and then the three walked side-by-side up the center aisle. The two guards stood back, a quiet respect in their posture, as the prisoner knelt at the open casket and then reached in to take the hand of his son, Lalo Camacho.

Ofelia slid into a pew two rows behind the family and watched the guards from Graterford Prison lead Lalo's father to the pew in front of his wife, two sons, and two daughters. Lalo had been the eldest. Lalo's father looked up at the casket a few seconds, as if there might be something he had missed, and then turned back, crying, to his family. Except for the tears there was no hint of emotion.

"This is what happens," he said, looking at the children. He looked up at the casket again, then back to the kids, and his eyes held what he had seen. He nodded once, as if that would enforce the words.

"This is what happens."

The youngest child, a girl of ten, shrunk into her mother's caress, hiding her face from her father and her dead brother. The mother held the girl tight and stroked her hair.

This is what happens, Ofelia was thinking, when the father isn't there to help raise the kids.

Ofelia scanned the faces of everyone in the room, as she had when they entered the church. About fifty people had come to Lalo's funeral, including the father who would immediately go back to prison in Montgomery County and serve out his sentence for a bank robbery, taking a new kind of guilt to sleep each night. Lalo had been seven when his father went to prison.

When she had seen everyone, focusing on the dozen or so teenagers, Ofelia looked up at the altar. Father Laetner, standing behind the casket, caught her glance and nodded. As she stood up to leave, Father Laetner began speaking.

"Across this world, across this country, and across this city, these are times that test our faith. Times when we find ourselves asking more and more, 'Where is God now?' "

Ofelia picked up her step, wanting to run but not letting herself. She struggled to the door as if she were paddling up through water, pushing toward the surface. When she was outside she threw her face to the sky, drawing deep breaths and wishing the rain onto her face. She pulled herself together, walked to the curb, and got into the black sedan.

"I didn't recognize anybody," she said.

Lieutenant Bagno looked straight ahead, as if there were something out there to see and only he could see it. He rolled his window down a crack, flicked a butt out, and blew smoke through the opening.

"You're sure?"

Ofelia took a deep breath and choked on the cigarette smoke that was still in the car.

"It's dark when I'm out," she said, wiping her brow with her sleeve, "and I don't look to memorize the faces. I just look to see if it's Gabriel or not."

Ofelia had called the police and asked to speak to somebody after Marisol told her Gabriel was a dealer. It was Lieutenant Bagno who called back and promised to meet with her.

Lieutenant Bagno started the car. He seemed to sense that she was uncomfortable with his silent reaction to her not recognizing any faces.

"All I was thinking," he said, making a U-turn and heading east on Lehigh, "is if one of the kids in there knew you, it might be easier for me to make him tell us where your son is. You know, the worried mother. Make him feel guilty with that."

He looked at Ofelia.

"Are you okay?"

Ofelia was trembling. When she tried to tell him she was fine, she cried.

Lieutenant Bagno pulled over at Ninth. He took her hand in his and patted the top of it.

Ofelia looked at his hand, not entirely comfortable with his gesture. His fingertips were yellow where he held cigarettes.

"He's a baby," she said, pulling her hand away.

Lieutenant Bagno wasn't sure if she meant Lalo or Gabriel.

She meant both.

She was sorry she'd gone into the church. Even though she had made herself look away from the casket, she could see Lalo's painted face even now, smooth and artificial. It was impossible not to change the face and imagine Gabriel in that coffin.

She shook away the thought and looked at Lieutenant Bagno. His skin was the color of too little sleep and too many cigarettes, and he had that look cops carry, the one that says nothing can surprise them. A black ball cap sat on the seat between them. The gold lettering over the bill said U.S. NAVY.

"Around here," Lieutenant Bagno said, his voice and manner true to his military training, "sixteen isn't young."

He reached into the glove compartment. In a way that seemed practiced, he pulled out a small box of tissues and handed her one. Something he'd done before, maybe for another mother. His movement reminded Ofelia of the movement of the guards as they took Lalo's father into the church.

"The paper said they beat him," Ofelia said. "Do you know why?"

Lieutenant Bagno frowned and looked away. "It's probably best you don't know everything about the way this works."

"Maybe," Ofelia said. "But I'd like to be the one who decides."

She could tell he respected her for that, whether he liked it or not.

"You ever hear Gabriel mention someone named Diablo?"

"No."

"Diablo's the asshole in charge of the Black Caps gang, excuse my language. He reports to a higher authority, but he's the street boss. One thing I can tell you, he is not human."

"And Lalo was in another gang?"

"No, Lalo was one of his."

Ofelia shook her head. "I don't get it. Why would he kill somebody on his own side?"

Lieutenant Bagno threw his head back to acknowledge the question. Ofelia could tell he loved explaining this sort of thing to civilians, and she could tell that's how he thought of everyone who wasn't a cop. They were civilians.

"Happens all the time," he said. "It's common. It's how they keep people in line. Scare the shit out of them, excuse my language."

Ofelia waved it off.

"I'd bet my house Diablo killed Lalo Camacho. The problem is the only people who saw it won't talk. Nobody ever talks."

Ofelia didn't see anything in there to respond to. Not at first. She wanted to ask him something though. Something she wasn't sure how to phrase. And then it just came out.

"You do this for everyone?"

The question pushed him away, which was fine. Ofelia's only experience with cops was at the diner, where all of them liked to get closer than they had a right to. She hadn't known one, married or not, who didn't make some remark about wanting something that wasn't on the menu.

"What do you mean?" Lieutenant Bagno asked.

They were still parked at Ninth and Lehigh. Lieutenant Bagno turned off the engine.

"Take them around," Ofelia said. "Ask questions like this. I called the police for four weeks, nobody would even come and take a report."

Lieutenant Bagno shook a cigarette loose and then put the pack to his mouth to pull it out. He began to light it, then stopped.

"I've seen you," he said with a half turn and a sideways glance.

She didn't follow him.

"What has it been, close to a month now? On the bike, I mean. I've seen you riding."

Ofelia felt uncomfortable with that. She drew closer to the window.

"Not like I was spying on you or anything," Lieutenant Bagno said. "I'm just out on the street at night is all. It'd be hard not to see you once or twice."

She nodded and he continued.

"When you called and you said you'd ridden around looking for your son, I knew it was you. There's not a lot of women ride bikes around here in the middle of the night."

She smiled and he returned it, as if her smile was his okay.

"You got a lot better," he said. "First couple of days, I didn't think you were going to make it. Now you look great. I mean, it looks like it's a breeze. Like you got in better shape or something."

Ofelia couldn't quite figure him out. If he was a nice guy, or if this was a come-on. She didn't know what to say, but he seemed to be waiting for something.

"So why didn't you say hello?" she said, disappointed in herself for the level of the remark. It almost sounded like a come-on of her own.

"Well it's none of my business, somebody's out riding a bike. Not unless they're selling drugs or whoring or something. I mean, excuse me. I didn't mean . . ."

Ofelia laughed a forgiving laugh. He wasn't too smooth.

"I understand," she said.

"Anyhow, to answer your question, there's different kinds of kids out here, Mrs. Santoro."

She thought of correcting him, but didn't. Technically, anyway, she was still Mrs.

"So tell me, Lieutenant," Ofelia said, her tone letting him know he couldn't bullshit her. "What are the different kinds of kids?"

Lieutenant Bagno lit the cigarette. Ofelia cracked her window open.

"This bother you?" he asked.

"Not if you blow it that way," she said.

"I'll just put it out," he said, stubbing it on the floor. "No problem."

She waited for him to continue.

"Believe me, there are people on these streets, I would throw the switch myself. Diablo's one of them. A real asshole, excuse my language. But they take some of these young kids who might not be all bad and get them started in this thing, a little bit at a time, and then the kids can't get out. Well let me tell you something. I know I can't stop this by myself, especially with that bitch of a federal judge and her prison cap bullshit, puttin' all these punks back out here ten minutes after I arrest them. Jesus, don't let me get started on her and the other fuckin' liberals. And then you've got the geniuses in Washington throwing money away in Colombia. Let me tell you something. If by some miracle they cut off the flow of drugs into this country, it'd take maybe twenty-four hours for a synthetic drug industry to spring up in this neighborhood. They want to spend money, give me some more cops out here, where it matters. And I'm not supposed to say this, because I'm a cop, but guess what. A kid's got to think there's at least a chance of getting a straight job some day, or we're never going to get him off the corner. Is that so fuckin' hard to figure out?"

He shook his head as if there was nothing dumber in the world than policy makers deciding things for the streets—his streets—without knowing what was out here.

"You wanna know what makes my day?" Lieutenant Bagno asked.

Ofelia didn't need to answer.

"It's some little old lady peeking out a window watching me handcuff one of these punks, and she smiles at me. That's what keeps me coming back here, that you can improve one little old lady's life for a half day, because I'll be goddamned if I'm going to let any one of these assholes scare the shit out of a whole neighborhood without me jamming this gun up their fucking nose every now and then. Excuse my language."

He was a little crazy, but Ofelia figured he probably had to be.

Lieutenant Bagno saw that he was only scaring her more and apologized for getting carried away. He told her he wasn't talking about Gabriel, if that's what she thought when he mentioned assholes.

It was still raining. Lieutenant Bagno started the car again. He looked over his shoulder and pulled into traffic, picking up his thoughts.

"I know it's the shits around here. The factories are closed, there's no jobs. Meanwhile, you got corners doing ten thousand dollars on a good night. But the people who let their kids come out here where the bullets are flying, so junior can give them money for a nice new television or VCR or whatever, as far as I'm concerned, they're the same kind of *cacatha* as Diablo. Worse, because it's their own kid's neck they're putting out here."

Ofelia felt bad enough about her bicycle without a lecture.

"What I'm saying," Lieutenant Bagno went on, "it doesn't look to me like you're one of those people, so I don't have a problem helping out. But I'm curious, if you don't mind. Why'd you ask why I'm helping you? You think I've got some kind of ulterior motive?"

The way he asked made her more convinced that he did.

"No," she said. She needed him on her side.

"Good then. Because I think we can help each other."

Ofelia played that over as Lieutenant Bagno turned right off of Lehigh, onto Hope Street, toward her house.

"What do you mean, help each other?" she asked.

"You know your son is a drug dealer, am I right?"

Ofelia looked into the drizzle. She couldn't answer.

"Anyhow," he continued, "Black happens to be the most violent gang in operation right now. I'm pretty sure your son witnessed the murder of Lalo Camacho."

He looked at her, to see how she was doing, before continuing.

"And I think he may be the next one they go after."

Ofelia knew he expected all of that to shock her. He seemed almost disappointed that it hadn't.

None of it was a surprise. In a part of her, she had known those things for weeks. It felt like she had known them since before they were determined. Still, the weight of the words squeezed down on the space Ofelia kept open for things to work out.

She felt a chill.

"If we can find him," Lieutenant Bagno continued, "not only do we save him, but maybe we can get this punk Diablo off the street. That's the problem, is nobody's ever willing to make the doer. What I'm asking is, you think we could get some cooperation from Gabriel, if it turns out he seen Diablo kill Lalo Camacho?"

He leaned toward her.

"Miss Santoro. You okay? Miss Santoro."

"I'm fine."

"You don't look too good."

"I'll be fine."

He didn't seem sure.

"Anyhow, you think we could get him to cooperate? Identify Diablo, I mean?"

He didn't want Gabriel except to get to Diablo. And maybe to her. But it didn't matter.

"You're sure?" she said. "You're sure he's this involved?"

Lieutenant Bagno dropped his head back again, as if to shake another piece of knowledge loose. "We have people on the street is the way we work," he said. "People who find it in their own interest sometimes to help us out."

"Sometimes," Ofelia said, "aren't they just saying what you want to hear? So as to protect themselves?"

"Look," Lieutenant Bagno said, "this is what we have on your son. We may not know everything, but we know he's not home at night doing homework, don't we?"

Ofelia looked away.

"I didn't mean it the way it sounded," he said.

Ofelia sighed. This was more like she'd expected it to be, the cop treating her like she was some kind of derelict parent. Like he knew all there was to know about her.

"You know where he's working?" she asked, an edge to her voice.

"They move around a lot. My information's he was at Third and Indiana last, but he probably disappeared himself by now. He'd go home, except he figures that's where they'd look. He might be afraid you could get hurt with him."

Lieutenant Bagno stopped in front of her house.

"What you could do," he said, "is let me know if he gets in contact with you. Or if you hear from that girl again. The girl he sees. At this point, he may be scared enough to at least call."

Ofelia nodded and opened her door.

"But listen," he said, grabbing her hand and holding it like he had done before. She pulled away quicker this time. "Riding out there on the bike, to Third and Indiana, I don't think that's too smart. This guy Diablo, to him it's enjoyment, hurting people. Killing them, even. You better just stay put."

It was the last sentence that did it, awakening something in her. Instead of getting out, Ofelia pulled her door closed and turned to face him.

"Lieutenant," she said, not sure what words would follow, but knowing something was there, "I was with a man for twelve years who never said what he was thinking and never had the balls to admit it. It's taken me two years to realize I'm better off without him, but it was too late to keep Gabriel from running away. It's nice that you're concerned for me. I'll be careful, and I'll do what I can to help you. But I'll be damned if I'm going to sit in this fucking house while my son is hunted like an animal."

Ofelia got out of the car, but leaned back in before closing the door.

"Excuse my language," she said.

Ofelia knew the moment she walked in the door that there was a presence in the house. There was nothing to suggest it, no noise, nothing out of place. But she knew. Someone was in here now, or had been. Someone or something.

She stood still just inside the kitchen door, waiting for it, whatever it was, to come to her. And she knew that it would. The premonition had started like this, somewhat like a feeling that she was being watched, and then it had all gone blue.

Ofelia dripped rain on the floor. She took off her jacket and threw it over a chair at the kitchen table.

She turned—something told her to look behind her.

The words were back on the wall: EL NADA EN LO OBSCURO. He swims in darkness.

Unless she had gone completely mad, she was sure she had erased those words. She had erased them three weeks ago. But here they were, in blue chalk, sitting above the thirty-five marks. In her handwriting.

Ofelia began to run through the possibilities.

She only thought she had erased them.

She had erased them, and forgot that she had written them again.

Somebody came in while she was away.

She was losing her mind.

This was all a dream.

No single possibility made more sense than another. When she was done running through them, Ofelia went to the sink for a sponge. As she rinsed it out, she thought she heard a noise behind her. She spun around, dropping the sponge.

Nothing.

Ofelia picked up the sponge and wiped in a fever, angry at the words. She bit hard on her bottom lip and sweat dripped off her face. She was out of breath and in tears.

When the words were gone she grabbed the chalk and added the thirty-sixth mark. A thin blue measure of time lost.

She stood back and moved about the kitchen, as if marking it off against the spirits that haunted her. She raised her arms and held them out at her sides. Slow footsteps on the floor, shadows on the wall. A dance for Lalo, a dance for Gabriel.

She felt closer to Gabriel than ever. And she felt free, for the first time, of her husband. Free of the way she had let him shape her image of herself.

Free of wanting him back.

She smiled, wondering if the lieutenant was coming on to her. His literal world was not for her. His neat arrangements of people and possibilities. He was the kind of man she could never be with. The kind who could explain everything.

Ofelia was given more to mystery and wonder, and she found them in simple things. All her life, she'd been hypnotized by the press of the city against people, of buildings against streets. Something as simple as changing light, sneaking through an alley or past a window, touching a memory, revealing a truth, could fill her with a sense of joy and sadness and power and futility.

She accepted all these things. She accepted the things she was made of.

She thought of her mother, who had willed her powers and limitations to Ofelia. For years, years long gone but close enough to touch now in this kitchen, her mother had tucked her into bed each night and sung the same song. A thousand times, she sang that song.

> It's only a paper moon
> Hanging over a cardboard sea
> But it wouldn't be make believe
> If you believed in me

Ofelia had sung that song for Gabriel when he was a baby. She had made a mobile and hung it over his bed, a mobile of moon and stars and clouds, and there were times when the two of them, through the magic of a good night kiss, had freed their souls to fly across the sky.

Thirty-six days.

The rain fell harder and the darkening sky swept into the room. Ofelia disappeared into it, still floating. There, in the darkness, she saw Gabriel and he called to her.

Twelve

Father Laetner walked slowly, hands in pockets, toward Third and Indiana. Ofelia had called and told him Gabriel was supposed to have been working at that intersection.

"I have to go to the diner for a few hours or they're going to fire me," Ofelia said. "But I'll be over there as soon as I get off."

In his five nights on the streets, Father Laetner had learned the drug business in all its detail. He knew what each of the four crew members did on a corner. He knew about the guns hidden in trash cans, the dime bags of cocaine nesting under the lip of a back bumper and the crack vials stuffed into a mailbox.

Every second or third block, another identical operation, another group of teenagers wearing gold chains, beepers clipped to their waists. And another stream of cars with plates from Pennsylvania, New Jersey, Delaware, Maryland, Virginia, and New York.

Small drive-by industries flourished along these routes. Boys as young as eight or nine sold needles and crack pipes, girls sold condoms. After midnight each night, a bespectacled boy of about seventeen made his rounds with a shopping cart full of guns concealed under bottles and cans. Everything from twenty-five-caliber relics to the latest in semiautomatics, new and used. All prices negotiable.

Most nights, a game of cat and mouse was played by the police and the hundreds of people who made a living off of drugs. Most of the workers could spot a cop at a hundred yards, even in an unmarked car, and a corner would dry up as the cop made a pass. But before the cop was out of sight, a signal would be made by a lookout—a wave, a nod, a call—and the operation was back in business.

Not that the drug dealers always won the game. At times, the warning system broke down, or police made an undercover buy, or they piled out of the back of a gas company truck or a phone company truck, guns drawn, and two or three of the dealers would take a ride to jail. But Father Laetner had seen replacements put a corner back in business within half an hour, and he had also seen men who were arrested return from custody in time to catch the tail end of their shift. The jails were overcrowded and the courts overwhelmed, and anyone caught with less than thirty thousand dollars' worth of drugs was released pending a hearing.

Every few blocks Father Laetner came across a house with a wheelchair ramp for someone who'd been paralyzed by a bullet. And just as often he'd see murals in the colors of fire, blood, and light, memorials to the dead.

IN LOVING MEMORY OF LUCY MARQUEZ, MOTHER, WIFE, FRIEND OF THE COMMUNITY, WHO DIED ON THIS SPOT WHILE BREAKING UP A FIGHT.

WE LOVE YOU SEXTO—YOUR BROTHERS AND SISTERS.

ANGEL ROJAS, 13—A SON AND A FRIEND—STOP THE KILLING.

Each night, Father Laetner felt angrier and more compelled to do something, and more confused as to what that might be. In a Sunday sermon at the Holy Ghost, he had worked himself into a lather, calling the abandonment of the inner city by politicians and diocesan officials "a conspiracy of silence by political whores and hypocrites."

The pastor, who happened to be swallowing at that moment, almost choked to death. He turned red and was patted on the back by the church deacon as he motioned to Father Laetner to pull back.

But Father Laetner didn't.

"There is money in the war on drugs to build more prisons, but not to reopen our libraries," he said. "And there is money for the church to defend priests accused of sexual misconduct, but no money to keep parishes open in the neighborhoods that need them most."

He closed by saying he was personally shamed by "America's lie to itself."

Father Laetner was put on notice that when Holy Ghost closed, he would be prohibited from representing the Catholic Church in any capacity while his status was reviewed. When he walked the streets at night, he didn't preach. He just asked everyone he saw if they knew of a boy named Gabriel Santoro.

It was dusk and there was a hint of winter in the air. Father Laetner zigzagged toward Third and Indiana, taking his time. Near Hancock Street, he saw a woman from his parish and followed. She was rail-thin and ghostly, all bones and teeth, and Father Laetner knew what that meant. He watched her knock at a door and disappear, and then he saw three more people walk up, knock, and enter the same house.

He decided to follow them in.

"Ten dollars," said a toothless old man who greeted him. He had the face of a Mississippi Delta bluesman.

"Ten dollars for what?" Father Laetner asked.

"To use the house," he said. "It's the cover charge."

"Do you own the house?" Father Laetner asked.

"Own it? Hell no I don't own it. I got no money to own me no house. I'm the gatekeeper."

When Father Laetner unzipped his jacket, the gatekeeper saw the white collar. Father Laetner felt safer with it when he worked the streets.

"A disciple of the Lord," the old man said respectfully. "My apologies. Make it five dollars."

Father Laetner moved past him without paying. The room was thick with a slow yellow smoke and smelled of incense and dope. A boy of about sixteen stood guard at a window, a Tec-9 in his hand. Two prep-school boys in jackets and ties sat on the living room sofa smoking crack. A woman of about fifty squatted in a corner, pulled her wilted left breast out of the top of her dress, and stabbed it with a hypodermic needle. In the kitchen, a woman kneeled before a man, his pants around his knees, his hands guiding her head.

The woman from his parish went upstairs and Father Laetner followed. She sat on a blanket on the floor and didn't look up, though she heard him enter. Ten dollars, she said, still not looking. Ten dollars and everybody pays first. No exceptions.

When she saw him, she apologized. But if there was any shame in her, she didn't show it. Her children? They were home. She had sold her food stamps to buy crack again, and so she came here to make some money for groceries.

Father Laetner went downstairs and left the house. The fresh air felt great.

A man walked up the street, holding a boy of about four by the hand, probably his grandson. Father Laetner saw a lot of that around here, grandparents taking care of children because the parents were addicted or in jail. The boy wore a Batman costume. Together, the man and the boy softened the street, and softened what Father Laetner had just seen. But as they drew closer to him, the man fell into that trance Father Laetner saw every day, the trance of law-abiding people who go everywhere in a hurry—the store, the subway station, the doctor's office—eyes turned away from everyone.

When they had walked past Father Laetner, a shot rang out a few blocks away. The little boy dropped to the ground and covered his head with his hands, a trained response, quick and smooth. He waited a few seconds, and when he heard nothing more, he stood and resumed his stroll, a little-boy bounce in his step as his grandfather tugged him along faster.

Father Laetner followed them as they crossed Lehigh, went down to Fifth, and entered a recreation center playground. Other kids were there in costume. Superman, a soldier, basketball players, a few doctors, a few nurses, several police officers. Halloween was a few days past, but it had been raining a lot. Their party must have been rescheduled.

As the kids gathered on the basketball courts, the adults combed the grass of the baseball fields. Father Laetner walked over and saw that they were clearing the field of crack vials, needles, condoms, and broken glass. "We started doing this a couple years ago," one of the parents explained to Father Laetner. "It's too dangerous to go trick-or-treating anymore, so we have something here instead."

Beyond the playground fences and across the street, Father Laetner saw a drug operation. The lookout was young enough to be involved in the parade.

When the adults were done clearing the field of drug paraphernalia and trash, two men carried a barbecue out to the field and lit a fire. Two women brought out bags of hot dogs, buns, and marshmallows.

Other adults called the kids together, a dozen or so kids in all, and led them on a Halloween march through the field. When they were done, they played carnival games. Tossing bean bags into buckets, and trying to bowl over aluminum cans with softballs. The prizes were brown lunchbags filled with candy and surprises.

Father Laetner left the playground even more committed to his new crusade. He had become convinced on his nightly excursions that nothing would change until decent people, cowering inside their homes, came outside. Until they realized it was more dangerous to do nothing.

That was his mission now. He would try to sell, in North Philadelphia and Kensington, the simple concept of strength in numbers. They would stand together in groups of ten at first, then twenty, and then a hundred, claiming the corners each night before the dealers did. That was how he envisioned it. In ten years as a priest, it was the closest he had come in believing in anything.

Father Laetner was only a block or two from Third and Indiana. Ofelia probably wouldn't be there yet, but he wanted to make sure he got there first. He worried about her. The image of Ofelia gliding along on the bicycle was his inspiration. He wanted to tell her that, and to thank her. She had come to him for guidance, and he had given less than he had taken.

The nights they'd gone out together, Ofelia would ride ahead of him and then circle back, catching up to him so they could share notes. One night, a lookout had told them Gabriel had been on the street a half hour earlier. But it only made them all the more frustrated, being that close, and still so far.

When Father Laetner got within half a block of Third and Indiana, he stopped and watched. It was like the other corners, only busier. And the neighborhood was worse. It literally looked as though it had been wiped out in an air raid. Half the houses were damaged, and people roamed the littered streets like dazed survivors at the end of the world.

Father Laetner picked the crew supervisor out of the crowd and walked right up to him.

"I'm looking for Gabriel Santoro," he said.

The supervisor was about twenty. He wore a Minnesota Vikings jacket, with gold chains around his neck and wrists. He didn't respond, and looked as though he didn't know what to make of this—a priest looking for someone. That was the angle Father Laetner usually worked on the streets. Putting people on the spot.

He tried again, his voice firm but polite. "Can you tell me where I could find Gabriel Santoro?"

The supervisor turned away, not in defiance, but because this had never come up. He didn't know what to do.

Father Laetner saw that and tried to use it. "You'd be much better off cooperating with me," he said. "Then I'll be gone and everything will be back to normal here. You can sell your drugs all night long. But I won't be leaving without the information I came for."

Still no response.

Father Laetner walked east on Indiana. He cupped his hands to his mouth and began to speak, broadcasting his message to no one in particular. There was nobody outside.

"We cannot let them run our lives. This is our street. These are our children locked in their own homes, afraid to step outside."

It felt good. He was surprised how good. He walked to the end of the block, repeating those words five times. At the corner, he asked the lookout, a boy of about twelve, if he knew Gabriel Santoro. The boy shook his head.

Father Laetner started back up Indiana. "We must not surrender our homes. We must not surrender our neighborhood. Join with me, with police, with clergy, with merchants, and let us together take back what has been stolen from us."

About half the houses on the block were occupied. Father Laetner looked onto porches and into windows, hoping to see a reaction. He saw a few lights go on, a few heads in windows, and that gave him more confidence.

He kept walking, and he kept preaching. Louder with each pass.

The supervisor was in a panic. He made a signal and the lookout went running toward him, sprinting the length of the block and passing Father Laetner midway. The supervisor said something and the boy disappeared south on Third Street, sprinting again.

When Father Laetner was almost back to Third and Indiana, he saw two more people looking out through windows.

"We can't wait for the president of the United States," Father Laetner said, warming to it a little more with each light that went on. "The politicians have written us off. We can't wait for Washington. We can't wait for the state or the city, because we're not a priority. We have only ourselves, and we can't wait any longer to unite."

He thought about going door to door and asking if anyone knew where he could find Gabriel. And asking, also, if they would join him in reclaiming the corner. But that might be too much to expect so soon. It probably would be wiser to set up a meeting and get organized.

In the ten minutes he had been on the street, a half dozen cars had driven by, slowed down, and then left because of him. He was scaring away customers.

The supervisor hadn't missed any of it, and he watched now as another car came up the street.

This time the driver stopped, and Father Laetner moved on it quickly. It was a charcoal BMW and the driver, fortyish, wore a gray suit and had an out-of-season tan.

"Good evening," Father Laetner said, beating the dealer to the car window. "I'm Father Laetner, and welcome to North Philadelphia."

The driver was more bothered than intimidated. He looked at Father Laetner and then at the dealer.

"We're taking back this street," Father Laetner said, as if there'd been a vote. "At this moment, one of my associates is taking down your license plate."

Before he finished the sentence, the driver hit the gas. As the car sped away, Father Laetner found himself shoulder to shoulder with the dealer. When the car had disappeared, Father Laetner turned to him and smiled, and then walked on toward the corner.

"Yes, we are afraid," he sang, talking to the whole street again. "They have guns and knives and clubs. But there is something that should frighten us more. We should be more afraid of what will happen if we continue to do nothing."

The lookout had returned from his errand, whatever it was. He said something to the supervisor and then ran back down to his end of the street.

Moments later, a car pulled up to the corner. A white Trans Am. Father Laetner watched the driver get out and walk up to the supervisor.

This must be the guy Ofelia told him about. The one named Diablo.

He wore a black denim jacket with the sleeves ripped off at the shoulders, his arms bare to the cold. A tattoo of a serpent slithered over the length of his right arm.

"We cannot let them take our streets from us," Father Laetner said aloud, knowing Diablo was watching.

The mere sight of him made Father Laetner nervous. But he couldn't stop now. Now was the time to go all out. He walked straight at Diablo.

"We will not be intimidated any longer. We will take back what is ours."

Father Laetner was close enough to hear Diablo ask the supervisor how long "the asshole priest" had been out here, and how many sales had been lost. The supervisor mumbled his answers.

"How long these people been watching?" Diablo asked.

The supervisor looked around. "What people?" he asked.

Diablo smacked him in the mouth with a backhand, drawing blood. "From the windows, fuckboy. People are looking from their windows, you blind bastard. I'm trying to run a business, I got fucking Stevie Wonder in charge of my best corner."

Father Laetner continued toward them, and Diablo turned to him. "Good evening, Padre," Diablo said, sweet as an altar boy. "Isn't it kind of late for services?"

"I'm looking for some information," Father Laetner said, seeing Diablo's face up close for the first time, and seeing that the man wore his disfigurement like a badge. "Maybe you can help me."

Diablo didn't answer.

"I'm looking for Gabriel Santoro."

Diablo smiled, but didn't respond.

"Do you know him?" Father Laetner asked.

Still no response.

"What's your name?" Father Laetner asked.

"Padre, ain't your fucking business, my name."

"Look, I don't care what your name is, Mr. Diablo. But if you could tell me where I might find Gabriel."

"What you want with him?"

"I'm helping his mother look for him."

Diablo laughed. "Gabriel's ours," he said.

This time Father Laetner laughed.

"What do you mean he's yours? You own the boy?"

"What you fucking want with him?"

"If you could just let us talk to him, so we know he's okay."

"Padre, you don't understand. The boy does what he wants. He wants to talk to you, he talks. He wants to go home, he goes home. Somebody must not of took good care of him, because he don't like it home. We're his family now. He's the one decided that."

Father Laetner looked down the block and saw more lights in the houses. Some people had come onto their porches.

"I think you're the one who doesn't understand," Father Laetner said. "This would be much easier for you if you'd just cooperate."

Father Laetner didn't wait for a response this time. He turned away, dishonoring Diablo, and started back down Indiana.

"We cannot let them run our lives," he said, starting in again, making it loud enough so people could hear him inside the houses.

More people came outside.

"We cannot let them take our streets, our corners, our parks. Together, we will take back what is ours."

Diablo called to him. Father Laetner ignored him.

"Padre," Diablo called again. "You take care of the church, I'll take care of the streets."

Father Laetner's back was to Diablo. He kept going.

"This a dangerous place," Diablo called after him. "Ain't no game. Ain't no place you wanna fuck with somebody."

The four crew members looked for Diablo's reaction to someone dissing him. They had never seen it happen, and they had never seen this expression—Diablo trying to hide the insult somewhere in that mess of scars that made up his face.

Father Laetner continued on down the street. He walked to Second and turned around, still chanting as he headed back.

A dozen people had come onto their porches. They had lived here long enough to be able to read every little movement on the block, every sound, and know what would follow. But this was something new.

When Father Laetner was halfway to the intersection, Diablo went to his Trans Am and opened the trunk. He sat on the lip of it, smoking a cigarette. The insult still sat with him, but the embarrassment of it was gone.

When Father Laetner was ten yards from the intersection, Diablo reached into his trunk and pulled out a two-foot length of rubber hose. He walked to a point in Father Laetner's path, took another drag on the cigarette, and then tossed it.

Father Laetner kept walking straight at Diablo, still chanting. When he was within two feet of him, Diablo drew back the hose.

Father Laetner stayed his course.

The impact rang through the hose. Father Laetner reached up with one hand and touched his head, feeling over the wound. But he didn't stop. He took his hand down now and kept walking, blocking out the pain, as if nothing had happened.

Diablo ran ahead and stood in front of him, raising the hose to swing again. There was a pause in him, as if he were giving Father Laetner a chance to reconsider.

Father Laetner kept moving and he kept chanting. "We will not back down. We will take back our street."

This time the blow stunned him. He wobbled for a moment and

then crashed to the pavement. He lay still except for the hand he brought up to his bloody head.

Father Laetner got to his hands and knees, shook away the cobwebs, and stood. Diablo was sitting on the lip of his trunk, watching. Father Laetner tugged at one sleeve and hitched up his pants.

His head rang like a bell and his ears felt like they were on fire. He looked down the block to see if enough people were on their porches to make this worthwhile. Everything was a blur, but he thought he could see some people.

And now he walked right at Diablo.

Diablo stood, still holding the hose, but he didn't draw it back this time. He looked as though he hadn't thought things out beyond hitting Father Laetner the first two times.

The punch was short and quick, pushed up from the legs, leveraged by a turn of the hips. Diablo flew back two steps and fell into the trunk of his car. The expression he carried into the trunk, a look of macho dismantled, was still with him when he looked up at Father Laetner. And it would stay frozen at this intersection, remembered forever by the people who saw this priest drop Diablo with a right cross to the chin.

There was applause from the porches. The four-man drug crew, which had gathered in close, drew back. If it were anyone else, they'd have attacked. But nobody was going to hit a priest.

Diablo got out of the trunk different than he'd gone in. He looked as if he'd been pushed farther into himself than he'd ever been, and crawled back out to show everyone he was even more evil than he knew.

He glowed.

Father Laetner stood in a defensive position, fists up, trying to figure out how he had managed to knock Diablo down. He had never hit anyone in his life.

Diablo was on him with the hose before he could react. The first blow caught him on the side of the head. He fell to one knee and threw his hands up for cover.

"Come on, Padre," Diablo said, taunting him. "Get up and let me make you a martyr. Let's go, fag boy. I'll make you a fucking saint."

Father Laetner was halfway up when the next shot came. The sound of this one was different. More like a pipe than a hose. It landed on top of his skull and Father Laetner tried to push through it and stand up, but another blow to the same spot drove him back down.

Halfway through the next ten shots he went numb. He heard the hose more than he felt it, and he heard Diablo's grunting and snorting, the rhythm quickening as the street went darker and darker and then disappeared.

Father Laetner lay still as Diablo drove away. He was drawn into himself, hands over his head to shield the next blow. Up and down both streets, Third and Indiana, the porches were empty.

The sketch was filled with motion. The priest on all fours, the hose at the top of its flight. Diablo's face not human.

Gabriel had seen the whole thing. He had been on his way to Third and Indiana to see if anybody would tell him what Diablo planned to do to him. A half block from his destination, he had seen the Trans Am and ducked into an abandoned house to hide.

He had watched through the window as Diablo got out of the car and the priest approached. This was the priest Marisol had told him about. The one who was helping his mother look for him.

And then the beating began. A priest he didn't even know was fighting Diablo. For Gabriel's sake.

Gabriel felt disengaged from himself. Looking through that window was like watching a movie of his life.

He began sketching because that was his answer to fear and uncertainty. He lived with a growing sense of things moving too fast, and of wisdom coming only when it was too late to do any good. And so he froze the frames he didn't understand or didn't want to lose.

When the priest picked himself up the first time, Gabriel wanted to yell to him to stay down. Diablo would beat him to death just like he had beaten Lalo to death.

Gabriel allowed himself a cheer when the priest knocked Diablo into the trunk. But he knew it was the wrong thing to do. It would only raise more of the savage in Diablo.

When it was finished, and Diablo had driven away, the priest lay curled up on the spot where Gabriel had sold drugs. He wanted to help him, but he was afraid to risk it. Maybe if he got to a phone and called an ambulance.

He had one foot out the door of the house when the bicycle went by.

His mother.

Gabriel threw himself back into the house, his heart pounding. If she hadn't been looking at the priest, she would have seen him. As she flew by on the bike, it occurred to Gabriel that she might have thought he was the one lying in the street.

She got off the bike without slowing down and it continued on without her. When it crashed into the curb and fell, she was already at the priest's side, bent over him. She turned him onto his back and was dabbing at his face with her sleeve, yelling something. He didn't respond.

Gabriel had to go out there. He couldn't stand back while his mother tried to revive a priest who'd been beaten because of him. He was two steps out the door this time when he was frightened back in again. This time by the appearance of Lieutenant Bagno.

Bagno's car screeched to a stop. He bent over the priest, too, and looked like he was prying his eyes open to see if there was anything left inside.

The lieutenant pulled the priest, feet dragging, to the car. Ofelia picked up her bike and Lieutenant Bagno threw it in the trunk and they drove away, Ofelia in the back seat with the priest.

Gabriel stood frozen for several minutes after they left. The corner was empty, but he stared down at Third and Indiana as if it were all still happening.

Maybe it was time just to give up. He'd walk over to the police station and tell Lieutenant Bagno everything he knew, and see if they could give him and his mother some protection. He was going over it in his head, still looking down at Third and Indiana, when he heard a voice behind him.

"Long time no see."

Diablo's breath gave him up before his voice did. And before Gabriel could even think of running, Diablo had the muzzle of the gun in his ear.

"Lucky me," Diablo said. "I heard they had a little disturbance up the corner there, and you know me, I gotta check it out before the blood dries. And who should I see standing here but my man?"

Gabriel was too upset with himself to be scared. Diablo loved watching his victims suffer. Gabriel should have known he wouldn't be far away.

"I was on my way to see you," Gabriel said. He still had his back to Diablo.

"This is what I figured," Diablo said. "Seeing as how you owe me two thousand dollars. You got that on you now?"

Gabriel guessed Diablo wouldn't shoot him here. He'd probably rather beat him in front of an audience, like he had done with Lalo. Especially since Gabriel had run from the gang, and was the one responsible for this harassment from the priest. Gabriel decided he would rather be shot.

He relaxed his body, as if to surrender. "I got the money right here," he said, patting his front pocket. "I was coming by to give it to you."

"I figured as much," Diablo said. "Because if you don't fuckin' have it, everybody dies. You, your mother, the fag priest, that fat fuck guitar man you been hanging with. Everybody goes swimming."

Diablo let go of Gabriel's neck and took a step back, giving him room to reach into his pocket for the money. When Gabriel turned toward him, Diablo was sticking the nose of his gun into his belt. This little game wouldn't be sick enough for him if he didn't give Gabriel a small chance.

Gabriel ran.

The corner was ten yards away. If he could reach it, he had a chance.

He heard two shots as he made the turn. He didn't think he was hit, but maybe that's what it was like when bullets passed through you. Maybe you didn't know you'd been hit, and you died wondering if you'd gotten away.

Gabriel exploded out of the turn, running in a crouch, hands cutting the wind like knives. He knew he couldn't make it to the end of the block before Diablo got a clear shot at him, and he was right. Two more shots rang past him. Gabriel ducked into an open row house, skidding on the crack vials that littered the floor. He raced through the abandoned house and jumped out the back, clearing the stairs. Already in a turn as he landed.

A half block down the alley he dived into the back of another abandoned house, sliding across the kitchen on his stomach. And now he lay still, listening. Diablo's footsteps filled the back alley. He was walking, looking and listening for anything that would tell him which house it was.

When Diablo had moved past the house, Gabriel crawled to the stairs in the middle of the first floor. He stood and walked upstairs, making his way to a bedroom at the front of the house. A blood-stained mattress was on the floor, surrounded by pipes, needles, crack vials, and condoms. Ants and roaches surrounded piles of chicken bones, and another trail of ants disappeared under a pile of blankets and rags.

Gabriel stepped over the pile and poked his head out the window just enough to see up the street. He drew back sharply when he saw Diablo. He'd gone to the end of the block and was making his way back, walking slowly down the street with his gun drawn, like in a western movie.

Gabriel took a step back and his feet got tangled in the pile of rags. He fell back and the floor creaked when he landed. The sound of it seemed to move like a fracture through the house.

Gabriel lay still, his feet on the pile of rags, his head on the floor. Wondering if Diablo heard him.

His hand had landed on something other than the floor. Something softer. He felt over it in the darkness, and then jerked back.

It was a hand, cold and clammy. There was a body under the pile of rags.

Gabriel started to roll away when he heard another footstep. This time it was in the house. Crack vials crunched under Diablo's shoes downstairs. Gabriel followed the sound across the first floor, past the stairs, into the kitchen. Then they turned and came back, pausing at the base of the stairs.

Gabriel looked at the hand.

The footsteps started up again, harder to follow this time. Gabriel thought they were coming up the stairs but they faded and now he heard nothing. Diablo must have gone back out the front.

If he got out of here alive, he could go to the police, tell them he saw

Diablo kill Lalo and beat the priest. They might arrest Diablo if Gabriel was willing to testify.

But Gabriel knew he wouldn't last a day. Diablo would have someone kill him, if not his mother and the others.

He waited fifteen or twenty minutes before sitting up. It had to be safe now.

Gabriel took hold of the blanket and peeled it back.

She was one of his regular customers, about twenty-five years old. Her eyes were open and there was nothing in them except the same plea she always had when she begged him to make it two dollars for a cap instead of three. He put his head to her chest and listened, and then he put the blanket back over her.

Gabriel went out the back. A light snow fell as he took off his Sixers cap and trotted down the alley, disappearing into the shadows.

Lieutenant Bagno sagged at the desk under a curtain of pale light, a cigarette between his fingers, a cup of cold coffee in front of him.

Everyone on his shift had been gone two hours, and he kept telling himself he should go, too. And then he'd look once more through the sketchpad. He had found it on the sidewalk at Fourth and Indiana when he went back after taking the priest to the hospital.

Most of the pages had been torn out. There were four pictures left.

Ofelia on the bicycle.

She was worried and lost, but beautiful and strong, too, with a sense of hope coming through the suffering. Each time Lieutenant Bagno looked, he saw something in Ofelia he hadn't seen before.

A man playing a guitar.

Scruffy beard, pudgy. He had a trace of the same lost look Gabriel had given his mother, but the pain was different. It wasn't the pain of things lost, but of things never found.

Diablo standing over the priest.

There was an obscenity to it that turned Lieutenant Bagno's stomach. He sealed this one in a plastic evidence bag.

The fourth sketch showed a trail of bodies, like the ones painted down the middle of Broad Street. All of them were outlines except for the last one, which had a face filled in. It was Lalo Camacho.

It was three in the morning when Lieutenant Bagno put the sketchbook in an evidence locker, turned out the light, and went home.

Thirteen

Gabriel pretended he was asleep. Eddie was on the phone telling Inverso there was no way in hell he was going in on it. And even if he did, he wouldn't bring the kid in.

"It's the fucking mayor," Eddie said. "You can't steal a ring off a dead mayor. It ain't right."

Inverso told Eddie he'd scoped out the funeral parlor and had a way to get in. There was a window out back, but it wasn't big enough for an adult to crawl through. A kid could slip in and out of there, though. No problem.

"Look," Eddie said. "I told you there's no fucking way. I'm not dragging him into this."

Gabriel waited several minutes after Eddie hung up before he walked into the living room. He sat on the flipchair, Eddie on the sofa, the two of them taking shape in the morning light.

Eddie was blocky and soft, a perfect ornament for the furniture. He was going puffy from all the grease at the Ritz, and his skin was taking on the color of unbaked bread.

Gabriel's slender body on the chair was like water descending steps. The bill of his Sixers cap sprayed a shadow over his already dark face as he yawned and stretched, the sleep flowing out of him.

The El came alive again, steady and familiar. The sound of the passing train brought a comfort to the room, making it easier to talk.

"Where'd you get the TV?" Gabriel asked, yawning again and rubbing his eyes. He let himself think, for a moment, that what had happened last night was only a dream. The priest getting smacked, his mother at the priest's side, Diablo chasing him into a house where ants crawled over a body.

"A friend was selling them," Eddie said, the word *friend* sounding wrong to him.

Gabriel nodded approval.

"It doesn't work," Eddie said. "I mean, it worked when I got it."

"When did you get it?"

"Yesterday." He said it as if that would be considered normal.

"What happened to it?" Gabriel asked.

"What?"

"The TV."

"I don't know. It just made a sound, like *poof,* and that was it."

Gabriel was getting to know him, so it didn't surprise him that Eddie could buy a TV, have it go out roughly ten minutes later, and not feel a need to explain beyond that. The only thing Eddie talked about in any detail, without being asked, was music.

Gabriel leaned closer to the set. "Orbitron?"

"It's the same as Sony," Eddie said. "They make them all in the same factory, the Japanese."

Gabriel nodded. Not that he gave a damn where they made Orbitron televisions. It was a polite nod, the kind that keeps conversations alive until you can get them to where they mean something. He needed to tell Eddie about the jam he was in. He didn't need advice, he just needed someone to know. But he had no idea where to begin. And he feared that if he tossed it out there, he'd lose Eddie.

"You been playing many jobs?" Gabriel asked, throwing a nod at the guitar.

Eddie shook his head. Shit, he'd played a Halloween dance and a paint store opening. But he wasn't going to sell out like Paulie Rego. In Eddie's mind, there was a clear distinction between playing music and being a musician. Musicians, for one thing, didn't get paid. The question was: How much pride do you really have?

"Damn," Eddie said, looking at the pawnshop guitar as if it were part of a conspiracy against him. "How am I supposed to play any jobs with this thing? This is like trying to be an auto mechanic with a pair of pliers."

Gabriel thought about Eddie's good guitar burning in the truck, and about how they had met. What were the odds? Of all the places that stupid chair could have flown off the truck. His mother would see something in it. She wouldn't know exactly what it meant, but she'd be convinced it meant something. Gabriel wasn't sure he believed that kind of stuff.

"A guitar like the one I had gets better as it ages," Eddie said. "The sound gets mellower."

Here he was again, lost in the memory of it. Almost in a trance. Gabriel wondered if Eddie liked it just a little bit that the guitar had got torched. It gave him a better explanation for his career.

Eddie closed his eyes and played. It sounded good to Gabriel. Better than his father ever sounded. He wondered how much better Eddie's other guitar could have been.

Gabriel ran his fingers over the scar under his eye. Something about it made him feel like a little boy again. He thought about his mother and father and strained to remember a time, a single moment, when they were together, side by side. He couldn't. First he tried the kitchen, then the living room. He could see one but not the other. Did they ever hold each other?

The motion of Eddie's right hand strumming the strings brought Gabriel out of the thought. He liked watching Eddie play. Not just hearing him, but watching him. It was magic, the way his fingers always knew exactly where to go, each one flying off to take care of its own little assignment.

His friends would laugh if they heard Eddie play. His friends, and Gabriel, too, were into a different kind of music. The music that pulsed from cars with heavy bass, a constant pounding you could feel in your chest. It was music about the streets and for the streets, an angry, rough kind of poetry.

Gabriel didn't know what you would call the stuff Eddie was playing right now, but he liked it. His mother would like it, too. She had a few old albums that sounded something like this. And she had a cassette she was playing a lot before he left home. It was from a movie.

"You know any songs about some mambo kings?" Gabriel asked. "It's like salsa."

Eddie didn't answer, but he went into something that sounded right.

"Yeah," Gabriel said, smiling. "That's it."

" 'Ran Kan Kan,' " Eddie said. "It's Tito Puente."

"Yeah. That's it."

A peacefulness came over Eddie when he played, the kind Gabriel felt when he drew. The tension in his face disappeared and he was off in a place where everything was okay. No lost trucks, no burning guitars, no missing girlfriends.

Eddie finished the song with a flourish and threw his hand in the air. "This guitar isn't really that bad," he said. "But I could get sound out of my Gibson you can't get out of just any guitar. Five, ten thousand it would cost, another guitar like that. Man, I could use some money."

"Yeah," Gabriel said, meaning it not for Eddie, but for himself. Eddie didn't pick up on it.

"You ever play Little League baseball?" Eddie asked.

Gabriel shook his head no. He wondered what Little League had to do with guitars and money, but he was sure Eddie had some kind of crazy connection.

"I played one year and we had this big game at the end of the season, the two first-place teams. Bases loaded, two outs. I could've won the game."

Eddie stopped the story there and began playing the guitar again. Thoughts sometimes came in pieces for him, like verses from unrelated songs.

"So what happened?" Gabriel asked. He would have wagered a week's pay that Eddie didn't come through in the clutch.

"My father was in the stands," Eddie said. "Everybody was cheering."

He definitely didn't come through, Gabriel thought.

"I struck out on three pitches."

Gabriel could almost hear the *whoosh.*

"You swang and missed three times?"

Eddie stirred on the sofa. The way he was screwing up his face, it was as if the strikeout happened yesterday.

"No," he said. "I didn't even swing. The pitches were right down the middle, and I just watched them. I couldn't swing the bat."

Gabriel nodded, not knowing what to say to someone who'd go through the trouble of signing up for Little League and then talk himself out of swinging the bat.

Eddie had qualities that reminded Gabriel of his mother, though Eddie wasn't quite as helpless. He was more the type to just say fuck it, after groveling and floundering a while, and move on to something else. And successful or not, he always had the music to disappear into.

"I think sports fuck kids up," Eddie said. "All that pressure. I think that's why so many people are messed up as adults. Youth sports."

Gabriel nodded again. It wasn't something to challenge him on.

"I've got this fear of performing. Also this fear that I won't be able to get the music out of me that's still in there. Or what would be worse, I already got all of it out."

Eddie had been talking into the rug. Now he looked at Gabriel with a wounded expression. "I think it all goes back to that game," he said. "I could have won it for my team and I didn't even swing the bat."

Gabriel held back as long as he could, and then it just fell out of him, a laugh that started in the middle.

"What's so funny?"

Gabriel couldn't answer.

"What?" Eddie said.

"That's pathetic," Gabriel said.

"What, that I didn't swing?"

"No. That you're forty, or whatever you are, and you can't play the guitar because thirty years ago you struck out in some Little League game."

Eddie was hurt, but stepped outside of it. He ran a hand through his beard again and nodded, as if he acknowledged Gabriel's observation. "All right," he said, smiling, the embarrassment showing through. "I guess it's pretty weak."

It was like permission for Gabriel to let loose, and he doubled over. Eddie realized he hadn't seen him laugh before. He had always been too dark, too cradled in his own thoughts. But now his eyes were shining and the white of his teeth darkened his hair and skin. The laugh moved through his body, turning him back into the kid that he was.

He was right, too. Eddie was using a lame Little League excuse for his shitty career. He tried not to laugh, but it rose up in him and they both roared, each of them letting go of something. It was the kind of laughing that almost looks and sounds like crying.

Eddie felt like he was cheating on his own kids, getting this close to Gabriel. But Gabriel had helped him realize he loved Anthony and Dominic more than he knew. Nothing was more important—including music—than being the father he had never been. He needed to set things right with them.

Eddie wondered what his kids would be like if they'd been raised here in this neighborhood, and what Gabriel would be like someplace else. Gabriel had a Main Line mind trapped in a Kensington body. He had a combination of intelligence and street sense that added up to more than the sum of those things, and he seemed to float above himself, quietly wise, tragically lost. An accidental prophet.

"You know," Eddie said, "somebody's been painting bodies on Broad Street every time a kid dies."

Gabriel nodded. He wasn't going to admit to anything. What was on Broad Street was between him and the kids who had died. And he sensed that the story would end the moment everyone knew who was doing it.

"There's a bunch of them," Eddie said. "All the kids that've been killed. Whoever's doing it, it's making people talk about it. The thing is, you drive over those painted bodies, no matter what neighborhood you're from, and you almost feel like they're your own kids and you're the one killing them. I freaked the first time."

Eddie was looking for something in Gabriel's eyes, some clue as to what it was Gabriel needed to tell him. He saw only the corner of it, nothing more. Eddie had a hunch Gabriel was the artist. His instincts told him not to ask.

"I knew a lot of them," Gabriel said.

"The kids on the street?"

"Yeah."

"Have you seen people die?" Eddie asked.

Gabriel nodded.

"How many?"

Gabriel shrugged.

"How'd they die?"

"I don't know."

"What do you mean you don't know?"

"They were shot. Beat. Stabbed. Plus some bodies that I don't know how they died because I didn't see it happen. I just saw them in a house, or under the bridge, by the tracks. A lot of bodies turn up by the tracks."

He said it calmly, and then looked to see if Eddie had anything else on his mind. Gabriel was tired of talking about bodies.

"You call your kids?" he asked.

"Last night," Eddie said. "I'm gonna go see them. Saturday, probably."

"Wha'd they say?"

Eddie didn't hear the question.

"I told them I miss them." He paused. "I told them I love them."

Gabriel knew Eddie was struggling.

"They said they wanted me to meet their mom's boyfriend. Maybe we could all go out to dinner or something. That's what they said."

Eddie looked at Gabriel as if he might have some advice.

"'You'd like my mother," Gabriel said. The thought of it settled in a comfortable place for him.

"Have you talked to her?" Eddie asked.

"I saw her last night," Gabriel said. It wasn't a lie. "So. Saturday? You're seeing your kids Saturday?"

"Yeah. If I live that long."

Eddie threw it out there as if weren't a real concern, but that only added to the weight of it.

They both stirred. Eddie looked at his guitar and then at Gabriel.

"I need to replace the truck that burned," he said. "You wouldn't happen to have ten thousand dollars you could loan me."

Gabriel smiled. He said he would if he could. And he meant it.

He had never really needed or wanted the money he got selling drugs. For a while, he'd thought about raising enough so he and his mother could move out of the neighborhood. But he had never figured out how he'd explain his riches.

Gabriel had pissed away most of his pay. He gave big tips to lookouts, especially if he knew their mothers were buying crack instead of food and clothes for the kids, and he loaned money to other kids in the gang. He bought an occasional pair of sneakers and some clothes, but mostly just so he'd have something to do.

His biggest expense was a pair of gold earrings he bought for Marisol. Two hundred dollars he paid, buying them from one of the more respectable fences in Kensington. He had hid them under the A Street bridge. There was a fort down there, sort of a clubhouse for runaways and drifters, and Gabriel had spent a few nights in it before he moved in with Eddie. He planned to give the earrings to Marisol next time he saw her. But he'd been through several next times and hadn't found the nerve.

Ten thousand dollars, Eddie needed. Gabriel added in his head how long that would take if he was still working a corner. Too long.

"What'll they do if you don't come up with the money?" Gabriel asked.

Eddie took a deep breath and forced it out through tight lips, like he was playing a trumpet. "It'll take a dentist and a surgeon to fix it. And that won't be the end of it." He didn't seem to be exaggerating. "They'll give me another couple days to come up with the money and then they'll come by, give me a tuneup."

"A tuneup?"

"Every week, they'll break something new. Nose, leg, arm, rib. They also like to break stuff they already broke. And when everything's all beat up, and you still can't pay, they whack you."

Gabriel thought of Lalo and got a chill.

"I need some money, too," he said, shaking his head. "Need it fast."

Eddie reached for his wallet.

"I got a couple of bucks," he said. "What do you need, something to eat?"

Gabriel's stomach fluttered.

"You wouldn't happen to have two thousand dollars."

Eddie didn't respond. He waited for Gabriel to explain.

Gabriel figured it had to happen sooner or later. "All right," he said, and then he told Eddie everything.

He told it without defending himself on any point, or suggesting reasons for anything he did or didn't do. Twenty minutes it took, ending with Diablo beating the priest and shooting at Gabriel.

Eddie stared through Gabriel the whole time. He listened to every word, but said nothing, and showed nothing in the way of surprise or anger. When Gabriel was done, the quiet was heavy.

Eddie stood and Gabriel studied him, hoping to see a sign that everything was okay. Eddie walked over to the window and then turned to Gabriel, his nostrils flared and his hands trembling.

"Out."

That was all. One word.

Gabriel threw himself against the back of the flipchair.

"I said get the fuck out of my house," Eddie said. There was more disappointment than anger in his voice. "Now! Get the fuck out."

He pointed to the window.

Gabriel stood up and made a pleading gesture. Eddie kept pointing at the window.

"Because I sold drugs?" Gabriel said. "I don't do it no more, if that's it."

"I don't want you here," Eddie said.

"I go out there, I'm dead," Gabriel said. "I go home, I'm dead. You don't understand this guy. He's an animal. He'll kill me."

Gabriel was hanging his head and looking up through those big sad eyes. Eddie shifted from one foot to the other and headed back to the living room. He paced a while and then fell face-first onto the sofa, the weight of the world driving his head down into the cushion. He began groaning, and then he popped up with a thought.

"What if they come after you?" Eddie asked.

"Nobody knows I'm here," Gabriel said.

And he was pretty sure they didn't. He hadn't told anyone. Not even Ralph. But Gabriel didn't tell Eddie that Diablo somehow knew about him, and had threatened to kill him along with everybody else. He couldn't tell him that.

Eddie sat up. "You've gotta just go to the police," he said. "Go to the cops and tell them everything."

"I can't," Gabriel said. "If I go to the police, I'm dead for sure. If they pick up Diablo, he'll have someone kill me, my mother. Everybody."

"Then why don't you just go get your mother and leave town?"

Even if they were able to, Diablo might go after Eddie. "We'll be dead before we get to the corner," Gabriel said. "If we're not, he'll come after us. This son of a bitch wants his two thousand dollars or somebody dies. That's the only way we might get out of this, is if I come up with the money."

Eddie dropped back down. "This is beautiful," he said. "I got no wife, no girlfriend, no kids, no guitar, no job. I live in fucking Puerto Rican Appalachia. The Mafia is after me, I need ten thousand dollars in two days, and I'm harboring a drug dealer with a contract on his head." Eddie rolled over again and stuck his head down in the cushion.

Gabriel went over and knelt at the sofa. He put his hand on Eddie's shoulder and spoke into the cushion.

"Eddie," he said.

No answer.

"Eddie. I can get the ring."

Eddie pulled his head up and looked straight at Gabriel, surprised. His hair stuck up like a crown.

"I can get it," Gabriel said again, his eyes wide and bright.

"What ring?"

"The mayor's ring. The dead mayor."

"What do you know about a ring?"

"I heard you talking to that guy on the phone. Perverso."

"Inverso."

"Yeah. I heard you."

"What did you hear?"

"About the window is too small for an adult."

"You heard that?"

"Also I heard you say there's no way you'd let me get involved."

Eddie sat up straight.

"What are you, fuckin' spying on me?"

"I wasn't trying to listen," Gabriel said. "I was asleep until I heard you tell Perverso to stuff his own midget ass through the window."

Eddie laughed, but it wasn't a funny joke kind of laugh. It was a fucking mess kind of laugh. "I'm not stealing a ring off the mayor," he said, crossing his arms to signal the end of the discussion.

Gabriel sat on the flipchair with one leg bent under him. "Why not?"

Eddie shook his head. "I never stole anything in my life," he said. "No bullshit. Nothing my whole life. I was surrounded by it, growing up. Everybody getting over on somebody else. I didn't do it. This was all I did." He grabbed the guitar by the neck. "My father drove an Amoroso's bread truck for twenty years and when he went to his grave, everybody knew he never took a roll. They had my mother run the Bingo games at Saint Thomas Aquinas because they knew she wouldn't skim a nickel. So maybe she became a slumlord, but the point is I grew up honest, and now I'm going to steal a ring off a dead man? I'm going to desecrate the body of the most famous guy in Philadelphia since Ben fucking Franklin?"

Gabriel listened closely. Not just to the words, but to the meaning behind them. It sounded to him like Eddie had already decided to steal the ring. The trick now was to make him feel good about the decision.

"Look," Gabriel said. "I didn't steal the money."

Eddie gave him a what-are-you-talking-about look. "What money?"

"The two thousand dollars. They say I stole two thousand dollars, is why they're after me. But I never stole a nickel."

"Then why do they say you did?" Eddie asked, his tone making Gabriel out to be a liar.

"My crew supervisor was afraid I'd take his job or something, so he told them I shorted him."

"What do you mean, supervisor? This guy have a fuckin' desk and a nameplate? It sounds like a corporation."

"It is," Gabriel said.

"And they just believed him? This Diablo guy believes it, just like that?"

"It's not like anybody plays fair," Gabriel said. "It's drugs. There's no rules in it. A friend of mine, they said the same thing about him, that he stole two thousand dollars."

"What happened to him?" Eddie asked.

Gabriel let the question sit. He was waiting for his response to be the only thing in the room.

"They killed him."

Eddie ran his fingers high on the neck of the guitar. The calluses on his fingertips came down on the strings like hammers. Gabriel could tell Eddie didn't know he was playing. It was automatic.

"It's just like with you," Gabriel said. "You didn't do nothing wrong. You borrowed a truck is all you did. It's not your fault it burned up like that."

Gabriel let Eddie consider that a while, and shook his head meanwhile at the injustice of it all. "It's not right," Gabriel said. "Both of us about to get killed when we didn't do nothing wrong."

That hit Eddie the wrong way. He stopped playing the guitar and turned sharply.

"Don't fucking try to compare us," Eddie said, out of breath the moment he stood up. His nostrils flared again and his hands shook. "Don't give me this bullshit about you didn't do anything wrong."

Gabriel became defensive.

"I'm telling the truth. I didn't take the money."

"Whether you took it or didn't, you were selling drugs. Nobody stuck a gun to your head, forced you into it. You volunteered. That's what was wrong, asshole, and that's what got you jammed up."

The word *volunteered* didn't sound right to Gabriel. It wasn't as simple as that. None of it was. And Gabriel could have argued that the right and wrong of things were different here than in the places Eddie knew. But he didn't. He didn't say anything, because there was truth in what Eddie said, and more than that, there was something comforting about the sound of it. Getting chewed out felt good.

"I made a mistake," Gabriel said.

"Fuckin'-A right you made a mistake," Eddie said. "And that's what this would be. Another mistake."

"What would be?"

"The ring," Eddie said. "Stealing the ring."

"It sounds simple to me," Gabriel said. It occurred to him, as he said it, that he wanted to do it for reasons that went beyond covering their debts. He wanted to do it because it would make them partners.

Eddie turned to him. "Nothing that involves Inverso is simple," he said. "The whole thing is fucked up."

"What's fucked up about it?"

"Let's say we get the ring," Eddie said. He looked at Gabriel for a response.

"Yeah?" Gabriel said. "So what's wrong?"

"So now what do we do with it?"

Gabriel shrugged. "We sell it," he said. "I heard you telling Perverso it was worth thousands, all the diamonds on it."

Eddie grinned. "What, go down Sansom Street, tell everybody on Jewelers Row, 'Hey, we just happened to come into this ring, maybe you folks would like to buy it?' Like that?"

Gabriel shook his head. Eddie was such an amateur. "You break it down," Gabriel said. "Whatever's on it, that's what you sell. The ring itself isn't worth that much. You take the stones off and sell them. Nobody knows what ring they came from."

Eddie listened the way a student listens to a good teacher.

"I know people who'd buy it," Gabriel said. "That part you could leave to me."

Eddie figured he must be crazy even to consider it. But he liked the idea of breaking it down and putting it in someone else's hands right away. Removing himself from the ring and the theft. And who would think to come snooping around Kensington?

"I don't know," Eddie said, arguing against his own leanings. "Besides, I don't think there's enough money in it for us to cover our debts."

"You could at least buy some time," Gabriel said. "That's what you need right now, is more time."

"I don't know," Eddie said.

"It's either that," Gabriel said, "or steal a truck and give that to him, this Thin Louie guy."

"Thin Jimmy."

"Yeah."

Eddie wanted to slap himself. Here he was with a drug dealer, trying to decide whether they should steal a ring off the mayor's body or just steal a truck. A lot had gone wrong in twenty-three days.

"How's Perverso know about the window?" Gabriel asked.

"The mayor's body is at Anthony Faggioli's Funeral Home," Eddie said. "We know Anthony."

"You know him?"

"We went to school with him," Eddie said. "His deal is, he doesn't want it to look like somebody working for him stole it."

Gabriel gave Eddie that what-an-amateur look again. "You mean he's in on it?"

"Yeah, well Inverso talked to him about it and he wanted a piece of it. He was the one had the idea for someone coming through the window, so it looks like an outside job all the way."

Gabriel shook his head.

"What?" Eddie said.

"South Philadelphia. Everyone's like this?"

"No," Eddie said, defensive now. "Not everyone's like this. I'm not like this. That's why I'm not doing it."

Gabriel had to reassure him. "It doesn't matter," he said. "That'll make it even easier, having the funeral guy involved."

"I don't know," Eddie said.

"When're they burying him?"

"Tomorrow. Tomorrow morning. It'd have to be tonight."

Eddie still wasn't hooked. Gabriel looked into his eyes the way he used to look into his father's eyes. He saw traces of a half dozen images, none of them clear. But one piece was easier to read than the rest. Gabriel knew it because he had seen it in his mother.

"You ever hear from Sarah anymore?" Gabriel asked.

The words startled Eddie—the way they eavesdropped on a private thought. He was imagining Sarah in the window again when Gabriel asked the question.

"No," Eddie said. "Why?"

"Just wondering. Seemed like you cared about her a lot."

Gabriel felt guilty about even bringing it up, but he suspected the injustice of being dumped by a lover would help Eddie rationalize the theft of the ring. Something had been stolen from him, and stealing the ring was almost a way of getting even with the world.

When Eddie finally looked up his eyes were clear. "Wha'd you think of the mayor?" he asked.

Gabriel grinned. "He was a crook."

Eddie smiled. He wouldn't admit it, but he believed Gabriel when he said he didn't steal the drug money. It'd be nice to get the mob off his back, but Eddie also wanted to get two thousand dollars for Gabriel and save him from this asshole Diablo.

He looked at Gabriel the way he had when he'd scolded him for selling drugs.

"Whatever happens," he said, pointing at him, "you gotta call your mother, let her know you're okay. I'll drag your ass over there myself, if you don't take care of it. You can't stay here forever."

Gabriel nodded, just to get Eddie to stop, but he fixed for a moment on the image of it. Eddie taking him home. Eddie meeting his mother.

"So it's tonight, the ring?" Gabriel said.

"Tonight."

"What do we do now, call Perverso?"

“Inverso.” Eddie shook his head. If only he hadn’t called Inverso about borrowing a truck that day.

“You really feel like crawling through a window?” Eddie asked as he went for the phone. He was still fighting it, or at least pretending to, looking for an argument that made sense. An argument that said he could steal the ring and somehow not betray himself.

Gabriel sensed this, again, and tried to simplify things. “It’s either crawl through a window,” he said, “or get beaten to death.” He stood up and put his hands in his pockets. He struck a casual pose. Nonchalant.

“It’s in the bag,” he said, trying to reassure Eddie. “We’ll have the money before anyone knows the ring is gone.”

Fourteen

The Anthony Faggioli Funeral Home sign had an extra *e* in it, making it "Funereal," a mistake few people brought to the attention of Anthony himself, who had inherited the business from his father. The home sat on South Broad Street near Emil's luncheonette, sharing a three-story brick building with Congressman Lou Fontanella, who had just won reelection despite an indictment for a case involving votes cast in the name of several dozen people who, in the previous two years, had passed through the building in the temporary care of Anthony Faggioli.

An alley ran behind the building, and Mike Inverso had told Eddie to park a few blocks away and meet him back there. The back of the funeral home sat in an alcove between another building and the garage where Anthony Faggioli parked one of his hearses.

Inverso was waiting when Eddie and Gabriel walked up. Eddie wasn't sure it was him at first, because Inverso wore a wig as a disguise.

They argued briefly about whether Inverso was early or Eddie was late. Now they were standing under two windows at the back of the building, arguing about which one was the right one.

Eddie had never seen Inverso this wound up. It was a cold night, but

Inverso had beads of sweat on his face, like rain on a freshly waxed car, and he hopped around like he had springs in his shoes.

"You look ridiculous in that wig," Eddie said. "You look like Liberace."

Gabriel had squatted down against the wall, wondering if it was all that smart to get involved with either of these two. Especially Inverso. He thought people like Inverso only existed in movies. When he first saw him, he thought he had palsy or something because of the way he talked out of the side of his mouth.

While Eddie and Inverso bantered, Gabriel jumped high enough to grab the ledge of a window and pull himself up to peek inside.

"It's this one," he said when he landed. "One of you guys wanna give me a boost?"

"Wait a minute," Inverso said. He reached into his pocket and pulled out a needle with a string through it.

"Listen to me," he said, his breath in white puffs. "You gotta take this in with you. Let me tell you about it."

"What the hell is this?" Eddie asked, trembling, but not from the cold.

"It's to get the ring off the mayor's finger," Inverso said. "Antny told me about it."

Inverso held the needle at eye level while explaining it to Gabriel. They were the same height, Eddie noticed. He wasn't so sure Inverso couldn't have fit through the window himself, although he did weigh thirty, forty pounds more than Gabriel.

"What happens," Inverso said, "the hand of a dead man gets a little stiff, maybe a little swollen, and the ring might be stuck, you see what I'm saying?"

Gabriel nodded. He ran his hand under his nose and wiped it on his pants.

"So if the ring don't come off, what you do, you stick the needle under the ring. You don't fuckin' stab the cocksucker, you just use the needle to slide the string under the ring. Then you pull up on the ends of the string and work it around the finger, so the ring breaks free from the flesh. Got it?"

Eddie made a face. He didn't have the stomach for this kind of thing, pulling a ring off a stiff. But Gabriel just kept nodding. Eddie could barely see his face under the Sixers cap.

There was still time to back out of this, Eddie was thinking. Time, at least, to tell Gabriel to get out of here. Send Inverso in there for the ring, get the money, and then give Gabriel what he needed anyway. He was feeling guilty about letting Gabriel in on it, although Gabriel was probably the only one cool enough to pull it off.

"Okay," Inverso said. "Now Antny, he says the mayor's in Chapel A. You go in this window, down the hall, then you go through Chapel B. Chapel B's got a side door, you go through that, bingo. You're in Chapel A and there's DeMarco, dumb fuckin' dead."

Eddie's teeth chattered.

"Capeesh?" Inverso said.

Gabriel shrugged, not knowing what that meant.

"You fuckin' understand?" Inverso translated.

Gabriel nodded and put the string in his shirt pocket. Inverso gave him a pair of gloves, cotton gardening gloves, and Gabriel put them on without asking what they were for.

Eddie moved under the window to give him a boost. He cupped his hands and Gabriel stepped in and rose up.

The window swung open from the bottom. It had been left unlocked, and Gabriel was snaking in now, his waist still outside, then just his legs, then just his feet. Like he was being swallowed.

Eddie and Inverso stood with rounded shoulders, hands in pockets, both of them listening for Gabriel's landing. Until this moment, it had just been a concept. Another South Philadelphia get-rich dream. Now the reality of it was sinking in.

Here they were in the shadows of a cold November night, Eddie Passarelli and Michael Inverso, a couple of paisans who grew up within six blocks of this place. A couple of nobodies, pulling off a heist like this. A heist that could end up in history books.

"You know what, Eddie?" Inverso said.

"What?"

"I don't fuckin' believe we're doing this."

Eddie laughed.

"Neither do I," he said. "As easy as it is, there's no way it can work."

Inverso said Anthony Faggioli told him some families decide to have jewelry buried with the deceased, but the DeMarco family wanted the ring. It was to be removed from the body after the final viewing, which was to take place during the morning mass. Mrs. DeMarco had told Anthony Faggioli that the ring would become a family heirloom, passed down through generations of DeMarcos.

Inverso blew on his hands. "Listen," he said, "Antny says chances are they won't even notice during the funeral. You're grieving like that, who's gonna inspect the fuckin' jewelry, even if it is a hairloom? The problem is he's under instructions to give them the ring before the burial. So what he's gonna do, he's gonna tell them after the mass. 'My god, Mrs. DeMarco, the ring! It's gone!' This way he buys us some time. They drop the body into the ground, they go back to the funeral home, and what do you know—the window's broken. And Antny comes with the 'Can you believe this, Mrs. DeMarco? What kind of sick human being breaks into a funeral home, steals a ring off the body of a great man like this? What kind of cocksucker can this be?' "

Good question, Eddie was thinking. What kind of cocksucker?

Eddie imagined how his mug shot would look. His chest hurt and it felt like arteries were snapping shut all through his body. He tried to say something and couldn't speak, but he didn't really have anything to say anyway. He felt like crawling through the window himself and dragging Gabriel out before he could get the ring. But by now he might already have it.

"Why couldn't an armored truck go over a bump and a sack of money falls out the back?" Eddie said.

"Yeah, like Joey Coyle," Inverso said. "Me, I wouldn't a had no moral dilemma there. That bag falls on the street in front of me, I'm in Atlantic City before the truck hits the corner. And they don't fuckin' catch my ass the way they caught Joey."

Inverso always had it all figured out. Everything. And he had a plan for the ring, too. He told Eddie to forget about selling it in Kensington. Too many crooks there, he said. And he didn't trust a kid with a job like that. He had arranged to meet with a pawnshop jeweler he knew, a former South Philly guy, on the Boardwalk in Atlantic City at nine in the morning. The jeweler told him the ring would be in eight pieces up and down the coast, from Boston to Miami, by the time Mayor DeMarco was in his grave.

The longer Gabriel was inside, the more improbable Eddie found the whole deal. But what could he do at this point? This thing had developed its own momentum. Wherever it was taking them, they were on their way.

Gabriel landed in a storage room so dark and quiet it scared him. He stood still until his eyes adjusted and the contents of the room came into focus. The top of a casket leaning upright against a wall. Several wreaths stacked in a corner. A vacuum cleaner. Boxes of candles, with matches thrown on top.

He took a book of matches and stepped through the room the way men walk on the moon. He was almost to the door when he caught something to his left, back in the corner. His heart jumped.

It looked like a man was standing there.

He listened for breathing. When he heard none, he took off the gloves and lit a match.

It was a mannequin. It looked like they must practice on it with a wig and clothes and whatnot.

Gabriel let out a sigh and waited for his heart to slow down. He opened the door, and the moment he did, the smell of flowers poured in. He was swimming in flowers.

The hall was black, silent as a cave. Gabriel lit a match. He preferred the sulfur smell to the scent of flowers. He didn't like flowers, in or out of a funeral home, because he associated them with death.

There was a kind of quiet in here that Gabriel hadn't heard before, and he wondered if dead people did that to a room. Drained it of everything. He tiptoed down the hall, trying not to make a sound. If he couldn't hear himself, maybe he wasn't here.

He opened the first door on his right and was hit again, harder this time, by flowers. Gabriel lit another match. This must be Chapel B.

In front of him and to the left, twenty feet away, a casket sat against the back wall. It caught the light of the match and held a warm, soft orange glow. Gabriel lit another match as he walked toward it. This time the flickering light fell on the face of a young boy.

Gabriel lit another match. Then another, and another. The boy lived and died each time.

He was in his early teens, skinnier than any boy Gabriel had ever seen. He looked like he had died of not eating. Maybe it was cancer. But he didn't look unhappy about it, whatever it was. Gabriel had seen at least a dozen people either dead or dying, but none of them looked as satisfied as this boy. If that was the expression he'd had when he died, he'd died happy. Gabriel wondered if it was for having been here, or for getting to leave.

A stack of cards was on a stand next to the casket. Gabriel picked one up.

JOEY NAPOLITANO, AGE 12.

The name was in big black letters. Under it was a poem.

All goes onward and outward, nothing collapses,
And to die is different from what anyone supposed, and luckier . . .
We ascend dazzling and tremendous as the sun,
We find our own O my soul in the calm and cool of the daybreak . . .
Failing to fetch me at first keep encouraged,
Missing me one place search another,
I stop somewhere waiting for you.

—*Song of Myself* by Walt Whitman, 1855

Gabriel slipped the card into his back pocket and looked at Joey Napolitano again. He realized he had never seen anyone in a casket. He had seen bodies on the pavement under a yellow street light, and on the ground next to the railroad tracks under the A Street Bridge. He had seen the woman under the blankets in the abandoned house. None of them had seemed like they had anywhere to go, but this boy did. The casket was like a ship and death was a trip to somewhere. Gabriel walked to the door, where he lit one more match and looked back at the casket. This time, it reminded him of the log ride at Hershey Park.

The door squeaked when it opened and the smell of the room hit him in a wave. It was flowers again, but the room also held the smell of people. A warm, musty smell of pressed bodies, perfume and cologne. Eddie had said fourteen thousand people had stood in line on Broad Street to pay respects to Mayor DeMarco. The line had gone south on Broad and turned right at Passyunk, all the way to the Melrose Diner.

Chapel A was at least twice the size of Chapel B. The casket was set against the back wall and a trail of flowers marked the path taken by those who came to view the body. Lilacs and heather, white roses and lilies.

The lights had been turned off in the boy's room, but they were left burning in here. Pale yellow light came from the ceiling, over the foot of the casket, and fell at an angle on the mayor's face, like slants of light breaking through clouds at sunset.

Gabriel stood there half a minute. He imagined the casket climbing the light, or being drawn up by it, through the ceiling and outside. Up to where it disappeared.

Gabriel had seen a story about the casket on the news at Eddie's house, after Inverso brought over a new Orbitron to replace the old one. On the news, Anthony Faggioli was in his showroom, describing the casket the mayor's family had chosen. Gabriel had thought it odd that Anthony Faggioli looked away from the reporter asking the questions, and spoke directly to viewers, as if it were a late-night TV commercial.

"This, my friend, is a triple-lid bronze sarcophagus, the regal sanctuary for a person of rare achievement, such as the mayor. It is handsomely fashioned from a special alloy designed to withstand the tests of time, much like the fine roofs of European cathedrals. One piece of the triple lid is covered in tufted velvet, another is a sheet of solid mahogany, and then we have the glass oval panel that hermetically seals the body. Twelve white-gloved pallbearers will carry His Honor to his eternal resting place in this twelve-hundred-pound vessel. It's the full couch, seamless, jointless. A Cadillac. And between you and me, it's the way to go."

The words that had stuck with Gabriel were *hermetically sealed*. He wasn't sure what that meant, but it gave him a shortness of breath.

Gabriel looked toward the main entrance of Chapel A to make sure no one was there, and then he took a step on the plush carpet. As he came closer, the mayor's profile seemed to draw itself.

Now Gabriel stood over him, struck by his size. He'd had no idea the mayor was this huge. His chest rose up strong and his face was made up of simple, oversize features, like a cartoon. His nose appeared to have been an afterthought, like someone just balled up some clay and threw it at him and it stuck where it stuck. A little off-center and crooked.

The mayor had a fixed expression Gabriel had seen on the streets a million times. The look of someone who was getting away with something.

Gabriel looked down at his hands. There it was.

The ring was gigantic, like the rest of the mayor. It looked more like a chandelier than a ring, a bouquet of diamonds sitting on little gold crowns.

Gabriel looked over his shoulder again at the entrance to the chapel and then he brought his right hand up, slow, to the edge of the casket. He intended to go right for the ring, but his hand held onto the lip of the coffin, as if it were making its own decisions.

Gabriel looked at the mayor's face, half thinking the man was going to open his eyes at any second. The mayor's hands were clasped at his stomach, and rosary beads were woven through his fingers. Nobody had said anything about rosary beads. It looked to Gabriel like he'd have to take the beads off to get the ring off.

He took a deep breath. He didn't really want to touch the beads or the ring, and he especially didn't want to touch the mayor's flesh. It wasn't the theft that bothered him, or the desecration. It was just the idea of touching somebody dead. It hadn't seemed like a problem before, when he'd told Eddie he could do it. But now he felt that by touching the dead mayor, he would somehow pass the ghost of death into his own body.

Gabriel could hear his own breathing. He felt hot, and had an itch under his collar.

He reminded himself the mayor was a crook. A big crook. Gabriel had never personally been hit up by a cop, but he knew of officers who still ran routine shakedowns. There was no way the corners could run as wide open and defiant as they did without some cops looking the other way now and then. There was actually an odd sort of respect for Lieutenant Bagno among dealers, because they knew he enjoyed locking up a crooked cop at least as much as he enjoyed nailing a dope dealer.

As for DeMarco, the word on the streets was that for all his bluster and swagger, he didn't have the guts to shake down dealers back when he was an officer. But he made out like a bandit when he was a squad leader and later as police commissioner—he'd always gotten the first piece of whatever his men stole from the dealers. His Society Hill mansion, registered by the federal government as a historic landmark and built by an eighteenth-century land baron, was a monument to corruption.

Gabriel took another breath and put his hand down fast over the mayor's hands.

The moment he made contact, Gabriel trembled. The mayor's hands were cold and clammy and sent a chill through Gabriel that settled on the back of his neck. He pulled away and looked at his hand. He wasn't sure what he expected to see, but he wished he could wash the hand right now.

Eddie and Inverso must be wondering what was taking him. Gabriel looked at the door again. He wiped his brow. Then he put his hand back over the mayor's hands, held it there a second, and then took hold of the rosary beads. He pulled at a loose end, trying to slip the beads free of the mayor's ring finger. But the beads were wedged tight between the closed fingers. He pulled a little harder, and all of a sudden something gave way.

The mayor's hand separated and fell apart. The left hand stayed where it was, on the mayor's stomach. But the whole right arm, moving as one piece, like a club, fell toward the edge of the coffin and banged the side of it with a thud. Gabriel ducked and his heart moved higher in his chest.

The mayor's hands had been held in place by the rosary beads. But even though Gabriel knew that, it was as if the mayor had come alive, just for a second, and taken a whack at him. Gabriel's stomach fluttered. He wanted to leave right now, find another exit, another window to crawl through, and never see Eddie or Inverso again.

He stood slowly, peeking over the edge of the casket.

Damn, it looked as if the mayor's expression had changed. Maybe the movement of his arm had pulled everything out of whack and shaped a frown on his face. Maybe it was just his imagination.

Gabriel reached inside the casket, wincing as he did, and pulled the mayor's arm up. The whole thing was stiff and hard. He put it back on his stomach and let go to see what would happen. It fell back again, thudding into the side of the coffin.

Gabriel lifted it back up and tied it to the other hand with the rosary beads. Then he went for the ring, trying to jimmy it loose. It wouldn't budge.

Maybe if he could separate the fingers a little more.

Damn, the fingers were hairy. Big and hairy and moist. The mayor was like some kind of beast crawled up from a bog. Gabriel held the mayor's pinky finger in his left hand and the middle finger in his right, separating them slightly from the ring finger. They were cool and slick, like hot dogs from a refrigerator. He tried the ring again and it still wouldn't budge. He'd have to use the needle.

Gabriel fumbled for the needle and string, wondering how long he'd been in the funeral home. Was it five minutes? Was it twenty-five? He had no idea.

He stuck the needle under the ring, careful not to puncture the skin. He wasn't sure what would leak out if he did, and he didn't want to know. Gabriel put his head down into the casket, to see the job better, and was almost bumping heads with the mayor. He looked again to make sure the eyes were still closed.

The needle was coming through the other side of the ring now. Gabriel pushed it all the way and took up the string. Then he worked it around, separating the ring from the flesh. He lifted the mayor's hand to pass the string underneath his finger, making a full circle. And then he made another, just to be sure the ring was free.

The ring was still tight, but it was moving now. It jammed at the first knuckle, but Gabriel turned it, like unscrewing a nut from a bolt, and it rode up over the joint.

As he moved the ring, it seemed as if the mayor's finger was changing color. Gabriel looked closer.

It was. The skin was getting darker. A dark brown. Gabriel looked at his own fingers and saw that the mayor's makeup had rubbed off on them.

It made him dizzy. He wiped his hand on his pants, as if he were wiping away death itself. He couldn't wait to get out of here.

But he was curious. Why had the mayor turned brown? Does everybody turn brown? Gabriel looked at the mayor's face. His face must be brown, too, under the makeup. That's why he looked a little weird. That, plus he was dead.

Gabriel went back to the ring and the rest of the way was easy. He slipped it off and put it in his pocket, and then he tried to put the rosary beads back the way they had been. It didn't look quite right, especially with the ring finger a different color than the other fingers. But it was the best he could do.

On his way through Chapel B, Gabriel waved to the boy in the coffin. It wasn't an empty gesture. He waved because he felt as if a part of the boy was still alive. A part of everybody who died was still alive, he figured, and a part of everybody alive was dead.

Gabriel wondered if there had ever been a story about the boy's death. Something on the TV or in the newspapers. Probably not. He wondered what it must be like, lying there while fourteen thousand people are looking at the guy next door.

He didn't know for sure. But he knew that was how he'd want it. There was something more dignified about going that way, not having your funeral turn into a parade.

When Gabriel pulled himself up to the window, Inverso was the first to speak.

"The hell you been junior? What did you, fuckin' embalm him again? I'm freezin' my balls out here."

Eddie helped him down.

"You all right?" he said.

"Yeah. I'm okay."

"You get it?" Inverso asked.

Gabriel reached into his pocket and pulled out the ring. He held it in his open hand.

The three of them looked at it, speechless. One of the diamonds caught a piece of light and threw it back. The ring must have had a dozen stones on it.

Inverso picked up a rock, nodded at Eddie and Gabriel, and hurled it through the window. They left in a brisk walk, Inverso patting his wig into place, Gabriel wiping his hands on his pants, and Eddie thinking it was all too easy.

Fifteen

"I were you, hon, I wouldn't be slingin' this slop, that's all I got to say."

"Stella, what am I going to do? I can't look for Gabriel twenty-four hours a day, and I can't sit in that house anymore. It's making me crazy. Besides, I'm just about broke. It's not like I have a choice."

They stood at the pickup station in their white uniforms, waiting for orders to slide through from the kitchen. Stella had a Lucille Ball figure, with reddish hair and fair skin. She made Ofelia all the darker just by standing next to her.

A busboy dropped a tray of dirty dishes down too hard on a cart and Niko yelled at him over the rattle, the voice booming from his two-hundred-fifty-pound body.

"What's her name again?" Niko asked Stella, nodding toward Ofelia. "Oh, wait a minute. It's coming back to me now. Ofelia, am I right? As in Hamlet? So nice to see you again."

Stella put her hand on her hip. Niko knew she was loading up.

"Hamlet," she said. "Isn't that where the hero sticks a fork in some fat slob?"

A plate of eggs and scrapple came up and Stella pulled two pieces of white out of the toaster and dropped them over the eggs. The next plate up was hers, too. Creamed chipped beef on toast.

"Eighteen years I'm serving this papier-mâché," Stella said to Ofelia, looking at the mound of milky beef. "And you know it's going to be the next health hazard in the workplace. Asbestos is going to turn out safe as tapioca compared to this stuff."

Ofelia hadn't slept more than an hour or two after a night of riding. It was eight thirty and she'd been drinking coffee since getting to the diner at six. She hated when she felt this way, tired and wired at the same time. But the routine of the diner was a comfort. And it felt good to be around Stella again. It always felt good.

Stella was one of those people who had it down. She lived simply, with few needs, and if she had impulses for suffering and self-torture, she didn't indulge them. Some might call her simple, but Ofelia was convinced it took superior intelligence for a person to have the good sense to avoid wrestling with things beyond human understanding. Stella's life was today. She lived for food and sex, without fear of indigestion or heartache. And Ofelia wished she had a little more of Stella in her.

When Father Laetner was beaten, Ofelia called Stella. She knew she'd wake her up, and that Stella had to be at work early, but she needed to hear her voice. She needed to be unalone.

Stella was at Ofelia's house in fifteen minutes, and held her hand while Ofelia cried over Father Laetner and the sketches Lieutenant Bagno had found. Gabriel had to have been right there, watching as the priest was beaten, and as Ofelia came to his aid. Why hadn't he come to her? What was so awful about Ofelia that her son couldn't be with her?

They had sat in the dark, and Stella told Ofelia over and over it was going to be all right. She said it enough that Ofelia believed her. "He loves you," Stella said, "and you love him. Sometimes that's all you can ask."

Ofelia watched Stella return from a table with an armful of dirty dishes, shaking her head to signal she had something to say. Stella was forty-five and she'd run out of ways to hide the years, especially around her eyes. But she was cute, too. She wore her hair in sort of a miniature beehive, an unintentional retro look, and her makeup was just short of being too much. She dropped the dishes into a tub and shoved them through the service window.

"These guys at number eight are at it again," she said. Ofelia looked over and saw them. The same five middle-aged men sat at the same table every day wearing thermal shirts under plaid flannel and talking about directions.

Stella began mocking their conversation.

" 'Wha'd you do over the weekend, Bob?'

" 'Went and seen my sister'n her kids, out in Schwenksville.'

" 'I used to go out that way to the auction at Zern's. Lot of good used tools, motor parts, that sort of thing. I'd get on Butler to Skippack Pike. How'd you go?' "

Ofelia laughed when she heard "How'd you go?" That was always the cue to hustle out of earshot of table eight.

Stella picked up the dialogue again. " 'Shot right out Three-oh-nine, no traffic at all, cut over to Seventy-three and took that all the way down, no problem. Beautyfull drive, made good time. What'd you do?'

" 'Me, I went out the Franklin Mills Mall, they got that store, it's the size of four football fields, everything marked down. A discount house is what it is.'

" 'How'd you go?'

" 'It's an easy shot up the Boulevard to Sixty-three, like nothin', boom. You're there before you know it.' "

Stella turned to Ofelia. "It's like they was in a nuclear accident and nobody told them. They do have some nice stores up there, though. You ever been to Franklin Mills Mall, hon?"

"No," Ofelia said. "But I feel like I've been to places before I knew it."

She meant it seriously. Stella rolled her eyes. "Listen, hon," she said. "If you ever see me sittin' around a table with friends, talkin' about how we got here or there, do me a favor, will you?"

"What?" Ofelia said.

"Shoot me."

Ofelia wished she hadn't missed so many days of work. Stella might have helped keep her sane.

Stella turned to the front door as a customer walked in. "Soldier boy here is yours, hon," she said.

Ofelia turned and saw Lieutenant Bagno sitting down at the counter. He set his U.S Navy cap on the seat next to him.

At first the familiar face was a comfort to Ofelia, but then she felt like an army wife getting a visit from the War Department. She took short steps toward him, her arms rigid at her sides. He watched her, his eyes giving nothing away.

When she spoke, her voice was low and the words felt like somebody else's. "What are you doing here?" she asked.

"What does anybody do here?" Lieutenant Bagno said. "I gotta eat."

His smile untied the knots inside of her. Ofelia almost cried, and turned away so he wouldn't see it.

"You want coffee?" she said, her back to him as she went for the pot.

"Cream and sugar," he said.

Her breathing was still quick, but she felt better. She blinked a few times and then walked over and filled his cup. He said nothing, as if that were all he had come in for—the coffee. He lit a cigarette, squinted through the smoke, and blew up at the ceiling.

Ofelia excused herself and picked up an order for table two. When she got back to top off his cup, Lieutenant Bagno asked if she'd heard from Gabriel.

"No," she said. "You have anything new?"

He shook his head and flicked ashes onto the saucer.

"The word on the street is nobody's seen him."

Ofelia leaned down, elbows on the counter. She looked around and then spoke softly.

"And this guy that was after him, Diablo, he's still after him?"

"Nobody's seen him either, last couple days," Lieutenant Bagno said. "I'm guessing he's laying low a while, because of beating the priest."

Ofelia walked over to see if any of her orders were up. She took a pot of coffee back to the counter and refilled Lieutenant Bagno's cup even though it was only down half an inch.

He picked it up and tipped it to her.

"I talked to Father Laetner last night," Ofelia said. "He might come in here this morning."

"How's he doing?"

"He said he felt pretty good."

Lieutenant Bagno shook his head.

"The padre's got himself a hard head or something," he said, lighting another cigarette. "He took a hell of a beating. A hell of a beating." He said it with admiration, but in a tone that also said it wouldn't have happened to a tougher man. Namely him.

Ofelia thought back on the scene at the hospital. They'd taken Father Laetner to Emergency at Temple, and the staff had dropped everything when they saw a priest being dragged in, all bloodied and slumped over.

"How many stitches was it?" Bagno asked.

"Twenty-three," Ofelia said. "Just under his hairline. And they said he had a slight concussion. They didn't know if it was from the hose or from hitting the pavement. You wouldn't think so, but a rubber hose can feel like a lead pipe."

Lieutenant Bagno had the coffee in his left hand, the cigarette in his right. He smiled. "I'll tell you something," he said. "That son of a bitch could make a difference out there."

Bagno raised his right hand, as if censoring himself. When he did, his jacket lifted and his gun peeked out from his belt. "I'm sorry," he said. "I don't mean to call him a son of a bitch. A priest and all. He's got balls though, I'll tell you that."

He stopped himself again.

"I guess I'm just on the street too much. What I mean to say, I think people might go for his thing, this coming out and taking the corners back. It's happened in a few other neighborhoods, but never one this tough."

Stella came by and put her hand on Ofelia's shoulder. "Who's our new friend?" she asked.

"Lieutenant Bagno, this is Stella."

Ofelia could tell that they saw possibilities in each other.

"Bill Bagno," Lieutenant Bagno said, standing up and reaching for Stella's hand. He did a little bow.

"Pleased to meet you," Stella said.

"The pleasure is all mine," Lieutenant Bagno answered, smiling at Stella as she wiggled away.

Ofelia rolled her eyes. They were meant for each other.

Lieutenant Bagno looked back at Ofelia and struggled to remember where he was.

"Taking back the corners," she said.

"Oh," he said. "It's the only way. The police can't do the job ourselves, even though we're expected to, and now I've got the goddamn mayor's office leaning on my ass."

His bloodshot eyes looked in the direction of City Hall.

"The mayor?"

"They're after my bosses about this art thing, you know? The bodies on Broad Street. They got reporters coming in here from all over the place. Washington, New York, Los Angeles. The national magazines, network TV, all kinds of assholes. They're trying to find out what we're doing so wrong that we got kids' bodies piling up in the streets. In my fuckin' district, no less."

"What are you going to do?" Ofelia said.

Lieutenant Bagno stubbed out a cigarette before it was half smoked. "I'm trying to get someone from the city out here to wipe these damn bodies off the street," he said. "That's what I'm doing. Because frankly, I don't need the distraction."

He saw that Ofelia was disappointed in him.

"But this priest," he said, trying to recover, "you get people out there to march with this priest, and the people start backing us up with good tips, we might make a dent in this thing. As long as they don't get crazy and try to take these punks on themselves, because let me tell you something. These animals will shoot you in the head and step over your body to sell a five-dollar cap to the next jerk standing in line."

He kept doing this. Reminding her how dangerous it was out there when he knew damn well she was afraid for Gabriel. It didn't seem like he was even aware of it. Ofelia excused herself again and took care of table three.

"More coffee?" she said to Lieutenant Bagno on her way back.

"No, thanks. This is good," he said. "I gotta go. Just wanted to check in, see if you'd heard anything."

Ofelia felt strange. She sort of wanted him to go and sort of wanted him to stay, too.

"You have any ideas where else I can look?" she asked.

"I'll try a couple of people today," Bagno said. "A couple of people who might know something. You might try this little girl he knows, the one works at the mom and pop."

Ofelia nodded.

"Oh," Bagno said. "Almost forgot. Those pictures I showed you the other night?"

"Yeah?"

"It still don't mean nothing to you, the guy with the guitar?"

Ofelia shook her head.

"All right," he said. "I'll be in touch."

Lieutenant Bagno walked out the way cops walk out of diners. Half his mind with the waitress he was leaving behind, half with the next crook he'd come across. Chest out for both.

The sketch of the man with the guitar had actually put Ofelia at ease somewhat. One thing with Gabriel's work, he could get character down on paper. And there was something in the man with the guitar, something in the way Gabriel drew him, that said he was a decent person. She could tell Gabriel respected him.

But it had made her sad, too, and kept her up at night. She wondered who he could possibly be, this man who knew her son, played music for him. She was jealous, and she wondered for the first time if she had been an awful parent. Not just a bad one but a dreadful one.

This guy, whoever he was, probably didn't make Gabriel come in to sit with him every night while he cried the sun right up into the sky. Maybe Gabriel just needed to be around a man. Somebody stronger.

Two hours after Lieutenant Bagno left, the men at table eight were still giving each other directions. Coming in the door now, bandage on his head, caution in his step, was Father Laetner. He wore blue jeans, a black ballcap, and a maroon Temple University sweatshirt. No white collar. He stopped at table six and slid into the booth as if he couldn't bend without pain.

Ofelia hurried to him.

"Hi."

"Hi."

He looked like a mental, Ofelia thought, with the black eye, the head bandage, the long hair. The one ear that stuck out. Nobody would ever guess he was a priest.

"How you feeling?" she asked.

"I'm good."

Ofelia gave him a don't-lie-to-me look.

"Really, I feel real good. I get a little dizzy is all, every now and then. And I get a little tired. But I'm fine."

Ofelia asked if he'd like something to eat.

"Just some tea," he said.

When Ofelia went for the tea, Stella asked who he was.

"That's him? Hon, he don't look like no priest to me."

Father Laetner's right eye was red and the tissue around it was a half dozen different colors, like meat gone bad. A white bandage dipped out from under the hat just above his left eye.

"You sure you should be out?" Ofelia asked.

"I just met with a City Council aide," Father Laetner said, "so I thought I'd drop by. We were on Broad Street, where the bodies are. You know there's some talk they're going to wash away the bodies because the city's worried about its image?"

Ofelia snickered.

"I heard," she said.

"Well I told this guy they can't do it. No way. We've finally got everybody talking about this thing nobody wants to talk about, people coming in from Washington and whatnot, and what do they do? Does the city use it to ask for a little more help from Harrisburg and Washington? No, they want to clean it up and send everybody home. I pleaded with this guy. Leave the bodies alone. You can trade them for better schools, more jobs. These bodies are valuable."

"What did he say?" Ofelia asked.

"He'll see what he can do."

She sat across from him in the booth and didn't seem to know what to do with her hands. She set them on the table and then put them in her lap. She felt a fondness for him, though not in a physical sense, really, although she found him attractive and probably would have flirted by now if he weren't a priest. He was a decent man. For two years, she had raised Gabriel alone, trying to steer him away from trouble. She felt like she had a partner in that now.

Ofelia still felt guilty about his beating. He wouldn't have been out there if not for her.

"Look," she said, "I just want to say . . ."

He interrupted her. "Really, I'm fine."

"Yeah, sure," Ofelia said, putting an elbow on the table and resting her head in her hand. "Look, just don't do anything stupid for a couple of days. Take a break, all right?"

"Well, I did go out a while last night."

"You what?"

"Just an hour or so. Two hours tops."

Ofelia had talked to him around nine, before she went out herself on the bike. He had said he was going to take it easy.

"What do you mean, you went out?"

Father Laetner pulled the bag out of his tea and squeezed lemon into the cup. He rang the sides of the cup as he stirred. "I went to Third and Indiana."

"Third and Indiana?"

He shrugged.

"What are you doing, going back out there?"

He slurped some tea and wiped his mouth with a napkin, gingerly. "It was important to go right back out," he said. "So the same people would see me. The people who saw what happened."

"Look," Ofelia said, "my son being out there's bad enough. I don't want to worry about you out there, too."

"They had to know I can't be scared away," Father Laetner said. "I'm just trying to let these people know they matter."

Ofelia shook her head. "What did you do out there?"

He smiled. "The same thing," he said. "I just went up and down Third, and then Indiana, saying the same stuff. We're taking our corners back."

Ofelia looked out the windows and across the street at a line of row houses, neat and symmetrical. "You're nuts," she said when she looked back at him. "You're out of your mind."

He was still smiling. It was a lopsided smile because of the stiffness and pain. "Well guess what," he said, a little-boy look crossing his face. "I've got some good news. It's sort of good news, I mean."

Ofelia had no idea what this could be.

"When I got back to the church, I got a call. It was someone from around Third and Indiana, and they said they had seen Gabriel."

Ofelia jumped. "They saw him?" she said. There were about a dozen people in the restaurant. Everyone turned.

She spoke more softly. "Who called? Who was it?"

"Look, don't get too excited," Father Laetner said. "They didn't give a name. It was a man, I don't know how old. Maybe fifty. He said his grandson used to be in one of Gabriel's classes or something, and he knew what Gabriel looked like. He said he was pretty sure he saw him, this was two or three weeks ago, in a pawnshop on Kensington Avenue. He was with a guy, he said, and they were looking at guitars."

"That's the man he drew," Ofelia said.

"And then he saw him again. He said he saw Gabriel with the same guy in a diner on Kensington Avenue."

Ofelia waited for more.

"That's all," Father Laetner said. "It's not the greatest scoop, but at least we know he's okay. You can tell Lieutenant Bagno, and if I can get a copy of the sketch Gabriel did, I can go to pawnshops and diners, see if anybody recognizes the guy. A picture of Gabriel would help, too. Maybe we'll get some leads."

Ofelia was trying not to let herself get too encouraged, but Gabriel had been gone five weeks, she'd ridden the bicycle every night for four weeks, and this was the closest she'd been to knowing anything.

She smiled at Father Laetner and shrugged. "If you don't watch out, you're going to restore my faith in the church," Ofelia said.

"I meant to ask you about that," he said. "You told me you never went to the Holy Ghost, right?"

"Yeah."

"There's two churches closer to your house. How come you came to us?"

Ofelia was embarrassed. "I looked in the yellow pages," she said.

He laughed and put his hand to his head. The laugh hurt.

"You okay?"

"Yeah, I'm fine," he said. "You're serious? You found us in the yellow pages?

"I liked the name. It scared me a little bit. You know, Holy Ghost. It's a pretty weird concept when you think about it."

"I never thought about it."

"Holy Ghost," Ofelia said again. She looked out the window, recalling the day she had ridden to the church.

"You know, you look great," Father Laetner said.

She looked for a place to put her hands, settling for her lap again. With most men, that was a come-on. She didn't think it was with him. With him, it just seemed nice.

"Really," he said. "I know you're scared, Ofelia, and I know how helpless you feel sometimes. But give yourself credit. You've got a lot of courage. And you seem like you've gotten stronger just in the time I've known you. It shows."

She smiled. Actually she was at least as frightened as she'd ever been, and had never felt more helpless about saving Gabriel. But it was true that she knew exactly what she wanted now, and exactly what she didn't. She'd gone from being pissed off at Ruben to being pissed off at herself, and it was like rising up from the grave.

"You think so?" Ofelia said to Father Laetner, unable to hold back a shy, flattered smile.

"Yeah, I think so."

"You do too," she said. "Seem more sure, I mean. That first time we talked, you weren't even sure why you were a priest."

He nodded. "I'm still not sure," he said. "But I don't think about it anymore."

He played with a napkin, folding the corners. "I talked to my family, back in California, and I couldn't explain what it was like here."

"What do you mean?"

"I told them I was doing some work against drugs, and they wanted to know what it was like. What the neighborhood was like." He looked up from the napkin. "How do you explain Third and Indiana? That it exists in America, a mile from the Liberty Bell? There's something prophetic about it. You know?"

Ofelia was staring out the window again. "You want some more tea?" she said.

"No, thanks."

Ofelia turned to look for Stella. Stella gave her a nod from the back of the restaurant, saying everything's under control, take your time.

Ofelia reached across the table and touched his hand. "I tried," she said. "I really tried. I was absorbed in myself after my husband left. But I still tried with Gabriel. It was all around us, the drugs, shootings, everything. I used to warn him. Don't hang out with these guys, don't go here, don't go there. It was hard after his father left. He was a little afraid of his father, I think, and never did anything to cross him. We were both kind of lost when his father left."

She drew her hand back. Father Laetner followed it across the table and grabbed it. He held and squeezed, then let go.

"For two years I had nothing but fears," Ofelia said. "Now I've got some dreams. The balance is better. Gabriel and I, when he comes home, we're going to leave. I'm going to take him someplace else."

Father Laetner finished his tea. "I have to get going," he said. "But tell me something. You ever go to the ocean?"

"Down the shore? Sometimes. I used to."

"We ought to just go there one day," he said. "That's what I used to do in California and after a while it was in my blood or something, having to go look at the ocean."

Ofelia knew exactly what he meant, but she played dumb. She wanted to hear him explain it. "Having to look at it?"

"It shrunk my problems, whatever they were," he said. "You know, it just puts things in perspective, because it's so big and so steady. I used to go to a forest, too, look at trees that are two hundred years old, rocks that were here a million years before you and they're going to be here a million years after you're gone. But the ocean . . . The smell of the air, the sound of the waves."

Ofelia watched him get lost in it. She saw him as a boy, Gabriel's age, going to the shore. Leaving footprints in the sand.

"This was California, right?"

"Yeah," he said.

"You think it could happen at the Jersey shore?"

He laughed.

"Not as well," he said. "I mean, the sun shouldn't rise out of an ocean, it should set on it, like in California. But the Atlantic is still an ocean, I guess."

Ofelia sat for a while with the idea of the sun rising on one ocean and setting on another, and she wondered what that must do to the way people look at things. "Even when science makes sense," she said, "it's a complete mystery."

"Like religion," Father Laetner said.

Five people walked into the restaurant and Ofelia slid out of the booth. "I better get back to work," she said.

"So maybe tomorrow?" Father Laetner said. "We go look at the ocean?"

"It'd be nice to get away for a few hours," Ofelia said. "But don't push it. Wait and see how you feel."

The moment Father Laetner was out the door, Stella was all over Ofelia. "Tell me he's not really a priest, hon. You gotta tell me he's not."

Ofelia smiled.

"Something about the religion, the bruises, the pain, the whole thing," Stella said. "This boy needs me, I can feel it in my bones. He needs a mature woman."

"He's too young for you," Ofelia said. "And he's a priest. I don't think he'll be a priest forever, but right now he's a priest."

"Ofelia, do you look at the papers, hon? They got priests all over this country doing it. Some of them even doing it with women."

They were back at the service window. Ofelia was thinking about the time Stella told her she'd had sex with dozens of men. Literally dozens. "But not one of them has fucked me," she had said. "I fucked them."

"I'll tell you something," Stella was saying now. "Both those men in here today, the soldier boy and the priest, they had eyes for you, hon."

"It's not like that," Ofelia said. "The cop, I don't care much for him. The priest, he could be a good friend. I like him."

"I like him a little different," Stella said.

"We're going down the shore," Ofelia said. "He said whatever your problems, it puts things in perspective, you know? It makes him feel smaller."

"I tell you what then," Stella said. "Tell him you'd rather go to the mountains."

It was eleven o'clock. Niko turned the radio up in the kitchen. A few seconds later, he came out and walked up to them.

"You're not going to believe it," he said. "Somebody stole a ring off the mayor's dead body."

Sixteen

Eddie lay awake a few minutes, waiting for dreams to stand clear of reality. He was almost certain now that it wasn't a dream. They had done it. They had stolen the ring.

He rolled from his left side to his right, staring at the fabric on the sofabed. He imagined the grooves as paths through a jungle and tried to disappear into it. He scratched his head, digging at an unconnected thought, something unsettling. There was an important point he had to make to himself, if he could just remember the subject. Now it came to him. Nothing profound, only a nagging concern. He'd left too much to Inverso.

Eddie looked up from the sofabed and saw Gabriel asleep in the dining room, Monk and Mingus curled up beside him. Eddie still felt guilty about having Gabriel in on the deal, but he didn't feel as bad as he thought he would about the heist itself. If everything went smoothly, maybe he'd be able to pay off Thin Jimmy and have enough left over to buy a new guitar.

All right. Maybe that was too optimistic. Hell, Inverso was even capable of stiffing him. But if he got enough to pay for the truck, or at least a good piece of it, he'd be happy. The other thing Eddie wanted out of the deal was to help Gabriel out of his jam with Diablo. The first two thousand dollars, he had decided, no matter how much he ended up with, would go to Gabriel.

It was ten thirty. Inverso had had a nine o'clock appointment in Atlantic City. He should be back in town soon.

Eddie put Monk and Mingus out back. They looked up at him before they stepped out, as if they had something to say, something unflattering. Eddie waited five minutes at the door while the dogs did their business. He looked out the window and over the rooftop of the house behind his, wondering if anyone out there knew by now about the ring. When he let the dogs back in, they hurried past him and trotted over to Gabriel, sprawling beside the flipchair.

Gabriel was still asleep. The scar on his cheek had become more defined and looked even more like Italy. Eddie walked past him with heavy steps, hoping he'd wake up. He still hadn't asked him what it was like in there, getting the ring. They had come home exhausted and too stressed, too frightened, to speak to each other, and so they both had lain awake, staring at the ceiling.

Eddie sat down with his guitar. He played Wayne Shorter's "Footprints," a song he always included in a set when he worked with a band. "Footprints" was just that—a walk, a stroll, dark and contemplative—leaving a trail of evidence.

Gabriel woke to the music and lay still, his eyes closed. It was different this time, Eddie's playing. The music was coming from Eddie instead of from the guitar. Gabriel imagined the life of the notes, each one rising up to a perfect peak and then parachuting down.

Gabriel felt a longing he had never known. He missed Marisol and ached to be with her again. Today, he would give her the earrings.

He began crying and tears rolled into his ear. He didn't know where it came from, exactly, but he knew what he felt. He felt ashamed for what he'd done to his mother. And he knew she had seen his death. In a way, he had seen his death, too. Every time he heard a gunshot, every time he watched someone die. He'd seen it with every new body on Broad Street. When he drew, he felt connected to it. He didn't just see physical things, he felt them, felt their future, too, and it scared him and intrigued him at the same time. He was more like his mother than she knew.

He would call her today. He would tell her he was in some trouble but he'd be home soon, if he could just think up a way to do it without getting everyone killed. And he'd tell her he had someone for her to meet. Somebody he knew she'd like. That's one thing he was sure of. His mother would like Eddie. Actually there were two things he was sure of. Eddie would like his mother, too.

All of these considerations went through Gabriel's mind before he played back the theft of the ring. It was there, at the edge of his thoughts, but he made it wait. He ran his thumbs over the pads of his fingers now to see if the feel of death was still on them.

Yes.

He rubbed them on his pants, wiped his tears, and waited a minute or two. He wanted to make sure his eyes were dry before he looked at Eddie.

"You hear from Inverso?" he called to him.

Eddie rose quickly and came into the room. He sat on the floor next to Gabriel, his guitar in his lap.

No. He hadn't called. But it was early yet.

"You were in there a long time last night," Eddie said.

Gabriel sat up. Monk and Mingus licked his face as he put on his Sixers cap and pulled it tight over his skull. "I had to use the needle," he said, folding up the flipchair and sitting on it to put on his sneakers. "The ring wouldn't come off."

Mingus was licking Gabriel's hands and Gabriel looked down to watch. Maybe the dog tasted the mayor.

"There was a kid, a boy, in the next chapel over," Gabriel said, his eyes on the boy now. Joey Napolitano.

"Were you scared?"

Gabriel scratched Mingus behind his ear.

"A little," he said, and then he told Eddie about the mayor's arm banging the side of the coffin like a club.

Eddie cringed. "I couldn't have done it," he said, shaking his head. "I'd rather have my head beat in by the wiseguys than have to do that."

Gabriel scratched his stomach and yawned. A nervous yawn. Eddie saw it and it made him yawn, too.

"You'll get your two thousand first," Eddie said. "So's you can get this asshole off your back."

Gabriel didn't say anything, but he was thinking it might be better to have the money in their hands before they started cutting it up.

"You figure out how you're going to get the money to this asshole?" Eddie asked. "Is there somebody you could give it to who'd give it to him?"

Gabriel nodded yes, but no, he didn't have anyone, and he had no idea how he'd get the money to Diablo. He hadn't thought it through.

Eddie, who had worked up an intense hatred of Diablo, was about to volunteer when the phone rang. He jumped for it, thinking it might be Inverso.

Wrong number.

"I'll go get us something to eat," Eddie said. "Why don't you stay here, in case Inverso calls? Also, so this Diablo doesn't see you. And listen, I can take the money to this cocksucker when we get it. I don't think he'll try to fuck with me. What is he, some wise-ass punk kid?"

Gabriel was touched. Eddie wasn't bullshitting. He probably would just march right up to Diablo with the money. Gabriel wondered what would make Eddie do it—concern for him, or guilt over his own kids. Either way, he liked it.

No, Gabriel said. Diablo was a punk, but not a kid. And he wasn't somebody to mess with. Gabriel wanted to thank Eddie anyway, but he couldn't. The words got stuck, just as they did whenever he wanted to tell his mother he loved her. It wasn't just that he was shy. He believed there were certain things that meant more if you didn't have to say them.

"What do you want?" Eddie asked.

"Bacon and egg on a roll, salt and pepper," Gabriel said. "And coffee."

Eddie looked at his watch. Eleven o'clock. He felt butterflies as he crawled out the window. By the time he hit the pavement, the flutter was a knot.

Gabriel patted Mingus on the head. Monk got jealous and came over to get some for himself. Gabriel kissed the tops of their heads and then went for the phone.

He wouldn't tell her where he was. She'd drop everything and come for him, and somebody might follow her, and the three of them would get whacked right here in Eddie's house.

Gabriel looked around. What a place to die. Not that there were any good places.

Gabriel dialed the first three numbers and hung up. He told himself not to get pissed off if she started yelling at him. She was probably going to yell, and she had a right. He dialed again. All seven numbers. And hung up on the first ring.

What would he say?

They'd always been able to talk about certain things. Light things. Like the Monet, and whether it was real. Or she would tell him stories about the characters in the diner and he'd ask her to tell him again about one of his favorites. She also liked to tease him about his clothes. She said there are always things you look back on later in life and you're humiliated, and she was sure he was going to be horrified one day about having worn pants halfway down his ass. She wanted to take pictures.

But they never talked much about other kinds of things. Important things. They hadn't even talked about his father leaving, except with hugs and tears. At times there was a respectful silence between them, and that was a way of communicating. But not a good way.

Gabriel decided just to tell his mother he loved her. Maybe it was something she ought to hear every once in a while, even though she knew it.

He dialed again and it rang a half dozen times. Ten times. Fifteen. He imagined the sound of it in the house, and he was able to put himself there. He saw the layout of the rooms. He saw his mother float through them, dressed all in black, heavy in her sorrow.

She must be at work. He'd call again later and tell her he loved her. It would be hard to say, but he would do it. He'd do it for her, and for himself.

The same young prostitute worked the corner under the El. Eddie had passed her dozens of times and she had taken to propositioning him with a different line each day, making a game of it.

"Hey," she said.

"What?"

"A man has to walk his dog. Take it out for some exercise." She wore a shirt unbuttoned to the middle of her chest despite the forty-five degrees, and she opened it now, exposing a breast. Eddie smiled and walked on by.

The hooker was looking better every day. She was sweet, Eddie thought, and then he caught himself. He'd gone from a middle-class marriage to a dead-end affair to lusting after a skid-row whore. His social life matching his career step for step.

Eddie had always seen a connection between his guitar and his women, similarities beyond the long neck, the curves, and the hole in the middle. The guitar had brought him some women and driven away others. And each time a relationship bombed, Eddie had said fuck it, at least I've got my guitar. Which lasted, on average, two weeks. At which point he'd blame the guitar for his lousy love life, go find another woman, and then blame her for delaying his destined appointment with artistic greatness.

A sharp breeze cut through Eddie in the shadows under the El. A train came by and the noise, all that rolling metal, made it seem colder. Eddie thought about the hooker's open shirt and her naked breast and he considered, momentarily, going back and offering to warm it.

The movement on the street calmed Eddie. Here was all this activity, as if it were a day like any other, and he was an anonymous, invisible part of it. He'd get a bacon and egg for Gabriel and maybe for himself, too, with cheese. And two coffees. He couldn't remember whether Gabriel took cream and sugar, so he'd get both.

As he walked along, Eddie dreamed about buying a new guitar. And if they really hit it big, there was a new gadget he might buy, so he could record his own compact discs. That's the kind of thing that could get his stuff out there and turn it around for him. The business was like that. You need money to make money. He had some ideas for new material, too, some of it inspired by the neighborhood. He'd thought about trying a piece that captured the sounds of the El and the other noises on the street. Sirens, car horns, trucks.

Who knows? If he turned the career around, maybe there was a chance of putting the marriage back together and being with the kids again. Not that he was sure he wanted to put it back together, but anything was possible. Good things could happen if he just had a few dollars in his pocket for a change.

Eddie had walked past the newsstand when something stopped him. The news vendor was usually inside the blue and white shack, but he was outside today, yelling something about a special edition of the *Daily News*.

Eddie turned and looked back. When he saw the paper, the blood drained from his face. The letters were the biggest he'd ever seen in a tabloid, the biggest he'd ever seen anywhere.

CROOKS BOOST RING
OFF DEAD MAYOR!!!

Eddie froze, his mouth open, his face locked in a silent shriek. He felt like he was drowning or suffocating or both. A buzzing started in his head, low at first and then it picked up speed and volume.

Eddie's first instinct, when he could think at all, was to hide. But that was ridiculous. Nobody knew it was him. They couldn't know.

Could they?

Don't panic, he told himself. Stay cool. He turned and continued down Kensington and the next thing he knew, he was at the counter inside the diner, but couldn't remember having walked in. Everyone in the place stared in his direction. The customers, the waitresses, the cook, the dishwasher. Everyone. They all looked shocked and disgusted.

Eddie was trying to decide what to do—run like hell or throw up his hands and confess—when he realized they weren't looking at him. They were looking at the television above him.

Eddie breathed deep and pushed it out. He did that three times and backed up, stiff as a board, so he could see the TV.

They were showing the back of the funeral home, and Anthony Faggioli was pointing up to the broken window, hanging his head as if disgusted, as if mortally wounded, by the inhumanity of the deed. The scene faded and the anchor said something about an exclusive interview, and now the TV at Puttin' on the Ritz was filled with the horrified, grief-stricken face of the mayor's wife. A reporter asked Mrs. DeMarco if there were words that could describe her feelings.

She wiped at a river of tears that ran black with mascara, glanced at a prepared statement, and then looked straight into the camera with the eyes of a hanging judge. Eddie backed away because he felt as if she were staring right at him, as if she had picked him out from among the one and a half million residents of Philadelphia.

"There are no words," she said, with raccoon eyes from the smudges, "to describe this, this . . ."

Her head suddenly dropped into her lap, as if she'd suffered a stroke. And then just as suddenly she was glaring back into the camera in a terrifying rage, straight at Eddie.

"This disgusting, ghoulish, animalistic act of cowardice and depravity."

Holy shit, Eddie muttered.

Next up was Police Commissioner Cosmo Banchini, whose Nazi-style getup, with high black boots and tasseled, scrambled egg epaulets, made him nearly as frightening as the mayor's wife. He promised an investigation like nothing ever seen in the history of Philadelphia.

"Are there any leads?" shouted a reporter.

"Any suspects?" shouted another.

"None that we can disclose at this time," Commissioner Banchini said. "But we are pursuing every possible angle, and would like to reiterate that the Italo-American Society has generously offered a ten-thousand-dollar reward for information leading to the arrest and conviction of the perpetrator or perpetrators. As well, a hotline has been set up to handle any and all tips. We ask that the public cooperate in helping us bring the responsibles to swift justice."

The back of Eddie's boxers were soaked through with sweat. His head throbbed, his eyes burned. He wanted to run out of the diner and back to the house, or possibly to Mexico or Canada, but he thought that would be too conspicuous. He cleared his throat and ordered two breakfast sandwiches and two cups of coffee, and he asked if he could have a glass of water while he waited.

When the station broke to a commercial, the customers all turned and spoke to each other in whispers appropriate to so unspeakable a crime.

"When they find them," said a white-haired lady in the first booth, "I hope they string them up by their business."

Eddie swallowed hard. How could this have made sense yesterday? How could it have made sense any day? They had pulled off the one crime that would have every boob in the city rooting for their arrest, conviction, and castration by hanging.

This was a pattern in his life. Not seeing things for what they were until it was too late. Getting into a hole and then making the kinds of decisions that only dug him in deeper.

Jesus fucking Christ, Eddie muttered. He was dumber than shit.

It wasn't that he hadn't expected the story to hit the papers. He just hadn't expected it to be this bad. He hadn't expected stealing the ring to seem so, so, what was the word? So wrong.

A police car went by as Eddie left the diner and it iced him. He ducked instinctively and tried to put other pedestrians between him and the squad car, and then realized that might not be the most brilliant strategy. That's the one thing that would take away his invisibility—acting like a suspect.

Eddie bought a *Daily News* to see if the police had any leads. But the paper flapped in the wind, so he tucked it under his arm and headed for home, looking into the eyes of everyone he passed to see if they saw something in him. Something that gave him away.

The hooker started toward Eddie when he turned his corner. "No," he barked before she could say a word.

He ran down the block and when he got to the house he called to Gabriel from the window.

"You're not going to believe it," he said, out of breath as he crawled in. "It's in the paper, it's on the television. This fuckin' thing is everywhere and the whole city is looking for the crooks." He held up the paper.

"Inverso called," Gabriel said, speaking in his usual low, calm voice.

"What'd he say?"

"I asked how much he got, he just said he'd be right over to talk about it. He's on his way."

Eddie was panting. "He didn't say anything else?"

"No."

"Do you see this?" Eddie asked, holding the paper up again.

Gabriel sat with Monk and Mingus at his feet, petting them. "What did you expect?" he asked.

Eddie's eyes bulged. The dogs sat at attention, waiting on Eddie's response.

"What did I expect? I didn't expect it to be in the fucking paper before they even buried the guy. I didn't expect to have the whole city itching to cut our hearts out. I didn't expect to walk down the street and feel like I had a sign on my head saying I'm the one."

Gabriel was still calm.

"I don't know," Eddie said, pacing and jingling the change in his pocket. "Maybe we should just go turn ourselves in."

Gabriel laughed like he had when Eddie told him about the Little League strikeout that turned his life around. "You're blowing it," Gabriel said. "Man, you gotta be cool or you're gonna screw it up."

"How'm I supposed to be cool when the mayor's wife is on television talking about the animals who violated her husband?"

"Look," Gabriel said, "we stole a ring off the mayor. Did you think they'd tell the story after sports and weather? It's a big deal, but don't forget why we did it."

"Why? Why? Tell me because I can't remember a reason that makes any sense."

Gabriel was losing his patience. "We did it because we were going to be killed."

"A bullet in the head would have been better," Eddie said. "Mayor DeMarco used to be police commissioner. You realize what that means? What the police would do if they got their hands on us? Shit, there's some old lady in the diner wants to string us up by our balls."

He was starting to scare Gabriel. "Look, nobody's going to catch us," Gabriel said, for his own good as much as Eddie's. "There's no way. Unless Inverso fucks up."

"Wonderful," Eddie said, throwing his hands up. "We're in good hands. Everything that little prick ever touched in his life got fucked up. Yo, he can get you a job. Yo, he can get you a truck. Yo, he can get you a ring. No problem. Well guess what. We got a problem."

Eddie put the bag down on the flipchair and Gabriel reached for it. He pulled out his bacon and egg and asked Eddie if he wanted his. Eddie didn't answer.

They heard a car door and then footsteps on the side of the house. They turned to the window and saw the top of Inverso's head, that unmistakable half inch of skin from hairline to eyebrows.

Eddie had left the window open and Inverso crawled in, his mouth already going.

"How many weeks is it, douchebag, and you can't fix the door of this fucking shack?"

Eddie held up the newspaper. "This thing's all over the news," he said, the voice of doom.

Inverso brushed off his slacks, ignoring Eddie.

Eddie shook the *Daily News* at him, but Inverso turned away.

"Yeah, I seen the fucking *News,* whadda you want me to do about it? So we stole the ring, it made the papers. Guess what. Big fuckin' deal. It don't mean nothing."

"How much did you get?" Eddie asked.

Inverso went toward the kitchen. "You got anything to eat?" he asked.

"What do you mean have I got anything to eat? How much fucking money did you get for the goddamn ring?"

"I smell fuckin' bacon, the kid's stuffin' his face, I'm asking do you got anything to eat?"

"How much did you get?"

Inverso wasn't himself. The smirk, the walk, the gyrations. All gone.

"I didn't get a penny," he said.

Eddie felt a shiver.

"Don't fuck with me," he said. "How much did we get?"

"I get into Atlantic City, the news was already out. This cocksucker wouldn't touch the fuckin' ring."

Eddie was about to blow.

"One of the DeMarcos goes to Antny's this morning with a pair of cufflinks they want the mayor to wear for the mass," Inverso said. "They look in the box, and *boom.* No fuckin' ring."

Gabriel slumped onto the flipchair. Eddie looked at him and then lunged at Inverso. Inverso backpedaled into the kitchen, trying to break free. Eddie had him by the shirt.

"You sold the fucking ring," Eddie said. "You sold it."

"Get your fucking hands off of me," Inverso said, his voice a squeal. "What are you, stupid? I told you I couldn't sell it. The guy wouldn't touch it."

Eddie threw him against the refrigerator. "Then where is it? Where's the ring, you lying sack of shit."

Inverso glared back at him. He waited a few seconds, then reached into his pocket.

"Here," he said, holding it at eye level, a foot from Eddie's face. "Right here's your ring, you prick fuck."

Inverso walked away. As an afterthought, he turned and threw the ring at Eddie. It bounced off his chest and danced across the dining room floor, glittering and shining until it disappeared into the pile of the muddy brown shag. All three of them followed the ring's path and then stared at the spot where it disappeared, a buried treasure.

"Just having the Mafia after me wasn't exciting enough," Eddie said, still looking at the spot. "What I needed was to have the Mafia after me and the cops, too. It's better this way. It's more interesting."

Eddie went off and sat in the living room. Inverso followed him, Gabriel followed Inverso, and the dogs followed Gabriel, who picked up the ring and sat on the floor in front of the sofa.

"We just sell it someplace else, that's all," Inverso said. "Somebody'll take it. If not, maybe we take a ride to Pittsburgh, Cleveland, Chicago, someplace where they don't fucking know about this thing. There's a sucker out there. You know there's always a sucker."

"I got about one day before Thin Jimmy breaks my head," Eddie said.

"So we bargain for a little time, that's all," Inverso said. "This ain't so bad as what it looks, you ask me. Everybody wants the ring, and we fuckin' got it. That puts us in the driver's seat."

Eddie gave him a look. "It puts us in jail," he said.

Nobody knew what to say. They looked at the floor and then at each other.

"I got a question," Eddie said. "What the hell were we thinking?"

Inverso got his smirk back. "Look, you stuttering prick, we did it, all right? We fuckin' did it so don't give me with the why did we do it. We got a little problem here is all, so instead of going into a fucking panic, let's put our heads together, come up with something intelligent."

On the word *intelligent,* Eddie and Inverso both turned to Gabriel. Gabriel wished they hadn't. "I could check around," he said, feeling the pressure. "It's going to be harder now, but there's a lot of crazy people out there."

"Yeah," Inverso said. "Yeah. We could probably unload the ring in ten minutes around here. What's anybody got to lose in this fucking neighborhood?"

Eddie wanted to hit him. Inverso saw it and backed off.

"I'll tell you what we should do," Eddie said. "We should give it back."

Inverso jumped up. He had it all back now. "Excuse me, Mrs. DeMarco? Hi, we're the crooks, we didn't actually mean to steal the ring off your fat fuck of a dead husband. We don't know what got into us but please, take it back. And just so you know there's no hard feelings, why don't you take one of these lovely flipchairs?"

"Fuck you," Eddie said. "We just leave the ring somewhere and tip off the police. Or we give it to Anthony, and he says he found it in the funeral home, the crook must've got scared and dropped it or something. Then it's all over."

"Then your fucking life's all over," Inverso said. "And mine, too. We're sittin' on a gold mine with this ring. We just gotta be patient is all, let the money come to us."

They agreed to let Gabriel make some contacts on the street, see what was out there. Eddie had reservations, but went along with it. He was worried that Gabriel might run into trouble, or bump into Diablo. Gabriel assured him he could handle it.

Inverso got up to leave and motioned for Eddie to come out with him. They crawled through the window and when they were outside, Inverso moved in close to Eddie.

"Look. They got a reward out, the Itlo-mericans. Ten thousand thin bones. You and me, our ass is on the line and guess what. We didn't go in there and take the fucking ring. You see what I'm saying?"

"No, what are you saying?"

"I'm saying this kid's okay. He understands *omertà.* They nab him, I don't think he talks. What I'm saying, worse comes to worse, we give up the kid, claim the reward. He's the one stole the fucking ring anyway."

Eddie didn't have to think about it this time. He snapped Inverso's head with a left to the nose. Inverso tried to say something but Eddie followed with another left and then a right, a big one.

Inverso was on the ground, his hands up in a plea for mercy as Eddie came for him again. Eddie hesitated half a second and then popped him with another right. Inverso slapped the pavement with his head, a solid smack. He was on all fours, crawling toward the street, when Eddie buried his foot in Inverso's ass.

Eddie crawled back through the window and didn't say a word to Gabriel, but Gabriel knew. He had been at the window, watching.

Seventeen

Gabriel rode the El all the way down through town and to the end of the Market-Frankford line in West Philadelphia. The motion had its own rhythm, the air of the car its own density. Sound was muffled. It must feel something like this, being hermetically sealed.

He stayed on the train and rode all the way back up, and then decided to do another round trip. It would relax him, make it easier to call Marisol and his mother. He had a lot to do today besides sell the ring.

The corner of the train window kept peeling back more of the city, telling a picture story. Gabriel thought about the time Mrs. Meketon showed him a book about Paul Cézanne and explained his theories about geometry. That's what Gabriel saw through the window now, not the cones and cylinders and spheres that Cézanne saw in the country but a city kind of geometry. Philadelphia was all lines and squares, brick and shadows.

Light fascinated Gabriel, and he usually tried to do something with that in his drawings. People seemed to change when they passed through shadows, like they'd entered a conspiracy and emerged only half aware of it. It was almost as if shadows toyed with people, knowing they were torn between wanting to disappear and needing to be found.

Gabriel did some sketches on the train. One of the boy in the casket, one of the mayor. He wondered where the boy was now.

He also drew Marisol, maybe the best sketch of her he'd ever done, and looking at it made him want to see her all the more.

He took his time on Eddie punching out Inverso, and when he was done he stared at it for several minutes. There was something good in Eddie, aside from the way he had come to Gabriel's defense. For all his bungling, all his troubles, Eddie liked himself well enough to respect other people. Eddie even respected the mayor and his family, and felt bad about stealing the ring because it was against a code he lived by.

Gabriel wondered if his father liked himself, and what code he lived by. He wondered where he was. Since Gabriel had run away, he hadn't sketched his father much.

On his way back to Kensington, Gabriel decided that if they got anything for the ring, Eddie should be paid first. The idea of the Mafia coming after Eddie scared Gabriel. They sounded at least as crazy as the Diablos of the drug world, and Gabriel didn't trust Eddie to be able to take care of himself.

He got off the train at Huntingdon and headed west, stopping at each intersection before turning a corner, scanning the block for Diablo or any of the other Black Caps bosses. He walked with the ring bulging in his front pocket, past newsstands with screaming headlines about the crooks who robbed the mayor. It was an odd feeling, holding a secret that big.

After thirty minutes Gabriel turned into an alley and went halfway down the block, past a row of garages. He knocked on a door and was let in by a tattooed man in a sleeveless leather vest.

Ralph had told him about this place, and Gabriel had bought Marisol's earrings here. It was sort of like a pawnshop, cluttered floor to ceiling with everything from beach chairs to shotguns, all of it stolen. It had struck Gabriel on his first visit that the shopowner's world didn't extend beyond these four walls, and he was gambling now that he wouldn't know about the mayor's ring. Or that, even if he did, he'd still buy it.

The fumes of a kerosene heater were making Gabriel dizzy. The man stood behind a glass case filled with guns. He had long greasy hair in a ponytail and a thick mustache crawled down the sides of his mouth.

"What'll it be?" he asked.

Gabriel asked if he was interested in some diamonds, and the man asked what he had.

Gabriel hesitated, then pulled the ring out of his pocket and put it in the man's open hand. It lay glittering on his palm, as if aware of its own celebrity. The man took an eyepiece out of a drawer and examined the ring.

Gabriel took a closer look at the guns. It might be a good idea to have one, but he wondered whether he could shoot Diablo, or for that matter, whether he could shoot anyone.

"Some serious stones," the man said, still looking through the eyepiece. "Come back later today or tomorrow. I'll make some calls, see if I can get rid of them."

"What do you think it's worth?" Gabriel asked.

"Depends," he said, "on how hungry you are. A couple thousand I could get you right away. You got the time, I'll see if we can do better."

Gabriel reached for the ring.

"You don't want me to shop it?" the man asked, pulling it back.

"Make the calls," Gabriel said, insisting on the ring and shoving it into his pocket. "You know what I've got. I'll be back."

On the way out, Gabriel threw another glance at the guns. He imagined himself aiming at Diablo and pulling the trigger.

He had his answer now.

Gabriel walked on, thinking about the offer. With two thousand dollars, he could pay off Diablo and beg for his life, and then go home to his mother. But if a fence was offering two thousand dollars, the ring had to be worth five times that.

Gabriel had walked for twenty minutes and found himself outside Episcopal Hospital. He went inside and got change for a dollar at the gift shop. There was a phone in the lobby.

Neither of these calls would be easy. But he couldn't stall anymore. He dropped in a quarter and dialed.

"Marisol. Gabriel."

Shit, maybe he should have planned it out, because he didn't know where to go from here. He pictured her on the other end, dark hair, brown skin, red lips. A white T-shirt.

Marisol helped him out. Instead of waiting for him to say something, she jumped on him, scolding him for not calling his mother.

"I tried calling her earlier," he said, his spirits lifted. She wouldn't be scolding him if she didn't like him.

"Listen," he said, deciding just to come out with it, because what did he have to lose? "I need to see you about something. The A Street Bridge. Yeah, that one. In about a hour. No, I can't go near my house right now. Yeah. Yeah. I'm calling her right now. No, I wouldn't lie to you. Okay, by the bridge about two thirty. Well I hope you can because it's really important."

Maybe he was wrong. It was possible she hated him, and he was about to make a fool of himself.

The gift shop clerk sat behind the cash register watching a small television. The camera zoomed in on the faces of the mayor's family at the cemetery. They stood next to the hole in the ground and watched as the casket was dropped onto it. The mayor's wife made a lunge toward the casket but was held back.

Gabriel wondered if the mayor's hands were still held together with the rosary beads. He also wondered if Joey Napolitano would be buried today. And he tried to imagine what that would be like for Joey's mother, watching her son go into the ground.

Gabriel put another quarter into the phone. She picked up on the first ring.

"Mom?"

"Gabriel!"

He couldn't talk for a while, neither could she. They both cried, listening to each other's sobs.

"I'm sorry," he finally said.

"I'm sorry too," she said.

He couldn't believe it. Not only was she not yelling at him, she was apologizing.

"I love you." There. He had said it. It felt good.

"I love you too."

"Look, I'm not sure why I—"

She stopped him. "No, Gabriel. Not now. We'll talk. We'll talk later. Just come and be with me. Please come home."

He told her he had a few things to work out, but he'd try to get home in a few days. "I don't know why I couldn't call you before," he said. "But I wanted you to know I'm fine now. I'm fine."

She cried again. "Call Lieutenant Bagno," she said. "Tell him you saw Diablo beat the priest and they'll arrest him. Tell him you saw Diablo kill Lalo."

Damn, she knew everything.

It was a little more complicated than that, he told her, but he took Lieutenant Bagno's number.

"Mom," he said. "I missed you."

"I missed you too. You sure you're all right?"

"Fine," he said. He told her he had a new friend, and that's where he'd been staying. He wanted her to meet him.

"I want you to come home now," she said, her tone changing.

"It'll be soon," he said.

"Now," she said. "Come home now, before you get hurt. They're after you, Gabriel. Come home now."

"I'll be fine," he said. "I love you, and I'll see you soon."

He kept his hand on the phone after he hung up, trying to hold onto her voice.

Gabriel took a deep breath and wiped away the last of his tears. Outside, the cold afternoon air made him feel better. He walked, head down, in the general direction of the A Street Bridge. He walked through shadows cast by three- and four-story buildings, disappearing and reemerging over and over again.

He stopped at a luncheonette with window service and ordered an Italian hoagie, oil and mayo, sweet peppers. He sat on a fire hydrant and ate the hoagie, watching the cars, watching the sun hang in the sky, watching people go by, seeing none of it. The sandwich was gone before he tasted it.

On his way to the A Street Bridge, Gabriel walked along a street with row houses on one side and an empty lot on the other. Three women worked the lot, gathering crack vials, needles, beer bottles, and condoms. They wore gloves and picked things up carefully, as if they might be alive.

Across from them, in front of the houses, a little girl played with a ball. She was about five, with curly black hair. She threw the ball against the front of a house and it bounced past her and across the street. When she started after it, one of the women looked up from the field and yelled, and the little girl froze with one foot in the gutter and one on the curb.

"You don't ever, ever, ever come over here. Do you hear me? How many times have I told you? Now get in the house." The girl wheeled back, head down. "Not ever," the woman yelled after her. "This is where the druggies come. Now get in the house."

The girl knew Gabriel was watching and she was embarrassed. She hurried into the house, pulling the door closed behind her.

Farther down the street, three more kids played on the sidewalk. Fifty feet beyond them, at the corner, was a drug operation. Gabriel thought he recognized the crew chief, who wore a beeper, but he wasn't sure. It wasn't a Black Caps crew, that much he knew. This had been a Blue corner since a shootout with Yellow about a month ago.

A car stopped and the driver made a buy. Another car followed, and then there were five or six more in line. A boy of about ten rode past the corner on a bicycle, undistracted.

The A Street Bridge took cars over the tracks of a dead rail line. The fort Gabriel had slept in a few times was under the bridge on the west side. He could see movement down there as he approached, and when he went down, he found five people.

Two whores in short skirts and bad makeup were asleep, flat on their backs, on the cold bare ground. A man in his thirties stood over a shopping cart filled with junk and smoked crack. A toothless couple who looked mentally ill or retarded or something sat on a sofa holding hands.

Gabriel still had about one hundred twenty-five dollars in drug money. He woke up the whores and offered them ten dollars each to leave. He did the same with the piper, and then he turned to the couple, who looked at him as if he were a TV game show host.

The man's clothes were too small and hers were too big. They were in their mid-twenties but looked twice that. Gabriel offered them twenty-five dollars to go up to the bridge and keep anyone from coming down to the fort for the next hour or so. If they kept everyone out, he told them, he'd make it fifty. The man put the money in his pocket before saying thank you.

When they left, Gabriel began straightening up the fort. There were two sofas and three armchairs, each one with stuffing coming out and springs exposed. A stuffed bear with a missing leg sat on one of the armchairs, looking over the fort and beyond, to the rise across the tracks where the women were still cleaning out the lot. Behind the amputee bear was a barbecue. Next to the bear, a milk crate served as an end table. It had some old magazines on it, including the "Best of Philly" issue of *Philadelphia* magazine. A bouquet of artificial flowers sprouted from a chunk of green Styrofoam.

The sleeping quarters were farther up the slope. Boxes from refrigerators and washers and dryers were used both as sleeping chambers and room dividers.

Gabriel took two flat pieces of cardboard and put them down in front of the nicest sofa, covering a soiled rug. He pulled the table with the magazines and flowers up next to the cardboard, then stood back to inspect the arrangement. It didn't look bad.

A mirror was propped up against one of the bridge supports. Gabriel looked into it, spit into his hands, and wiped some dirt off his face. Then he sniffed his underarms and patted his hair down in the back, where it came out from under his Sixers cap. Shit, he should have showered at Eddie's.

Gabriel went down to the tracks and headed north, his sneakers finding every other railroad tie. After about forty steps, he saw the raised spike that was his marker and turned toward the slope. He picked up a rusted can to use as a shovel, and walked up to a patch of weeds under a small tree. When he was sure nobody was looking, he got down on his knees and began digging.

About eight inches down, he hit the jar and pulled it out of the hole. Wrapped in some newspaper were Marisol's earrings.

Gabriel wiped them on his pants, then put them in his pocket, not the pocket with the mayor's ring, but the other one. Then he went up on the bridge to wait for her. She should be here any minute, if she was coming.

He checked the top button on his shirt, hung the pants a little lower on his butt, and looked for the proper pose against the concrete bridge railing.

One foot in front of the other? No.

Sitting on the bridge? That wasn't it, either.

Leaning against it, feet crossed, hands in pockets.

Yes. Very cool.

Twenty minutes passed. The lookout couple turned his way and smiled politely. A block and a half away, someone moved closer. This could be it. It was a girl, right height, right color. She was closer now, dark hair, a bit of a wiggle. Marisol?

Damn. It was a woman in her twenties and as she crossed the bridge, Gabriel's heart fell into his shoes.

He thought about running to a phone and calling again, but that wouldn't be right. He had it bad for her, but you had to hold part of yourself back in these situations, not come off as pathetic. You had to hold on to your pride.

Twenty minutes later, there was none left. He felt stupid for ever thinking he had a chance with a girl like her. He walked toward the couple to give them the rest of their money, and was almost there when she turned a corner.

"Sorry," Marisol said. "We had a bunch of people come for lunch."

She'd done it again. She was more beautiful than he remembered her. Gabriel tried not to show his elation. He worked for a look that said it was nice of her to show up, but he wouldn't have killed himself or anything if she hadn't.

"So what's the big deal that I gotta meet you here?" she asked.

Maybe she really had no idea what was up. Shit, he was going to look like an idiot when he gave her the earrings. She might even slap him or something. Or worse, laugh at him.

She seemed to have redone her lipstick, though. That was a good sign. Gabriel nodded to the couple and led Marisol down under the bridge.

"What's going on?" she said in mild protest, looking back at the couple for a clue. "I heard about this place but I never been here," she said. "People live here?"

"They just stay here sometimes," Gabriel said. He sat down on the sofa, expecting her to join him, but she stood there, looking over the place as if rearranging the layout in her head.

"It ain't that bad," she said, finally taking a seat next to him. A cloud of her scent rose when she sat down, the smell of her skin and hair that he'd tried to re-create in his mind a thousand times.

She left a good eighteen inches between them, which Gabriel took as a bad sign. It was worse, even, than if she had sat farther away. Eighteen inches said we're friends and I don't have to worry about you hitting on me.

"You still being a jerk and not calling your mother?" she asked.

"I just called her," he said, drumming the heel of his sneaker on the cardboard floor, shaping a little dent.

"Yeah, sure."

"I'm going home," he said, looking into her eyes. "I've got some things to straighten out, then I'm going back. School, too. I'm going back to school."

She didn't respond, and that was all it took, this one little pause, and the whole thing went awkward on them, the silence growing. Gabriel wondered if she was waiting for him to make a move. Maybe he was blowing it.

"What'd you say to her?" Marisol asked, breaking the quiet.

Gabriel saw an opportunity in the question. He knew he could get somewhere with his answer. "I told her I love her," he said, looking up to see if that did what it was supposed to do.

She knew he wouldn't lie about something like that, and the edge went out of her. This was his opening. But every time he swallowed to clear his throat, it felt like marbles going down.

He ran his hand over the lump of the earrings in his pocket. Just do it, he told himself. Just give them to her and see what happens.

He couldn't. Not yet. He had to loosen her up a little more. He had to say something, anything, that would let her know he had feelings for her without actually saying he had feelings for her. Maybe he wasn't clever enough for this stuff.

He stared over the railroad tracks, feeling roughly as intelligent as the amputee bear. It seemed like he hadn't spoken in about six hours and he worried that they'd do maybe another ten minutes of this and then she'd get up and thank him for a really wonderful fucking time and never so much as look at him again the rest of her life.

Lost in worry, he hadn't felt Marisol narrow those eighteen inches. And he hadn't felt the sofa move until she was straddling him on her knees and putting her hands first on his shoulders and then the back of his neck. She had a smile he had never seen built into an expression he had never imagined.

All weight drained out of him and he was unable, for the moment, to do anything but float under her. She was kissing him and the touch of her lips to his, the smell of her breath, sent both a tremble and a calm through him. While they kissed, Marisol snuck her hand inside his jacket, undid his shirt, and ran a finger in circles around his nipple. Then she slipped the finger between his lips and into his mouth, sliding it in and out, and dropped the finger back to his chest and teased it, wet, over his nipple.

All of which led Gabriel to believe that, unlike him, she'd done this before.

Marisol wore a denim jacket over a sweatshirt and Gabriel slipped both hands inside the jacket and under the sweatshirt, running them up over her tight stomach to her breasts. She wore no bra and her breasts were small and firm. She arched her back as he ran his open hands lightly over her nipples.

In one piece, hands inside each other's clothes, they slid off the sofa and onto the cardboard floor, Gabriel still wearing his Sixers cap, and then they rolled onto their sides and undid each other's pants.

Gabriel climbed on top of her. Something told him he was supposed to wait, take it slow, maybe even talk to her. But there was nothing either of them needed to say, and as he realized that, she took hold of him and squeezed tight, making him feel huge. Then she guided him inside of her.

Gabriel felt as if he'd poked his head through a cloud and discovered another universe. He made himself perfectly still for a moment and leaned down to kiss her. Then he put one hand under her bottom and pulled himself into her, and everything else in the world fell away.

When they were done, Gabriel wondered if she was impressed that it had taken him less than a minute, but he thought it probably wasn't cool to ask. Besides, she didn't look disappointed or anything. They put their clothes back on without conversation and then Gabriel reached into his back pocket and took out the picture he'd drawn of her on the El.

"This is for you," he said.

She seemed touched.

"And this is what I called to give you." He handed her the earrings.

Marisol looked at them and breathed the way she did when he was first inside of her. She ducked under the bill of his Sixers cap, which he had kept on the entire time, and kissed him.

A soft kiss, sweet.

"I love you," she said.

And Gabriel floated.

Eighteen

Ofelia was on her steps, keys in hand, when the feeling came over her. She fumbled with the keys, dropping them on the top step, and then put the wrong key in the door.

She told herself to hurry, only half aware of the reason.

Inside the house, she rushed to the phone on the kitchen table. The marks on the wall were at her back. Thirty-seven of them. The bicycle was behind her, too.

The room waited with her.

Ofelia draped her jacket over the back of a chair. She swept her hair back with her hand and a toss of her head. And when the phone rang she knew it was Gabriel.

His voice had changed. It was deeper and sounded vaguely like his father's voice.

He said he loved her.

And there it was, after more than a month of worrying, wondering, searching. He was alive and she was grateful. She was elated. And she was angry, too. Angry that he'd made her wait this long. Angry that it wasn't over yet.

Ofelia put her elbows on the table and her face in her hands. The afternoon light, sliced by the blinds, fell at her feet.

She drifted.

The moment Gabriel was born she feared his death. When he first walked, she danced. When he first spoke, she sang.

His ninth birthday, his eyes closed, she led him down to the basement, walking him up to the easel with the canvas, dipping the brush in the paint and handing it to him. His stroke was natural, effortless, a bird gliding low over a river. And the look it drew out of him, as if the brush were everything he needed, as if that canvas were a window and he realized he had the power to give himself whatever view he wanted.

He must have known before she did that his father was leaving. He went through a period in which he painted nothing else. His father sitting in the living room. His father walking home at the end of a workday. His father playing the guitar.

As if it were a way of stopping time. A way of holding him there.

Ofelia turned the chair so she faced the center of the kitchen. If he was coming home soon, maybe she should clean the house. She looked at a pile of dishes in the sink, the wastebasket overflowing with pizza boxes. She looked up at the cobwebs in the corners of the ceiling, hanging like moss from trees in a rain forest.

It was probably best, she told herself, to leave things alone. He'd be more comfortable returning to the house he'd left.

They'd do new things together, now that she had changed, now that she would no longer mope around the house wallowing in self-pity, a woman betrayed. She couldn't wait to show him she had changed. They'd go to dinner at places they'd never been to. She'd take him to a Sixers game like his father had. She'd take him to the art museum and they'd take a close look at the Monets.

Maybe they'd catch one of those double-decker buses to Atlantic City and laugh at the weirdos dropping paychecks into shiny machines and onto emerald tables. At night they'd put on sweaters and walk along the edge of the continent, and maybe the moon would throw a funnel of silver light over the water, laying it down as if it were a sidewalk to the center of the sea.

Ofelia lifted her head and she wondered, in her guilt and her fear, if he was ever coming home. She walked to the counter and turned on the radio.

Police were still on the trail of the crooks who stole the ring off the dead mayor. Ofelia couldn't imagine how anyone would do such a thing, but she figured DeMarco probably had it coming.

Another story now. A sixteen-year-old drug dealer shot dead on a corner in Hunting Park in what appeared to be a feud among rival gangs; a nine-year-old girl, jumping rope when the fight broke out, shot in the back, dead at her doorstep. The father of the girl, who went after his daughter's killer with a baseball bat, was turned on by a gang and savagely beaten with his own bat. He was in critical but stable condition at Temple University Hospital, where his wife was being treated for shock.

With new deaths among children, the announcer said, the painted bodies on Broad Street were expected to reach Spring Garden Avenue, a full mile of bodies tumbling down on everyone's conscience. Teachers at two art colleges, Tyler and Moore, were calling the Broad Street bodies one of the most powerful public art projects since the Vietnam Veterans Memorial in Washington. A public television crew was in town from Washington to film the Broad Street bodies as part of a documentary on the failed strategy of America's war on drugs. The story was fueled by the unknown identity of the artist.

The mystery artist.

Ofelia turned off the radio and thought about the sketches Lieutenant Bagno had found near Third and Indiana. If she had suspected, back then, that Gabriel was the Broad Street artist, it was only a passing thought. But now it was clear, not a possibility, but a truth. Gabriel. Her son. He was the artist everyone was talking about. The start of a smile quivered at her mouth. It held there a moment, unsure, and then it spread.

She wondered if Gabriel was aware of the commotion. He had to be. But the way he was, low-key, quiet, kind of withdrawn, it probably wouldn't stroke his ego that much. He might happen by, blend into the crowd of people watching a TV news crew, and be comfortable with the anonymity. He was an artist, not a performer. But he had a passion and a rage, and it occurred to Ofelia that maybe he hadn't run from her, but from the reality of a life like this, surrounded by death.

She had to tell somebody. Ofelia reached for the phone to call Stella. And the moment she touched it she felt him again, heard his voice again.

I miss you. I've got a couple of things to work out. I'll be home in a few days. I love you.

She drew her hand away and cried, the weight of each tear pulling her head down a little more until she rested it in the crease of her arm and floated at the edge of sleep. She sees a boy and even through the blue haze there is no mistaking it, his father's lean body, his mother's dark skin, those slow sad eyes that see too much and know too much. He plays with shadows under the El, mesmerized by his own movement, and her heart jumps each time he disappears.

The scene shifts. The corner is the same, but the time much earlier. A man in an overcoat and motorman's cap walks with purpose at the end of a workday, tips his hat to the pretzel vendor, nods to the beat cop with the broad chest and great belly, and takes a place in line at the newsstand. Ofelia watches as her father drops his nickel when he moves up to the window. The nickel lands on its edge—what are the odds of that?—and rolls down the sidewalk, past the cop, past the pretzel vendor. Ofelia's father walks after it, bent over, like an actor in a silent movie. Finally he stops it with the sole of his boot, picks it up, and goes back to the newsstand, where he waits in line again to buy his racing form. He plays the ponies because that's the only way, he always says. That's the only chance they have to ever get ahead. Luck is what it will take. And now with his eyes down on the page, his concentration given to the long shot that would lift his family beyond its means, he steps onto the avenue and into the path of the approaching trolley.

For months, Ofelia's mother abused herself. If only she had called her husband at work that afternoon to tell him about her premonition. On better days she gave herself a break, wondering how anyone is supposed to distinguish between a vision, a hunch, a fear of lost love. They run together, she would tell Ofelia. How can anyone know? And what kind of place is this that a man drops a nickel and the thirty seconds it takes him to pick it up changes a half dozen lives forever?

Ofelia tries to get Gabriel's attention, but he is oblivious, floating deeper into the blue haze at Third and Indiana. Another man is behind him, the man who beat Father Laetner.

Ofelia calls out and Gabriel moves closer, his hand at his ear as if he is straining to hear her voice. And when he has taken shape, when he has moved close enough that she can almost touch him, a sudden darkness grows over him, consumes him like a windblown fire, turning everything a deep and bottomless black, and he floats once more now through the fog, disappearing into himself and falling through the centuries.

She sees his immortality in the tiniest things. The way he runs a finger sideways over his lips when lost in thought. The way he wears his clothes to bed. The way he holds back a part of each smile, and the way his eyes travel over things, searching for what everyone else has missed. She sees the circle of his life, her son the mystery artist, sees the gift of it as never before, and she finds the smallest piece of strength in the knowledge that unlike his father, he ran because of love.

Nineteen

He'd done it. He'd made love to Marisol.

Here he was, walking down the street with a target on his head, a crazed drug boss after him, and he could push that aside for the moment because the greatest thing in his life had just happened. It wasn't the sex so much—not that he had any complaints about the sex, and she didn't seem to, either. But her wanting him, that was the best part. Finding out she had the same kind of feelings for him that he had for her, after all these months.

Marisol had put the earrings on right before he left and then she'd smiled. He ran his hand through her hair and lightly touched the back of her neck, raising a shiver. He kissed her and her dark eyes filled, and Gabriel would not forget what the tears did to her skin, the way the wetness created a color he hadn't known.

Marisol. He was even in love with her name. Sea and sun, it meant. Sea and sun.

Gabriel went back to the fence he had shopped the ring to, but the man said he couldn't help him. He tried two more fences, but they didn't want it either, and with each failed try, the Mayor DeMarco heirloom grew in size and weight and bulged in Gabriel's pocket as if a part of the mayor were still attached to it.

This was getting too risky. Gabriel hoped that if the fences knew about the mayor's ring, they'd never suspect a kid to be carrying it around the Badlands. But there was a ten-thousand-dollar reward out there, and if they recognized the ring from television, or if they were the least bit suspicious, they were sure to call the police.

It had been dark about an hour. Gabriel zipped up his green army jacket as he passed a newsstand on Kensington and saw that the *Philadelphia Inquirer* had put out a special evening edition devoted entirely to the heist. A sketch of the ring, about four inches square, ran above the fold, but Gabriel didn't think it was all that good. He could have done a better job.

He bought a copy of the paper and ducked into a diner. Under the sketch of the ring was a big photograph of the family standing over the casket at the cemetery. Gabriel scanned the stories, nervous about what he might find, but it didn't look like the police had a clue. A story across the bottom of the page said the theft was making news all over the world. In Moscow, Istanbul, Baghdad, Sydney, and practically every city in Italy. Another story said the DeMarco family had held a press conference to announce the hiring of a team of private detectives.

Gabriel took the long way around to Eddie's, traveling streets where he was pretty sure he wouldn't see Diablo or anybody who worked for him. He knew that the longer he eluded Diablo, the more set Diablo would be on killing him. For a guy like Diablo, having a nobody like Gabriel defy you was like having your dick shrink another inch every day. Gabriel figured the Mafia operated on the same principle, and Eddie must not have much time, either, with Thin Jimmy. Whether it was the Mafia or the drug gangs, the punishment went way beyond the crime just for the sake of scaring the shit out of everyone else. Break a man's legs, his knuckles. Put him in a car trunk, bound and gagged, a bullet behind his ear. Something to get everyone's attention. The only way to rule by intimidation was to carry out threats, whether those threatened were guilty or not. Hell, it worked even better if they weren't.

Gabriel wondered why he and Eddie had ended up in this mess together. They weren't saints, exactly, but they weren't bad guys, either, just a couple of lost souls who had stumbled upon each other one day and got into something that immediately slipped beyond their control. He wasn't sure there was somebody in the heavens pulling strings so that this person bumped into that one, but he believed something had to be out there.

When he drew, he felt connected to something beyond himself, beyond the world. When he painted the bodies on Broad Street, sometimes the whole line of them, three dozen kids, would rise up off the pavement and march in silence down the dark and empty street, their souls rising into the starlit sky. From up there, they would watch over the people they loved and wait to be with them again.

A white Trans Am turned the corner and moved slowly up the street. Gabriel ducked behind a car that was stripped and torched, and peeked through the knocked-out windows as the Trans Am passed. It wasn't Diablo, and Gabriel didn't recognize the driver, but he was pretty sure it was Diablo's car.

Diablo was probably staying off the streets as much as possible, hiding out in one drug house or another. He knew bail would be high for beating a priest, and he knew he'd do time if he were convicted. But it wasn't as if the operation suffered with Diablo in hiding. He had a half dozen men under him, a loyal pack of Dobermans, some just as cold-blooded as Diablo himself, if not as ugly, all of them scared to death of him. If Diablo told them to, they'd kill anybody. If he told them to, they'd shoot themselves in the head. They were dumber than shit, every last one of them.

Even if he came up with the two thousand dollars, Gabriel knew the chances of it saving him were slim. Diablo would probably take the money and waste him anyway. Gabriel had run from Diablo the night the priest was beaten, and Diablo wouldn't let that go.

Still, Gabriel had to get the money and pay him off. If he didn't, Diablo might kill his mother, and Eddie, too.

The hooker was working Kensington and Huntingdon again as Gabriel approached. She seemed to be studying him, and when he was a few feet away she smiled.

"You got it," she said.

Gabriel stopped.

"What?"

"You got it."

He didn't know what she was talking about. He touched his pocket where the ring was.

"You got laid," she said, looking into his eyes as if it was written in there. "Damn, he didn't just get laid, he fell in love. The boy's a lady killer. I could tell you was a killer." She stretched out the word *love,* turning it into a little song. Gabriel was amazed at the way she read him. "What are you talking about?" he said.

"Don't lie to me," she said. "I can see it. You got a look. You and your baggy-ass self."

Gabriel fought off a smile and kept on going.

"And here I was," she shouted after him, "saving myself for you."

Eddie was pacing the dining room when Gabriel crawled through the window. He looked as if he'd made several attempts to pull his hair straight up out of his head. And he was smoking.

Monk and Mingus jumped on Gabriel as if they'd been waiting twenty years.

"You sell the ring?" Eddie asked. Judging by his expression, it didn't look like he was sure what answer he wanted to hear.

Gabriel reached into his pocket. He held the ring in his open palm, big as a crown.

Eddie groaned and collapsed on the flipchair, as if the sight of it made him too heavy to hold himself up. He sucked on the cigarette again and coughed, taking a swig of Yuengling like it was medicine. There were three empties at his feet.

"You don't smoke," Gabriel said.

"I started."

"When'd you start?"

"I started two hours ago and it feels great," Eddie said, coughing harder this time. "I wish I started years ago so I could be dying now."

"Take it easy," Gabriel said. "You gotta relax."

"Relax? I got two fuckin' developments for you, Mr. Take It Easy. What one you want first, the good news or the bad?"

Gabriel didn't answer.

"The good news," Eddie said, "they fished Thin Jimmy out of the fuckin' Delaware last night."

"They what?"

"He's dead. Thin Jimmy, the guy's truck it is. They found him floating in the river, a bullet in his head."

"You're sure?"

"It's on the news," Eddie said. "Mostly the news is about DeMarco and the stupid crooks everybody wants to hang. But they had something about Jimmy, too. He crossed the wrong guys downtown. The way it is now, it's not like the old days. These young guys, the turks, they kill each other for nothing."

"So you're off the hook," Gabriel said, wondering why Eddie wasn't celebrating.

"Some guys," Eddie said, holding the cigarette the way people do when they don't know how to smoke, "they fall into a bucket of shit and come up smelling like flowers. Me, it's always the other way around."

"What's the bad news?" Gabriel asked.

Eddie looked up without moving his head, giving Gabriel the tops of his eyes. Monk and Mingus sat on their haunches on either side of Gabriel, waiting for the rest of it.

"They brought Anthony Faggioli in for questioning."

"Who?"

"Anthony, the funeral guy. The cops, they called him in."

"How do you know?"

Eddie walked across the room and back. "What do you mean how do I know? Inverso called. That's how I fuckin' know. He said a dozen cop cars pulled up to the funeral home, Anthony gets in, they take him to the Roundhouse. That's two hours ago now."

Gabriel stuck the ring back in his pocket and sat down on the floor. "Let me have a cigarette," he said.

"It's bad for you," Eddie said.

"I know," Gabriel said, lighting up.

Gabriel didn't know how to smoke, either. He was wheezing and Eddie sounded like he was about to cough up a lung. They both flicked the cigarettes on the floor and the ashes disappeared into the shag.

Nobody said anything for going on ten minutes. The sound of a passing train brought the whole city into the room. All of a sudden Gabriel started giggling.

"What?" Eddie said. "What?"

Gabriel broke into a laugh and then it was half laughing and half coughing. "Man we fucked up," Gabriel said when he could speak. "Whose idea was this, anyway?"

"Inverso, the stupid fuck," Eddie said. "It was his idea. And you're the one insisted we do it."

Gabriel tried to make a straight face, but it only split him up more. "You realize the whole world is waiting to find out who took the ring?" Gabriel said.

"What do you mean?"

"The *Inquirer*'s got a story, about all these different countries trying to follow it."

"Great," Eddie said. "We're internationally known crooks. Maybe they can do a TV miniseries about us."

"The DeMarco family hired a bunch of private detectives," Gabriel said.

Eddie started to laugh too. "Beautiful," he said. "Two weeks ago my biggest worry is whether some dive bar hires my band for two hundred bucks on a Friday night. Now I got this."

"And it turns out you didn't even need a ring," Gabriel said, "now that Thin Jimmy's dead."

They laughed together until it went from feeling good to sounding pathetic. Eddie shook his head. "Who knew?" he said, smiling like the king of losers.

"We should have just killed him ourselves instead of stealing the ring," Gabriel said. "We could have gone down to South Philly, killed Thin Jimmy, then come back up here and killed Diablo. We'd be in good shape now."

"Good shape? We might have gotten medals or something," Eddie said. "We would have done the city a favor. Two favors."

Gabriel wondered if Eddie thought he was serious about killing Thin Jimmy and Diablo. Probably not. But Gabriel was. He was half-serious, at least.

"So this Anthony guy, what do you think?" Gabriel said. He had a bit of a buzz from the cigarette.

"I don't know," Eddie said, the smile disappearing as he shook his head. "Probably they're offering some kind of deal. You know, he gives us up, they go easy on him."

Gabriel stared at the wall, looking for something wrong with Eddie's theory. "They don't have shit," Gabriel said. "But there's all this pressure with the whole world watching, so they took a wild guess it was an inside job. All this guy has to do, Anthony, is say he doesn't know what they're talking about."

"Yeah, well cross your fingers and say a prayer," Eddie said. "The cops are liable to beat it out of him."

Gabriel didn't take Eddie literally, but he thought about the prayer. "It's kind of weird," he said, "my mother hanging out with this priest."

Eddie reached for his guitar.

"She's not even religious," Gabriel said. "Not in a church way."

"Me neither," Eddie said. As an afterthought, he asked: "How old's your mother?"

"Your age," Gabriel said.

If Eddie had a reaction to that, he didn't show it. He started playing the guitar. "The only thing that ever made sense to me, a rabbi said it," Eddie was saying as he strummed.

"You're Jewish?"

"Jewish? I'm a fuckin' dago. But one time I played a weekend job at a summer camp and one night they bring this rabbi in to tell the kids they ought to encourage their families to join synagogues, if they're not already in one. Anyhow, what should happen but this one kid raises his hand, he tells the rabbi he wants to join for the social activities, the idea of a community, all that stuff, but he isn't sure he believes in God. He doesn't even know who to pray to, he says, so he's asking what's the point of joining a religious organization."

Gabriel waited for more. Eddie was pulling that thing again, where he started a story and then floated off into his music.

"What did he say?"

"The rabbi? He tells the guy to forget the conventional idea of who

God is and where he is and all of that bullshit. What you can do, he says, is pray to something inside yourself instead of something outside, because maybe that's what God is. It's your sense of right and wrong, good and bad, all that. It's your conscience. It's inside of you instead of up in the clouds. I mean, there might be a God up there somewhere, but the way to get to him is through yourself."

Gabriel stopped smoking and just listened.

"What do you think?" he asked Eddie.

"What do I think? I think I paid too much for this guitar," Eddie said, inspecting a loose fret bar that made the strings hum.

"What do you think about what the rabbi said?"

"Fuck if I know," Eddie said. "Guess what. Nobody knows a thing about where we come from or where we're going. Religion is an invention. It's a way of dealing with the fear of death."

Gabriel liked what the rabbi had to say better than what Eddie was saying. "So you think the guy was full of shit?"

Eddie looked up from the guitar, annoyed. "What is this, fucking catechism here?"

Eddie saw that Gabriel was put off by that. He thought about Anthony and Dominic, and his conversations with them. He always cut them off, too. Treated them as if they weren't worth the effort.

"Here's what I think," Eddie said. "I think that's what you do when you pray. You talk to something inside yourself, some kind of spiritual force. Like when your kid's sick or something, or about to die, what do you do? You say, Dear God, if he makes it, I'll always do this, or I'll never do that . . . Am I right? You sort of bargain with the universe. Me, I went to Catholic school twelve years, this fuckin' Schlomo made more sense of the whole thing in two minutes."

Gabriel was quiet again, working it out. "So why didn't you join up? You know, become a Jew? For Sarah?"

"I don't need it," Eddie said. "First of all, religion is responsible for more wars, more death, and more hatred than any plague or natural disaster in the history of the world. Second of all, any religion that divides people in love isn't worth the time. You see this guitar?" He held it up by the neck. "This is my religion. Music."

"You still love her," Gabriel said. Not a question, a statement.

"No. Not like you love what's-her-name," Eddie said, grinning.

Gabriel didn't follow.

"Whoever it is left her lipstick all up under your ear," Eddie said.

Gabriel's hand flew up to his neck without him sending it there. A blush came over him like a shade pulled over a window. He wiped at the smudge, missing the spot entirely. Shit, he had Marisol's lipstick all over himself.

Eddie decided to give him a break and change the subject. "So what are we going to do with this ring?" he asked.

"Fuck if I know," Gabriel said. "I tried three places. Nobody wants to touch a ring right now."

"One thing," Eddie said, "we can't keep it here. Anthony tells them what happened, the cops will be here in two minutes. If we're holding the ring, it's all over."

Gabriel thought about the spot where he buried Marisol's earrings.

"I can hide it somewhere," he said.

Eddie laid the guitar against the flipchair and leaned forward. The angle of the lean said he had something important on his mind. "Listen," he said. "Don't worry. Thin Jimmy's dead, but we're still going to take care of your guy."

"I'm all right," Gabriel said.

"Look," Eddie said. "Who do you think you're dealing with, some dumb fuckin' guinea? This is Eddie Joe Pass you're dealing with. I can talk to this guy, Diablo."

"Talk to him?"

"Pay a little visit, tell him look, you cocksucker, Gabriel didn't take none of your fuckin' money, all right? Lay the fuck off him or you gotta deal with me, you prick. You know, muscle him a little bit. Drop a few names from downtown." He said the whole thing the way Inverso would say it, the words falling off the side of his mouth. It was meant to sound tough.

Gabriel shook his head. "You can't do that," he said. "He'd kill you in a minute and dump your body off a pier."

Eddie was momentarily insulted. "Well how about if I tell him you just need a little more time to get the money together? Then we get on a train, you and me, and go someplace where we can sell this damn ring. What do you say?"

Gabriel had to look away. Shit, Eddie could have ditched him with Thin Jimmy dead. It wasn't Eddie's problem that Diablo wanted two thousand dollars from Gabriel. But he still wanted to help.

It worried Gabriel. Eddie was naïve enough to get hurt.

"Look, this is not somebody you can talk to," Gabriel said. "He's not gonna give you a payment plan, like it's Sears or something. He'll follow you back here and kill the two of us. He's bagged a dozen people, easy, they're like trophies for him. He's got a different grin for every one of them."

Eddie worked his hand through his beard. At first it looked to Gabriel like he was mad. But it was frustration, not anger.

"I can't believe it," Eddie said, "that someone smart as you was dumb enough to start selling drugs. What the hell were you thinking? You're not like these other kids, you're smarter than that, and now you've got this asshole after you. We gotta get you out of this neighborhood."

"They're all smart," Gabriel argued. "You gonna get all the kids out?"

"They're not like you," Eddie said.

"They are like me. The only difference is they all think they're going to die, so they don't give a shit about anything. Me, I think I'm going to live."

"Well if you wanna live, you gotta get out of here. You and your mother both."

Gabriel knew Eddie meant well by that, but something about it didn't sit right with him. "When I first got involved," he said, "that's what I thought I was doing. I was going to make enough money so me and my mother could move somewhere. But it's not that easy, and even if it was, it doesn't change what's here."

Gabriel told Eddie he'd seen a story in the paper about a woman in Bosnia. Her town kept getting bombed by the Serbs and the reporter asked why she didn't get on a bus or a train and leave like some of the other people. "She said this was the town where she was born, where her family grew up. This was her place on the planet. She said if human beings were fucked up enough to bomb innocent women and children and nobody lifted a hand to stop it, she'd rather die in her home than survive anywhere in a world that crazy."

Eddie listened, and then he downed about half his beer, hoping there might be some wisdom in the bottle. Sometimes it was hard to keep up with Gabriel.

"I don't know about fuckin' Bosnia," Eddie said, "but there's too many kids dying here. I hear shooting every night, and these bodies on Broad Street somebody's painting, they're almost all the way to City Hall now."

Gabriel still hadn't done the last three bodies. The sixteen-year-old dealer who'd got shot and the nine-year-old girl who'd been in the wrong place. And he still had to do Lalo.

Gabriel wondered what his art teacher would say about his Broad Street project, and the thought of it stirred another thought. Not that long ago, that's what he had been—a student. It'd be nice if it were as simple as that again. Going to school, being with his mother, hanging out with Marisol. But even if he were in school, he wouldn't tell Mrs. Meketon about the bodies. He wasn't sure why, but he didn't want anyone to know. Everything seemed so big sometimes, it was nice having something no one else had. Holding on to a secret. He wasn't even going to tell Eddie.

As for Eddie giving him shit about selling drugs, what could he say? Yeah, he'd made some mistakes. It wasn't right, though, that a little mistake, instead of being something you learned from, could be the last thing you ever did.

Gabriel looked at Eddie.

"That was cool, what you said," Gabriel told him. "Bargain with the universe. I like that."

Twenty

Night crept into the house and emptied it, erasing Ofelia as she dozed at the kitchen table. Two hours passed. Three. Stillness. And then the telephone rang.

Ofelia woke with a start. Her heart swelled and raced and the phone sounded as if it were ringing inside her head. Ofelia chased the retreating edge of her own memory, afraid to follow it too far, afraid not to follow it far enough.

Had she dreamed of Gabriel's death? Had she seen it? The house's signature scent, last week's pork and beans, hung like smoke.

Ofelia stood, put a hand on the wall, and followed it blindly to the light switch, anxious to locate and strangle the screaming phone. The light was a yellow spray, sudden as shattering glass. Ofelia closed her eyes until the flash stopped repeating itself in her head, and then she picked up the phone.

"It's me."

His voice didn't register at first.

"Oh, Father Laetner. Sorry. I was asleep."

Ofelia grabbed at a kink in her neck. She'd slept awkwardly, her head in her arms on the table.

"I'm sorry. I didn't mean to wake you."

"No, no, it's fine," she said, squinting out the light. "What time is it?"

"Let's see." She heard his chair squeak and she imagined him turning to the clock in the kitchen of the rectory, where they had their first talk. "About nine, I guess. Yeah, just after nine."

"I should've been out there already," Ofelia said.

She looked toward her bike, but her eyes settled on the wall instead. Eight clusters. Thirty-eight marks.

The thirty-eighth, which she didn't remember drawing, seemed more punctuation than a measure of time. Ofelia looked at it the way she might peek around a corner at something feared or unknown. Something capable of looking back.

"So listen," Father Laetner said, "Lieutenant Bagno called. I'm going in for a lineup tomorrow morning. Either a lineup or they show me some photos, see if I can pick out Diablo. If they find him, they do a lineup, but nobody's seen him on the street. Looks like he's hiding out. Lieutenant Bagno says he thinks something's up, the start of a new turf war or something. Things are too quiet."

His voice dragged a bit.

"Are you okay?" Ofelia asked.

"I'm fine, a little sore is all. I'm just going to do an hour or two tonight and then get some sleep."

"Look," Ofelia said, pointing her bike toward the door, "what have I known you, a week? Not long, but you oughta start listening to me. You gotta take this slow because nothing's going to change overnight. You think this started yesterday, all the drugs, all the blood? You gotta pace yourself, you know? That was a warning, what they did to you. They'll come after you again, trust me, and they'll do you worse next time. Being a priest won't save you in this neighborhood."

Silence on the other end. Maybe she was too harsh. Maybe she had offended or scared him. But it was for his own good. He had to know these guys had no rules. Besides, she had enough problems without having to feel responsible for what happened to him out there.

"Listen," she said, "I'm going to check with the pawnshops and the diners, see if anybody remembers Gabriel or the guitar man."

"And what about you?" Father Laetner asked. "You think you're safe out there on your bicycle, investigating this guy's drug operation every night, asking everybody where your son is? You think he's going to leave you alone because you're a woman?"

If there was a suggestion in that, any suggestion at all, that she shouldn't go out there, she would have jumped on Father Laetner the way she jumped on Lieutenant Bagno the other day. But there wasn't. He was just telling her to be careful. He knew she was going out no matter what he said. And she knew the same about him.

"Come by Niko's tomorrow morning after the lineup," Ofelia said, "tell me how it went."

"All right."

"And hey, you busy tomorrow afternoon?" she asked.

"I don't think so."

"When did you say we were going down the shore?"

His voice brightened. "Tomorrow afternoon all right?" he asked.

Ofelia smiled. "That'd be great."

"And listen. Gabriel's going to be all right. I don't know how to explain it, but I have a feeling about him."

"What do you mean?"

"It's hard to describe. I guess it's just a feeling that this has all happened for a reason, and something good will come of it."

"It sounds like you're starting to believe again," Ofelia said.

He paused. "I believe Gabriel's going to be okay."

Ofelia wiped away a tear. She looked at the wall.

EL NADA EN LO OBSCURO.

She wanted to believe Father Laetner. But there it was, truer than faith. He Swims in Darkness. She took a deep breath. "Listen," she said.

"Yeah?"

"You're sweet." The compliment embarrassed him and she knew it. "That's all," Ofelia said. "I just wanted to say you're sweet. And please be careful."

"Yeah," he said. "You too."

Ofelia was aware of the cold but didn't feel it. The night was crisp, the sky clear, and the stars burned through the halo of light that hung over the city.

There was none of the embarrassment Ofelia had felt those first nights she rode the bicycle. So much had changed. The way she looked at herself, the things she thought were important. It was hard to imagine that just over a month ago she had still cared enough about her husband that she had used the Thighmaster regularly and had a fleeting urge to kill him. Complete disinterest, that was what she had now. He could be dead, he could be a millionaire, he could be drilling the Queen of England. It didn't matter. Just as she knew she could never be with a man like Lieutenant Bagno, someone who knew everything—she knew she could never be with a man like her husband, who said nothing. She rode like the wind on her red bicycle, and felt like she could ride all night.

Ofelia didn't let her thoughts drift, the way she normally did, because she was afraid of where they would take her. Instead she pushed them to where she wanted to go. Back to eighth grade, and one of those June days when school ought to be out but isn't. The Catholic school kids always got out for summer break sooner than the public school kids, and took every opportunity to tease them. Ofelia and a friend decided they'd had enough of that. They caught the El downtown, boarded a bus, and cut school for a day down the shore.

Ofelia had never been there before, although she'd been taken by the very concept of oceans ever since a seventh-grade geography class. She couldn't imagine what it would look like where the land ends and the water begins. She wondered if she'd feel as though she were falling off the edge of the earth, and she wondered if, on a clear day, you could look out over the water and spot Portugal or England, one of those countries, rising up out of the sea.

When they got off the bus Ofelia saw a vendor selling something called a knish, and she bought one out of curiosity. It was sort of heavy and kind of plain, but she liked it okay at first and then more and more, almost as much as the fresh bagel she tried next. She told her friend she could see herself living happily in Atlantic City, and that was before she even saw the beach.

The salt air hit them first, making Ofelia go light in the head. And then the ocean came into view, spreading wide and lapping at the sky, a show of light and color like nothing Ofelia had imagined. The sea held magic and mystery and danger, mostly danger, and Ofelia was in love with it from that moment, in love with the way it made her feel important and irrelevant at the same time.

Ofelia sat on the beach that night eating knishes, and when the stars moved into the sky and the breath of the ocean turned cool, she lay back on the sand and felt as if she were at the door to the mysteries of the universe. Eyes closed, she reached down and touched herself, her fingers running slow at first, a circular motion, the circle tightening, then faster and more firm. The wave came from the other side of the world, a weightless, gathering rush, and when Ofelia opened her eyes the stars exploded.

The next day, she had three knishes before noon and then headed back to Philadelphia, where her parents grounded her for a month and she sat in her room doing little seashore sketches and surprising herself with how much she liked them. Since then, every time she looked at the ocean it was like discovering it all over again. She couldn't wait to go there tomorrow with Father Laetner. She had to get away from this, if only for a few hours.

The pawnshops stayed open late, but they didn't stay open all night. Ofelia was coming up on Dauphin Street, pedaling fast, and the city spun by as if it were on a wheel. Everything ran together, the graffiti, the murals to dead kids, the barrel fires that warmed the winos in their mismatched shoes and knit caps. She had loved the neighborhood when others hadn't, had seen a beauty in it that escaped them, but now she didn't know why. It had probably been nothing more than wanting it to be for Gabriel what it had been for her.

These days the neighborhood was defined by the locked doors of the library, the cars at the bottom of the rec center swimming pools, and the rusty chains that dangled from swing sets. It was defined by the uselessness in the slow step of a man, hands in pockets, walking past the boarded-up factory where he once worked. By the posture and movements of a tactless teenage boy, preening for a girl he didn't know how to respect, and the willing eyes of the girl, who didn't know it any other way. By the fat necks and cinderblock heads of pit bulls on short chains. By the occasional block that stood out, proud, defiant, because it was painted and swept and free of smashed cars and broken glass. By the sight of children on their way home from school, backpacks strapped over their shoulders, as they passed a drug corner without a break in their conversation, without looking up, without knowing it isn't supposed to be this way.

She would take Gabriel away from here when he came home. She didn't know how. Maybe work two jobs. Whatever it took, she would take him away.

Ofelia knew of three pawnshops on Kensington Avenue, and the first was coming up on her right. She lifted the bike onto the curb and pushed it into the shop ahead of her, coming face to face with a man who peered through an opening in a cage, as if from prison.

He had a shiny bald head, droopy eyes, a bulbous schnoz, and a gray face that hadn't known a moment of pleasure in forty years, and dollars filled his eyes as he studied Ofelia's bicycle, thinking she'd come in to hawk it. The shop was a honeycomb of rejects. Every inch of shelf space was occupied. Televisions, radios, boom boxes, tools, jewelry. Guitars, saxophones, and trumpets hung from wires looped across the ceiling.

Ofelia pulled the sketch of Eddie and the photograph of Gabriel from her pocket and put them on the ledge under the man's nose. It was Gabriel's eighth-grade school photo, with a line on his forehead dug by the Sixers cap he had just removed.

"I'm looking for some people who might have been in here," she said. "Can you tell me, do you recognize either one of them?"

The man looked at Eddie and Gabriel, stoic, and then at Ofelia.

"A lot of people come in here, doll," he said, shaking his head.

The second pawnshop didn't work out, either, but in the third, the shopkeeper paused over Gabriel.

"You recognize him?" Ofelia asked excitedly.

The man was about sixty, lanky face, bird eyes, with spaces in his brilliantined hair from a big-tooth comb. He had a friendlier way about him than the other two men, and he bounced around the counter and stood next to Ofelia.

"I lost my boy when he was twelve," he said, looking at the photo of Gabriel. "Leukemia."

"I'm sorry," Ofelia said.

"He's still with me though. You know what I mean?"

Ofelia nodded.

"You do this?" he asked, looking at the sketch.

"No, my son. The boy in the picture did it."

That brought a smile to his face. "You got yourself a talented boy there."

Ofelia nodded politely, impatiently. "You think you've seen them, either one? They would have bought a guitar."

He looked at the sketch again and then back at Gabriel. "I might have," he said. "The boy, he looks familiar, actually. There was a boy in here that looked a little like him. Yeah, I remember thinking about my own boy when I saw him. Something's different, though. I think the kid in here had on a ball cap. Eagles or Phillies."

"Sixers?"

"Might have been."

"That's him," Ofelia said, unsure why she was just as frightened as she was encouraged.

"Do you keep records?" she asked.

"No," he said. "If you pawn something, yeah. But not if you buy."

"What if the man wrote a check for the guitar? Would you still have the check, maybe, or a credit-card receipt?"

"I don't accept no checks or credit cards," he said. "You kidding, a neighborhood like this?"

Ofelia's hopes sank as quickly as they had risen.

"So you wouldn't remember a name or anything?"

"I'm sorry," he said. "What I can do is give you a call if I see them. You want, you could leave a number."

Ofelia pedaled two blocks and came to a diner on a corner. She leaned the bike against the cigarette machine just inside the front door and took a seat at the counter.

"Coffee, please," she said before the waitress got to her. "Black."

The waitress came back with a cup and a pot. Her eyes seemed to be closed, but it was clear by the way she moved that she could do this job in her sleep. The upper half of her body floated behind the counter as if she were on a rail, like one of those metal cutouts in a shooting gallery. She had her name on her pocket.

Jackie.

This wasn't too promising, Ofelia thought. If the woman walked through the day with her eyes closed, what were the chances she could identify someone in a photo or a sketch?

She looked for another waitress, but Jackie was it. "Excuse me," Ofelia said. "You recognize this person?" She showed her the sketch of Eddie.

"Yeah," she said. "He kind of stands out in here."

"What do you mean?"

"Number one, he ain't bad-looking. Number two, he's got teeth." Jackie talked just like Stella. "What did he, run out on you, hon?"

"And this boy. Have you seen him?"

"That's his son," the waitress said. "Generally I work mornings. That's when I see them."

"His son? Did he tell you this is his son?"

"No, he don't tell me nothin'. I just assumed, since they're in here together."

Ofelia took a sip of coffee, her hand trembling, and clanged the cup back down on the saucer.

"You all right, hon?" Jackie asked.

Ofelia gave her a wave that meant she was fine. "You know where I can find them?"

Jackie thought about it. "I don't know their names or nothing. One time though, this guy stiffed me, not your guy but some other meatball, and I ran out after him. The cheap bastard disappears in the crowd, but while I'm out there, I seen this guy, the one with the guitar here, he's turning the corner. It's about three blocks up from here, he turns right."

Ofelia thanked Jackie and pushed two dollar bills under the saucer. She rode three blocks up Kensington, under the El, and came to a corner worked by a hooker. As Ofelia started toward her, the hooker retreated.

"I'm looking for someone," Ofelia said.

"I don't know nothing about it," the hooker said.

"Please."

The hooker turned her back to Ofelia and put her hands up. "I don't know nothing about no husbands and boyfriends," she said, walking away.

"It's my son," Ofelia said. "My son ran away. I'm looking for him."

The hooker turned. She pouted and frowned, but let Ofelia get in close enough to hand her the photo and the sketch. She looked at Eddie first and then at Gabriel, and then she looked at Ofelia, trying to make a decision.

"On the left," she said. "The sixth or seventh house down."

"Thanks," Ofelia said.

"Don't thank me," the hooker said. "You didn't get nothing from me."

There was a break in the row of houses between the sixth and seventh. The seventh house had a side yard and Ofelia saw a light through a side window. She walked up the front steps and knocked.

She could hear footsteps drawing close, and then a voice behind the door. "Inverso?"

She didn't know what that meant.

"Inverso?" said the voice again.

"My name's Ofelia," she said. "Ofelia Santoro."

It was quiet behind the door.

"I'm looking for my son," Ofelia said. "Gabriel."

Ofelia heard the footsteps fall away from the door. Maybe this was the wrong house. She walked down to the sidewalk and looked back at the hooker. She might have heard wrong.

Ofelia had started back toward the corner when he appeared from the side of the house. It was the man in the sketch.

"Mrs. Santoro?" he said.

They stood facing each other, cautious, curious. Scared. Ofelia couldn't speak.

He was younger than she had expected, even with the salt-and-pepper beard, and the neighborhood hadn't put its hard and tired look all over him like it had on so many of the glassy-eyed, yellow-skinned cigarette junkies who wandered the avenue under the El. Something wasn't right with him, though, and she couldn't put her finger on it at first. The guitar maybe. Yes. In Gabriel's sketch, the guitar was so right, so much an extension of him, he didn't look like himself without it.

She was bigger than he had imagined, and everything on her was black—the skirt, the sweater, the sneakers, eyes, hair. The darkness only added to her mystery, and so did her voice. It was raspy. Sexy. And the longer Eddie looked, the prettier she got, a kind of pretty that sneaks up on you. She was one of those women you just said yes to, no matter what the question, because whatever her spell was, good or bad, you didn't want to break it.

"You wanna come in?"

Ofelia cleared her throat. "Is Gabriel here?" she asked, her voice squeaky.

"Not right now, but you can wait for him here."

"Thanks," Ofelia said, and she began following him around the side of the house.

This was it. It'd been over a month, and finally she'd found him. So why did she feel so faint?

Almost to the window, Eddie realized there was no smooth way to help her crawl through it, and no easy way to explain the situation. He stopped. "Tell you what," he said. "You go around front, I'll go in and open the door for you."

It struck her as strange, but what could she say?

She was standing at the front door when she heard his footsteps. Then he grunted as he yanked on the door. Nothing. She wondered if he might have suffered a hernia.

She heard him take a few steps back, and then make a run at the door. The thud was followed by a moment of silence, and then he opened the door as if it had never been a problem. He seemed stunned as he let her in, but tried to act as if everything was normal.

Ofelia stepped in and leaned her bike against a wall. When she looked around, she felt instantly better about her own house. Compared to this, she had a furniture showroom.

"My name's Eddie," he said, holding out his hand. "Eddie Passarelli."

She took his hand and managed a smile.

He seemed to think he had to give her a tour and apologize at the same time. "I just moved in. It's kind of temporary," he was saying as he led her into the dining room. "This here's Gabriel's room. This is where he sleeps."

He pointed to the flipchair and she looked at it with some confusion. "Oh, it opens up," Eddie said.

She watched him jerk the chair so it flipped out. Something Jackie had said in the diner was bugging her now. The comment about Eddie eating breakfast there with Gabriel, his son.

"Gabriel went out," he said, realizing the statement was so obvious it was stupid. He felt so awkward, he didn't know what to say. "But he might be back in a while."

The words *might be back* separated themselves from the others. Damn, Eddie thought, what a dumb thing to tell her. Yeah, your son stays here, but who knows where the hell he is or when he's coming back? Eddie felt like an irresponsible parent.

Ofelia could smell Gabriel. The sweaty ballcap. The lingering odor from inside his sneakers. She looked at Eddie with gratitude, suspicion, and contempt, in that order, each emotion growing bigger than the last. Here was this stranger, some second-rate musician living in a dark, mildewy dump with a trick door, telling her things about her own son. She felt cheated, violated. Insulted. The old Ofelia, the one who let men push her around, even if they were assholes, would have let it pass. But the old Ofelia was dead.

"Look," she said, taking a step back and throwing her hair over her shoulder, a move that was the equivalent of rolling up her sleeves. "I don't mean to be rude or anything, but would you mind telling me what he's doing here in the first place, and what you mean when you say he might be back in a while?"

Here it is, Eddie thought. And he had it coming, violating a law of nature, as he had. He had come between a mother and her son.

She was all over him now, warming up to the fight. Her eyes raced and her body tensed. She was erupting.

"Listen," Eddie said, trying to calm her down, but she cut him off.

"No," Ofelia said, inching closer and stabbing a finger into his chest. "You fuckin' listen to me."

Eddie was on his heels.

"This is my son. You understand that? My son. He's gone over a month, and you don't have the sense, you don't have the fucking decency, to have him call me, or to call me yourself and let me know he's alive?"

She had backed him against the wall and was still stabbing at him. Eddie could tell she didn't know where this was going.

"I'm his fucking mother," she screamed. She dropped her right hand to her left hip and came up hard with a sweeping rage, smacking him in the face with a backhand that surprised her as much as it did him.

There were two sounds. Skin on skin. And head on wall. Eddie kept his head turned that way, the way of the slap, letting her have this. Letting her have this moment. The pain ate up some of his guilt.

"I ought to call the police," she said. "Every fucking night I'm all over this shit neighborhood on a bicycle trying to find him, scared to death he'll have his head blown off before I can get to him, and you're in here playing the guitar for him like it's summer camp. What have you got in your fucking head?"

When she turned away from him, Eddie saw Gabriel, just a glimpse, in the way she moved. He put his hand to his face, soothing the sting. Ofelia had walked to the dining room window and was looking out. He invited her back into the living room and she followed without speaking. They sat on opposite ends of the sofa, Ofelia on the left, Eddie on the right. The TV was on low and the light of it pulsed blue against the wall.

He was prepared to say "It's okay" when she apologized, but she never did, and that was okay, too. She didn't have to apologize for being afraid or for being angry or whatever she was.

She had a pretty good punch. Eddie touched his face again. Welts had risen.

"So how'd you find the place?" he asked.

She seemed to be wondering whether to feel insulted by the question, as if it implied she didn't have a right to track down her own son. "I asked around," she said, glaring back at him.

Eddie nodded.

There was a scratching at the back door and Ofelia bolted off the sofa, her heart full.

"It's my dogs," Eddie said.

When Ofelia sat back down, it sent a little wave through the sofa and over to his side. To Eddie, she was one of those women whose weight wasn't a turnoff. It was proportioned, sexy. In a way, she was a sturdier Sarah, dark, intense. Her hair had a habit of falling forward and she would push it back, tilting her head as she did, revealing the dark skin of her neck.

Ofelia looked to her left, at the milk crate end table. And at the photos of Anthony and Dominic.

Eddie saw that the pictures seemed to change something in her. The guy she had just smacked in the face might not be a complete bum. She had hit somebody who was a father, and however bad he was, he couldn't be a worse father than her husband had been.

"Your kids?" she asked.

"Anthony and Dominic," he said.

"How old?"

"Eleven and nine."

Ofelia looked around for any sign that they lived here.

"They're with their mom right now," Eddie said. "We're split up."

Ofelia shook her head in a way that asked if there were any families left in America that lived under one roof.

"You see them much?"

He smiled. "Tomorrow," he said. "I'm seeing them tomorrow."

His face changed at the thought, and Ofelia saw the decency that had come through in Gabriel's sketch of him. It gave her a trace of guilt for smacking him, but no more than a trace.

"Gabriel stayed on me about it," Eddie said. "He wanted to know if I'd called them and when I was going to see them."

A single tear streaked down Ofelia's cheek to the corner of her mouth, and a few more followed. Eddie imagined the taste of salt.

Ofelia wiped her face. She could see it now. Some of it, anyway. Eddie had been Gabriel's stand-in father, and Gabriel was the sons Eddie hadn't known how to love. She felt left out, slighted by the privacy and intimacy of that. But she was proud of Gabriel. The world, to him, was an unfinished puzzle, and he walked through it trying to match one lost piece to another.

"Listen," Eddie said, standing up and facing her. "You're absolutely right and I'm sorry. I should have called. I should have done something."

She looked at him, then looked away. "You wouldn't happen to have a drink," she said.

He went into the kitchen and hurried back with two Yuenglings. Ofelia chugged about half of hers without a breath.

Eddie couldn't take his eyes off of her. Whichever way she moved, the changing light always found her and reinvented her, prettier each time. He had to say something, but he didn't know what. She was hard to read. If he had to guess, he'd say she was one-third relieved, one-third scared, and one-third dying to smack him again.

"It was a tough time for me, a tough time for him, and we just hit it off," Eddie said. "He's a great kid, and he got me thinking about stuff, like when he talked about his drawings, or when he asked about my kids. We just got along real well."

Ofelia knew he was trying to be nice, but the whole thing was still offensive. She didn't need to hear from a stranger that she had a great kid. And she didn't need to hear that Gabriel, after walking out on her, was having the time of his life with someone else.

She took a swig of Yuengling. "How'd you meet him?" she asked, pushing her hair back again. Eddie watched it fall and then told her the story of the flipchairs and sofa flying off the truck.

"When Gabriel started staying over, he said you and your husband were having problems and needed some time alone. Later on, I figured there had to be more to it. I told him he couldn't stay if he didn't let you know where he was."

She didn't seem satisfied with the explanation.

"Anyhow, I'm sorry. I should have handled it different."

"You know where he went?" Ofelia asked.

Eddie realized he'd gone ten minutes, probably for the first time in two days, without thinking about the ring. Now he really felt like shit. Gabriel had gone out to hide the ring. He had said he was going to stash it under the bridge and then take care of something. Probably go see the girl again, Eddie figured. But now that his mother was sitting here, it seemed all the more stupid and irresponsible to have dragged

Gabriel into the DeMarco heist. Eddie wished Ofelia had smacked him harder.

"Do you know?" Ofelia asked again, with an edge to her voice. "Do you know where my son went?"

"He said he had to see somebody, but he'd be back pretty quick."

"Well, he's in some trouble," Ofelia said. "I don't know if you're aware of it, but he's got some problems."

She didn't know the half of it. Eddie waited for her to continue. She didn't.

"I'll tell you something," Eddie said. "I don't know how you raise a kid in this neighborhood."

"I could have done better," Ofelia said.

"I don't know," Eddie said. "But he's going to be okay. I'm trying to raise a little money for him, pay off this guy that's after him."

"Diablo," Ofelia said.

"Tell you the truth, Mrs. Santoro—"

"Miss."

"I'd like to fuckin' nail that bastard myself."

He looked up, ready to apologize for his language, but saw that he didn't need to.

"You're not from around here, are you?" she asked.

"South Philly," he said.

"Why would anybody come up here?"

"This is my mother's place," he said. "She rents it out."

"So what do you mean, nail him?" she asked.

"Look, I don't know exactly how Gabriel got involved in this. That was his first mistake, I told him. But he's trying to get out. Gabriel says a lot of kids don't realize what they're getting into. They figure it's easy. You just stand on a corner a while, somebody puts a hundred dollars in your pocket, and everybody else is doing it anyway so what's the big deal? They don't stop to think that once you're in, you can't get out. Gabriel's case, what happened, they say he stole money from them but he didn't. I know he didn't."

None of this came as a surprise to Ofelia, but it was upsetting just the same.

"I told Gabriel look, just let me talk to this guy," Eddie said. "This Diablo guy."

"What did he say?"

"He says I don't understand. It's not like I think it is. You cross him, he says, and he'll come after you and everybody you know. That's why Gabriel's been staying here. He's afraid if he goes home, they'll come after him and you'll get hurt. He would have called you sooner, but he's ashamed. He's ashamed that he let you down."

Ofelia's face fell and she began to cry. "I go out every night," she said, as if she were repeating it to herself rather than letting him in on something. "I go out on the bike after dark, a different place each night. I ride through the neighborhoods and I look for my son."

In Eddie's mind, it was a song, desperate and beautiful. He closed his eyes and could see her riding through the streets.

"I ask if anybody's seen him, if they know where I can find him. I go to all the drug corners, I hear gunfire. Sometimes I think I've seen him die. It's a dream or a vision or something. A few weeks ago, he died. Tonight he died again."

Eddie just listened. He wanted to move over and hold her but he didn't think it would be right.

"He loves you," Eddie said. "He loves you more than anything."

It was quiet now. So quiet.

They both turned to the television when the music for the eleven-o'clock news came on. Ofelia because there were often stories of kids being killed, Eddie because he knew that if Anthony Faggioli had talked, that would be the big story. Shit, if Anthony Faggioli had talked, the police could be knocking down the door any second.

The anchorman said there had been a plane crash in a country Eddie never heard of, SEPTA fares were going up a quarter to pay for improvements to the El, and there were no new leads in the theft of Mayor Michael Angelo DeMarco's ring.

"But the big story," said the anchor, "involves a new level of shocking, cold-blooded violence in the North Philadelphia area known as the Badlands. We've learned that a priest, known as a crusader against drugs and a critic of the church's plans to close parishes and abandon the poorest neighborhoods in the city, was shot and killed tonight at Third and Indiana."

Ofelia heard it, but it didn't sink in. "Could you turn this up?" she asked. It was a tone Eddie hadn't heard her use.

She sat up straight.

The station went live to a reporter who stood in front of a crowd of people. There must have been two hundred of them on the streets, chanting. The reporter stuck a microphone in someone's face and asked him to explain what was going on.

"We're not hiding in our houses no more," said a man named Efraín. "We're taking back the streets. They murdered this priest, who fought for us and for our children, but that ain't gonna scare us back inside. We're out here to stay."

The air went out of the room. Ofelia, sobbing, held her hands to her face.

The reporter said no name had been officially realeased, but sources identified the slain clergyman as a Father Laetner of the Holy Ghost Catholic Church on Lehigh Avenue. A church, the reporter said, that was scheduled to be closed in two months, one of several that would be shut down because of declining revenues and attendance in the area known as the Badlands. According to the sources, Father Laetner, a recent transfer to Philadelphia, had enraged archdiocesan officials by protesting the impending closure. He also had taken to the streets nightly to campaign for the safe return of the neighborhood to people who wanted to live in peace.

Ofelia sat in horror. Eddie moved closer to her and asked if she was okay. She put her hand up to quiet him as the station cut to a woman in the crowd.

"He only came out like, I don't know, a week ago," she said. "He didn't seem to know he was supposed to be afraid. Two nights ago they beat him with a hose, right here on this very spot, and he was back last night. That's when a lot of people took notice."

Then the reporter introduced Lieutenant Bagno and asked if police had a motive or a suspect. Bagno took off his U.S. Navy cap to answer the question. "At this juncture of the investigation, any comment would be premature, but we are investigating the possibility that the priest was murdered because of his antidrug work in the community. We do know that once before, a couple of nights ago, he was severely beaten."

"Did you personally know Father Laetner?"

"He was a friend of the police and a friend of the good people in this neighborhood who live in fear, terrorized night and day by drug dealers who have no respect for personal property or human life. It appears that Father Laetner died instantly and without suffering. My sincere hope is that his killer will not."

Ofelia was bent over, head on her knees. Eddie moved over and put his hand on her back. When she didn't object, he reached all the way around and held her in a hug. She lifted herself and turned toward him, eyes red, and hugged back.

"You know him," Eddie whispered.

"I know him," she whispered back.

"He's your priest?"

"We're going down the shore tomorrow," she said. "He's been helping me look for Gabriel. He's my friend."

They held each other for several minutes before Ofelia pulled away. She seemed to be looking inside herself for strength, and when she found enough, she asked Eddie if he could take her somewhere.

The heater in Eddie's Cutlass was broken and he shivered. Ofelia didn't. She told Eddie about Gabriel giving her the bicycle for her birthday. She spoke with an eerie detachment that scared him. "I didn't want to use it," she said. "I figured he bought it with drug money. Besides, I was big as a house. I knew I'd look ridiculous riding around town on that thing. When he was gone a week, that's when I started."

They took Kensington to Lehigh.

"I ended up right here the first night," Ofelia said, laughing at herself. "I could barely drive the damn thing. Right here though, this intersection, I thought I could feel Gabriel. You know, like he was close by. You ever have a feeling like that?"

Her saying it made Eddie feel as if Gabriel were there now. "Yes," he said. "I think I know what you mean."

They went past a drug operation a few blocks down on Lehigh. "These kids," Ofelia said. "Look at them. Fifteen-year-old dealers with beepers, eleven-year-old lookouts with gold chains. This is where I grew up."

Eddie thought she wanted to go to Third and Indiana, but instead she directed him to Broad Street and told him to turn left. "This is where the bodies start," Eddie said. "They don't know who's doing it." He wasn't going to tell her he thought it was Gabriel. He didn't feel it was his place.

"Drive down to the last one," Ofelia said, the smile gone, her voice thinner.

They drove about a mile, the Center City skyline growing in front of them, before the bodies stopped.

"You can pull over right here," she said.

Ofelia got out and Eddie followed her into the middle of the street, where she surveyed the last three bodies. One body had a number sixteen in it. The next, a little girl with a skirt, had a nine. Then another sixteen.

"Lalo," Ofelia said, standing over the second sixteen.

"What?" Eddie asked.

Ofelia kneeled in the street and touched Lalo's outline, then looked at her fingers. The paint wasn't dry.

Ofelia looked back up Broad Street and then down a side street. Still kneeling, she looked at Eddie.

"We just missed him."

Twenty-one

When he finished painting Lalo, Gabriel caught a bus back up Broad Street and sat with his face pressed against the window, watching the bodies float by. He looked at his right index finger and ran his thumb over the indented circle left by the spray nozzle. He remembered looking toward City Hall when he was done painting Lalo, wondering who would fill the next space.

There wasn't much traffic on North Broad Street late at night. Gabriel had been spotted more than once while painting a body, and car tires had smudged some of his work. But the people who drove through this part of town at this hour tended to fall into two categories; those who didn't care what somebody might be doing in the middle of the street, and those who were too afraid to find out. All you really had to worry about was the police. The police, and anyone who might be trying to figure out who the mystery artist was.

Gabriel pulled a torn *Daily News* clipping from his pocket. It was a story about the Hunting Park shooting that killed the sixteen-year-old dealer and the nine-year-old girl who was jumping rope. Gabriel had used the pictures as a guide for the paintings.

The sixteen-year-old looked like a sawed-off little guy, judging from the mugshot, with a squashed, fat face, a low hairline, and spiked hair with the sides shaved. He wore three gold necklaces.

The girl, pretty, and narrow in the face, was smiling. Her hair was braided into pigtails and her eyes, almond-shaped and dark, were radiant. She was looking off to her right, as if to a friend who'd just said something funny.

Gabriel had painted the boy first, trying not to let any judgment show, though he held him partly responsible for the girl's death. He held himself partly responsible, too.

Two cars drove by, one traveling north, one south, as Gabriel did the girl. He stopped each time and waited on the sidewalk, hands in his pockets, until the cars passed.

When he was done with the girl, he went back over each one, as he always did, making the lines thicker and fuller. He put the sixteen in the middle of the boy's chest, the nine in a corner of the little girl's skirt.

And then he did Lalo.

Gabriel tried to give Lalo that same look of valiant surrender he wore the night Diablo walked toward him on the street, slapping the meat of the baseball bat against the palm of his hand. Lalo had died with dignity, and there was a certain dignity to his spray-painted ghost—Lalo's arms outstretched crucifixion style.

Gabriel got off the bus at Lehigh and walked eight blocks to Episcopal Hospital, back to the phone near the gift shop. It was late to be calling Marisol. Gabriel hoped she would answer, and not her parents.

She picked up on the first ring, relieved at the sound of his voice. "Where you been at?" she asked. She sounded upset. Not mad upset, scared upset.

"Why, what's wrong?" Gabriel asked.

"Ralph came by the store," she said.

Gabriel hadn't seen Ralph since the night Lalo was killed. He had wanted to get together, not just because they were friends, but because Ralph might be able to tell him about Diablo's plans. But he knew that to make contact was to put Ralph in danger.

"What'd he want?" Gabriel asked.

"He said he needed to find you fast." She paused, and then: "Diablo's after you."

Diablo being after him wasn't news. He knew it, and she knew he knew it. "So?"

"It ain't just you he's after," Marisol said. "Ralph says Diablo's ready to kill everybody."

"Everybody?"

"You, the priest, your mother, that guy's house you stay at. Ralph said he needed to find you, warn you of it."

Marisol was getting worked up, but Gabriel wasn't ready to be alarmed yet. Diablo had already threatened all of that, the night he chased Gabriel.

"What'd you tell him?" he asked.

"I didn't tell him nothing. Said I ain't seen you."

"Why?" Gabriel asked.

"Why? 'Cuz I don't trust him's why. He ain't coming to warn you. He's coming to kill you."

Gabriel noticed the smell of the hospital now for the first time, the smell of sickness and medicine, the two of them indistinguishable. The double doors leading to one of the wards burst open and a woman in a wheelchair was rolled out by a black nurse in a white uniform. A plastic bag hung from a rack over the chair and a clear liquid dripped into her body.

It hadn't occurred to him, but yes, he could see it. Ralph coming after him either to kill him or to set him up for somebody else. It wasn't something Ralph would have decided on his own, but if he got an order, he wouldn't have any choice.

What Gabriel couldn't see was them going after his mother and Eddie and the priest. Couldn't see it or didn't want to see it. Diablo was out of his mind, but was he that vicious? If one of them got in the way while they were coming after him, sure, Diablo would blow them away without a thought. But Gabriel didn't see them being targets.

He asked Marisol what she thought.

"You didn't hear?"

"Hear what?"

"They killed the priest tonight."

Gabriel sagged against the wall, slid down it. He couldn't speak for a moment. Couldn't move. He wondered if his mother had been on the street with the priest, but was afraid to ask.

"You all right?" Marisol asked.

"My mother," he said, "she okay?" The question so fragile.

"They killed the priest's all," Marisol said. "That's all they killed tonight. But all of you know stuff about Diablo, about drugs, about him beating the priest, and the fucker's crazy. I don't know him, but everything I hear, he'd kill his own mother."

Gabriel was partly responsible for the priest's murder. He stood up again, dizzy. The smell of the hospital made him feel like he had to vomit.

A simple mistake, going out on the street when his mother told him not to, had brought all this. There was no balance to it. Everything was on a tilt in the Badlands.

All Gabriel wanted to do was go home, be with his mother, be with Marisol. He wanted to go to school, draw, sleep in his own bed, eat in his kitchen, even if it was pork and beans. He wanted Eddie to come over and sit in the living room and play the guitar and just hang out and be a part of things, and who knows what might happen? He wanted to see Marisol after school, take her to movies, kiss her. Make love. He wanted to tell his mother that his father was gone and he wasn't coming back and it didn't matter. They didn't need him anymore.

"I'm tired," he said, his voice low and draggy. "Tired of hiding, tired of this whole thing."

"Gabriel?"

He didn't answer.

"Listen to me," Marisol said, frightened by his tone, by the surrender in it. "It'll work out."

"When did Ralph come over?" Gabriel asked.

"About three hours ago," she said. "Where you at right now?"

"On my way to the bridge. I wanted to see you."

"Fifteen minutes," she said.

"No," he said, some strength back in his voice. "Not now. They might be following you. They might add you to the list." Gabriel meant it, but he hoped she wouldn't listen to him.

"I'm on my way," she said, hanging up without waiting for a response, and he thought of how beautiful she was and how, each time he saw her, she was more beautiful than he remembered.

Gabriel left the hospital and looked up at the sky as a jet lumbered over the city, connecting the stars, all those people escaping one thing for another. Something about it lifted his spirits for an instant. There had to be a way through this. But what it was, he didn't know yet.

A sudden breeze picked up and something in it suggested rain, even though the sky was clear. Gabriel buttoned his army jacket and headed north toward the bridge, keeping an eye out for anything or anyone suspicious. Ordinarily he wouldn't wear his Sixers cap around here, not since he'd been on the run. But he was Gabriel with or without it, and right now he wanted the small comfort it brought.

Fifteen minutes. Gabriel wondered if that was enough time to make it to the fence who had all the guns. It was late, but Gabriel was sure the guy slept in the garage to guard his property.

It wasn't smart to be unarmed anymore. The problem with a gun was even if he killed somebody, say one of Diablo's ignorant Dobermans, or even Diablo himself, it didn't mean he was in the clear. It just made it all the more likely that he'd die the same way.

But there'd be the satisfaction he got from killing one of them. Not Ralph, or one of the others who would have gotten out if they could have, but one of the ones like Diablo. That was how Gabriel felt now, not just that he could kill, but that he wanted to. That's what Diablo threatening to kill his mother did to him. And the satisfaction would go beyond whoever fell dead with a bullet in him. It would be like shooting a piece of this stinking, fucking neighborhood. Nothing that happened here suggested you should live by the rules they gave you, anyway, because nothing that happened here suggested you should expect to be around tomorrow. With a gun, there was a chance he could save his mother, or Marisol, or Eddie, if not himself. Maybe they could get out, all of them, and start all over somewhere else.

Gabriel started trotting in the direction of the fence. He could actually throw them off, he thought. Surprise them. Go after them instead of waiting for them to come after him. He imagined the gun in his hand and liked the weight of it, the weight and the power behind the weight. He imagined the gun as a paintbrush, and he remembered the feeling he'd had when his mother blindfolded him and led him down to the basement and stood him in front of his first easel. He remembered excitement and fear. The fear that came with being able to create your own world.

Gabriel was suspicious of every car. He wished it was summer and the windows were down, so he could make out the faces. All he saw was glare from the streetlights, and shadows behind the glass. He could be killed by one of those shadows before he had a chance to react.

He picked up the pace and then, just as quickly, he stopped. He didn't want Marisol waiting out there for him. Gabriel turned and ran toward the bridge. He'd get the gun after he saw Marisol.

When he slowed to a walk, to catch his breath, Gabriel felt over the bump in his pocket. The ring had grown comfortable there. He reached in and touched it, the ring the whole city knew about and wanted back. And a thought occurred.

He could confess. That's it, just walk into a police station, pull it out of his pocket, and offer his wrists for the handcuffs.

How bad could it be? He was a kid, and maybe they wouldn't go too hard on him. An adult, especially an adult from the neighborhood, they'd probably throw away the key. But the most they could keep a kid in jail would be until he turned twenty-one. That was only seven years, and he'd be safe. Safer, anyway, than he was out here. And Eddie would be off the hook. He could save Eddie.

Gabriel half slid down the hill by the bridge, desperate to see Marisol and already panicking at the thought of not finding her there.

She had arranged things the way they were the last time, exactly, except for a candle that burned on the table made of crates. There was nothing to say, nothing to do but hold each other, and Gabriel felt as if the whole world was balanced on this embrace.

Everything was pushed away, all problems, all fears, by the smell of her hair and her skin and the taste of her kisses, and he was tearing through her clothes, rougher than he should, but unable to control himself, and she only encouraged it with nervous hurried breathing and with her touch, one hand on the middle of his back and the other on his butt, pulling him deeper into her.

Gabriel dragged his tongue over her face and flicked it inside her mouth, swallowing her gasps, and the light of the candle flickered on her wet face. After he had come, he let all his weight down on her and lay his face at her breast, content beyond all dreams. At the sound of her heart, he closed his eyes and floated in her, safe from everything.

They had been lying still for several minutes, Gabriel still inside of her, when Marisol kissed him and then put her mouth to his ear.

"Don't do it," she whispered. "Don't go out there."

He rolled off and lay next to her and the light of the flame caught both their faces. Above them was the underside of the bridge, but off to the right, toward Center City, they could see the open night and they held hands as a light rain began to fall, bringing up the smell of the earth.

"Go to the police," she said. "Call the police."

Gabriel squeezed her hand and she squeezed back.

"What do you know about the priest?" he asked.

"Just that he was shot, somewhere around Third and Indiana. They said he was getting people together, an antidrug thing."

"They didn't arrest anyone?"

"Nobody seen it's what I heard. They didn't have no witnesses. They never have no witnesses."

Gabriel wondered what the chances were that Diablo had done it himself. His guess was Diablo knew better than to pull the trigger. He probably sent somebody out and told him to kill or be killed.

"Look," he said to Marisol, "you gotta be careful now."

"What do you mean?"

"Nobody was watching you when you left the store?"

"Nobody."

"You have to make sure, every time you go anywhere. You gotta be careful." He lifted himself onto his side, disturbed about something. "Man, how'd they even know?" he asked.

"Know what?"

"About me'n you."

"Wasn't me," she said. "Probably you were talking to one of your stupid drug-dealer buddies."

Shit. Gabriel had told Ralph about Marisol. He hadn't told him a lot, but he'd told him he thought he loved her, and Ralph, pretending he wasn't a virgin himself, had told Gabriel there was a difference between being in love and needing to get laid.

Gabriel didn't want to think about the possibility that his closest friend was trying to set him up. He looked back at Marisol and ran a finger down the middle of her chest, between her breasts. He ran it down past her waist and over her thigh and then he lay back again.

"All those times I was in the store," he said, "you were interested?"

They both looked out at the rain. She giggled. "No," she said, and then she laughed at the face he made. "Not until you started reading the business section," she said.

"What, you thought I was smart?" It had worked. He was proud of himself.

"No," she said again. "I thought you was pathetic. But it was cute, that you were trying to impress me. You were already cute, but when you were trying to look grown-up, that's when I started thinking about it."

This was embarrassing. He must be pretty simple, for people to be able to read him this easily. He remembered the hooker on the corner, taking one look at him and knowing he'd just made love to Marisol.

"Plus the coffee," she said.

"What do you mean plus the coffee?"

"You drank coffee," she said.

"I like coffee," he protested. "I always drank coffee."

"Coffee and the business page. I thought you was gonna start coming in there with a suit and a fucking briefcase."

"What makes you think I wasn't really reading the business page?"

"A artist don't read no business page," she said.

"Why not?"

"Because," she said. "Because he's a artist."

Gabriel liked the answer. He liked everything about her.

"I knew about Broad Street in June," she said.

"You what?"

"I knew who was painting the bodies."

She kept surprising him.

"How?"

"I knew. Couple times, you drew them on napkins."

"Why didn't you say anything?"

"I liked the secret," she said. "You had a secret, that you was doing it. I had a secret, that I knew."

"Marisol," he said, not looking at her. He waited, half wanting to say it, half afraid. And then it just came out. "I love you."

"I know," she said before it was even out of his mouth. "You know that time you came to the store all beat up?"

"Yeah?"

"That was when I fell in love. If you weren't so fucked up, I would've done you right there."

He turned to her with a look of bad-boy guilt. "Did I hurt you tonight?"

"Were you trying to?"

"No. I just couldn't hold back."

"Neither could I."

The rain fell harder. If they could just stay here, Gabriel thought, side by side, forever.

"I wondered," he said. "I wondered if you knew, all those times I went in the store. I wondered if you knew I was interested. You're the most beautiful girl I ever saw."

He didn't look at her when he said it, but he knew her response. She was crying, not for what he said, but for what he was going to do.

"I can't go to the police," he said. "What do I tell them? I'm a drug dealer and another drug dealer's trying to kill me?"

"You tell them Diablo beat the priest," Marisol said. "You saw that. And you tell them he killed Lalo, because you saw that too."

Gabriel shook his head. "What do you think my chances are, staying alive, if they arrest Diablo because I say he murdered somebody? You think I'll ever go to court? You think I'll last ten minutes?"

She cried harder and turned on her side, leaning on her elbow to look at him. "Well what else can you do? Killing Diablo don't fixing nothing neither."

"Why not?"

"Because it's not a person, it's the neighborhood. You can't kill the fucking neighborhood."

They both sat up.

"What do you do then?" he asked.

She put her arms around him at his shoulders. "I don't know," she said. A gust knocked over the candle and killed the flame, and the wind blew a light spray of rain over them.

He touched the lump in his pocket, and he was tempted to tell Marisol the whole story. "You know about the mayor's ring?" he asked.

"Who don't know about that?"

"What do you think they're going to do if they catch the guy?"

"Fuckin' Italians'll drag his ass out of jail, haul him up to the City Hall tower, and hang him from Billy Penn's hat."

"You think so?"

"I don't know. Cut off his balls, maybe. First, the cops'll beat the shit out of him before he even gets to the station. And the DA, I saw him on TV tonight after they showed the story on the priest, he says all the charges you could get for stealing off a corpse and all, you could get twenty, twenty-five years."

Twenty-five years.

Suddenly a thought took shape. It came from a distance and as it got closer Gabriel knew it had been there all along, waiting for him to see it.

It was a risky idea, but if it worked, it might save them all.

Twenty-two

Every night at two, Diablo waited at the base house for the night's take. At the end of the shift, each crew supervisor would deliver the money and the leftover drugs to the boss and Diablo would preside over these reckonings as if he were the chairman of the board of a corporation, which, for all intents and purposes, he was. That had been the system when Gabriel worked for the Black Caps gang, and he didn't imagine anything had changed except the location of the house. So finding Diablo would be simple. All he had to do was follow a crew captain.

Gabriel asked Marisol if she had any quarters. Yes, she said. Four. He left her with two, and with Lieutenant Bagno's direct line.

"Call Bagno in the next few minutes," he said. "Don't say who you are. Don't say you know me. Tell him to be at Third and Indiana at three. Tell him Diablo will be there with a shitload of crack hidden in his Trans Am. And tell him to be careful, because Diablo will be carrying."

"What are you going to do?" she asked.

"I'm not sure yet," he said.

Gabriel looked at Marisol one last time and saw her the way he had seen her the day of his promotion, the day she took care of him after he was beaten on the El, the day she told him not to leave, not to go out there and become a dealer because once you did you didn't control your life anymore. The sun had caught her that day as he opened the door of the store and it lit her like an angel.

"If Bagno doesn't answer, wait about twenty minutes and try again. He should be around, though, working on the priest's murder."

"If you don't come back . . . ," she said, taking his hand, not sure what to say.

"I'll be back," he said. "I'll be back. You be careful."

Gabriel started off in the rain, headed toward the fence with the guns. He wasn't halfway there when he saw the guy who made the nightly rounds to the drug corners with all sorts of new and used artillery hidden in a shopping cart. He was small and wiry and half his teeth were broken off to jagged yellow edges that hurt to look at. Gabriel figured him for a one-hundred-dollar-a-day man, the way his eyes sat like glass in his head. But he was one of those people who could still manage okay on crack.

"What you need, man?"

"All I got's twenty-five dollars," Gabriel said.

"Shit, that's light."

"That's all I got."

"Fifty, man. Fifty and I could get you a thirty-eight, do you some damage. Man, you don't want no fuckin' pop gun, you see what I'm saying?"

"It's all I got."

"All right, man."

He dug under the hills of cans and bottles in the cart and pulled out a nicked steel-gray revolver. He handed it to Gabriel and said it was loaded. He was throwing in the bullets for free.

Gabriel held it as if he were considering not just the gun, but the act of shooting somebody with it.

"It works?"

The guy grabbed the gun out of his hand and looked up and down Lehigh for cop cars. When he saw none, he aimed at a streetlamp across the street, squeezed the trigger, and blew out the light. "Five shots left," he said, putting the gun back in Gabriel's hand. A thin column of smoke rose from the muzzle.

Gabriel kept his hand on the gun inside his army jacket pocket. With his other hand, he touched the ring. Something had started now, and he was going to follow it. There was a relief in that, in not having to decide anything anymore.

He stopped at a mini-mart pay phone.

"Eddie. Gabriel."

"Where the fuck are you?"

"You told me to hide the ring. I'm hiding the ring."

"Where you hiding it, China?"

"Listen to me, I don't have much time. You gotta be careful. There's a chance Diablo's coming after us all."

"They killed the priest," Eddie said.

"I know," Gabriel said. "But there's no witnesses. I don't think they can even pick Diablo up, because nobody saw it, and he might be coming after us. You, my mother, me, everybody who knows something about him."

"What's he want me for?" Eddie asked, more out of curiosity than fear.

"Look, I need you to go over my mom's, let her know to watch out. Tell her to call and tell the police or something, I don't know."

"Gabriel."

"Eddie you gotta do this. You gotta watch out for my mother, because I don't know when I'm getting back. She doesn't have anybody."

"Gabriel, she's here."

"What?"

"Your mother. Your mother's here. She tracked us down. I got her here waiting for you."

She had found him.

"You want me to put her on?"

Gabriel stood in the fluorescent glow of the store window, warmed by the thought of his mother and Eddie together. "No, don't put her on," he said. And then he remembered the priest, her friend. "She all right?"

"Yeah, she's all right. Look, she's torn up about the priest. She's worried because you're not here, too, and she was pissed I didn't call her, let her know where you were. But she's okay, I think. She's amazing, your mother."

Gabriel couldn't talk. He hoped Eddie would say something, because he knew he couldn't talk.

"When you coming over?" Eddie asked.

Gabriel covered the mouthpiece with his hand and took a deep breath. "Later," he said, feeling over the gun in his pocket. "I gotta take care of something. If it works out, I'll be over around four."

"What do you mean if it works out? If what works out?"

Gabriel looked at the clock inside the store. He had to get going. "You still seeing your kids tomorrow?" he asked.

"Yeah. In the morning."

"Eddie," Gabriel said, his voice softer. "Tell my mother something for me."

"I'll get her," Eddie said.

"No." He wouldn't be able to talk.

There were a half dozen things he wanted to tell her. That he loved her. That he wanted to be with her. That he wanted to get out of this town. That he was in love with Marisol. That he was the Broad Street artist. That he was sorry. That he was scared.

"Just tell her I'll see her soon," Gabriel said, and he hung up with Eddie asking where he was and his mother asking Eddie for the phone.

At quarter to two, Gabriel crept to within a block of Fourth and Cambria and watched the crew close out a shift. He didn't recognize any of the four, even though it was a Black corner. The rain fell on them and they stood with hands in pockets, doing business once every two minutes or so. The license plates were from outside the city, from places where people got high but nobody brought down a corner and nobody hid inside his house because of what was on the street.

This was a risky time to work—rain, snow, any kind of bad weather, because it was a dead giveaway. The cops knew you wouldn't be standing in the weather if there wasn't money in it. But all the safeguards were in place. You didn't carry a gun if you carried drugs. You didn't carry drugs if you carried money. If the cops told you to get your ass out of there, all you did was move to the nearest block another crew wasn't already working.

It was twisted, the way laws designed to protect innocent people gave more protection to the dirtballs. The way the cops knew exactly what was up but had no authority to stop it. It only made the cops tougher and more lawless. You grab a cop by the balls like this, fuck with him, and he'll bust your head every chance.

As Gabriel watched the crew, he couldn't see himself out there, not anymore. They were pathetic, everyone on the corner, and he watched half with sympathy, half with disgust. He wanted to tell them they were better than that, but he had learned it wasn't something you could find out from somebody else.

Gabriel pulled his sketchpad and pencil out of his back pocket and wrote a note to Diablo. *Got your money. Meet me at three o'clock, Third and Indiana. Gabriel.*

At two, the Fourth and Cambria crew gathered at the corner. The captain said something and his three workers walked off, two in one direction, one in another. The captain went east on Cambria, and Gabriel followed from a safe distance. When the captain turned right on American, Gabriel figured this was his best shot. He ran up behind him.

"Yo," he said.

The captain turned, cautious. He was about twenty-two and heavy, head shaved on the sides except for a BC carving. Black Caps was expanding and this was one of Diablo's new hires, a perfect company man, it seemed, attitude crawling up from every cell in his body to say "Don't fuck with me."

"Man, you wanna do me a favor?" Gabriel asked. No answer. "Give this to Diablo, will you?"

The supervisor looked at the folded piece of paper. Raindrops fell on it.

"I owe him some money," Gabriel said.

The supervisor took the paper without commenting and continued on his way. Gabriel headed in the other direction, but snuck back when it was safe and tailed him.

Down Lehigh, left on Front, into an abandoned house near the railroad tracks. Gabriel stood a half block away, in the doorway of a house destroyed by fire, and watched the other crew supervisors arrive one by one and disappear into the house. He figured Diablo had read the note by now, and that the itch had started, the itch that could only be satisfied by killing somebody.

Gabriel checked up and down the block for the Trans Am, ducking behind cars as he went by the house. It wasn't here. He went around the block to Hope Street, and it wasn't there either. Then he remembered the garages along Gurney Street, where Diablo had once held a meeting. They were more like sheds than garages, barely high enough to stand up in, and they lined the ridge against the railroad tracks. Black Caps sometimes used one to stash drugs or weapons. Diablo kept a mattress in there, too, and would take his women in and fuck them dog-style, then come out with the fuck still fresh on his bragging landslide of a melted face.

Twenty or thirty garages sat in a row, all of them with wooden doors painted green, all of them with padlocks, and Gabriel wasn't sure which it was. He looked behind him, hoping something in the view, something in the grid of streets, would help him remember.

Gabriel's jacket was soaked through and a chill crept into his body. He walked to the first garage on his left, then moved to another, two to the right of it. He tried to pull the lock hard enough to see through the crack between the double doors, but there wasn't enough play in them. He looked around once and then took the gun out of his pocket and shot the lock.

Gabriel didn't bother to look around and see if anybody had heard anything. The rain would help cover the sound, and this was a neighborhood where people heard enough gunshots that they didn't run outside to investigate every one. Gabriel threw open the door. Nothing but televisions and stereos.

He moved one garage to the left and shot that lock. Only three shots left, he was thinking as he pulled open the door. And there, looking back at him, the grille like a smiling face, was the white Trans Am.

Gabriel closed the doors behind him and felt his way in the darkness to the passenger side of the car. The ceiling light came on when he opened the door and he sat down, slipping his hand into his pocket for the ring. He dried and polished it with his shirt, then held it by the edges and examined it for fingerprints. Clean.

Gabriel reached into his back pocket and pulled out Joey

Napolitano's holy card, remembering Joey in the casket, propped up like he was on a log ride into the next world. Gabriel thought he heard something and looked to the garage door. Nothing. It was probably the rain. He looked at the card again and read the Walt Whitman poem.

All goes onward and outward, nothing collapses,
And to die is different from what anyone supposed, and luckier . . .
We ascend dazzling and tremendous as the sun,
We find our own O my soul in the calm and cool of the daybreak . . .
Failing to fetch me at first keep encouraged,
Missing me one place search another,
I stop somewhere waiting for you.

Gabriel opened the glove compartment and laid the ring and the card inside. Then he got out of the car and closed the door, throwing the garage into darkness again. This was easier than he had thought it would be. All he had to do now was run down to Third and Indiana and hide out someplace where he could watch Diablo drive into Lieutenant Bagno's arms and get hauled off to jail for the crime of the century.

This was even better than killing Diablo, although Gabriel was prepared to do that if he had to. If Diablo had spotted him following the crew supervisors, Gabriel would have shot it out with him right there, though he would have preferred to have Diablo give chase, like he did the night he beat the priest with the hose, and then Gabriel would tiptoe into an empty house like before, only this time, when Diablo came slithering inside, he'd find a gun at his neck. Gabriel didn't know why, but he thought he'd like to shoot Diablo in the neck, and then, if he was still twitching, smile at him and put one between his eyes. But this was better, having him go down as the thief who stole the ring off the dead mayor, better because Diablo would be despised by an entire city and do time for a crime he didn't commit, if he was lucky enough not to be dragged out of his cell and lynched.

Gabriel gently pushed the garage door open, hoping Marisol had taken care of her part. As soon as Diablo got nailed at Third and Indiana, he'd run to Eddie's place and tell his mother they still had to be careful, but it probably was safe to go home. He'd pull Eddie aside and tell him the ring wasn't their problem anymore.

It was all set. All Diablo had to do was get in the car and drive down to Third and Indiana. All Lieutenant Bagno had to do was a routine search of the Trans Am. No jury would ever believe Diablo, who wasn't much bigger than Gabriel and could just as easily have crawled through the window at the Anthony Faggioli Funeral Home.

Gabriel closed the garage doors and tossed the shot-up lock over the roof. Diablo would know somebody had been there, but he wouldn't think to look in the glove compartment. Gabriel was congratulating himself for devising this plan—it seemed to have come to him in pieces throughout the night—when he heard a noise that didn't sound like rain, and before he could turn, he felt a gun at his neck.

His heart stopped.

Gabriel's gun was in his right jacket pocket but there was no way to get his hand down there and even if he could, there wasn't time to turn and pull the trigger. He'd be dead on the spot.

Gabriel put his hands over his head and took a slow turn to his right, ready to tell Diablo he'd just put the two thousand dollars in the car and everything was cool.

But it wasn't Diablo. It was Ralph.

"The fuck you doing?" Ralph said, soaking wet and shivering.

Gabriel didn't answer. He didn't know what to say.

"Come on, you gotta come with me," Ralph said, standing back three feet and holding the gun on Gabriel.

"Come where?"

"Why'd you shoot the fuckin' lock? They heard the shots and sent me out to see what it was."

Ralph wasn't into this at all, and Gabriel tried to figure out what he could do with that. "So tell them you couldn't find anything," he said.

Ralph raised his aim, pointing the gun at Gabriel's head.

"Why'd you come looking for me earlier?" Gabriel asked, letting his arms drop as he spoke.

"Keep your fucking hands up," Ralph said. He seemed more afraid of himself than of Gabriel. "I was supposed to bring you back," he said. "Either kill you or take you to Diablo, so he could kill you. Fucker went crazy, man, he's goofy in the head, you know? Worse than before. Way worse."

"And if you fuck up," Gabriel said, "he kills you, right? Either you bring me in or he kills you?"

Ralph was sobbing. "He's killing everybody. Says he going to kill your mother, kill that guy. He says he's going to rape Marisol in front of you, fuck her up the ass while he makes you watch, and then blow your head off in front of her."

That was it. Gabriel wanted to kill. He was prepared to push his way past Ralph, take his weapon, and storm into the drug house, guns blazing. He wanted to empty both guns into Diablo's head.

Gabriel turned, only thinking about one thing. He had to get to a phone and warn Marisol.

"Don't fuckin' move," Ralph shouted, his finger on the trigger.

Gabriel stopped cold.

"Fuckin' Diablo lost his mind," Ralph was saying, "and we can't get out. Maceo comes five minutes late one night to his corner, the motherfucker drove out there and shot up his feet. Maceo's all fucked up, can't even walk. Tonight Diablo sends one of the new kids out, kill the fucking priest, he tells him. You come back here and the priest is alive, you're a dead man. You gotta kill everybody, even your friends. It's fucked up, man."

There wasn't much time. If Diablo was driving down to Third and Indiana, he'd be coming out soon.

"Ralph," Gabriel said, "I'm putting my hands down."

Ralph stiffened and pointed the gun between Gabriel's eyes, more frightened than ever now. "Don't fuck with me," he shouted. "Don't fuckin' fuck with me. I'll do you, man. I gotta whack you or they whack me. I don't wanna die, you fuck. I don't wanna fuckin' die."

He was about to lose it. He was going to shoot any second now.

"Listen to me," Gabriel said. "There's enough people trying to kill us, we don't need to kill each other. In ten minutes, Diablo's getting arrested and he's going away. It's all set up. I gotta walk away right now though or it doesn't happen. Diablo comes out here right now and sees me, the whole thing's fucked."

"The fuck you doing in the garage, man. Wha'd you do to the car?"

"It's all set up, trust me. Ten minutes, this is all over, you're not his slave anymore."

"Don't fuck with me, man. I got two days to kill you," Ralph wailed. "Two more days and then he fuckin' kills me. I'm fifteen years old, man. Fifteen."

Gabriel could see it. Ralph was going to pull the trigger.

He had two choices. Get to his own gun, if Ralph gave him the time. Or turn and walk away. Diablo could be out here any second.

Gabriel moved his hand toward his gun, watching for Ralph's reaction as he did. In Ralph's face, he saw Lalo and he saw all the other kids who died and he saw all the bodies on Broad Street, washed by the rain.

He couldn't shoot Ralph. He was going to just turn and run.

The second he did, he heard the shot. It broke him at the knees and his hand went up to the back of his head to see if he'd been hit. Feeling nothing, he turned to see Ralph flat on his back, blood gurgling out of his mouth.

He'd shot himself. His eyes were open and he tried to talk but nothing came out and then his eyes went blank.

Gabriel picked Ralph up by his arms and dragged him into the open house across the street. Diablo would be out here soon, and if he saw Ralph's body, he might not go to Third and Indiana. He might stay here, looking for the killer.

Gabriel laid Ralph's body just inside the door and he paused for a moment to look at his friend, to imagine his body on Broad Street. He leaned down, kissed Ralph on the forehead, and then he was running through the rain, running toward Third and Indiana. He had covered three blocks when he heard the car coming up behind him, Diablo's car, and saw his own shadow stretched out in front of him, a shadow thrown by the headlights of the Trans Am. It grew darker and longer and more defined, and Gabriel saw there was no alley here, no abandoned house that he could duck into, nowhere for the shadow to disappear. There was only the rain in front of him and the car behind him, and his one chance was to make it to Third and Indiana, another few blocks, and hope Lieutenant Bagno was already there and that Diablo would drive right into the trap. He knew that Diablo would. He knew that when Diablo saw Lieutenant Bagno, he'd ditch his gun somewhere and drive right up to the cop, unable to resist a chance to throw it in Bagno's face.

Gabriel heard the first shot when he hit American Street, and it made him think of Ralph. His last words: "I'm fifteen years old, man. Fifteen." Ralph had shot himself because that made more sense than living in a world where an animal drug boss rules your life and you can't go home and the only way to survive is to shoot your friend. Gabriel envied Ralph the way he envied Lalo, and for the first time he saw his own body painted on Broad Street and saw himself rising up at night with the others and walking into the dreams of the people he loved. He saw himself with his mother, and with Eddie. And he saw himself with Marisol.

The next shot hit Gabriel square in the back and he went down face first, skidding through puddles with his arms outstretched, his Sixers cap flying off. When he came to a stop, feeling no pain, he picked himself up and ran again, not sure he'd been hit. He was only two blocks away from Third and Indiana, and he couldn't hear the car behind him anymore, but up ahead he saw headlights and he ran for them. The street tilted left and then right and the row houses on either side went fuzzy, and as the headlights grew brighter Gabriel felt as if he were running against a river instead of through the rain. There was some pain now but mostly just a numbness, like the edge of sleep. He was never this tired, but he told himself not to give up, keep running, Diablo might still be behind him. Just keep going, he said, whispering it, and then the lights were all he saw and he disappeared into them and heard a familiar voice. He felt himself in someone's arms, content now, finally, no more running. It was over.

Twenty-three

Ofelia sat in the street at Third and Indiana cradling Gabriel in her arms, and the rain washed over both of them, camouflaging Ofelia's tears.

She showed no horror, only love for her sleeping child. She ran her fingers through his hair, styling it as if preparing him for the first day of school, and now she pulled his face to hers and whispered to him, rocking gently and closing her eyes so she could see what she wanted to see.

The ambulance was close now and the siren was a long sad cry. The rain ran red under Ofelia.

The people of the neighborhood came onto their porches and looked at this. Two shootings in one night, first the priest and now a boy in his mother's arms. Most of them went back inside because it was wet and cold, and too much to look at.

Lieutenant Bagno shouted into the little microphone at the end of a tangled cord, calling in the hit and trying to get a squad car to the neighborhood to look for the shooter. He was cursing everyone he could think of, the police commissioner, the mayor, the governor, because they were short again tonight and there were two robberies in progress in the district and there wasn't a car within two miles of Third and Indiana. And now Lieutenant Bagno was yelling at Eddie, telling him he was out of his fucking mind if he thought he was going to wander in the direction Gabriel had run from and accomplish anything other than to get his own sorry ass shot.

"What are you going to do," Bagno asked. "Hit somebody with your fucking guitar?"

The ambulance arrived and the paramedics stepped out in the manner of men whose sense of outrage had been stolen. "This is cute," one of them said. "Third and Indiana twice in one night."

Eddie ran toward Ofelia and Gabriel to see if he could help the paramedics. Halfway there, he stopped with a fright. He'd almost stepped on the detectives' chalk outline of Father Laetner's body. They were everywhere in this city, down alleys, in empty lots, up and down Broad Street. Everywhere, ghosts.

Father Laetner's ghost has almost disappeared in the rain, and the blood had washed away. Eddie looked toward Gabriel and imagined the blood of the two of them—the priest and the boy he'd been looking for—running together under the city.

A paramedic pulled back Gabriel's eyelids, put an ear to his chest, and told his partner to hurry. "This one's still alive."

Eddie felt sick as he watched them lift Gabriel onto the gurney. His shiny wet face had lost all color and his sneakers pointed to the sky. Eddie heard Gabriel's last question on the phone. "You seeing your kids tomorrow?"

They slid Gabriel into the ambulance and Ofelia climbed in after him, more shaken now that he was no longer in her arms. Eddie stepped up after her but one of the paramedics waved him back. "You family?"

Eddie shook his head.

"I'll see you at the hospital," he said, and Ofelia nodded. Eddie reached for her hand and she gave it to him and they squeezed, passing strength to each other. She seemed strangely resigned to this, Eddie thought. Almost as if she had already lived through it. When the ambulance wheeled away Eddie saw her through the window, dark in the pale yellow light.

And then Lieutenant Bagno was talking to him.

"So that's all he said when he called, that he had something to do?"

Eddie thought back on the conversation. "I think so."

"So how'd you know to come here?" Bagno asked, impatient and frustrated. Eddie thought Bagno was mad at him, not realizing the lieutenant was mad at himself anytime anybody got shot out here, because he wanted to think he could save them all.

"We didn't know where to go. We were driving around trying to find him and then his mother gets this feeling. Like a premonition or something. 'Go to Third and Indiana,' she says. 'That's where he is. Third and Indiana.' "

Lieutenant Bagno had already been at the intersection when Eddie and Ofelia pulled up. "How'd you know to come here?" Eddie asked.

Lieutenant Bagno looked at him the way a soldier looks at a civilian who never served. "We got a call," he said. "A call that this fucking shitbag Diablo's supposed to be here."

Eddie looked around for a car. The rain, slanting with the wind, drove into him with a chill. Lieutenant Bagno stood at his open car door in his U.S. Navy ball cap, a general waiting for the enemy to come across the battlefield.

"How long you gonna wait?" Eddie asked.

"Till he comes," Lieutenant Bagno said, cupping his hand over a cigarette as he lit it. "He'll come, too, the crazy motherfucker." A pause. "He'll come."

Eddie started walking.

"The fuck you doing?" Lieutenant Bagno called out.

Eddie didn't stop. He wanted to go back to where Gabriel was when he wasn't shot yet, when he was still a boy of fourteen, scared maybe, but brave and alive, an artist. Three blocks into the rain he saw the Sixers cap and picked it up. It still held the shape of Gabriel's head. He walked another half block and looked around, wondering if, when Gabriel was here, right here, everything was still okay.

It occurred to Eddie that Gabriel never blamed anyone for his predicament. Not his mother. Not his father. Not Diablo. Not this bombed-out fucking neighborhood with its bloody streets and shitty schools and shut-down factories. He had laughed when Eddie blamed his own failures on a Little League strikeout thirty years ago. But he hadn't laughed when Eddie told him about praying to something inside yourself. What idea was it that Gabriel said he liked?

Bargain with the universe.

When Eddie got back to Third and Indiana, he could see Lieutenant Bagno straightening up as a car approached. In his posture he was saying, "This is it."

Eddie watched as the white Trans Am pulled over and the driver got out. He was the ugliest human Eddie had ever seen. Diablo.

"What seems to be the problem, officer?" the drug boss asked Bagno. "Some type of mishap here this evening?"

Eddie clenched his fists without knowing it and moved in next to Lieutenant Bagno, who pushed him aside.

"No big deal, you drug-dealing sack of shit. Just a couple of bodies laid out with bullets in their backs. The priest and the boy. You wouldn't know anything about that, would you?"

Diablo threw his hands out, a mocking gesture of innocence.

"What priest? What boy?" He grinned, showing his fucked-up teeth. "I don't even fuckin' carry since I joined the regular workforce," he said, patting himself down.

Eddie could see that Lieutenant Bagno despised Diablo even more than Eddie did. He wondered, if he weren't out here to watch, what Bagno might do to the dealer.

"Well if you're not carrying then you wouldn't mind I take a look inside your trunk, am I right, fuckface?"

"No problema. You got a search warrant, no problema."

Bagno reached for his gun. He didn't take it out, just touched where it was, tucked into the back of his pants.

"I got my search warrant right here, fuckface. You wanna see the cocksucker? I could book you right now, you son of a bitch, for two homicides."

"I don't know nothing about no homicides, except that you don't got no fucking evidence on either one. Listen, man, I went straight, got me a nine-to-five in the post office. But I tell you what I'm gonna do. Gonna make a goodwill gesture, man, so you leave me alone and I can raise my family, pay my taxes to support the five-ohs because let me tell you, we need a little more police presence out here, man, it's fucking dangerous. You wanna see inside my trunk, go ahead. Crawl inside the fucker, it makes you happy. I'm a clean motherfucker. *No tengo nada.*"

Lieutenant Bagno was about to choke on the bullshit. He shoved Diablo against the Trans Am and frisked him. Nothing.

He wondered what had happened to the help he'd called for on the radio, and he looked around, not for the help, but to see if Diablo had anybody else out here. The call he'd gotten at two o'clock, from some young girl, could have been a setup. Diablo would love nothing more than to do Bagno.

Of course it also made sense that Diablo, sick fuck that he was, would have some kind of perverted need to drop by the spot where two of his victims had fallen in one night. He was like an arsonist who shows up and plays with himself while people jump from a building he torched. Diablo, a psycho killer, was in love with the feel of it and the smell of it, and he liked to rub it in the cops' noses, taunt them, tell them they couldn't touch him.

But would he be here now, Bagno wondered, if he had a trunk full of dope? It didn't add up.

"Nice fuckin' car," Bagno said, walking back to the trunk. "What's your dick, about two inches long?"

Diablo lost his grin. "The fuck you saying?"

"This car you got. Fuckin' penis extender. That's what all the car dealers tell me. Everyone buys one of these things, loaded with all the extras, their dick's two inches long."

"Man, don't fuck with me," Diablo said.

"Open the goddamn trunk," Bagno said, pulling his gun out of his pants and using it as a pointer.

Diablo wasn't over the insult but he put that grin back on his face because he couldn't go two minutes without making it look like he had the best of Bagno. He popped the trunk, did a little half turn, and held out his hands—*nada*—cocky as ever.

Nothing inside but a spare tire and a crowbar. Bagno lifted the tire, looking for drugs, or the rubber hose Diablo had used to beat up Father Laetner. He found neither. "How about the little compartment in there?" Bagno said, pointing to the wheel well.

"Qué dice?" Diablo said. "What you talkin' about, man?"

"Under the rug, fuckface. And don't fuck with me or I'll stick this gun up your nose and blow your brains out of your fucking head."

Diablo pulled up the rug. Underneath was a locked hatch about the size of a glove compartment. Diablo picked a key out of his ring, looked at Lieutenant Bagno as if this was it, Bagno had finally nailed him, and then he opened it.

Nothing.

Diablo was having a great time. "How about you come look inside my house now too?" he suggested.

"How about I look up your fuckin' asshole with my size twelve, you murdering sack of shit?" They were at the passenger door and Bagno, pissed off, told him to open it. He was just going to harass the shit out of him now.

Diablo told Bagno he didn't have any more time to watch him embarrass himself. He said he had to go read bedtime stories to his kids and then get up and go to work and pay his taxes.

Bagno told him to open the door or he'd crack his fucking head.

Diablo opened it, slid inside the car, and sat in the passenger seat. He was laughing at Bagno's frustration as the lieutenant popped the glove compartment and reached inside.

"What do we have here?" the lieutenant said, pulling out the ring.

Diablo's grin disappeared. "What the fuck is that?" he asked.

Bagno, his gun still drawn, touched it to Diablo's nose and said: "Let me tell you how this works, dick nose. I ask the questions and you fucking answer them, all right?" He reached back into the glove compartment and pulled out Joey Napolitano's funeral card. He held the ring and the card under the ceiling light so he could see them better.

"Son of a bitch," Bagno said. "Son of a fucking bitch." He straightened up and turned to Eddie with the face of a child on Christmas morning. "Look at this," he said, opening his palm to reveal the jewel. "It's the fucking mayor's ring."

Eddie choked and tried to clear his throat. Diablo was climbing out of the car and Bagno was doing a little jig in the rain, waving his gun at the sky and celebrating as Diablo said he didn't know nothing about no fucking ring.

It still hadn't sunk in for Eddie.

"Let me see that," he said.

Lieutenant Bagno held it out for him again. Eddie looked at the ring, then at Lieutenant Bagno, then at Diablo, who looked as if he'd seen a ghost.

He was unbelievable, Eddie was thinking. Gabriel was unbelievable.

Lieutenant Bagno, beaming, held the ring out once more. "Is that it, or is that it?" he asked.

Eddie gave it another look. "Yeah, that looks like it," Eddie said. "I mean, that's what I seen on TV."

Bagno took out a handkerchief, wrapped the ring and the holy card in it, and slipped it into the inside breast pocket of his jacket. He turned to Diablo with the same fuck-you grin Diablo had been giving him. "What seems to be the problem, officer?" Lieutenant Bagno said, mocking the tone Diablo had used on him. "We got ourselves a mishap here? I'll tell you what we got, shit for brains. We got ourselves the dumbest fuckin' crook in the history of crooks."

"You're fuckin' crazy," Diablo protested. "Somebody settin' me up."

"So tell me," Bagno said, his face in Diablo's. "Ten thousand dollars a day in crack, that's not enough for you? You need to rob a corpse, get yourself a little trophy? You do it yourself, or you send one of your boys in there?"

"I didn't take no fuckin' ring," Diablo was saying, but the way he looked, he knew he might as well have.

Bagno shoved him against the car, jerked his arms back, and cuffed him. "You have the right to remain stupid," he said. "You fuck."

"Man, I never touched DeMarco. I wouldn't dirty my hands on that fuckin' pig."

Lieutenant Bagno whipped his gun out of his pants and cracked Diablo on the back of the head. "Listen to me," he said, pushing Diablo's cuffed hands halfway up his back and then rapping him again with the gun, this time on the side of the head. "That was a fuckin' man of honor. He was a man who could kick your faggot ass before you knew what hit you, just like I could kick your faggot ass. You say another word about him I'm gonna stick your fuckin' head in the door here and slam it till the rocks fall out. Now get your slimy, dope-dealing, ring-stealing motherfucking ass in there."

Bagno looked at Eddie and grinned. An odd grin, almost a wink. Eddie wondered if Lieutenant Bagno knew. If he was just playing along.

Eddie watched him take Diablo by his belt, push his head down, and then boot him into the back of his squad car. Then he got on the radio to say he was bringing in the man who stole Mayor DeMarco's ring.

Eddie was stunned by it all. Not just the ring, but everything. He was broken up for Ofelia, and he felt a love for Gabriel and a sadness and a guilt like nothing he'd ever known. And then a rage started to grow in him. It was sweet, watching Diablo get nailed like this, but it wasn't justice enough. Gabriel was bleeding to death right now, and one way or another, by his own hand or by his order, Diablo was the prick who shot him in the back. Eddie wanted a piece of him right now.

"Listen," he said, pulling Lieutenant Bagno away from the car. "Give me five minutes with this guy. Five minutes."

Bagno laughed. "What are you, fuckin' nuts? This kid's a crocodile."

Eddie begged, and Bagno saw something in his eyes. Something he respected. He looked back at Diablo and then at Eddie again. Then he looked down Indiana. Everybody was back inside because of the time and the weather. The rain still fell in sheets.

"Look," Lieutenant Bagno said, leaning into his car to light another cigarette, "just give him a quick pop and we're out of here."

"Five minutes," Eddie repeated, more an order than a request.

"I can't let him out of the car."

"Take off his cuffs. I'll get in there with him."

Bagno shook his head. This was against his better judgment. But he was planning to beat the shit out of Diablo himself before taking him in, so he might as well let Eddie tune him up first.

Bagno opened the back door and reached for Diablo's hands. "You shouldn't have done this," he said.

"Done what?" Diablo asked.

"Resisted arrest," Bagno said.

Eddie got in the other side and closed the door. He looked into Diablo's eyes for half a minute, trying to figure out how to explain to a jerk like this what he'd just done. He wanted to tell him about the kind of kid Gabriel was. But he realized Diablo was too low to get it, and so he just went nuts.

It was like fighting in a phone booth turned sideways. Diablo got in a couple of shots but Eddie, powered by rage, hammered him. Lieutenant Bagno watched through the window at first, but when he realized Eddie could take care of himself, he turned his back.

Eddie had Diablo by the collar with one hand and was popping him with the other, hockey-style, when Diablo spit in his face. Eddie pulled back and wiped it off. His eyes went homicidal and he smacked Diablo with backhands. Then, grabbing him by the collar with one hand and pushing his face with the other, Eddie drove Diablo's head through the side window. Glass exploded and flew everywhere.

"All right, that's enough," Lieutenant Bagno said, fairly impressed. The glass was supposed to be shatterproof. He shoved Diablo's head back into the car and then opened the door and cuffed him again. "Yes, captain, he resisted arrest's how he got banged up there a little bit, but order was quickly restored."

Eddie climbed out, still crazy.

"This motherfucker's nuts," Diablo said, glass in his hair and blood on his face. "Get him out of here."

Eddie flew back into the car and grabbed Diablo by the throat. "If Gabriel doesn't make it," he said, "look for me. I'm gonna visit you in jail and pull your fucking head through the bars."

Twenty-four

Ofelia heard it was nice down the shore in southern Delaware. Bethany, Rehoboth, that area. Maybe that's where they'd move if she could find a job. Away from here, a fresh start, a second chance. She and Gabriel would buy saltwater taffy and walk on the beach when the day's afterglow lingered in the clouds.

She looked at Gabriel and asked if that was okay with him.

"Fine then," she said, tapping his hand. "That's what we'll do."

She suspected Gabriel might already be there, judging by the expression on his face. It showed no discomfort, but it wasn't at rest, either. It was as if, floating between living and dying, he was trying to figure out which was the bigger mystery.

He wore a light blue gown stamped ST. CHRISTOPHER'S HOSPITAL FOR CHILDREN and lay on his back on a white-sheeted bed with high-rise metal bars. Ofelia pretended not to see the heart monitor and the tubes that ran in and out of him because that was not her son. Her son needed no attachments and would be moving with her down the shore, where he would impress the art teacher at his new school with his ability to see things others didn't see. He would come home each day, drop his bookbag on the kitchen table, and ask what was for dinner.

Bagels and milk shakes, she would say. Let's go to the beach.

Ofelia looked at the big clock on the wall as if it were part of a conspiracy. Six o'clock. Gabriel had been hanging on for fifteen hours, but the doctors held out little hope. A miracle, one doctor told Ofelia—that's what it would take. He was in surgery for three hours, with doctors working close to his spine to remove a nine-milimeter bullet, and they'd pumped fourteen pints of blood into him.

A miracle. It was a wonderful idea, Ofelia thought, that there was a force of good out there, somebody or something that brought justice from a place beyond human understanding. It was probably the force of everyone who ever feared losing someone. She prayed to those people and to Gabriel, too, as he lay unconscious, with his world being decided for him.

Ofelia wanted to sing to Gabriel, sing "Paper Moon" like she did when he was a baby, but she decided it was better to keep the memory sweet. She touched his hair the way she had when she cradled him in her arms at Third and Indiana, and remembered thinking that despite it all, it felt so good to hold him again. She leaned over the bed, kissed him on the forehead, and whispered that she loved him.

And she knew that he heard.

Ofelia left the room to see if Eddie was back yet. He'd been good to her, getting her a change of clothes and then staying with her through the night, holding her when she needed to be held, telling her things about Gabriel when she needed to hear them. He had left at ten in the morning to be with his kids, but promised to come back, and twice he had called and asked first how Gabriel was doing and then if she was okay.

She found him alone in the waiting room watching the six-o'clock news. They led with a photo of Diablo followed by a graphic listing all his previous arrests. Lieutenant Bagno was being called a hero for subduing Diablo when the suspect assaulted the officer and attempted to flee after the mayor's ring was discovered in a routine traffic stop. In an interview, Bagno said he was pleased, for the sake of the city and for the mayor's family, that one of the most violent drug lords, who routinely terrorized the decent citizens of North Philadelphia and Kensington, "now stands a good chance of being removed from the streets for a lengthy period of time."

Bagno called the theft of the ring "an act of terrorism against not just the mayor's family, but against society." He said Diablo was also a suspect in the beating of the priest who had later been killed at Third and Indiana, as well as in several murders involving members of drug gangs.

Eddie, lost in the report, didn't see Ofelia when she first entered the room. Seeing her now, he stood. "I just saw one of the doctors," Eddie said. "He said no change."

Ofelia nodded and Eddie saw the exhaustion in her. Her exhaustion, and her struggle to keep reality from crashing through the protection she'd built up.

Ofelia sat next to Eddie and looked at the television. Mayor DeMarco's daughter was on, expressing "relief and gratitude" at the return of the ring, but the mayor's wife said it was no cause for leniency, and she demanded that Diablo, whom she called a despicable character of subhuman qualities, be prosecuted to the full extent of the law. "I'm just disappointed," Mrs. DeMarco said, "that under the law, they can't fry him."

The reporter said nothing to follow that and the anchor let it sit there, too, his pause an endorsement of the idea.

Eddie felt Ofelia's eyes on him.

"Why do you think someone like Diablo would go all the way down to South Philly and do that?" she asked.

Eddie was afraid of the question. He wondered if she knew, or if she suspected, just as he had wondered if Lieutenant Bagno knew. Eddie had determined that no matter what, he wasn't going to tell Ofelia a thing about it.

"A guy like that can never get enough," Eddie said.

She looked at the bumps and bruises on Eddie's face. Diablo had gotten more than he gave, but he had given a few.

"You all right?" she asked.

Eddie nodded. He'd told her he had helped Lieutenant Bagno wrestle Diablo to the ground when he tried to run, and she seemed to suspect that something was wrong with that part of the story, too.

"Marisol was here," Ofelia said, changing the subject. "She left about an hour ago, said she couldn't stand it. Another friend of theirs,

Ralph, he was killed last night. Not far from Third and Indiana." She spoke with a growing distance from it all, something in her stare dragging out the seconds, trying to make time slow to a stop.

"Your kids," she said. "What did you guys do?" She seemed to recover a bit with her question.

"We had a great time," Eddie said. "We went to the Wissahickon, walked through the covered bridge. You ever been there?"

"No," she said. "I'd like to."

"It's great," Eddie said. "I'll take you sometime. There's a red covered bridge over the creek, a waterfall under it. We went down and skipped rocks and Monk and Mingus fetched sticks out of the water. It stopped raining, you know, but the creek was wild, all the rainwater rushing through it."

"You go there a lot?" she asked.

"I used to," he said. "It helps, you know? Everything's so old, so big. So quiet."

Eddie wanted to hold her, and there was something else he wanted to do, too. He wanted to tell Ofelia it had never felt better to see his kids. "I'm gonna work out a custody thing," he said, "see them regular days and stuff. It'll be hard, you know, getting my career going again and all. But I'm going to see them weekends, plus some weeknights."

She smiled.

"It was good, you know? It's the first time in a few years I was with them. I mean really with them. The one, my little guy, he says he's worried I might be lonely by myself. He says he wants to come back with me so I won't be lonely."

Ofelia took his hand, and when Eddie looked into her eyes the sadness in them made her so beautiful he ached.

One of the doctors appeared, though neither of them had seen him coming. In a low voice he called to Ofelia and she stood slowly, rising up through the weight of the world and all its history, and went with him.

Five minutes passed. Ten. Fifteen.

Footsteps now in the hall. Eddie knew the sound and weight of her walk. With each step his heart fell.

She was a hundred years older, cold black stones for eyes, and she wore Gabriel's death.

Eddie hurried to her and she collapsed into him crying, all of it coming now. Eddie held her tight, a hand on her head, and she cried into his chest. He guided her toward the chairs, and held her as they sat for half an hour, Ofelia bent at the waist and burying her head in her lap, rocking and moaning. And then Ofelia looked up at Eddie as if she'd just remembered something, and she asked if he could take her to his house to get her bicycle.

"I could just bring it over to you tomorrow," he said, but Ofelia said she wanted it now if he didn't mind.

It was a short ride to Eddie's and neither of them said anything, there was nothing to say. They got the bike out of Eddie's living room and Ofelia asked if he could put it in the trunk and take her home.

When they stopped at her house on Diamond Street, Eddie got her bike out and walked her to the door. She said thanks, and told him she needed to be alone.

"You going to be all right here tonight?" he asked.

"Thank you for everything," she said. "I'll call tomorrow and tell you about the arrangements."

Ofelia went into the kitchen, turned on the light, looked at the wall. No thirty-eight marks, no EL NADA EN LA OSCURIDAD. She wondered if there ever had been.

She went into the basement and came back up with a can of spray paint. And then she rolled her bicycle outside and locked the door behind her.

It was the same outfit she had worn the first night, her signature black uniform, except for a jacket and black sneakers instead of sandals. It was cold now, very cold, but it felt good.

Ofelia pedaled with perfect balance, her skirt rippling in the breeze and her hair flying behind her, glowing in the yellow light of the streetlamps. She closed her eyes, excited by the danger, lost in the dream of a sleep so deep it raised the dead.

Ofelia banked onto Broad Street and picked up speed on the straightaway. She veered right when the bodies started, making sure not to ride over them. Blocks and blocks of bodies piled north to south, bodies that had made national news and had everybody talking about what was wrong and how to fix it. She would never tell a soul that Gabriel was the artist. It was their secret to keep. Gabriel and Ofelia and Eddie. If everyone knew, the story would grow old eventually. This way, wrapped in mystery, it would live forever, and Gabriel with it.

When she got to the last body, Lalo's, Ofelia leaned her bike against a parked car and pulled the can of white spray paint from her pocket. She walked back a half block, studying the last two or three bodies, and then she was ready.

She did Ralph first, then Gabriel.

She did Gabriel's head, his arms, his body, his legs. And then she went back over it a couple of times, filling in and thickening the line, and she painted a Sixers cap on his head. Then she leaned over the torso, holding the can closer to the ground, and painted the number fourteen.

That's all he was, her boy. Fourteen years old. At least half a century stolen from him.

Ofelia stood back to take a look, and shook her head in awe. Something about the power of young voices silenced, human futures wasted. They looked as if they could rise up and walk through dreams.

She would watch for them, Ofelia thought as she got on her bicycle and started riding back up Broad Street. She would watch for Gabriel, and she would talk to him, see what he thought about moving to the shore. And even if he said no, they'd at least go there more often because they both loved the smell of the salt water and the sound of the waves and the mystery and magic of the ocean. At night they'd put on sweaters and walk along the edge of the continent, and maybe the moon would throw a funnel of silver light over the water for them, an invitation, laying it down as if it were a sidewalk to the center of the sea.